YESTERDAY
TODAY
and
TOMORROW

COOKBOOK

A collection of favorite recipes
compiled by
Charles Baddour

APPRECIATION

To all those who contributed their favorite recipes or gave of their time to help with this book, we are sincerely grateful.

Whether or not you chose to include your name, we are indebted because you took the time to send us your recipe. Limited space prevented our using all submitted, but every effort was made to include a variety of favorite selections.

For their many hours of dedicated hard work in compiling the recipes and in preparing the book for publication, we give an extra special thanks to Carol Higgins, Marie Baddour Albertson, and Eulalee Dacus.

The proceeds from the sale of this book will go to Baddour Memorial Center, a residential community for mentally retarded adults.

Printed in the USA by

WIMMER
The Wimmer Companies, Inc.
Memphis • Dallas

2

This book is lovingly dedicated to the memory of

Oneida Smith Baddour

A gentle person whose greatest joys resulted from her activities at home, devoted to her family, an inspiration to all who knew her, whose memory we wish to honor by sharing favorite recipes. May the use of this book continue the kind of fellowship and loving friendship which her life exemplified.

And to the memory of

Charles Baddour

A devoted husband and father who lived a distinctive life as a businessman and philanthropist. His interest in cooking birthday cakes for more than 500 people each year for many years enabled him to offer one of the best cake sections ever presented in a cookbook. "Mr. Charles," as he was affectionately called, conceived the idea for this cookbook and compiled it in order to help the mentally retarded adults of Baddour Center.

The Fifth Printing Made Possible By

Eli and Rose Saleeby

As a token of their high esteem and great love for Mr. Charles Baddour and for the ministry of Baddour Center, Mr. and Mrs. Eli Saleeby contributed the necessary funds for the fifth printing of this cookbook. Mrs. Rose Saleeby is the sister of Mr. Charles Baddour. The Saleebys reside in Salisbury, North Carolina, where they are recognized as gracious and caring people who give liberally and humbly to help others have better and more fulfilling lives.

CONTENTS

The Gateway marks the entrance to Baddour Memorial Center, a residential community for 150 mildly and moderately retarded adults, located in Senatobia, Mississippi. For them, it represents entrance into a life of dignity and fulfillment. For parents and guardians, Baddour Center offers the caring, Christian environment they seek for their loved ones. This Gateway symbolizes what Baddour Center is: a beacon to light the way, a model for others who also wish to recognize and encourage the talents, abilities and worth of these special people.

"The people that walked in darkness have seen a great light."

Isaiah 9:2

PARTY FOODS

Gateway, Baddour Memorial Center

COFFEE PUNCH

5 tablespoons instant coffee
2 cups hot water
1 cup sugar
½ teaspoon salt
6 cups cold water

½ teaspoon almond extract
1 pint Half and Half
½ gallon vanilla ice cream
½ gallon chocolate ice cream

Dissolve instant coffee in hot water. Add sugar and salt and stir until dissolved. Add cold water and almond extract. Chill. When ready to serve add Half and Half and pour over ice cream. *Serves 40-50.*

June Spotts

A big hit with non-coffee drinkers.

HOT CHOCOLATE MIX

2½ quarts powdered milk
4 ounces Nestles Quick cocoa mix

4 ounces powdered coffee cream
4 ounces powdered sugar

Mix the above. When ready to serve, combine ⅓ cup of the mix and ⅔ cup of hot water.

Donna Poteet

PARTY PUNCH

3 bananas, mashed
1 package unsweetened cherry
Kool-Aid
1 package unsweetened orange
Kool-Aid
½ cup lemon juice

1 46-ounce can unsweetened
pineapple juice
1½ quarts water
2½ cups sugar
48 ounces 7-Up

Mix bananas, Kool-Aid, juices, water and sugar well. Freeze in empty milk cartons. Thaw 4-6 hours before serving and add 7-Up.

June Spotts

SWEET AND SOUR MEATBALLS

1 8-ounce jar grape jam   2 pounds ground chuck
1 12-ounce jar chili sauce

Mix grape jam and chili sauce in large heavy pan. Roll meat into very small meatballs. Cook in sauce for 1 hour. Serve hot over rice or serve with toothpicks for party.

Mrs. Harold Tannen

DRUNK WEINERS

1 16-ounce package weiners   ¼ cup prepared mustard
1 10-ounce jar guava jelly

Melt jelly and add mustard. Stir well and heat again in fondue to boiling point (not bubbling). Cut weiners into one inch pieces. Add to liquid, boil for about 10 minutes, and serve.

Donna Frangenberg

A non-alcoholic variation.

SAUSAGE BALLS

2 pounds hot sausage   ½ cup ketchup
½ cup wine vinegar   1 tablespoon soy sauce
½ teaspoon ginger   ½ cup brown sugar

Roll sausage into small balls (will shrink about ⅓ size). Place on cookie sheet and bake 30-40 minutes in oven at 375°. Combine vinegar, ginger, ketchup, soy sauce, and brown sugar to make sauce. Pour sauce over balls and let set overnight in refrigerator. Heat and serve.

Mrs. John Jenkins

CHEESE SAUSAGE BALLS

3 cups Bisquick flour   12 ounces Cheddar cheese, grated
1 pound hot sausage

Mix together and roll into balls. Bake on cookie sheet at 350° until crispy.

Mrs. Fred Martin

7

BARBECUED SAUSAGE BALLS

1 pound hot pork sausage
1 egg, slightly beaten
⅓ cup fine dry bread crumbs
½ teaspoon sage

½ cup catsup
1 tablespoon vinegar
1 tablespoon soy sauce

Mix sausage, egg, bread crumbs and sage. Shape in balls the size of walnuts. Brown balls slowly on all sides about 15 minutes, pouring off excess fat. Combine catsup, vinegar and soy sauce and pour over meat. Cover and simmer 30 minutes. Stir occasionally to coat meatballs. Serve with toothpicks.

Patti Upton

JO ANN CURI'S MEATBALLS

5 pounds mixture of beef, pork, veal
3 cloves garlic, pressed
3 tablespoons parsley, chopped
1 tablespoon salt

Pepper to taste
1½ cups fine bread crumbs
3 eggs
1 large can Hunts tomato sauce

Blend meat, garlic, parsley, salt and pepper, bread crumbs and eggs, kneading with fingers until smooth. Form into balls. Fry slowly in olive oil until well brown. Put meatballs in pot. Add tomato sauce and simmer slowly 30 minutes until meatballs are well cooked. *Or* fry meatballs slowly until well cooked. Serve with hot Hunts tomato sauce. Serve over rice or use as an hors d'oeuvres.

Jo Ann Curi

6-PENNY NAIL CHICKEN

24 deboned chicken thighs
Garlic salt
24 aluminum 6-penny nails

$10,000 Barbeque Sauce (page 73)
Kraft Barbeque sauce

Sprinkle inside of each chicken thigh generously with garlic salt. Roll in jellyroll fashion, securing each with a 6-penny nail. Place chicken, seam side down (to seal the chicken), over a glowing fire on the grill. Don't turn it over until the top begins to change color, then turn often, basting each time with the $10,000 Barbeque Sauce. When ¾ done, move to cooler side of the grill, and baste again. When chicken is done, take off grill and remove nails (make sure to get them all) and put in a baking dish. Baste generously with Kraft Barbeque sauce and place in 150° oven for 1 hour. Serve warm.

Charles Baddour

CHICKEN-HAM PINWHEELS

2   chicken breasts, skinned and
    boned
⅛   teaspoon dried, crushed basil
    leaves
⅛   teaspoon salt

Dash pepper
Dash garlic salt
3   thin slices cooked ham
2   teaspoons lemon juice
Paprika

Place chicken on board and pound to ¼-inch thick. Combine seasonings and sprinkle on chicken. Place 1½ slices ham on each breast and roll up. Place rolls, seam down, in dish and sprinkle with lemon juice and paprika. Bake at 350° for 40 minutes. Chill and slice into ¼″ slices. Serve with bread or crackers. *Makes 24 slices.*

Anita M. Slaughter

Also excellent, using whole breast, as main course.

INDIAN CHICKEN BALLS

4   ounces cream cheese
2   tablespoons mayonnaise
1   cup chicken, finely chopped
1   cup pecans (or almonds),
    chopped

1   tablespoon chutney, chopped
½   teaspoon salt
1   tablespoon curry powder
½   cup fine grated coconut

Mix cream cheese and mayonnaise. Add chicken, nuts, chutney, salt and curry powder. Shape into balls. Roll in coconut. Chill and serve. *(40 balls)*

Hita Jo Pryor

HONEY CHICKEN WINGS APPETIZER

3   pounds chicken wings
Salt and pepper
1   cup honey
½   cup soy sauce

2   tablespoons vegetable oil
2   tablespoons catsup
½   garlic clove, chopped

Cut off and discard chicken wing tips. Cut each wing into two parts and sprinkle with salt and pepper. Combine remaining ingredients and mix well. Place wings in slow cooker and pour sauce over. Cook all day on low setting. Or, preheat oven to 375°. Place wings in shallow casserole, pour sauce over and bake 1 hour, until chicken is well done and sauce is caramelized. *Serves 10.*

9

HAM CUBES

2 tablespoons prepared
  horseradish
2 tablespoons mayonnaise
1 teaspoon Worcestershire
½ teaspoon seasoned salt

⅛ teaspoon pepper
1 8-ounce package cream cheese,
  softened
6 thin slices boiled ham

Beat horseradish, mayonnaise, Worcestershire, seasoned salt, pepper, and cream cheese together until creamy and of spreading consistency. Place one ham slice on a piece of waxed paper. With a spatula, spread some of the creamed mixture over it. Place another slice of ham on top of creamed mixture and spread with more of the cheese. Repeat, ending with ham slice on top. Wrap all securely in waxed paper and place in freezer for 2 hours or more. One hour before serving, remove and cut into small cubes. Pierce each with a colored toothpick. *Makes about 36 appetizers.*

Brenda Naifeh

PARTY PIZZA

1 pound hot sausage
1 pound Velveeta cheese

Oregano
Party rye bread

Brown sausage and stir in cheese (don't drain the grease). Sprinkle with oregano and spread on bread. Broil until toasted.

Patti Upton

PARTY PIZZA

1 pound ground beef
1 pound hot or mild sausage
1 pound Velveeta cheese,
  cut in chunks

1½ tablespoons Worcestershire sauce
2 teaspoons garlic salt
2 loaves party rye bread

Brown meat in a large skillet. Spoon off most of the grease. Add cheese and stir until melted. Add Worcestershire and garlic salt and allow to cool. Spread on rye rounds. Bake at 400° for 10 minutes.

Mrs. Charles Adams, Jr.

ORIENTAL HORS D'OEUVRES

2 10-ounce cans water chestnuts   1 pound bacon
1 bottle soy sauce

Marinate water chestnuts in soy sauce for at least two hours. Wrap each in ½ strip bacon without stretching the bacon. Secure with toothpicks. Bake at 400° for 15-20 minutes or until bacon is crisp. Serve hot. Can be made ahead and refrigerated until time to bake. Chicken livers may be substituted for water chestnuts.

Doris Lanford

Different and delicious!

STUFFED MUSHROOMS

Fresh mushrooms   Sliced American cheese
Regular pork sausage (not hot)

Remove stems from mushrooms and wash; hollow out mushrooms and stuff sausage in hole. Bake in 375° oven until sausage is done. Remove and cover sausage with cheese. Cut oven off and run mushrooms back in until cheese melts; drain on paper towels after cheese melts. Serve while hot.

Joy Melton

Quick and delicious.

STUFFED MUSHROOMS

6   tablespoons butter   1½ cups small bread cubes
½ pound mushroom caps   ½ teaspoon salt
¼ cup green pepper, chopped   ½ teaspoon pepper
¼ cup onion, chopped   ¼ teaspoon Tabasco

Sauté mushrooms in half the butter. Transfer to baking dish. In remaining butter, sauté pepper, onion, and bread cubes. Add salt, pepper and Tabasco. Stuff mushrooms with this mixture and bake at 350° for 15 minutes.

FLAKY APPETIZERS

3   3-ounce packages cream cheese,   Almost ½ pound mushrooms, chopped
    softened   ¼   teaspoon thyme
½ cup butter, softened   ½   teaspoon salt
1½ cups flour   Ground pepper
3   tablespoons butter   2   tablespoons flour
1½ large onions, finely chopped   1½ cups sour cream

To make crust, mix together cream cheese, butter, and flour. Refrigerate.
Mix filling by sautéeing onions in butter, adding mushrooms, seasoning,
then flour and sour cream. Divide dough into 3-4 parts. Roll each one and cut
circles with glass or round cookie cutter. Place about 1 teaspoon filling on ½
of each round and fold over and crimp. Bake for 10 minutes at 350° and
freeze. When ready to serve, thaw some and bake at 350° another 10-15
minutes, until golden. *Makes 4 dozen.*

Dorrie Weiner

WALNUT SOUR CREAM DIAMONDS

Sour Cream Pastry:

1½ cups all-purpose flour, sifted   ½ cup butter or margarine
¾ teaspoon salt   ½ cup dairy sour cream
¼ teaspoon paprika

Filling:

¾ cup toasted walnuts, chopped   ¾ cup Cheddar cheese, grated
¾ cup pimento-stuffed green olives,   2 tablespoons mayonnaise
   chopped

For pastry, resift flour with salt and paprika into mixing bowl. Cut in butter.
Add sour cream and mix until well blended. Cover and chill dough 30 minutes or longer before using.

While dough is chilling assemble filling ingredients. Mix together walnuts,
olives, cheese and mayonnaise. Divide dough in half. Roll each half to a
rectangle 8x15 inches; then cut into two 4-inch strips. Spread center of each
strip with filling. Fold edges over to enclose it completely, moistening edges
which overlap so they will seal. Invert onto baking sheet, seam-side down.
Bake at 400° until crisp and golden brown, about 10 minutes. Cool and cut in
diagonal slices to make diamonds. *Makes about 3 dozen.*

Mrs. R. L. Burns

We make in advance and freeze and cook when needed.

STUFFED PARTY ROLLS

5 dozen party size finger rolls
1 pound Cheddar cheese (½ sharp,
   ½ mild)
1 4½-ounce can ripe olives,
   chopped
6 eggs, hard boiled

1 4-ounce can green chilies
1 cup tomato sauce
1 teaspoon celery salt
1 medium onion
¼ pound butter

Scoop out centers of rolls with sharp knife, and reserve crumbs. Grind together all other ingredients including ⅓ of the reserved crumbs from the centers of the rolls. Mix well. Stuff rolls and bake at 400° for about 10 or 15 minutes, until lightly browned on top. Can be frozen before baking.

Lee Ellis
Mrs. Burton W. Renager

CHEESE TRIANGLES

¼ cup butter
3 tablespoons flour
2 cups hot milk
1 cup Muenster cheese, grated (or
   Swiss or Monterey Jack)

1 pound cream cheese, softened
3 egg yolks
2 tablespoons parsley, chopped
1 cup butter, melted
1 box Filo pastry sheets

Melt butter in saucepan and add flour. Stir constantly until cooked but not brown. Add the hot milk and cook until thickened. Cool. Add cheeses, eggs, parsley, and 3 tablespoons butter to cooled sauce and mix well. Lay one sheet of the pastry on a flat surface and brush with melted butter. Cut into strips 2 inches wide. Spread a teaspoonful of cheese mixture on one end of pastry strips. Fold corner of pastry over to meet other side, forming a triangle. Continue folding over and over in shape of triangle. Repeat with remaining pastry and cheese mixture. Bake at 375° for 15-20 minutes.

Marie Baddour Albertson

13

CHEESE CAPERS

¼ cup green onions or scallions
2 tablespoons pitted green olives
1 tablespoon pimento
1 teaspoon capers

2 cups sharp Cheddar cheese, grated
½ cup mayonnaise
6 English muffins, halved
1 tablespoon Parmesan cheese

Thinly slice the onions, including green part. Drain the olives, pimento and capers well, then chop. Combine onions, olives, pimento, capers, cheese and mayonnaise and spread evenly over muffin halves. Cut each muffin into quarters. Sprinkle with Parmesan. Place on baking sheet and bake at 350° for 25 minutes or until cheese is bubbling. *Makes 48 appetizers.* May be refrigerated for up to 24 hours or frozen. Bring to room temperature before baking.

Rose Baddour Saleeby

Bet you can't eat just one!

HOT CHEESE PUFFS

½ cup butter
2 cups Cheddar or Mozzarella
  cheese, shredded

1 cup flour
⅛ teaspoon salt
¼ teaspoon paprika

Cream butter with cheese. Add flour, salt and paprika. Shape into 1-inch balls. Flash freeze on baking sheet. Store in freezer bag or container. Bake on ungreased pan at 350° for 15 minutes. *Makes about 30-36 puffs.* Sometimes puffs are more flat, then "puff" after baking.

Dorrie Weiner

CHEESE WAFERS

2 cups cheese, grated
2 sticks butter or
  margarine

2 cups flour
¼ teaspoon ground red pepper
2 cups Rice Krispies cereal

Cream cheese and butter, add sifted flour that has been sifted 3 times with red pepper, add Rice Krispies. Make into small balls the size of a nickel — flatten with finger. Bake on an ungreased cookie tin for 10 minutes at 350°. These will keep well in a tin for a week, also they freeze well (heat in a low oven to be sure they are crisp) before serving.

CHEESE RICE BALLS

1 cup rice
1 egg, beaten
1 cup sharp Cheddar cheese,
  grated

¼ teaspoon paprika
Cracker crumbs

Cook rice according to package directions. To cooked rice, add egg, cheese and paprika. Form into small balls, roll in fine cracker crumbs, and fry in deep fat until brown. Watch carefully, as they brown quickly. Serve hot.

Louise Westley

OLIVE CHEESE BALLS

1 cup cheese, grated
¼ cup oleo
¾ cup flour

⅛ teaspoon salt
½ teaspoon paprika
Large stuffed olives

Mix cheese and oleo well. Add flour, salt and paprika. Shape dough around a large stuffed olive. Place on ungreased cookie sheet. Bake at 400° for 10 minutes.

Mrs. Albert J. Thomas

CHEESE STRAWS

¼ pound butter or margarine
1 pound sharp Cheddar cheese,
  grated
1 egg
1 tablespoon cold water

Few dashes Worcestershire sauce
1¾ cups sifted all-purpose flour
½ teaspoon salt
¼ teaspoon cayenne pepper
½ teaspoon paprika

With mixer at medium to high speed, cream butter and cheese until soft. Add egg, water, and Worcestershire, and beat well. Sift flour, salt, cayenne, and paprika together; add in 3 additions; beat well after each addition. Shape dough into 2 rolls; wrap in plastic film or foil; refrigerate 30-60 minutes. (If refrigerated longer than 1 hour, allow dough to stand at room temperature about 15-20 minutes.) Put dough through a cookie press, using the small star; or through a Super Shooter, using a decorator tip; or roll out thin and cut with a small biscuit cutter. Bake at 350° about 16-17 minutes, or until just starting to turn light brown at edges. *Makes about 8 dozen 3-inch straws.*

Ann Basore

CHEESE STRAWS

1   stick of butter
½ pound sharp cheese
1   teaspoon salt

Paprika (about 3 shakes of can)
Dash of red pepper – to your taste
2   cups flour, sifted

Use butter and cheese at room temperature. Mix well, add salt, paprika, red pepper, then add flour; mix well (by hand). Press through a cookie press. Bake until golden brown at 375°.

Marie Hartfield

Very tasty.

SPINACH BALLS

2   packages frozen chopped
     spinach
2   cups herbed stuffing mix
2   medium onions, chopped fine
½ cup celery or water chestnuts,
     chopped
6   eggs, beaten

¾ cup margarine, melted
½ cup grated Parmesan cheese
1   tablespoon garlic salt
½ teaspoon thyme
½ tablespoon pepper
Dash of MSG
Tabasco to taste

Cook spinach and drain well. Mix all ingredients. Chill, form into small balls. Bake at 350° for 20 minutes.

Amy Denny

DIRTY SOCK CHEESE

2   4-ounce wedges of Blue cheese
2   6-ounce glasses English
     Cheddar cheese
1   6-ounce glass or roll smoked
     cheese spread
1   6-ounce roll garlic cheese

Juice of 2 lemons
2   teaspoons Worcestershire sauce
Hot sauce
1   large clove garlic
Paprika

Mix together softened cheeses, lemon juice, Worcestershire, and hot sauce. Split the clove of garlic, and rub the cut side over a large sheet of wax paper. Sprinkle heavily with paprika. Blend cheese mixture again and drop onto wax paper. Shape into a roll and when all sides of the roll are covered with paprika, stick a piece of the garlic in each end, roll it up in the paper and let mellow overnight in refrigerator. *Serves 50-75 guests.*

Louise Westley

JALAPENO CHEESE DIP

1 pound Velveeta cheese
¾ cup xx cream
4 rounded tablespoons
   mayonnaise

Dash cayenne
3 to 5 jalapeno peppers, chopped fine
Dash paprika
Salt and pepper to taste

Melt cheese in double boiler. Add other ingredients. Cool. Serve with Fritos.

Variation: 3 rounded tablespoons mayonnaise, and 1 rounded tablespoon Durkees sauce.

Billy and Barbara Mills

JALAPENO DIP

2 pounds Old English cheese
10 jalapeno peppers

3 cups Miracle Whip salad dressing
5 cloves garlic, pressed

Grate cheese into a mixing bowl. Drain peppers, reserving liquid. Chop peppers, and add to cheese. Add salad dressing and garlic. Add 2 tablespoons reserved pepper juice, or enough to thin. Mix well. Serve with king size Fritos.

Homazelle Ashford

BILLY MILLS' REALLY, REALLY GOOD CHEESE DIP

1 pound Velveeta cheese
1 tablespoon mayonnaise
1 heaping teaspoon cumin powder
1 teaspoon paprika
¼ teaspoon black pepper
½ teaspoon chili powder

¼ teaspoon dry mustard
1 clove garlic, put through garlic
   press
4 ounces Snappy Tom
4 ounces water
1 jalapeno pepper

Melt cheese in double boiler. In separate bowl, combine mayonnaise, cumin, paprika, pepper, chili powder, mustard, and garlic. Mix well. Add Snappy Tom (do not substitute) and water; mix well. Add to melted cheese and stir. Pour into blender and add jalapeno pepper. Blend well. Let set overnight in refrigerator before serving.

Billy and Barbara Mills

17

FIESTA DIP

1 can bean and bacon soup
1 cup sour cream
½ cup Cheddar cheese, grated

2 tablespoons dry taco seasoning
   mix
½ teaspoon instant minced onion

Combine all ingredients in 1½-quart bowl. Cook uncovered in microwave 2 minutes or until bubbly. Serve hot with Doritos.

June Spotts

MEXICAN DIP

1 can Cheddar cheese soup
2 tablespoons catsup
Dash of instant minced garlic

2 jalapeno peppers, chopped
¼ teaspoon cumin

In 1½-quart bowl, mix all ingredients. Cook uncovered in microwave for 2 minutes or until bubbly. Serve hot or cold.

June Spotts

I make this by the gallon, because I can't keep it on hand.

ROSE'S SURPRISE SPREAD

2 3-ounce packages cream cheese,
   softened
1 ounce Blue cheese, crumbled
½ cup nuts, chopped

¼ teaspoon onion, grated
½ teaspoon Worcestershire sauce
¼ teaspoon salt
⅓ cup mayonnaise

Combine cream cheese and Blue cheese. Add other ingredients and mix well. *Makes 1½ cups.*

Rose Baddour Saleeby

CHEESE BALLS

1 cup cheese, grated
1 stick oleo
1 cup flour, unsifted
½ teaspoon salt
⅛ teaspoon red pepper

Few drops of Lea & Perrin
   Worcestershire sauce
1 tablespoon milk
Pecans (optional)

Combine cheese, oleo, flour, salt, pepper and Lea & Perrin. If too dry to stick together, add milk. Roll into size of large marbles. Press out flat. Press pecans on top if desired. Bake 1 hour at 275°.

Rebecca Barrett

CRUNCHY CHEESE BALL

1 8-ounce package cream cheese,
   softened
¼ cup mayonnaise
2 cups cooked ham, ground
2 tablespoons chopped parsley

1 teaspoon onion, minced
¼ teaspoon dry mustard
¼ teaspoon Tabasco
½ cup nuts, chopped

Beat cream cheese and mayonnaise til smooth. Stir in ham, parsley, onion, mustard, and Tabasco. Cover and chill several hours. Form into ball. Roll in nuts to coat. Serve with crackers.

Randy Caldwell

HORSERADISH CHEESE BALL

2 8-ounce packages cream cheese,
   softened
4 teaspoons onion, grated
2 tablespoons Worcestershire

4 tablespoons pure horseradish
2 tablespoons mayonnaise
1 teaspoon salt
4 ounces dried beef

Mix all ingredients except dried beef together until thoroughly blended. Shape into a ball and refrigerate. Shred dried beef and put on large piece of waxed paper. Roll ball in dried beef to cover and then refrigerate until time to serve. Serve with assorted crackers.

Mrs. Donald Foster

PINEAPPLE CHEESE BALL

2   8-ounce packages cream cheese
1   8½-ounce can crushed
    pineapple, drained
1½ cups pecans, chopped
¼   cup bell pepper, chopped
2   tablespoons onion, finely chopped
1   tablespoon seasoning salt

In medium bowl mix cream cheese with pineapple until smooth. Stir in half of pecans and other ingredients. Shape into ball or 2 small balls and roll in remaining pecans. Serve with Triscuits or Sociables crackers. (Can be frozen.)

Sissy Rieves

SMOKED OYSTER ROLL

1   8-ounce package cream cheese,
    softened
2-3 dashes Worcestershire
Dash of garlic salt
1   can chopped smoked oysters
Paprika

Mix cream cheese, Worcestershire, and garlic salt thoroughly. Spread into rectangle on waxed paper. Cover with smoked oysters. Roll jellyroll fashion and sprinkle with paprika.

Mrs. James Robertson

OYSTER SPREAD

1   3½-ounce can smoked oysters,
    drained
1   8-ounce package cream cheese,
    softened
1   teaspoon lemon juice
Grated onion to taste
Hot sauce to taste
Worcestershire sauce to taste
Chopped parsley

Mash oysters with a fork to make a paste. Blend cream cheese and oysters with a fork until smooth. Add lemon juice, onion, hot sauce, and Worcestershire. Mix well. Chill 3 hours. Roll into a ball and cover with chopped parsley. Serve with crackers.

Mary Jane Baddour Chandler

GOURMET OYSTER IMPROMPTU

½ cup butter	2 pints oysters
1½ cups green onions, chopped, tops included	1 teaspoon salt
	½ teaspoon hot sauce
1 cup parsley, chopped	1½ cups Italian-style bread crumbs

Melt butter in heavy skillet. Sauté onions and parsley in butter until onions are tender. Add oysters and liquid, cooking until edges curl. Add salt and hot sauce, mixing well. Stir in crumbs. Heat thoroughly. Serve in chafing dish with round buttery crackers or toast. *Yield: 8-10 servings.*

Sara Massey

LOBSTER MOUSSE

1 can tomato soup	2 envelopes Knox gelatin
8 ounces cream cheese	1 cup cold water
1 cup celery, chopped	1 can lobster, shredded
½ cup green pepper, chopped	Salt, pepper, parsley (to taste)
2 tablespoons onion, grated	

Heat soup in saucepan. Add cream cheese, celery, green peppers and onions. Dissolve gelatin in water and add. Heat until cream cheese is melted. Add lobster and seasonings. Pour into greased ring mold. Serve with snack crackers.

Mrs. C. S. Sanders, Jr.

GRACE'S WONDERFUL SHRIMP BALL

1 8-ounce package cream cheese, softened	4-5 shakes of Worcestershire sauce
	½ teaspoon garlic salt
1 4½-ounce can medium shrimp	3-4 teaspoons horseradish
1 medium onion, grated	3-4 teaspoons shrimp sauce
4-5 shakes Tabasco sauce	

Mix all ingredients, except shrimp sauce, together. Shape into a ball, chill well before serving — spread with shrimp sauce.

Grace Knolton

21

BARBARA MILLS' FRIED SHRIMP

Shrimp
Salt and pepper
Lemon juice
Bacon

Egg
Milk
Flour

Wash and shell shrimp. Sprinkle with salt and pepper and a little lemon juice. Wrap each shrimp in ⅓ of piece of bacon and secure with toothpick. Mix eggs and milk together. Dip shrimp in milk, then in flour. Deep fry until golden brown.

Billy and Barbara Mills

PICKLED SHRIMP

1 cup Wesson oil
¾ cup wine vinegar
1 teaspoon salt
1 teaspoon black pepper
2 teaspoons horseradish

2 tablespoons prepared mustard
2 stalks celery, chopped
Few drops of red food coloring
1 pound shrimp, cooked and peeled

In mixing bowl, combine oil, vinegar, salt, pepper, horseradish, mustard, celery and food coloring. Pour over shrimp and refrigerate 24 hours.

Mrs. Stewart Vail

MARINATED SHRIMP

5 pounds uncooked shrimp
1 cup celery tops
3 tablespoons salt
3 tablespoons sugar
1 bag shrimp boil
4 cups red or white onions, thinly sliced
14 bay leaves

2½ cups salad oil
1½ cups white vinegar
3 teaspoons salt
5 teaspoons celery seed
5 tablespoons capers and juice
1 teaspoon Tabasco
1 tablespoon Lea & Perrin's Worcestershire sauce

Cover shrimp with boiling water. Add celery, salt, sugar and bag of shrimp boil. Cook shrimp 10 to 12 minutes. Clean shrimp and alternate shrimp and sliced onions and bay leaves in a shallow bowl. Combine in a separate bowl the salad oil, vinegar, salt, celery seed, capers, Tabasco, and Lea & Perrin. Mix well and pour over shrimp. Cover and refrigerate for 24 hours. *Serves 20.*

Sara M. Hart

SHRIMP JEWEL CANAPÉS

2   envelopes unflavored gelatin
1½   cups consommé
1   cup Rhine wine
Dash Tabasco
½   teaspoon salt

¼   teaspoon Worcestershire
30   small shrimp, cooked
30   Melba Toast rounds
Mayonnaise

Soften gelatin in ¼ cup cold consommé. Heat remaining consommé and add to gelatin, stirring until dissolved. Cool. Add wine. Add Tabasco, salt and Worcestershire. Oil 30 small muffin cups (1¼ inches bottom diameter); place 1 shrimp in bottom of each cup. Add just enough gelatin mixture to barely cover shrimp. Chill until firm. Unmold. Spread Melba Toast rounds with mayonnaise and top with the shrimp aspic. A tiny dab of mayonnaise on top is optional.

Lee Ellis

SHRIMP DIP

1   8-ounce package cream cheese
1   tablespoon vinegar
1   4½-ounce can shrimp
4   tablespoons mayonnaise

2   teaspoons seasoning salt
2   teaspoons onion, chopped
Thin with milk

Mix all ingredients in blender. Chill. Serve with chips or crackers.

Jeanne Kendall

SHRIMP DIP

1   can Campbell's shrimp soup
8-ounce package cream cheese
½   pound cooked shrimp, diced
1   small can ripe olives, chopped
Juice of 1 lemon

1   teaspoon Tabasco sauce
1   tablespoon Lea & Perrins
     Worcestershire sauce
¼   teaspoon curry or sherry (optional)

Heat soup and cream cheese in double boiler until melted. Add shrimp, olives, and seasonings. Serve warm with Fritos and chips. *Serves 12.*

SHRIMP SPREAD

1 3-ounce package cream cheese
1 teaspoon grated onion (or juice)
1 tablespoon cream
½ teaspoon lemon juice
½ teaspoon Worcestershire sauce

½ pound de-veined, cooked shrimp
½ cup mayonnaise (more or less, to
    make for easy spreading)
Salt and pepper to taste

Combine cream cheese, grated onion, cream, lemon juice, and Worcestershire sauce. Add shrimp (crumbled with fingers or mashed with fork), mayonnaise, salt and pepper.

Mrs. Ford Turner

SHRIMP MOLD

10½-ounce can tomato soup,
    undiluted
1 envelope Knox unflavored
    gelatin
¼ cup warm water
8-ounce package cream cheese

1 cup celery, chopped
1 cup pecans, chopped (optional)
¼ cup onion, chopped
1 cup mayonnaise
2 cans small size shrimp, drained
    and mashed

Heat soup in saucepan. Dissolve gelatin in water, and add to hot soup. Stir in cream cheese, and heat until melted. Add celery, pecans, onion, mayonnaise, and shrimp. Mix well. Pour into mold and refrigerate. Serve with assorted crackers.

Jan Richardson

SHRIMP MOUSSE

1 can tomato soup
1 envelope gelatin
⅓ cup water
2 3-ounce packages cream cheese
½ cup mayonnaise

1½ cups celery, minced
½ cup green onion, minced
    (use green part only)
2 4½-ounce cans shrimp

Heat soup to boiling. Soften gelatin in water and add to hot soup. Beat till dissolved. Cut cheese in small cubes. Gradually add cheese to soup. Beat until smooth with mixer. Blend in mayonnaise until smooth. Add celery, onion, shrimp, and blend. Pour into Jello mold (may need to spray mold with *Pam*). Refrigerate. This recipe can be made 2 days ahead. Serve with crackers.

Nina Martin

CHEESE AND CRABMEAT DIP

1 clove garlic
4 ounces cream cheese, softened
½ pint sour cream

1 teaspoon curry powder
1 small can crabmeat

Put garlic through garlic press. Mix with cream cheese. Add sour cream, curry and crabmeat. Serve with chips or crackers.

CRAB MEAT DIP

1 7½-ounce can crab meat
⅔ cup sour cream
2 teaspoons horseradish

½ teaspoon pepper
2 tablespoons Italian dressing

Mix all ingredients together. Serve with chips or crackers of your choice.

HOT CRAB DIP

3 8-ounce packages cream cheese, softened
1 pound frozen or 2 cans crab meat
½ cup mayonnaise
2 tablespoons prepared mustard

Seasoned salt to taste
1 teaspoon powdered sugar
1 clove garlic, mashed or chopped fine
1 teaspoon onion juice
¼ cup sherry

Combine all ingredients in double boiler. Stir well and heat. Serve in chafing dish with crackers or chips.

Mrs. Stewart Vail

HOT CRAB MEAT APPETIZER

1 8-ounce package cream cheese
1 6½-ounce can crab meat
1 tablespoon milk
2 tablespoons onions, chopped

½ teaspoon horseradish
¼ teaspoon salt
½ cup sliced almonds, toasted (optional)

Combine all ingredients except almonds and mix well. Pour into 9-inch pie pan and sprinkle almonds over top. Bake at 375° for 15 minutes. Prepare bread rounds and spread or serve on crackers, etc.

Brenda Cole

CURRIED CHICKEN LOG

2   8-ounce packages cream
    cheese, softened
1   tablespoon bottled steak sauce
½   teaspoon curry powder

1½ cups cooked chicken, minced
½   cup celery, minced
3   tablespoons fresh parsley, minced
½   cup toasted almonds, chopped

Beat cream cheese, steak sauce and curry powder together. Blend in chicken, celery and parsley. Shape into a 9-inch log (or 2 shorter logs). Wrap in waxed paper and chill 4 hours or overnight. When ready to serve, coat log in almonds. Serve with crackers.

Marie Baddour Albertson

CHIPPED BEEF SPREAD

8   ounces cream cheese, softened
¼   cup grated Parmesan cheese
1   tablespoon mayonnaise
⅓   cup stuffed olives, chopped
1   tablespoon horseradish

½   teaspoon Worcestershire
1   tablespoon parsley, minced
1   tablespoon onion, chopped
1   package dried beef

Combine all ingredients except beef and shape into loaf. Shred dried beef and cover top of loaf. Serve with crackers.

Mrs. John Whalen

DEVILED HAM MOLD

2   cans deviled ham
8-10 olives, chopped
1   tablespoon mustard

Dash horseradish
Cream cheese, softened
Parsley and sliced carrots

Mix ham, olives, mustard, and horseradish. Put in mold and freeze. Remove from mold and ice with softened cream cheese. Garnish with parsley and carrot slices. Return to refrigerator. Serve thawed.

Amy Denny

MUSHROOM DIP

4 tablespoons butter
1 clove garlic, minced
1 pound mushrooms, sliced
2 tablespoons dried parsley

1 teaspoon salt
¼ teaspoon pepper
1 cup sour cream

Melt butter. Add garlic, mushrooms, parsley, salt and pepper. Cook, stirring often until mushrooms are tender. Fold in sour cream and serve in chafing dish with melba toast.

Mrs. James Robertson

MARINATED ONION AND BLUE CHEESE

½ cup olive oil or vegetable oil
2 tablespoons lemon juice
1 teaspoon salt
Dash of pepper
Dash of paprika

½ teaspoon sugar
¼ cup crumbled Blue cheese
2 cups large red or yellow onions,
    thickly sliced

Mix oil, lemon juice, seasonings and sugar. Stir in cheese, pour over onions, cover and chill at least 2 days. *Makes 6 to 8 servings.* Delicious with thin, buttered slices of pumpernickel.

Rose Baddour Saleeby

ANTAPASTA DIP

1 14-ounce can artichoke hearts
1 small jar pimento
1 small jar olives
¼ cup bell pepper
½ cup celery
2 4-ounce cans mushroom stems
    and pieces
⅔ cup white vinegar
⅔ cup oil

¼ cup minced dry onion
2½ teaspoons Italian seasoning
1 teaspoon salt
1 teaspoon seasoned salt
1 teaspoon garlic salt
1 teaspoon onion salt
1 teaspoon sugar
1 teaspoon Accent
½ teaspoon seasoned pepper

Drain artichokes, pimento, and olives. Chop all vegetables and put in bowl. In saucepan, mix vinegar, oil, onion, and seasonings. Bring to a boil. Cool. Pour over chopped vegetables. Refrigerate overnight. Serve with Wheat Thins.

Doris Fisackerly

GUACAMOLE DIP

Salt
1 clove garlic, sliced in half
1 large avocado
¼ teaspoon chili powder
¼ teaspoon garlic salt
1 teaspoon lemon juice

2 teaspoons onion, minced or chopped
1 ripe tomato, diced and seeded
Mayonnaise
4 ounces Cheddar cheese, shredded

Sprinkle bowl with salt and rub with garlic. Mash avocado and add chili powder, lemon juice, onion, and tomato. (Use spices to personal taste.) Cover with mayonnaise if left standing out. When ready to use, mix and cover with cheese. Serve with fresh-made tortilla chips (or packaged).

Dorrie Weiner

CHILI DIP

1½ pounds lean ground beef
1 large onion, chopped
Salt to taste
1 teaspoon ground cumin

1 teaspoon chili powder
1 large can chili (no beans)
1 pound Cheddar cheese, grated

Cook ground beef and onion till meat is done but not brown and onion is clear. Add salt, cumin, chili powder and chili. Cook for about 20 minutes. Transfer to crock-pot or chafing dish; add cheese. Stir occasionally. Serve with Fritos or Doritos.

Mrs. Boyce Billingsley

BEAN SPREAD

1 can kidney beans, drained and rinsed
1 medium onion, minced fine
¼ cup mayonnaise
1 dash dry mustard

1 dash Worcestershire sauce
1 teaspoon horseradish
1 clove garlic, minced fine
¼ cup sweet relish
Salt and pepper to taste

Mix all ingredients in bowl. Refrigerate for 1 hour. Tastes better if left at least overnight — better yet, for a day or two. Use as appetizer or side dish.

Dorrie Weiner

A man pleaser.

CURRY DIP

1 cup mayonnaise	1 teaspoon onion powder
1 teaspoon curry powder	1 teaspoon horseradish
1 teaspoon garlic salt	Yellow food coloring
1 teaspoon Tarragon vinegar	

Combine all ingredients. Add enough yellow food coloring to make deep yellow. Chill — can make 2 days ahead. Serve with cauliflower, celery, carrots or any fresh vegetables.

CURRY DIP

1 cup mayonnaise	1 tablespoon curry powder
3 tablespoons catsup	½ teaspoon Tabasco
1 tablespoon Worcestershire	Salt to taste
2 tablespoons onion, grated	

Mix all ingredients well and chill 4 or 5 days for best flavor.

Louise Westley, Joy Melton,
Mrs. Albert Thomas

Good with raw cauliflower, turnips, carrots and celery. Also on ham and beef.

ARTICHOKE DIP

1 can artichoke hearts, drained
1 cup Parmesan cheese, grated

1 cup Hellman's mayonnaise
Dash garlic salt

Break up artichoke hearts with fork and mix with remaining ingredients. Bake in greased casserole at 350° for 15-20 minutes or until brown. Serve with Triscuits or Waverly Wafers.

Sissy Rieves, Doris Lanford,
Carol Thompson

ARTICHOKE DIP

1 14-ounce can artichokes
1 cup mayonnaise

1 package Ranch Style Creamy
   Italian dressing

Drain and chop artichokes very fine. Mix with mayonnaise and dressing. Keeps well.

HOT BROCCOLI DIP

2 packages frozen chopped
   broccoli
1 medium onion, grated
1 stick oleo
1 can mushroom soup

1 small can chopped mushrooms,
   drained
1 roll garlic cheese
Sliced almonds, toasted

Cook broccoli as directed on package, and drain. Sauté onion in oleo until soft. Combine onion, soup, and mushrooms. Mix with broccoli. Add crumbled cheese and heat until cheese melts, stirring constantly. Should be made at least 3 days before serving. Keep refrigerated and heat before serving, stirring well. Sprinkle almonds on top before serving. *Serves 25.*

Minnie Miller

SYBLE'S DIP

1 cup mayonnaise
1 cup sour cream
1 can water chestnuts, chopped

12 green onions, chopped
Dash lemon pepper
Dash seasoned salt

Mix all ingredients together. Chill.

June Spotts

PARTY POPCORN

1 cup pecan halves
1 cup blanched almonds
12 cups popped corn (¾ cup
   popcorn)

½ cup packed dark brown sugar
½ cup butter
½ teaspoon salt

Preheat oven to 350°. In 13x10½ roasting pan, spread nuts in single layer. Bake 10 to 15 minutes, stirring occasionally until nuts are lightly browned. Remove pan from oven. Add popped corn. Meanwhile in small pan over medium heat, melt sugar, butter or margarine. Stir into popcorn mixture with salt until well-coated. Bake 10 minutes longer or until golden, stirring once. Cool in pan. Store in tightly covered container. *Makes 14 cups.*

Mrs. Walter Scott

31

HOT BECHAMEL CANAPE

2 cups hot white sauce
1 pound ground beef, cooked
1 pound gruyere cheese
½ cup dry white wine
1 clove garlic, minced

1 egg, slightly beaten
Salt
Pepper
Nutmeg
Bread

Into white sauce that cooked ground beef has been added, stir in cheese, wine, garlic, egg, salt, pepper, and nutmeg. Toast round of bread on one side. Spread the untoasted side with the cheese mixture, leaving a ¼ inch border all around so that the cheese will not run over the sides. Cheese side up, broil on cookie sheet or bake in hot oven 450°.

CHICKEN DIP

2 cups chicken, minced
5 tablespoons mayonnaise
2 tablespoons chili sauce
1 tablespoon prepared mustard
1 tablespoon grated onion

2 teaspoons Worcestershire sauce
2 tablespoons pickle relish
4 dashes hot pepper sauce
1 teaspoon salt

Boil the chicken until very done. Remove from bones and mince. Add all other ingredients, mixing well. *Yields 2 cups.* If not thin enough, add more chili sauce and mayonnaise.

Oneida Baddour

The Baddour Memorial Chapel provides the setting for regular inter-denominational services. Here, residents learn that everyone is worthy of God's love and concern. A chaplain guides their spiritual growth and development and offers consolation when sadness and disappointments enter their lives, and he gives reassurance when doubts and fears arise. Here, also, staff "Prayer Pilgrims" daily kneel and praise God for the blessings He bestows on Baddour Center and ask His direction and help as the Center works to influence others for good and for God.

*"One thing have I desired of the Lord, that will
I seek after: that I may dwell in the house of the
Lord all the days of my life, to behold the beauty
of the Lord, and to inquire in His temple."*
Psalms 27:4

SOUPS & SANDWICHES

Memorial Chapel

CREAM-OF-FRESH-ASPARAGUS SOUP

2 pounds fresh asparagus	⅛ teaspoon pepper
1 13¾-ounce can chicken broth	½ cup light cream
½ teaspoon lemon juice	1 tablespoon chopped parsley
¾ teaspoon salt	

Break or cut off tough ends of asparagus stalks. Wash asparagus tips well with cold water; if necessary, use a soft brush to remove grit. With vegetable parer, scrape scales from lower part of the stalk only. Cut into ½-inch pieces. In boiling chicken broth in 5-quart Dutch oven, cook asparagus with lemon juice, salt and pepper over medium heat, covered, until mushy — about 15 minutes. Remove from heat. Blend cooked asparagus mixture in an electric blender or press through a food mill until smooth. Return to Dutch oven. Add cream. Cook over medium heat, stirring just until hot. Serve sprinkled with parsley. *Makes 6 servings.*

Marie Baddour Albertson

CORN CHOWDER

2 tablespoons salt pork or bacon, diced	4 cups potatoes, diced
	2½ cups cream style corn
3 tablespoons onion, chopped	Salt and pepper
1 quart milk	2 tablespoons chopped parsley

Cook salt pork or bacon slightly. Add onion. Cook about 10 minutes or until soft, but not browned. Add milk and potatoes. Boil gently about 20 minutes or until potatoes are tender. Add corn, season to taste. Sprinkle each serving with parsley.

Mrs. E. D. Welden

GAZPACHO SOUP

½ cup oil	6 drops Worcestershire
¼ cup lemon juice	2 teaspoons salt
6 cups Hunt's tomato juice	¼ teaspoon ground pepper
½ cup onion, finely minced	2 green peppers, finely chopped
2 tomatoes, peeled and chopped	2 cucumbers, peeled, seeded and diced
2 cups celery, finely chopped	
6 drops Tabasco	Fresh mushrooms, sliced (optional)

Beat oil and lemon juice with blender. Slowly add tomato juice (must be Hunt's). Add all other ingredients and stir. Serve cold. *Serves 8 to 10.* Keeps for a week in the refrigerator.

Doris Lanford

Try this on a very hot day.

MATZO BALL SOUP

3 eggs, separated	1 ¾ cups matzo meal
1 ⅔ cups water	6 cups chicken broth
1 teaspoon salt	2 tablespoons parsley, chopped
2 tablespoons chicken fat	

Beat egg yolks and water together. Add salt, chicken fat, and matzo meal. Mix well, then fold in stiffly beaten egg whites. Put into the refrigerator for at least 1 hour to make dough easy to handle. Bring chicken broth to a boil in a large saucepan. Dampen hands to keep dough from sticking and form dough into balls the size of golf balls. Drop them into boiling chicken broth along with parsley. When balls have been added, cover the pan and cook for 15 minutes. The balls will swell and rise to top when they are done. Put one ball in each soup bowl and then fill the bowl with broth. *Makes 12 matzo balls.*

Mavis Zuckerman

SQUASH SOUP

3 to 4 medium size squash	Dash pepper
1 quart milk	¼ teaspoon celery salt
1 slice onion	2 tablespoons butter
1 teaspoon salt	3 tablespoons flour

Scrub squash to clean, and grate. Cook in small amount of water for 10 to 15 minutes — drain well. Scald milk with onion slice, remove onion, add milk to squash, add remaining seasonings. Melt butter and stir in flour until smooth. Stir in squash mixture and cook until slightly thickened.

YELLOW SQUASH SOUP

2 pounds crooked neck squash, sliced	¼ teaspoon dried marjoram
4 scallions, sliced	1 tablespoon honey
1½ quarts chicken stock or bouillon	Salt and pepper to taste

Simmer the vegetables in the stock, covered, until tender, about 30 minutes. Cool slightly, puree, return to saucepan, add marjoram and honey, and salt and pepper to taste. Stir well, reheat, and serve. *Serves 6-8.*

HOT TOMATO SOUP

3 tablespoons oleo or butter
¼ cup onions, chopped
¼ cup celery, chopped
¼ cup carrots, chopped
1 bay leaf

½ teaspoon white pepper
1 teaspoon salt
⅛ teaspoon thyme
6 whole cloves
4 cups tomato juice
2 cups beef bouillon

Cook onions, celery, and carrots in butter for 5 minutes. Add bay leaf, pepper, salt, thyme, cloves, and tomato juice and simmer for 1 hour. Strain and add bouillon.

Mary Jane Baddour Chandler

GROUND BEEF VEGETABLE SOUP

1 pound ground beef
1 tablespoon margarine
1 large onion, chopped
4 Irish potatoes, diced
⅓ cup raw rice
1 can tomato sauce
3 cups water

1 large can tomato juice
1 small can peas and carrots
1 tablespoon salt
½ teaspoon pepper
1 tablespoon Worcestershire
Dash of Tabasco

Over low heat, brown ground beef lightly in margarine in Dutch oven, stirring often. Mix in remaining ingredients, and bring to boil. Reduce to simmer and cook about 2 hours until desired thickness is achieved. Adjust seasoning if necessary. *Serves 8.*

Edwin Goodman

HOME-MADE VEGETABLE SOUP

1 pound round steak or roast
3 large onions, chopped
3 cups celery, chopped
5 cups water
8 chicken bouillon cubes
2 #2 cans tomatoes

¾ teaspoon black pepper
3 carrots, diced
1 cup frozen lima beans
2 Irish potatoes, diced
1 #2 can cream style white corn
1 cup hot water

Cube beef and place in 5 or 6 quart pot. Add onions, celery, water, bouillon cubes, tomatoes and pepper. Boil for 1 hour, starting on high til begins to boil, then turn to medium low. After one hour, add carrots and lima beans and boil for another hour on medium low. Then add potatoes and let boil for another 30 minutes. Next add corn and cup of hot water. Let simmer for 30 minutes.

Pam Baddour

VEGETABLE SOUP

3   quarts water
3   medium soup bones with
    meat on them
1   ham bone with meat
3-4 pounds meaty beef short ribs
2   large onions, chopped
6-8 celery stalks and tops, cut into
    2" pieces
2   large bay leaves
3-4 pound beef roast or round
    steak
1½-2 quarts water
2   packages Ronco soup mix
4   large cans tomatoes
2   large cans tomato sauce
2   small cans tomato paste

4   cans cream style white or yellow
    corn
2   cans hominy
4   cans cut okra
2   cans speckled butter beans
2   cans green beans
2   cans green peas
2   teaspoons sugar
2   small bay leaves
4-6 dashes Tabasco sauce
2   dashes A-1 sauce
2   dashes Worcestershire sauce
Salt and pepper to taste
2-3 carrots, sliced
2-3 potatoes, quartered (optional)

In a large pot, place water, soup bones, ham bones, short ribs (trim suet and fat away), onions, celery, and bay leaves. Boil hard 5 minutes, then turn down and boil gently for 2 hours or until all the meat has come off the bones. Stir frequently to keep them from sticking. Cut roast or steak into 2" pieces and trim off all suet, add to pot, and gently boil until meat is tender. Let cool completely or refrigerate overnight. When cool, remove all fat on top and discard. Remove bay leaves. Re-heat slowly, adding water. After heated, divide into 2 large pots, and divide remaining ingredients, except carrots and potatoes, between the 2 pots. You may substitute any leftover vegetables from ice box, or fresh or frozen vegetables. Simmer for 1½ hours or more, stirring often. About 30-45 minutes before serving, add carrots and potatoes. Serve with cornbread. Freezes well; to heat frozen soup, add tomato juice and few dashes Tabasco sauce.

Eulalee B. Dacus

STEAK SOUP

2   pounds ground chuck
1   quart water
2   cans consommé
1   onion, chopped

2   medium potatoes, diced
2   small cans tomato sauce
Salt and pepper

Brown meat very well in heavy iron soup pot. Add water, consommé, onion, and potatoes. Cook one hour covered or until vegetables are done. Add tomato sauce, salt and pepper.

Diane Fair

LENTIL SUPER SOUP

1 pound dried lentils	2 quarts water
2 medium onions, chopped	1 tablespoon salt
1 stick celery, diced	¾ teaspoon liquid hot pepper sauce
1 tablespoon parsley, chopped	1 pound (about 8) frankfurters
1 16-ounce can stewed tomatoes	1 teaspoon oil
2 beef bouillon cubes	

Pick over lentils, wash and drain. Combine with remaining ingredients except frankfurters and oil in 5 or 6 quart saucepan. Cover and simmer over low heat for 2 hours stirring occasionally. Brown frankfurters in oil and slice. Add to soup and cook 10 minutes longer. *Makes 3½ quarts.*
Variation: Ham bone or beef bone may be used in the cooking water. If used, omit bouillon cubes.

Rose Baddour Saleeby

Especially good on a cold day.

POTATO SOUP

3 to 4 medium size potatoes	4 tablespoons butter
2 slices onion	1 teaspoon salt
4 cups milk	1 teaspoon celery salt
2 tablespoons flour	

Cook onion with potatoes. Mash potatoes. Scald milk. In saucepan cook flour and butter, stirring until smooth. Add 1 cup scalded milk, salt and celery salt. Blend well. Add remaining milk and potatoes and boil 1 minute. Strain and thin to proper consistency with additional hot milk. Serve hot.

Chloe W. Dacus

SHRIMP BISQUE

1 cup water	2 cups milk
1 cup celery, chopped	3 tablespoons flour
1 cup potatoes, diced	1 4½-ounce can shrimp, drained and
½ cup onions, chopped	chopped
½ teaspoon salt	2 tablespoons butter
Dash pepper	Snipped parsley

In saucepan, combine water, celery, potato, onion, salt and pepper. Simmer covered for 15 minutes or until potatoes are tender. Combine milk and flour until smooth. Stir into mixture along with shrimp and butter. Cook and stir until thick and bubbly. Garnish with snipped parsley. *Makes 4 servings.*

Beverly Reeves

Doubles as entree.

CHEESEBURGERS

1½ pounds ground beef	2 large onions
¼ pound lean pork	10 slices cheese
1 teaspoon salt	3 medium tomatoes, peeled and
½ teaspoon black pepper	sliced
1 cup milk	Hamburger buns

Grind meat together. Mix in a bowl, with salt and pepper. Gradually add milk and work with hands until well mixed. Form into balls, allowing 2 for each burger and pat out the size of buns. Place half the patties in large baking pan. Slice onions into round thin rings and arrange several on meat. Top with one slice of cheese and slice of tomato. Cover with another meat patty. Bake in 400° oven for 20 minutes. Heat buns and dip them in juice from the burgers.

Nona Ash

OPEN-FACED SUPREME SANDWICH

1 large slice rye bread	3 tablespoons parsley, chopped
Swiss or Mozzarella cheese	1 hard cooked egg, chopped
Sliced turkey or chicken	1 pint mayonnaise
Tomato slices	1½ tablespoons dry mustard
3 slices of bacon, fried and	1 medium onion, grated
crumbled	Juice of one lemon
Shredded lettuce	Garlic salt to taste
4 tablespoons Kosher dill pickles,	Pinch of sugar
chopped	

Make open-faced sandwich with bread, cheese, meat, tomato, bacon and lettuce. Combine remaining ingredients and add pickle juice to thin if needed. Use as topping for sandwich. *Makes enough dressing for 6 servings.*

Mrs. Charles Adams, Jr.

FRENCH-STYLE PEANUT PANWICHES

Peanut butter, plain or crunchy	1 teaspoon sugar
Jelly or jam	¼ teaspoon salt
12 slices thin bread	¼ cup milk
4 egg yolks	

Spread peanut butter and jelly on 6 slices of bread. Top with remaining slices to make the sandwiches. Beat egg yolks, sugar and salt together and stir in milk. Dip sandwiches into egg mixture, coating well. Soak sandwiches in egg mixture until they take up all the liquid. Brown in bacon drippings or oil, turning to brown both sides. Serve with honey or syrup or alone, as you like. Fried apples are good with these. *Serves 6.*

Eulalee B. Dacus

39

QUICK CORN SOUP

1 can cream style corn
1 cup milk
1 cup light cream
2 chicken bouillon cubes

Salt and white pepper to taste
½ stick oleo
Chopped parsley

Blend corn in blender. Combine milk, cream and bouillon. Add pepper and salt. Pour in saucepan; bring to boil, stirring constantly. Add oleo. Garnish with parsley. *Serves 4 to 6.*

Jennie Yaeger

An Amphitheater is located north of the Administration Building in a picturesque setting. The stage is used by the surrounding communities as well as for Baddour Center functions, such as a community-wide, Easter Sunrise Service, concerts, and special presentations. The 300-seat entertainment center is a memorial to Oneida Smith (Mrs. Charles) Baddour, who gave enthusiasm and loving direction in the planning and creation of Baddour Center. Mrs. Baddour died before the Center was completed in 1978.

"Because the road was steep and long
  And through a dark and lonely land,
God set upon my lips a song
  And put a lantern in my hand."
      –"Love's Lantern," Joyce Kilmer

SALADS & DRESSINGS

Oneida Baddour Amphitheater

APRICOT AND CHEESE SALAD

1 #2 can apricots	3 tablespoons flour
1 #2 can crushed pineapple	1 egg, beaten
2 cups hot water	2 tablespoons butter
2 packages orange Jello	1 cup whipping cream
1 package plain gelatin	¾ cup cheese, grated
½ cup sugar	

Drain apricots and pineapples, reserving juice. Dissolve Jello and gelatin in hot water and add 2 cups of the reserved juices. Cool slightly, and stir in fruit. Let stand until firm. To make topping, combine sugar, flour and eggs in top of double boiler. Stir in 1 cup of reserved fruit juices and cook over low heat until thick. Stir in butter and cook well. Whip cream and fold in. Spread on top of Jello and sprinkle with cheese.

Lilly Baddour Icenhour

APRICOT JELLO DELIGHT

2 packages apricot Jello	2 tablespoons flour
3½ cups boiling water	1 egg, beaten
1 #2 can crushed pineapple	1 tablespoon butter
1 cup miniature marshmallows	3 ounces cream cheese
2 bananas, mashed	1 package Dream Whip
1 cup sugar	

Dissolve Jello in water and let stand until syrupy. Drain pineapple well, reserving juice. Add pineapple, marshmallows and bananas to Jello. Pour into large flat glass dish. In saucepan, combine sugar, flour, egg, butter and ½ cup reserved pineapple juice. Cook until thick. Add cream cheese and cool. Prepare Dream Whip according to package directions and fold into cooled sauce. Spread over congealed Jello. *Serves 12*.

Dottie Schoettle

COOL SUMMER SALAD

1 box pistachio pudding mix	1½ cups Cool Whip
1 cup miniature marshallows	½ cup cherries, chopped
½ cup pecans, chopped	1 large can crushed pineapple,
1½ cups sour cream	drained

Mix all ingredients well and chill 4 or 5 days for best flavor.

Mary Simpson

This salad holds up well and may be made well in advance of serving.

FROZEN FRUIT SALAD

1 cup mayonnaise
1 8-ounce package cream cheese
3 tablespoons confectioners sugar
1 cup pineapple tidbits, drained
1 cup apricots, chopped

½ cup cherries, halved
2 cups miniature marshmallows
1 cup whipped cream
Few drops red food coloring

Gradually add mayonnaise to cream cheese. Mix until smooth and well blended. Add confectioners sugar, pineapple, apricots, cherries and marshmallows. Fold in whipped cream, add food color and freeze. *Serves 8.*

Mrs. Frank Steudlein

FROZEN FRUIT SALAD

¾ cup sugar
4 ounces cream cheese
½ cup pecans, chopped
2 bananas, sliced and covered
   with lemon juice

1 can pineapple tidbits, drained
1 10-ounce package frozen
   strawberries and juice
1 large carton Cool Whip

Cream sugar and cheese. Fold in other ingredients. Freeze.

Joyce T. Ferguson,
Mrs. Ben G. Hines

STRAWBERRY SURPRISE

1 3-ounce package strawberry
   gelatin
1 cup boiling water
1 10-ounce package frozen
   strawberries

1 small can crushed pineapple,
   drained
2 bananas, mashed
½ cup pecans, chopped
½ cup sour cream

Dissolve gelatin in boiling water; add strawberries, pineapple, bananas and pecans. Chill half the mixture until thickened; spread with sour cream. Cover with remaining gelatin mixture; chill until firm. *Serves 4-6.*

Cheryl Grace

CHERRY SALAD

2   packages cherry Jello
2½ cups boiling water
1   can pineapple juice
1   can cranberry sauce

1   can pineapple chunks
1   cup celery, chopped
¾   cup nuts, chopped

Dissolve Jello in water and pineapple juice. Allow to cool. Stir in chopped cranberry sauce, pineapple, celery and nuts. Chill.

Mrs. James H. Wright

BLACK BING CHERRY SALAD

1   package cherry Jello
1   cup cherry juice
1   cup Port Wine or ½ Port and ½
    sherry

1   can Bing cherries
1   3-ounce package cream cheese
Pecan halves

Dissolve Jello in cup of hot cherry juice. Add the wine. Line a mold with cherries stuffed with cream cheese and pecan halves. Pour in Jello mixture and let congeal before serving.

RASPBERRY SALAD

2   small packages or 1 large
    package raspberry Jello
1½ cups hot water
2   cups orange juice

1   jar cranberry-orange relish
1   small can crushed pineapple
½   cup nuts, chopped (optional)

Dissolve Jello in hot water and add orange juice. Chill until it begins to set. Stir in relish, pineapple, and nuts. Chill.

Grace Knolton

BANANA-PEACH-MARSHMALLOW SALAD

2   tablespoons Knox gelatin
½ cup cold water
1   cup peach juice
1   cup miniature marshmallows
¾ cup sugar
1   cup peaches, diced

1   cup bananas, diced
¼ cup lemon juice
2   egg whites, beaten
1   cup whipping cream
⅛ teaspoon salt

Dissolve gelatin in water. In double boiler, bring peach juice to boiling. Add gelatin, marshmallows, and sugar. Cook until congealed lightly, and add fruit and lemon juice. Fold in egg whites, whipped cream and salt. Chill.

Mrs. L. E. Burch, Jr.

PEACH CONGEALED SALAD

1   3-ounce package peach Jello
2   large ripe peaches
½ cup celery, finely chopped
½ cup pecans, chopped

1   cup whipped cream
½ cup miniature marshmallows
⅓ cup mayonnaise

Make Jello as directions on package. Congeal. Beat until light and fluffy. Chop peaches, and combine with remaining ingredients. Stir into whipped Jello. Pour in Jello mold. Chill until firm. Serve on lettuce leaves. *Yield: about 6 servings.*

Virginia M. Steinek

SNOW AND GOLD SALAD

1   9-ounce package Cool Whip
1   regular package orange Jello
1   cup small curd cottage cheese

1   29-ounce can sliced peaches
Chopped nuts

Mix Cool Whip and Jello well. Fold in cottage cheese. Drain peaches in a paper towel after draining in a colander, then dry individually with paper towels. Add to salad. Pour into large dish and top with chopped nuts.

Myrtle Burks
Hazel Smith

ORANGE SHERBET SALAD

1 #2 can crushed pineapple
2 packages orange gelatin
Boiling water
1 pint orange sherbet

1 #11 can mandarin oranges,
   drained and diced
2 bananas, mashed

Drain juice from pineapple and add enough boiling water to make 2 cups. Dissolve gelatin in this liquid. Add sherbet and stir until melted. Add fruit and chill.

Beth Vail

ORANGE CONGEALED SALAD

1 small package orange Jello
1 cup hot water
1 small can crushed pineapple
1 banana, sliced
1 cup miniature marshmallows
½ cup pecans, chopped

½ cup sugar
2 tablespoons flour
1 egg
3 ounces cream cheese
1 package Dream Whip

Dissolve Jello in hot water. After the Jello is dissolved, add 7 ice cubes and let these melt. Drain the crushed pineapple and reserve the juice for the topping. Add the crushed pineapple, banana, marshmallows and chopped nuts to gelatin and let gel, stirring occasionally.

For topping, combine sugar, flour, egg and reserved pineapple juice in saucepan, and cook over low heat until it thickens, stirring constantly. After it thickens, add cream cheese. Mix until creamy and put into refrigerator until cold. Mix Dream Whip according to directions on package. Fold cold topping mixture into Dream Whip. Pour over gelatin mixture.

Mrs. William Sanford

PINK SALAD

1 20-ounce can crushed pineapple
24 large marshmallows
1 package strawberry gelatin

2 cups cottage cheese
1 cup pecans, chopped
½ pint whipping cream, whipped

Combine juice from pineapple with marshmallows. Place over low heat. Add gelatin and stir until all are dissolved. Remove from heat and cool slightly. Add cottage cheese, pineapple and pecans. Fold in whipped cream.

Gladys Jones

LIME JELLO SALAD

1 small box lime Jello
1 small box lemon Jello
2 cups boiling water
16 ounces cream cheese
1 small can Eagle Brand
   condensed milk

1 tablespoon mayonnaise
1 small can crushed pineapple
1 cup pecans, chopped

Dissolve Jello in boiling water. Add cream cheese, Eagle Brand milk and mayonnaise. Mix with electric mixer at slow speed for 3 minutes. Add remaining ingredients and let gel for 2 hours.

Connie Banks

LEMON LIME SALAD

1 package lemon Jello
1 package lime Jello
1 pint hot water
1 cup salad dressing
2 teaspoons horseradish

1 carton cottage cheese
½ cup Eagle Brand milk
1 can crushed pineapple
1 cup nuts

Dissolve Jello in water. Cool. Combine remaining ingredients and stir into partially set Jello. To make firmer salad, add 1 package Knox gelatin to Jello and hot water.

Mrs. E. H. Clarke, Sr.

CONGEALED FRUIT SALAD

1 #2 can crushed pineapple,
   drained
½ cup juice from pineapple
1 package Knox gelatin
2 tablespoons sugar

2 tablespoons mayonnaise
1 medium bottle cherries, sliced
   round
Dash salt
1 cup whipped cream

Pour juice over gelatin in top of double boiler and dissolve. Let set until cool. Then add sugar, mayonnaise, cherries, pineapple and salt. Now fold in whipped cream, place in refrigerator to congeal. Cut in squares and serve on lettuce.

Mrs. L. E. Burch, Jr.

EASY FRUIT SALAD

1-pound can pineapple chunks
1-pound can fruit cocktail
1-pound can peach slices
1 large or 2 small apples, peeled
2 bananas

1 cup red grapes
1 cup miniature marshmallows
½ cup pecans, chopped (optional)
Salt to taste

Drain pineapple, fruit cocktail and peach slices. Dice apple and bananas. Remove seeds from grapes. Combine fruits and remaining ingredients. Chill. *Serves 10-12.*

Amanda Wise

FRUIT SALAD

1 cup green seedless grapes
1 cup bananas, diced
1 cup pineapple, diced
1 cup maraschino cherries
1 cup peaches, diced
1 cup orange sections
2 cups marshmallows

2 eggs
2 tablespoons sugar
2 tablespoons orange juice
2 tablespoons vinegar
1 tablespoon butter
Dash salt
2 cups sour cream

Mix fruit and marshmallows together. May use canned fruit except grapes. For dressing, in a small pan combine eggs, sugar, orange juice, and vinegar. Cook, stirring constantly, until thick. Remove from heat, stir in butter and salt. Cool. Add sour cream.

Anita M. Slaughter

OUT OF THIS WORLD SALAD

1 package lemon Jello
1 cup hot water
1 8-ounce package cream cheese, softened
1 small can crushed pineapple

1 teaspoon sugar
1 teaspoon vanilla
½ cup pecans
1 cup Seven-up

Dissolve Jello in water. Add cream cheese, and stir until dissolved. Cool; add pineapple, sugar, vanilla and pecans. Stir. Add Seven-up, stir well, and chill until set.

Jackie Taylor

FRUIT SALAD

1 quart strawberries or
  blueberries, sliced
1 14½-ounce can pineapple
  chunks
1 medium can pears, chopped

1 can mandarin oranges
1 cup maraschino cherries, cut in
  half
2 bananas, sliced
1 can peach pie filling

Drain all fruit well, at least 30 minutes. Mix well with the peach pie filling. Chill and serve on lettuce.

Mrs. Burton W. Renager

GEORGIE'S CONFETTI SALAD

2 packages lemon or orange
  flavored gelatin
2 cups tart apple, chopped

2 cups orange sections
4-5 green onions

Make gelatin as directed on package. Do not peel apple before chopping. Remove all membrane from oranges. If sections are large, cut them in half. Chop green onions, including green tops. Add apples, oranges and onions to gelatin. Pour into a 2-quart pyrex casserole and chill. *Serves 8-10.*

Ann Basore

Very old recipe. From Joe Neff's grandmother.

JELLO SALAD – WITH TOPPING

1 cup marshmallows
2 cups hot water
1 package lemon Jello
1 cup crushed pineapple, drained
3 bananas, sliced
½ cup sugar

2 tablespoons cornstarch or flour
1 egg, beaten
1 cup pineapple juice (add water to
  juice to make 1 cup)
1 package Dream Whip, whipped
1 cup cheese or coconut, grated

Melt marshmallows in hot water. Add Jello, pineapple and bananas. Place in refrigerator to set. In saucepan, mix sugar, cornstarch or flour, egg and pineapple juice. Stir and cook until thick over medium heat. When cool, fold in Dream Whip. Pour on top of Jello. Top with grated cheese or coconut and place in refrigerator to chill.

Mrs. Henry Harmon

FRUIT SALAD

1 large package Cool Whip
1 large or 2 small boxes orange Jello
1 can mandarin orange segments, drained
½ cup coconut

1 cup small curd cottage cheese
1 large can crushed pineapple, drained
1 cup pecans, chopped
1 apple, peeled and diced

Mix Cool Whip and Jello together until Jello is no longer grainy. Add other ingredients and mix well. Chill.

Mrs. Jack Atkins, Jr.

HARVEST FRUIT MOLD

1 11-ounce package mixed dried fruit
⅓ cup sugar

2 3-ounce packages orange Jello
2 cups boiling water

Place fruit in saucepan, and add enough water to cover. Simmer gently in covered pan 25 minutes, adding sugar for last 5 minutes. Drain fruit, reserving syrup to make 2 cups. Dissolve Jello in the boiling water and stir in the reserved syrup. Chill til partially set. Cut fruit into small pieces and fold into Jello. Chill in individual molds or one large mold. *Serves 10.*

Mrs. J. E. Craig

STEWED GRAPEFRUIT

3 grapefruit
1 cup sugar

½ cup water

Peel and remove membrane from grapefruit; remove sections while holding over a bowl to catch the juice. Sliver 2 tablespoons of the yellow part of the rind, add sugar and water. Cook over low heat, without stirring, until consistency of corn syrup. Pour hot syrup over the grapefruit sections, stir gently and chill thoroughly. *Serves four.*

Ruby Alperin

HOT FRUIT SALAD

1 medium can peach halves
1 medium can pear halves
1 medium can apricot halves
1 medium can pineapple slices
1 medium can apple rings

1 medium can maraschino cherries,
   halved
2 tablespoons cornstarch
1 cup brown sugar
1 cup sherry

Drain fruit, reserving liquid. Arrange fruit in large baking dish. To liquid add cornstarch, sugar and sherry. Cook over hot water, stirring constantly, until thick. Pour over fruit. Bake at 350° for 30 minutes. May be refrigerated for several days.

Amy Denny

CURRIED FRUIT CASSEROLE

1 29-ounce can peach halves
1 small can apricots
1 29-ounce can pears
3 small cans pineapple pieces

10 maraschino cherries
⅓ cup butter, melted
¾ cup brown sugar
4 teaspoons curry powder

Drain fruit well. Mix butter, brown sugar and curry powder. Lay fruit in a shallow baking dish, hollow side up. Dot all over with butter and sugar mixture. Bake at 325° for 1 hour, basting frequently. Cool and refrigerate for at least 1 day. Warm over at 350° for ½ hour. *Serves 10.*

Elizabeth and Catherine Baddour

Pretty, different, and easy to make.

APRICOT CASSEROLE

1 #2½ can peeled apricots
½ box light brown sugar
3 tablespoons lemon juice

½ box Cheese Ritz crackers
½ stick oleo, melted

Remove seeds from apricots and drain in colander for 1-1½ hours. Turn apricot, cavity up, in pyrex dish and sprinkle with sugar and lemon juice. Marinate overnight in refrigerator. Just before cooking crumble crackers coarsely over apricots; drizzle with butter and bake at 350° for 40-50 minutes.

Elizabeth and Catherine Baddour

Delightful with any meats.

51

ANTIPASTA

1 small cauliflower head, broken into flowerettes
2 carrots, cut into 2-inch strips
2 stalks celery, cut into 1-inch pieces
1 green pepper, cut into 2-inch strips
1 jar pimento or fresh red pepper, cut into 2-inch strips
1 jar pitted green olives, drained
1 can ripe olives, drained
1 cup small yellow squash, sliced (optional)
16 ounces Kraft Italian dressing
1 teaspoon sugar
Wine vinegar

Combine vegetables in bowl with air-tight top. Add Italian dressing. If vegetables aren't completely covered, add sugar and enough vinegar to cover. Place top on bowl and refrigerate. Will keep at least a month.

Mrs. Stewart Vail

ASPARAGUS SALAD

1 pound fresh asparagus
8 tablespoons soy sauce
1 tablespoon sesame oil
1 tablespoon vegetable oil
1 tablespoon vinegar
Dash pepper
Dash MSG (optional)
¼ tablespoon onion powder

Cut off tough ends of asparagus and wash. In large saucepan, boil 1½ quarts of water. Add asparagus and cook one minute. Drain and plunge asparagus into cold water until thoroughly chilled. Drain well. Cut into one-inch pieces. In bowl, mix soy sauce, sesame oil, vegetable oil, vinegar, pepper, MSG and onion powder. Combine sauce and asparagus just before serving. *Makes six servings.*

Doris Lanford

CONGEALED ASPARAGUS SALAD

1 17-ounce jar green asparagus
1 3-ounce package cream cheese
⅓ pint mayonnaise
1 3-ounce package lemon gelatin dessert
½ pint boiling water
¼ cup slivered almonds
2 teaspoons almond extract

Whip asparagus juice into cream cheese, add well-mashed asparagus and mayonnaise. Dissolve lemon gelatin in water. Cool. Add asparagus mixture, almonds and almond extract. Spoon into slightly greased mold.

Mrs. William M. Forman

DELICIOUS MOLDED ASPARAGUS SALAD

¾ cup sugar
½ cup vinegar
1 tablespoon lemon juice
1 cup water
½ teaspoon salt
1 envelope unflavored gelatin
½ cup cold water

1 cup celery, chopped
½ cup pecans, chopped
2 whole pimentos, chopped
1 10½-ounce can cut asparagus, drained
2 teaspoons onion, grated
½ cup stuffed olives, chopped

Combine sugar, vinegar, lemon juice, water and salt; bring to a boil, and boil 2 minutes. Soften gelatin in cold water; add to vinegar mixture, stirring until dissolved. Chill until consistency of unbeaten egg white. Fold in remaining ingredients, spoon into mold, and chill until firm.

Nellie George Baddour

SWEET-SOUR BEANS

2 cans whole green beans, drained
1 cup sugar
¾ cup water
¾ cup red vinegar

4 tablespoons salad oil
2 cloves garlic, chopped
2 large white onions, sliced

Rinse beans and drain. Combine sugar, water, vinegar, oil, garlic and onions and add beans. Let stand overnight in refrigerator. Before serving add salt and pepper to taste.

Gladys Jones

BEAN SALAD

1 can French style green beans
1 can English peas
1 onion, cut in rings
1 green pepper, sliced in strips
1 can water chestnuts, sliced
1 cup celery, chopped

½ cup water
1¼ cups white vinegar
¼ cup oil
1 cup white sugar
3 teaspoons salt

Drain vegetables and put in container. Mix dressing and pour over vegetables. Marinate overnight.

Mrs. Malcolm Graham

53

GAGA'S VEGETABLE SALAD

1 can cut green beans, drained
1 can English peas, drained
1 small can mixed vegetables, drained
1 jar mushrooms, drained
1 medium jar cut pimento
¾ cup celery, chopped

1 bell pepper, chopped
3 bunches green onions, chopped
1 tablespoon mustard
1 teaspoon salt
1 cup vinegar
1 cup sugar
½ cup salad oil

Place all vegetables in a bowl. Mix mustard, salt, vinegar, sugar, and oil together. Pour over vegetables, and marinate overnight. *Serves 8-10.*

Carol Higgins

My mother-in-law's "special occasion" salad.

3-BEAN SALAD

1 can green beans, drained
1 can wax beans, drained
1 can kidney beans, drained
1 large white onion, chopped
1 green pepper, chopped
½ cup sugar

½ cup vinegar
½ cup Wesson oil
1 teaspoon salt
¼ teaspoon pepper
1 pimento, chopped

Put all vegetables in bowl. Combine sugar, vinegar, oil, salt, pepper, and pimento. Pour over vegetables. Marinate 5-6 hours before serving. *Serves 10.*

Carolyn Chalk
Mrs. Woods C. Eastland

BROCCOLI SALAD

1 package frozen broccoli
1 envelope unflavored gelatin
¼ cup cold water
1 can beef consommé, heated
1 cup mayonnaise

6 hard cooked eggs, sliced
½ teaspoon salt
1 teaspoon onion juice
Juice of one lemon
1 teaspoon Worcestershire

Cook broccoli according to package directions. Cool and cut into small pieces. Soak gelatin in cold water; dissolve in hot consommé. Cool completely. Add remaining ingredients and pour into individual molds. Chill until firm. *Serves 12.*

Barbara Petty

CAESAR SALAD OF THE KINGS

Romaine lettuce
3 large garlic cloves
½ cup olive oil
3 slices French bread
1 egg

2 drops Tabasco
¼ teaspoon Worcestershire sauce
Salt and pepper
1 lime
¼-½ cup Parmesan cheese

Use only the small crisp leaves of lettuce. Wash and drain lettuce and place in refrigerator until ready to prepare salad. Crush 1 clove of garlic in 1 jigger of oil. Set aside for 2 hours. Cut bread into ½-inch cubes. Sauté lightly in remaining olive oil with a clove of garlic. Place on a baking sheet and toast in 200° oven for 2 hours. Coddle the egg by dropping it in boiling water for 1 minute and immediately putting it in cold water. When cooled, break the egg into a small bowl, add Tabasco and Worcestershire, and beat. In a wooden salad bowl, sprinkle some salt and rub the inside of the bowl with a garlic clove. Add lettuce and salt and pepper to taste. Mixing well after each addition, add in order: juice from lime, coddled egg, reserved olive oil, and Parmesan cheese. Top with croutons and serve immediately.

Barney Holt

CAESAR SALAD

1 large head romaine lettuce, washed and broken
6 cups croutons
Salt and ground black pepper
1½ cloves garlic, minced
¾ cup olive oil
¼ cup wine vinegar

2 tablespoons lemon juice
1 cup anchovies, drained and cut
1 tablespoon capers and juice
1 egg, coddled for 1 minute
2 tablespoons Worcestershire sauce
3 tablespoons Parmesan cheese

Place greens and croutons in large bowl, then salt and pepper to taste. Mix garlic, olive oil, vinegar, lemon juice, anchovies, capers, egg, and Worcestershire together. Pour over croutons and greens, and add Parmesan cheese. Toss to distribute dressing, and serve immediately. *Serves 6.*

Sara M. Hart

RAW BROCCOLI SALAD

1 tomato
1 bunch of broccoli
3 or 4 green onions, chopped
½ cup mayonnaise

½ cup sour cream
1 tablespoon lemon juice
Salt to taste

Cut tomato and broccoli flowerets into bite-size pieces. Add green onions. Combine mayonnaise, sour cream, lemon juice, and salt, and pour over the vegetables. Let stand in refrigerator overnight.

Billy and Barbara Mills

COPPER PENNIES

5 cups carrots, sliced
1 onion, sliced into rings
2 small bell peppers (optional)
1 can cream of tomato soup
½ cup salad oil
1 cup sugar

¾ cup vinegar
1 teaspoon prepared mustard
1 teaspoon Worcestershire sauce
1 teaspoon salt
1 teaspoon black pepper

Cook carrots until tender. Drain and cool. Add onion rings and peppers. Mix other ingredients together and pour over carrots. Let set 12 hours. Keeps well.

Mrs. Carlton Stubbs, Brenda Vick
Mrs. Albert L. Waring

Will keep as long as two weeks in the refrigerator.

CHICKEN SALAD DELUXE

3   cups chicken, cooked and diced
½   cup toasted pecans
1   cup celery, chopped
½   cup coconut
½   cup seedless grapes, halved

¼   cup sour cream
1   teaspoon mustard
½   teaspoon salt
½   cup mayonnaise
Juice from half a lemon

Combine chicken, pecans, celery, coconut and grapes. Mix together the sour cream, mustard, salt, mayonnaise, and lemon juice to make dressing. Serve on lettuce or halved avocado. Surround with pineapple or other fruit. Garnish with olives or cherries.

Gertrude Dacus

A complete luncheon plate.

CURRIED CHICKEN AND PECAN SALAD

2   cups cooked or canned chicken, cubed
1½   cups cooked rice
½   cup crushed pineapple, drained well
Small can sliced pineapple, cut in small pieces
1   tablespoon red wine vinegar
2   tablespoons salad oil

1   teaspoon salt
¾   teaspoon curry powder
1   cup celery, diced
¼   cup green pepper, chopped
¾   cup pecans, broken
½ to ¾ cup mayonnaise
Lettuce
Pecan halves

Combine chicken, rice, pineapple, vinegar, salad oil, salt and curry powder. Chill 2 hours or longer. Fold in celery, green pepper, broken pecans and enough mayonnaise to moisten. To serve, pile on crisp lettuce and garnish with pecan halves.

Hita Jo Pryor

HOT CHICKEN SALAD

2   cups chicken breasts, cooked, deboned and chopped
1½   cups celery, chopped fine
1   cup Hellman's mayonnaise (do not substitute)
2   tablespoons lemon juice

2   teaspoons onion, grated
½   teaspoon salt
½ to ¾ cup toasted almonds
1   cup American cheese, grated
1   cup potato chips, crushed

Combine chicken, celery, mayonnaise, lemon juice, onion, and salt. Toss lightly. Put in 2-quart flat casserole. Top with almonds, cheese and potato chips. Bake at 350° for 20 minutes or until hot.

Mrs. Bill Lunsford

CUCUMBERS IN SOUR CREAM

1 small clove garlic
¾ teaspoon salt
1 carton sour cream
2 tablespoons distilled red
  vinegar

¼ teaspoon pepper
2 cucumbers, washed and scored

Mash garlic and salt together. Combine sour cream, salt-garlic mixture, vinegar and pepper. Slice cucumbers ⅛" thick. Toss with sour cream mixture and chill.

Mrs. Robert Homra

This always makes a hit.

JELLIED SOUR CREAM CUCUMBERS

2 medium cucumbers
1 teaspoon salt
Dash pepper
1 cup sour cream
3 tablespoons vinegar

2 tablespoons chives or green onion
  tops, minced
1 package unflavored gelatin
¼ cup cold water
Mayonnaise

Peel and grate cucumbers and remove seed. Season with salt and good dash of pepper. Mix together sour cream, vinegar, chives or green onion tops. Soften gelatin in cold water, dissolve over hot water and add to sour cream mixture. Add chopped cucumbers and mix well. Mold in ring mold. Serve with a dab of mayonnaise.

Mildred F. Fall

POTATO SALAD

6 large potatoes
6 eggs, hard boiled and chopped
1 large onion, chopped
1½ cups celery, chopped

1 tablespoon mustard
1½ teaspoons salt
4 cups mayonnaise
Paprika

Boil potatoes with jackets on. Then peel and cut in small cubes. In serving bowl, layer: potatoes, eggs, celery, onion, and mayonnaise. Repeat. Stir well. Sprinkle with paprika.

Mrs. James H. Wright

SERSTAH'S SALAD

1 cup mayonnaise
1 tablespoon lemon juice
1 teaspoon soy sauce
⅛ teaspoon curry powder
2 small cans tuna, drained
1 cup celery, chopped

1 box frozen peas, defrosted but not cooked
1 10-ounce jar cocktail onions, halved
1 can chow mein noodles
1 bag slivered almonds

Mix mayonnaise, lemon juice, soy sauce, and curry together to make dressing. Let set 24 hours. At time of serving, combine tuna, celery, peas, and onions. Add chow mein noodles, almonds, and dressing.

Carol Thompson

Good for a luncheon.

ROQUEFORT TUNA SALAD

1 7-ounce can tuna, drained and flaked
1 cup celery, diced
1¼-ounce wedge of Roquefort cheese, cubed

1 tablespoon onion, minced
⅛ teaspoon pepper
¾ cup mayonnaise

Mix all ingredients thoroughly and serve on crisp lettuce cups. *Serves 2 to 3.*

Oneida Baddour

LILLIAN'S SALMON PARTY SALAD

1 envelope gelatin
¼ cup cold water
¾ cup boiling water
2 tablespoons sugar
1 tablespoon fresh lemon juice
2 tablespoons onion, grated
½ teaspoon horseradish
½ teaspoon salt
1 #1 can Merrimac red salmon, drained and flaked

½ cup mayonnaise
⅓ cup ripe olives, sliced
¼ cup celery, finely chopped
1 avocado, mashed
½ cup sour cream
½ teaspoon salt
Dash of lemon juice

Soften gelatin in cold water. Add boiling water and mix well. Add sugar, lemon juice, onion, horseradish and salt. If this mixture is not tart enough, add 1 tablespoon vinegar. Chill until partially set. Stir in salmon, mayonnaise, olives and celery. Pour into mold. Let set overnight. Serve with avocado dressing, made by mixing mashed avocado, sour cream, salt, and dash of lemon juice.

Mrs. L. H. Polk

BAR-B-Q SLAW

1 medium head cabbage	1 cup vinegar
1 small onion	¾ cup sugar
2 stems of celery	1 teaspoon salt
1 green bell pepper	1 tablespoon white mustard seed
1 carrot	½ teaspoon turmeric or curry powder

Put vegetables in blender. Cover with water and chop into bite-size pieces. Drain. Heat vinegar, sugar, salt, mustard seed and turmeric or curry. Pour over vegetables. Seal in jars and refrigerate. Keeps very well.

Elizabeth and Catherine Baddour

SLAW

3 small onions, sliced thin	½ cup vinegar
1 small cabbage, shredded thin	½ cup sugar
2 cucumbers, sliced thin	¼ cup Wesson oil

Mix onions, cabbage, and cucumbers together and soak in ice water until crisp. Drain well. Combine vinegar, sugar and oil. Pour over vegetables and let set overnight.

Amanda Wise

SLAW

1 head cabbage, shredded	1 cup sugar
1 teaspoon grated onion or more if desired	1 teaspoon turmeric
	1 teaspoon mustard seed
1 bell pepper, chopped	1 teaspoon salt
1 cup vinegar	

Combine cabbage, onion and pepper. Bring vinegar, sugar, turmeric, mustard seed and salt to a boil and pour over cabbage mixture. Let stand til cool. Refrigerate overnight. Keeps for weeks.

Mrs. Frank Steudlein

The beauty of this recipe is that it can be kept in the refrigerator for weeks and still be as fresh as the day it's made.

SARA CLARK'S SLAW

½ head cabbage, shredded
½ onion, chopped
1 large sweet pepper, chopped
1 3-ounce jar pimento-stuffed
   olives, whole
1 teaspoon salt

1 teaspoon celery seed
½ cup oil
½ cup red vinegar
½ cup sugar
½ cup sweet relish
1 teaspoon prepared mustard

Combine cabbage, onions, pepper, olives, salt and celery seed. Boil oil, vinegar and sugar until sugar is dissolved. Add relish and mustard when cool and pour over slaw. Chill. *Makes 8-10 servings.* This keeps about 10 days in the refrigerator.

Mrs. Kent Ingram

CABBAGE SLAW

1 large cabbage, chopped
1 large onion, chopped
1 cup vinegar
1 tablespoon celery seed

1 tablespoon prepared mustard
1 cup oil
¾ cup sugar

Mix cabbage and onion together in large container. Bring to a boil the vinegar, celery seed and mustard. Add oil and sugar and bring to a second boil. Pour this over cabbage. Let stand (covered) outside refrigerator overnight. Next morning refrigerate. Keeps for weeks.

Barbara Petty

FABULOUS COLE SLAW

1 head cabbage
1 jar Kraft Miracle French
   Dressing
½ cup sweet mix pickle juice
2 tablespoons vinegar

½ cup sweet mix pickle, chopped
1 jar pimento, chopped
¼ cup sugar
Salt and celery seed to taste

Shred cabbage. Add remainder of ingredients and let marinate at least four hours. Do not make any substitutions of French dressing—that is the secret to the tangy taste.

61

PERKY CAULIFLOWER SLAW

1 small head cauliflower, chopped
2 tablespoons onions, finely
   chopped
2 tablespoons radishes, grated
1 tablespoon lemon juice

1 teaspoon prepared horseradish
½ teaspoon salt
⅛ teaspoon black pepper
1 tablespoon mayonnaise

Toss together in a large bowl chopped cauliflower, onion, and grated radishes. Blend together the lemon juice, horseradish, salt, pepper and mayonnaise. Toss with vegetables until well blended. Chill covered in refrigerator several hours before serving. Serve in lettuce cups. Sprinkle each with snipped parsley. *4 to 6 servings.*

Rose Baddour Saleeby

Unusual flavor. Garnish with tomato wedges.

SAUERKRAUT SALAD

1 large can chopped sauerkraut
¾ cup sugar
1 cup celery, diced
1 cup bell pepper, diced
¼ cup onion, diced

3 tablespoons red vinegar
½ teaspoon salt
⅛ teaspoon pepper
1 teaspoon celery seed
3 tablespoons pimentos, diced

Drain kraut for 15 minutes. Place in large bowl. Add remaining ingredients and mix well. Store in refrigerator for at least 24 hours. This salad keeps indefinitely. *Serves 15 to 20.*

Mrs. Robert Homra

PICKLE AND NUT SALAD

3 cups water
1 cup sugar
12 cloves
3 tablespoons gelatin

1 cup nuts
1 cup sweet cucumber pickles, sliced
   thin

Boil 2 cups water, sugar, and cloves until clear. Soak gelatin in one cup cold water, and add first mixture. Stir in nuts and pickles. Pour in molds and let congeal.

Mrs. James H. Wright

HYDE PARK SALAD

2 potatoes, cooked and diced	2 hard-cooked eggs, diced
1 cup carrots, sliced and cooked	Homemade mayonnaise
1 cup green peas, cooked	Salt and pepper to taste
2 large sour pickles, diced	

Combine potatoes, carrots, peas, pickles and hard-cooked eggs in a bowl. Moisten with mayonnaise; season with salt and pepper. *Yield: 4 servings*

CALICO SALAD BOWL

1 cup potatoes, cooked and diced	1 cup green peas
1 cup carrots, cooked and diced	¼ cup French dressing
2 tablespoons parsley, chopped	½ head lettuce
1 can pimento, chopped	Mayonnaise
2 tablespoons onions, chopped	

Combine vegetables, chill and marinate in French dressing one hour. Break lettuce into bite size pieces. Add vegetables, toss lightly. Serve with mayonnaise.

Mrs. James H. Wright

LAYERED SALAD

1 head of lettuce, shredded to bite size	1 package frozen peas
	1 pint Hellman's mayonnaise
1 green pepper, finely chopped	1 tablespoon sugar
1 cup celery, finely chopped	1 cup cheese, grated
1 Spanish onion, finely chopped	8 strips bacon

Place lettuce in 9x13 pan or glass pyrex dish followed by green pepper, and celery, and then onion. Then add peas, which have been cooked and drained. Spread mayonnaise on top and seal edges. Sprinkle sugar over mayonnaise. Fry bacon crisp, crumble and sprinkle over. Then sprinkle cheese over bacon. Cover with Saran Wrap and chill overnight. Cut into squares. Lift out of dish with a spatula. *Serves 12-15*.

Mrs. L. E. Burch, Jr., Lilly Baddour Icenhour,
Syble Bollinger, Nina Martin, Julian Neal

GUACAMOLE SALAD

1 avocado, mashed
1 tomato, finely chopped
1 teaspoon onion, finely chopped
Tabasco sauce to taste

1 tablespoon salad dressing
Salt to taste
Dash of lemon juice

Mix together and serve on shredded lettuce.

Mrs. Hugh Dillahunty

GOOD GREEN PEA SALAD

1 package frozen green peas
1½ cups mayonnaise
½ cup green onions, chopped
½ cup celery, chopped
¼ cup green pepper, chopped

1 teaspoon sugar
1 teaspoon salt
½ teaspooon pepper
1 head lettuce
8 slices bacon, fried

Cook and drain peas. Mix peas, mayonnaise, onions, celery, green pepper, sugar, salt and pepper together. Chill. Shred lettuce into 3-quart casserole. Spoon peas over lettuce and sprinkle with crumbled bacon.

June Smith

CHINESE SALAD

1 #2 can French style green beans
1 #2 can LeSeur peas
1 #2 can Chinese mixed vegetables
1 flat can water chestnuts, sliced
1 cup celery, finely chopped

2 medium white onions, chopped
1 small can button mushrooms
½ cup sugar
½ cup vinegar
¼ cup Wesson oil

Drain all vegetables. Mix sugar, vinegar and Wesson oil and pour over vegetables. Refrigerate overnight. Will keep for weeks.

Mrs. Albert L. Waring

TOMATO ASPIC

4 cups tomato juice
1 bay leaf
1 teaspoon onion juice
¼ cup vinegar

1 teaspoon sugar
1 teaspoon salt
Ground red pepper
2 packages lemon Jello

Boil tomato juice, bay leaf, and onion juice for 5 minutes. Add vinegar, sugar, salt, and pepper to taste. Pour over Jello and stir until dissolved. Pour into mold and refrigerate.

Grace Wesson

TOMATO ASPIC

Juice of 2 lemons
3½ cups tomato juice
1 tablespoon onion, grated
¼ teaspoon Tabasco
1 teaspoon Worcestershire
½ teaspoon salt

2 packages lemon Jello
1 cup celery, chopped fine
½ bell pepper, chopped fine
1 small jar stuffed olives, chopped fine

In saucepan, combine lemon juice, tomato juice, onion, Tabasco, Worcestershire, and salt. Bring to a boil, and add Jello. Remove from heat, let set 5 minutes, and strain. Refrigerate until it begins to thicken. Add celery, bell pepper, and olives. Refrigerate overnight. *Serves 8-10.*

Mrs. Bill Lunsford

RED RING SALAD MOLD

1 14½-ounce can Hunt's stewed
   tomatoes
1 package strawberry flavored
   gelatin

1 tablespoon vinegar
1 tablespoon lemon juice

Break up tomatoes. Heat until bubbly. Add gelatin, vinegar and lemon juice. Pour into ring mold. Chill until firm. (Double recipe fills 9-inch ring mold). Serve with:

Horseradish Sauce:

½ cup mayonnaise
½ cup sour cream

¼ cup prepared horseradish, drained

Ann Basore

65

BLEU CHEESE DRESSING

1   3-ounce package Bleu cheese,   1   cup mayonnaise
    grated   1   teaspoon garlic salt
1   cup buttermilk   Juice of 1 lemon

Mix all ingredients a day ahead for blending for flavors. Store in refrigerator. *Makes 3 cups.*

Oneida Baddour

A true bleu cheese dressing.

BLUE CHEESE BUTTERMILK SALAD DRESSING

1   cup cottage cheese   1   tablespoon chopped parsley
2   tablespoons Blue cheese,   2   tablespoons onion, grated
    crumbled   ½   teaspoon salt
1   tablespoon lemon juice   ¾   cup buttermilk

In a mixing bowl combine cottage cheese, Blue cheese, lemon juice, parsley,
onion and salt; beat well until well blended. Stir in buttermilk. *Yield: 2 cups.*
(Will keep refrigerated for 2 weeks.)

Homazelle Ashford

BLUE CHEESE DRESSING

8   ounce package cream cheese   ⅛   teaspoon garlic salt
1   small can evaporated milk   8   ounces Blue cheese or less
1   teaspoon celery seed

Soften cream cheese. Blend with milk a little at a time. Add spices and Blue
cheese (8 ounces of Blue cheese makes a very thick dressing.) If it becomes
too thick, add more milk.

Rosemond Deeb

GREEN GODDESS DRESSING

1   clove garlic
4   anchovy fillets, finely cut
2   tablespoons onion, chopped
1   teaspoon parsley

1   teaspoon tarragon
1   teaspoon chives
1   teaspoon tarragon vinegar
1 ½   cups mayonnaise

Mix together and serve.

Anita M. Slaughter

ROQUEFORT DRESSING

1   cup sour cream
1   cup mayonnaise
2   -ounce wedge of Roquefort
     (or to taste)
2   teaspoons lemon juice

1   teaspoon horseradish
Few drops Worcestershire sauce
Dash of Tabasco
2   tablespoons sherry

Mix all ingredients together. Chill.

Mildred Earney

ROTISSERIE DRESSING

1   pint mayonnaise
½   cup chili sauce
½   cup catsup
1   cup salad oil

1   teaspoon black pepper
2   tablespoons Worcestershire sauce
1   small onion, grated
3   cloves garlic, chopped fine

Mix well. Let set 24 hours before using.

Mrs. C. D. Williams

ALFRED'S 1000 ISLAND DRESSING

8   ounces heavy firm mayonnaise
2   ounces ketchup
2   ounces chili sauce
2   ounces relish

½   ounce capers, chopped
½   ounce mustard
½   teaspoon chives, chopped
½   teaspoon parsley, chopped

Mix thoroughly together. Makes 1 pint.

Palm Beach Kennel Club Chef

BEACON SALAD DRESSING

1¾ cups Stewarts salad dressing	1 tablespoon Lea & Perrins
1 can Heinz tomato soup	Worcestershire sauce
¼ can water	½ teaspoon garlic salt
¼ can vinegar	½ cup + 2 tablespoons Wesson oil
3 tablespoons sugar	

Mix well.

Marguerite Baddour

From the old Beacon restaurant in Memphis.

CUCUMBER SALAD DRESSING

1 large cucumber	1½ tablespoons lemon juice
1 medium white onion	⅛ teaspoon green food color
1 pint mayonnaise	1 tablespoon Worcestershire sauce
2 tablespoons sugar	⅛ teaspoon garlic powder
⅛ teaspoon Accent	

Slice cucumber and onion into blender. Add other ingredients and blend until smooth. Pour into container and refrigerate.

Bettye Mooneyhan

DRESSING FOR SALAD

¼ cup tomato sauce	1 teaspoon Worcestershire
⅓ cup red wine vinegar	¼ teaspoon dry mustard
1 cup salad oil	¼ teaspoon pepper
1 tablespoon sugar	½ teaspoon hot pepper sauce
1 teaspoon basil	1 clove garlic

Combine all the ingredients in a processor or blender and blend until smooth and the garlic is minced. Chill in a cruet until ready to use. *Makes 1⅔ cup dressing.*

Patricia Maxwell

SHRIMP SAUCE FOR MUSHROOM SOUFFLE OR VEGETABLES

¼ cup shrimp, chopped very fine
1 can cream of shrimp soup
1 3-ounce package cream cheese
1 tablespoon onion juice
1 tablespoon lemon juice
1 teaspoon Tabasco
½ teaspoon white pepper

Mix all ingredients together and heat in pan until smooth and melted. Very good over asparagus, broccoli, brussels sprouts or mushroom souffle. *Makes 2 cups.*

Mrs. William M. Forman

SAUCE FOR GREEN VEGETABLES

2 cups mayonnaise
1 small onion, grated
1 teaspoon prepared mustard
8 tablespoons olive oil
Big dash Tabasco sauce
1 teaspoon Worcestershire sauce
4 to 6 hard boiled eggs, mashed fine
Salt to taste

Mix all ingredients together. Especially good on green beans and meat sandwiches.

Amanda Wise

YOGURT HOLLANDAISE SAUCE

1 cup unflavored yogurt
4 egg yolks or 2 whole eggs
¾ teaspoon salt
2 teaspoons sugar
¼ teaspoon liquid hot pepper seasoning

In top of a double boiler, stir together the yogurt and egg yolks (or whole eggs) with a wire whip; then add the salt, sugar and liquid hot pepper seasoning. Place over barely simmering water and cook, stirring constantly with a wire whip, until thickened, about 8 to 10 minutes. Serve hot; or cool, cover and refrigerate up to two days. Reheat in the top of a double boiler, stirring over hot (not boiling) water. *Makes about 1⅓ cups.*

Hita Jo Pryor

"K's" MAYONNAISE

1 egg yolk
1 pint Mazola oil
3 tablespoons tarragon vinegar or
2 tablespoons tarragon vinegar
and 1 tablespoon lemon juice

1 or 2 slivers of garlic, crushed
½ teaspoon salt

Not good if you use any other vinegar. Beat egg yolk gradually, add oil — little at a time, then vinegar and then rest of ingredients.

Mrs. R. A. Caldwell, Sr.

Wonderful with cucumber sandwiches.

REMOULADE SAUCE

1 cup mayonnaise
1 clove garlic, pressed
1 small onion, finely chopped
1 hard boiled egg, finely chopped
1 dill pickle, finely chopped
4 sprigs parsley, finely chopped

1 teaspoon tarragon
1 teaspoon dried mustard
½ teaspoon paprika
1 teaspoon black pepper, freshly
ground

Combine mayonnaise, garlic, onion, egg, dill pickle and parsley in a bowl. Add tarragon, mustard, paprika and pepper. Blend well and let stand for one hour before using.

Jackie Edwards

REMOULADE SAUCE

1 pint Hellman's mayonnaise
½ clove garlic, pressed
¼ teaspoon tarragon
¼ teaspoon basil
1 tablespoon wine vinegar

½ medium onion, chopped fine
2 teaspoons horseradish
1 tablespoon lemon juice
Salt and pepper to taste

Mix all ingredients together. Store in refrigerator at least overnight. Keeps indefinitely. Serve over shrimp or other seafood that has been placed on a bed of shredded lettuce. Garnish with celery sticks, radishes, wedges of hard boiled eggs and tomatoes.

Eulalee B. Dacus

QUICK BROWN SAUCE

3 tablespoons butter	½ teaspoon thyme
3 tablespoons flour	Sprig parsley
1½ cups canned bouillon, soup stock or vegetable stock	Salt and freshly ground pepper

Melt the butter in a heavy saucepan over low heat. Add flour and blend well over medium heat. Reduce the heat and simmer for several minutes. Heat the bouillon or stock, stir into the flour and butter mixture and continue stirring until the sauce thickens. Add herbs, reduce heat and simmer for several minutes. Correct the seasoning. Serve as it is with meats or other dishes or use as a base for Madeira sauce.

James A. Beard

MADEIRA SAUCE

Combine 1½ cups Brown sauce with ½ cup Madeira wine and simmer till reduced by almost a third. Correct the seasoning. Serve over Cornish game hen or other baked fowl.

James A. Beard

BECHAMEL SAUCE

1 tablespoon onion, minced	2 cups milk, scalded
3 tablespoons butter	¼ teaspoon salt
¼ cup flour	Dash white pepper

In a saucepan sauté onion in butter until soft. Stir in flour and cook over low heat, stirring, for 3 minutes. Remove pan from heat, add scalded milk in a stream — whisking vigorously until mixture is thick and smooth. Add salt and pepper. Simmer sauce for 15 minutes. Strain sauce through a fine sieve and cover it with buttered waxed paper.

CANNED CHILI SAUCE

2 dozen large ripe tomatoes	1 tablespoon nutmeg
3 green peppers	1 tablespoon ginger
3 large onions	1 tablespoon allspice
½ cup sugar	1 quart vinegar
1 tablespoon cloves	2 tablespoons salt

Scald tomatoes, peel and cut into small pieces. Put all in enamel saucepan. Cook slowly for 3 hours. Bottle and seal.

Mrs. Frank Baddour

JESSIE'S MARINADE

1 cup Burgundy red wine
1 cup oil
1 tablespoon A-1 sauce

1 clove garlic, crushed
2 tablespoons Worcestershire sauce
2 teaspoons soy sauce

Marinate meat at room temperature for 2 hours before cooking. Use this same marinade to baste roast — very often. Cook at 300°. Use meat thermometer for desired doneness. Serve with mushroom gravy (use remaining marinade — add mushrooms and thickening.)

Jessie Blackwell

WHITE SAUCE WITH WINE

6 tablespoons butter
6 tablespoons flour
1 cup chicken broth
1 cup heavy cream

1 tablespoon cooking sherry or dry
   white wine
1 teaspoon white pepper

Melt butter. Remove from heat; blend in flour, then broth. Bring to a boil; simmer until thick, stirring constantly. Gradually blend in cream, then sherry or wine. Season to taste. Serve immediately over chicken, fish or egg dishes.

MARCHAND DE VIN SAUCE

1 cup dry red wine (Claret)
2 tablespoons green onions,
   minced
Fresh black pepper
1½ cups beef bouillon
2 4-ounce cans mushrooms
Garlic

1 scant teaspoon meat extract
   (optional)
Parsley
1 stick butter
Juice of ½ lemon
1 tablespoon cornstarch

Combine wine and onions in saucepan. Cook until onions are done. Add black pepper, bouillon, mushrooms (undrained), garlic, meat extract, parsley, butter and lemon juice. Boil for a minute then add cornstarch mixed with little water to thicken slightly. Pour over steak.

Billy and Barbara Mills

LILLIAN JACKSON'S SUPERIOR BARBECUE SAUCE

1   cup very strong black coffee
2   cups Worcestershire sauce
1¼ cups tomato ketchup
¼   pound butter
1   tablespoon salt

4   teaspoons sugar
1 to 2 tablespoons freshly ground
    black pepper (the larger amount
    will make the sauce spicer)

Combine all the ingredients in a heavy pot or kettle and bring to a boil over low heat. Cook, stirring frequently, at least 30 minutes. Brush on foods as they are grilled. *Yield: about 4½ cups.*

CHARLES' TEN THOUSAND DOLLAR BAR-B-QUE SAUCE

6   bottles Louisiana Hot Sauce
⅓ cup ground black pepper
¼   cup ground (not cayenne) red
    pepper

2   tablespoons crushed red pepper
6 to 8 squirts Lea & Perrin
    Worchestershire sauce
Red or white distilled vinegar

Put the above ingredients in a 1 gallon jar. Fill the jar with distilled red vinegar to make one gallon.

Charles Baddour

You'll never get burned meat from this sauce.

BARBECUE SAUCE

1   small box black pepper
1   small box red powdered pepper
1   box paprika
1   tablespoon flour

1   teaspoon sugar
2   tablespoons Wesson oil
1   quart vinegar
1   teaspoon salt

Bring to boil. Boil about 10 minutes. Makes very hot sauce. Good with barbecue of any kind.

Elizabeth and Catherine Baddour

COCKTAIL SAUCE (SHRIMP)

12 tablespoons chili sauce
4   tablespoons lemon juice
3   tablespoons horseradish
2   teaspoons Worcestershire

½   teaspoon onions, grated
4   drops Tabasco sauce
Salt to taste

Combine ingredients and chill for several hours if possible. *Makes 1 cup.*

Oneida Baddour

APRICOT DELIGHT

1 large package apricot Jello
2 cups boiling water
2 cups cold water
Pecan bits
Miniature marshmallows
½ cup pineapple juice

½ cup sugar
1 egg, beaten
1 teaspoon vanilla
8 ounces cream cheese, softened
1 package Dream Whip

Dissolve Jello in boiling water. Stir in cold water and pour into 9½x13 pan. Sprinkle top with pecan bits and marshmallows. Let stand overnight. Combine pineapple juice, sugar, egg and vanilla. Cook about 5 minutes. Stir in cream cheese and cream well. Cool. Prepare Dream Whip according to package directions. Fold into cooled cream cheese mixture. Spread over Jello, and refrigerate several hours before serving.

Chloe W. Dacus

Delicious as a salad or dessert.

In the Administration Building, offices and a large conference room give evidence of the need for staff who plan and direct the programs at Baddour Center. At the Center, staff are encouraged to pray and play, to laugh and love while going about their assigned responsibilities: all to create a loving, supportive atmosphere for the residents. Included in the building also are an all-weather pool, an exercise room, and a full size gymnasium. The American Flag, waving welcome to all those who enter, gives statement to the Center's emphasis on patriotism.

"Now the heart is so full that a drop
overfills it
We are happy now because God
wills it."

—"The Vision of Sir Launfal," James Russell Lowell

EGGS & CHEESE

Administration Building

PICKLED EGGS

8 eggs, hard boiled	4 whole black peppers
2 cups cider vinegar	1 whole clove
2 tablespoons sugar	¼ teaspoon caraway seed
1 teaspoon salt	1 garlic slice

Remove shell from eggs and cool. Place in 1-quart jar with tight lid. Bring vinegar and spices to a boil. Reduce heat and simmer 10 minutes uncovered. Strain and discard spices and garlic. Pour hot liquid over eggs. Cover tightly. Refrigerate 2 days to develop flavor.

Mrs. Frank Baddour

PICKLED EGGS

12 eggs, hard boiled	1 teaspoon ground mustard
48 cloves	1 teaspoon salt
1 bay leaf	1 teaspoon pepper
1 jalapeno pepper	1-1½ cups boiling vinegar

Prepare eggs. Shell and stick 4 whole cloves into each egg. At the bottom of a wide mouth quart mayonnaise jar, put whole bay leaf and whole jalapeno pepper. Add eggs. Mix mustard, salt, pepper, and vinegar. Pour over eggs and let cool. To keep jar top from rusting, put Saran Wrap over jar before putting lid on. After jar cools, put in refrigerator for 2 weeks. Good to use with cold plates, cold cuts, and in salads.

Laura Pope

OMELET

8 eggs	Cooked leftover vegetables (especially
Salt	squash, asparagus or green beans)
Pepper	½ stick butter
3 or 4 slices ham, ground	

Beat eggs well. Add salt and pepper. Add ham and vegetables and mix well. In 9" iron skillet (handle must be heat proof), melt butter. Pour egg mixture into it. Let set on low heat for about 10 minutes. Put in 350° oven until all omelet is set. Turn out on plate and cut in wedges. Serve with a green salad for lunch.

Louise Pearson

DEVILED EGG MOLD

1 envelope Knox unflavored gelatin	¾ cup mayonnaise
½ cup water	1½ teaspoons onion, grated
1 teaspoon salt	½ cup celery, finely diced
2 tablespoons lemon juice	¼ cup bell pepper, finely diced
¼ teaspoon Worcestershire sauce	¼ cup pimento-stuffed green olives, chopped
⅛ teaspoon cayenne pepper	4 hard cooked eggs, chopped

In a saucepan, sprinkle gelatin on water to soften. Place over low heat. Stir until gelatin is dissolved. Remove from heat. Add salt, lemon juice, Worcestershire sauce and cayenne pepper. Cool. Stir in mayonnaise. Fold in onion, celery, pepper, olives and eggs. Turn into a 3 cup mold and chill until firm.

I prepare my mold by brushing the inside lightly with mayonnaise. To unmold, dip mold in medium hot water for a few seconds. With a knife, loosen mold at some point. Place serving dish on top and unmold. *Serves 6.*

Martha Whitington

This is a good way to use leftover Easter eggs.

SHRIMP STUFFED EGGS

8 eggs, hard boiled	2 tablespoons onion, minced
2 tablespoons mayonnaise	2 tablespoons celery, minced
2 tablespoons Durkees dressing	2 tablespoons dill pickle, minced
1 cup shrimp, cooked and shredded	Salt and paprika

Slice eggs in half lengthwise and remove yolks. Mash yolks with mayonnaise and Durkees; blend with shrimp, onion, celery, pickle, salt and paprika. Spoon mixture into egg whites. Garnish with olives and paprika.

Virginia M. Steinek

RING AROUND THE EGG

2 tablespoons butter	1 egg
1 slice bread	Jelly

Melt butter in skillet. With 2-inch biscuit cutter, cut hole in center of slice of bread. Place bread in skillet and crack egg into the hole. Brown on both sides. Serve with jelly spread on the bread.

Gwenda M. Smith

77

DEVILED EGG CASSEROLE

12 eggs	1 stick butter
¾ cup mayonnaise	8 tablespoons flour
1 cup olives, chopped or 1 cup ham, chopped	1 quart milk
	1 roll smoked cheese
⅛ teaspoon curry powder	1 roll sharp cheese

Cook eggs to hard boiled. Cut in half, remove the yolks and combine yolks with mayonnaise, olives or ham, and curry powder. Stuff eggs with this mixture and put halves together to make whole eggs. Place in bottom of casserole. Make cheese sauce by melting butter, adding flour and gradually stirring in milk. Cook, stirring often, until thickened. Cut up the cheese and add to the sauce. Cook until melted. Pour the cheese sauce over the eggs and bake at 350° for 20 minutes or until bubbly.

Dena Burns

COMPANY EGGS

¼ cup butter	1 can mushroom soup
12 eggs	¼ cup sherry (or milk)
½ cup milk	½ cup cheese, grated
Salt and pepper	

Melt butter. Add and scramble eggs mixed with milk, salt and pepper. Put into buttered casserole dish. Mix the soup, sherry, and cheese together and pour over eggs. Refrigerate at least 6 hours, overnight is better. Bake at 300° for 40 minutes or until hot.

June Spotts

EGGS IN TOMATOES

Select tomatoes ripe but firm. Plunge into boiling water for a moment to remove skin. Cut out hard stem ends, making in each a hollow large enough to hold a broken egg; into each hollow add a broken egg without breaking yolk. Season with salt and pepper and butter. Bake in moderate oven until the tomatoes are tender and the eggs are set. Serve on rounds of buttered toast with cream or cheese sauce.

Mrs. Hugh Dillahunty

A delicious dish to serve at a brunch.

78

EGG CASSEROLE

¼ cup oleo or butter	1 pound sharp cheese, grated
¼ cup flour	1½ dozen eggs, hard boiled
2 cups Half and Half	1 pound bacon, cooked, drained
1 teaspoon thyme	and crumbled
1 teaspoon basil	¼ cup parsley
1 teaspoon marjoram	Buttered bread crumbs

In saucepan, melt butter. Add flour and Half and Half and cook until thick. Stir in thyme, basil, marjoram and cheese. Slice half of eggs in bottom of 9x13 pyrex dish. Add a layer of bacon, half the sauce and half the parsley. Repeat. Top with bread crumbs. Bake at 350° for 20-30 minutes or until bubbly. Can be prepared the day ahead. *Serves 8-12.*

Martha Whitington

BRUNCH PARTY EGGS

3 dozen eggs	¼ cup sherry
2 cans cream of mushroom soup	½ cup onion, finely chopped
2 cups mushrooms, sliced	½ cup green pepper, finely chopped
2 cups sharp cheese, grated	Salt and pepper to taste

Using two large skillets, scramble eggs til just set. Transfer to 3-quart casserole. Add all other ingredients. Mix well. Bake in 350° oven for 30 minutes. May be done the day before and refrigerate, covered with foil. Bring to room temperature before baking. *Serves 15-16.*

Mrs. Boyce Billingsley

SWISS EGGS

1½ cups Cheddar cheese, coarsley shredded	¾ teaspoon salt
	Dash of cayenne
6 large eggs	3 tablespoons butter or margarine
½ cup light cream	Bacon or ham
1½ teaspoons powdered mustard	

Sprinkle cheese over the bottom of a well-buttered 11¼x7½x1½-inch baking pan. Break eggs over cheese, being careful not to break yolks. Combine cream, mustard, salt and cayenne and pour over eggs. Dot with butter or margarine. Bake in a preheated 350° oven for 15 minutes or until eggs are set and cheese has melted. Serve hot with bacon or ham for breakfast or brunch.

Ann Basore

QUICHE LORRAINE

2 cups sifted flour	1 can mushrooms (optional)
1 teaspoon salt	4 eggs
4 tablespoons butter	1 cup heavy cream
4 tablespoons shortening	½ cup milk
3 tablespoons ice water	Dash salt and pepper
1 cup diced cooked ham (or bacon)	Pinch of nutmeg
1 onion, chopped	⅔ cup Swiss cheese, finely grated

Mix flour, salt, butter and shortening until mixture looks like bread crumbs. Sprinkle ice water over dough and work gently. Wrap and chill about 1 hour in refrigerator. Roll out and line deep pie pan. Bake 10 minutes at 400°. Brown diced ham, onion and mushrooms. Put in pie shell. Mix remaining ingredients, pour into pie shell. Bake 25-30 mintues at 350°. Serve warm as main course or as an appetizer.

Carol Higgins

QUICK QUICHE

½ cup biscuit mix	Crisp bacon bits
4 eggs	2 cups milk
3 tablespoons butter	½ pound Swiss, American or
Onion, chopped or instant	Cheddar cheese

Put all ingredients in blender and mix well. Pour into 9-inch buttered pie plate. Bake at 400° for 30-40 minutes.

Ann Basore

SPINACH QUICHE

1 10-ounce package frozen spinach	3 eggs, beaten
	1 cup heavy cream
2 tablespoons onion, minced	1 Deep-Dish Pet Ritz Pie Shell
½ teaspoon salt	4 ounces Swiss cheese, grated
⅛ teaspoon pepper	

Cook spinach and drain to very dry. Mix spinach, onions, salt and pepper together. Add eggs and cream. Pour into unbaked pie shell. Sprinkle cheese over top. Bake at 375° until set — about 30 minutes.

Mary Virginia Gaines

CHEESE PUDDING

2 cups sharp Cheddar cheese
2 cups soft bread crumbs
2 eggs
2 cups milk

1 teaspoon mustard
1 teaspoon salt
¼ teaspoon pepper
Buttered crumbs

Chop or grate cheese. Have ready soft bread crumbs. Put layers of cheese and bread in 1-quart baking dish. Mix together the well-beaten eggs, milk, mustard, salt and pepper. Pour over cheese and bread. Sprinkle with buttered crumbs (optional). Bake 1 hour at 350° or until firm. *Serves 4-6.*

Mrs. Roy R. Morley

CHEESE CASSEROLE

12 ounces large curd cottage cheese
8 ounces sharp Cheddar cheese, crumbled
1 pound Velveeta, chunked

4 eggs, beaten
2 tablespoons flour
½ stick butter, chunked

Mix all together. Bake in 9x9 pyrex dish at 350° for 25 minutes or until hot, bubbly and just turning brown on top. Let sit for 5 to 10 minutes so that it solidifies somewhat.

Dr. Patty Calvert

FRIED MOZZARELLA

¼" slices Mozzarella cheese
Flour
1 egg, beaten

¼ cup butter
¼ cup olive oil

Coat cheese slices with flour. Dip in beaten egg and fry in combined butter and olive oil until golden brown. Serve immediately.

Variation: For sandwiches, cut slices of thin bread the same size as the cheese. Soak the sandwich in the beaten egg for 15 minutes on each side. Press together tightly. Fry in butter and olive oil.

Billy and Barbara Mills

BRUNCH SOUFFLE

8 slices white bread
¾ pound sharp cheese, grated
½ pound link sausage, cooked and
  sliced
4 eggs

3 cups milk
¾ teaspoon prepared mustard
½ teaspoon salt
1 cup mushroom soup
1 cup mushrooms

Remove crusts from bread and cut into cubes. Place in 9x13 casserole. Top with cheese and sausage. Beat eggs, 2½ cups milk, mustard and salt together. Pour over sausage. Let stand overnight. Combine soup, mushrooms and remaining ½ cup milk. Pour over casserole. Bake at 300° for 1½ hours. *Serves 6-8.*

Mildred Fall
Mrs. Lowell Taylor, Jr.

For so long, society has looked at obvious handicaps and overlooked the character and personality of the individual. At Baddour Center, residents comfortably express their individuality within the family setting of a group home. The home coordinators deserve and receive admiration and thanks for their efforts. Often, the unseen accomplishments in the areas of socialization and life skills take place quietly under the tireless direction of coordinators. Some residents live in "transitional" homes with less supervision, and others live independently of direct, daily supervision.

"But every house where Love abides
* And Friendship is a guest*
Is surely home, and home,
* sweet home,*
For there the heart can rest."
* –"Home Song," Henry Van Dyke*

BREADS

Home at Baddour Center

One marvelous point about bread baking is the simplicity of the tools. Bread is one of the oldest and simplest of all foods—it's been baked on open fires. Bread was baked before recorded history and originated (as did wheat) in the fertile valleys of the Middle East. The Lebanese Pita bread is a descendant of the earliest breads. The enthusiastic response of family and friends when served fresh baked bread is one of the real joys of life.

Al Berthouex

BASIC WHITE LOAF

2 packages granular yeast
2¼ cups warm water
⅜ cup honey or ¼ cup sugar
1 tablespoon salt

¼ cup soft shortening or corn oil or safflower oil
7½ cups unbleached white flour (with or without wheat germ)

In a large bowl, combine water, yeast, and honey. Stir to dissolve yeast and honey. Let it stand until bubbly. (This is called proofing the yeast.) Add salt and shortening, and stir to dissolve. Add and beat in half of flour. Add remaining flour gradually and work in as much as possible. When dough becomes too stiff to stir, turn out on a lightly floured board or area and work in remaining flour. You will use more or less 7½ cups, depending on humidity, climate, and your own hands. At this point you can let the dough "rest" for about ten minutes, but this is not really necessary. Knead the dough until it is smooth and elastic. You cannot overhandle the dough. Enjoy the kneading — it is good therapy!!! Put the dough in a greased bowl and turn it over in the bowl so that the dough has a light coating of oil on top of it. Cover the bowl with a cloth and let rise until it is double in bulk, or until dough will hold impression of your finger when gently poked. This will take about 1 to 2 hours. Punch down the dough. Form into two loaves and place in greased 8" or 9" loaf pans. Cover and let rise until double again, about 45 minutes. Preheat oven to 375° during second rising. Bake for 35 to 45 minutes. Check after about 30 minutes. When you think they are done, take one out, turn it out of pan, and thump the bottom. If it is done it will make an unmistakable hollow "thunk". If it isn't done, put it back in the pan and back in the oven. It won't affect the quality. Bread slices better when it is allowed to cool — but it always seems to taste better hot from the oven. Let your conscience be your guide. Real butter adds a special flavor.

Variation: Whole Wheat Bread: Use ¼ cup black strap molasses (unsulphured) and ¼ cup honey for sweetener. Replace 3 cups white flour with same amount of whole wheat flour. Add ½ cup wheat germ.

Variation: Use milk as liquid in proportions ½ cup warm water (to dissolve yeast) and 1¾ cups scalded milk. This makes a richer bread and a much browner crust.

Al Berthouex

FAMILY STYLE WHITE BREAD

1 cup skim milk	1 cup warm (not hot) water
3 tablespoons sugar	2 envelopes active dry yeast
2 teaspoons salt	6-6¼ cups sifted all-purpose flour
⅓ cup Wesson oil	

Heat milk just to boiling. Remove from heat. Stir in sugar, salt, Wesson oil. Cool to lukewarm. Measure water into 3 quart bowl; sprinkle in yeast; stir till dissolved. Add lukewarm milk mixture. Sift 3 cups of flour over yeast mixture, stir in, then beat until smooth. Add rest of flour to make soft dough. Turn out on lightly-floured board. Knead until smooth and elastic. Place in oiled bowl. Brush top with Wesson oil. Cover, let rise in warm place until double in bulk, about 1¼ hours. Punch down, turn on lightly-floured board. Divide dough in half. Form each half into a smooth ball. Place in oiled 9"x5"x3" loaf pans. Cover and let rise in warm place until doubled again in bulk, about 1 hour. Bake at 400° about 50 minutes. *Makes 2 loaves.* 60 calories per slice.

Mrs. John R. Booth

GRANDMA'S BREAD

2 packages dry yeast	1 cup boiling water
½ cup warm water	1 cup cold water
1 stick oleo	2 eggs
½ cup sugar	8½ cups flour
2 teaspoons salt	

Dissolve yeast. In large mixing bowl place oleo, sugar and salt. Add boiling water and stir until melted. Add cold water, eggs, yeast and 4½ cups flour. Beat by hand three minutes. Add remaining 4 cups flour. Stir and beat by hand three minutes. If to be used as refrigerator dough, cover with plastic wrap over bowl and refrigerate until ready for use. To bake bread or rolls same day: Let rise until double in bulk (1½-2 hours). Shape into 2 large or 4 small loaves. Place in buttered loaf pans. Let rise until double in bulk. Bake in 350° oven for 30-35 minutes. Remove from pans and brush lightly with melted butter, wrap in towel and place on rack to cool.

Rolls or Cinnamon Rolls: Shape into desired shape, let rise until double bulk. Bake at 350° until brown (about 30 min.)

This is a light dough. Handle gently when shaping on floured board.

Dottie Schoettle

JAMES BEARD'S BASIC BREAD

1 package dry yeast	4 cups unbleached flour
½ cup warm water	1 tablespoon salt
2 teaspoons sugar	1½ cups water

Dissolve yeast and sugar in water. Let yeast bubble. Add flour, salt, and water. Knead well. Let rise until double in bulk. Punch down and knead briefly. Put in buttered loaf pan. Bake 35 minutes at 400°. Or: Make 4 small loaves and bake 22 minutes at 400°. When you take bread out of oven, brush with melted butter.

Billy and Barbara Mills

SALLY LUNN

2 packages yeast	⅜ to ½ cup honey
2 cups warm milk	3 large eggs or 4 small eggs, beaten
1 cup shortening (liquid safflower oil or butter)	2 teaspoons salt
	7-8 cups unbleached white flour

Scald milk, add shortening and cool to lukewarm. Add honey and yeast to milk. Add salt to milk. Stir in eggs. Add the flour and mix well. *NO KNEAD-ING!!!* Let rise until double. Punch down. Spoon dough into 10" tube pans or loaf pans or muffin tins. Let rise until double. Preheat oven to 350° during rising.

Bake: loaf pan 35-45 minutes
      tube pan 35-40 minutes
      muffins 15-20 minutes

This makes a wonderful, light, textured bread. It bakes up to a beautiful, light brown handsome loaf. A delicious rich bread to serve at meal time.

Al Berthouex

BATTER BREAD

3½ cups flour	1½ cups water
½ cup dry milk	1 package yeast
2 teaspoons salt	2 eggs
1 cup oats	¼ cup butter, melted

Mix flour, dry milk, salt and oats. Melt yeast in ¼ cup warm water. Add eggs and yeast to dry ingredients and mix well. Spread dough in well-greased 9x13-inch pan. Let rise 1 hour. Bake at 350°.

Lillie Bryant

STOVE PIPE BREAD

3½ cups 100% stone ground whole   ½ cup salad oil
     wheat flour, unbleached   ¼ cup sugar
1   package active dry yeast   1 teaspoon salt
½   cup sweet milk   2 eggs
½   cup water   Oleo

Place 1½ cups flour into large bowl of mixer. Add yeast and blend at low speed ½ minute. Combine milk, water, oil, sugar and salt in saucepan and heat until warm. Add to dry ingredients in mixer bowl, and beat at low speed until smooth. Add eggs and beat at medium speed until blended. Gradually add 1 cup flour at lowest speed, and beat until smooth and well blended. Scrape beaters, remove bowl from mixer and stir in remaining flour (1 cup) with a wooden spoon. This will make a soft dough or stiff batter. If extra stiff, add a small amount of warm water. Spoon into two well-buttered coffee cans (1 pound). Cover with greased plastic lids and let stand in warm place, draft free. When dough has risen almost to tops of cans, remove lids. Bake in 375° preheated oven for 30-35 minutes, or until brown. Cool about 10 minutes in can before removing to rack to cool. Delicious served toasted for breakfast, or spread with cream cheese mixed with crushed pineapple. Freezes well — double recipe when freezing.

Mrs. Burton W. Renager

BUTTER BREAD

2 packages yeast   ⅔ cup sugar
1 cup cold water   1 cup boiling water
2 sticks butter or Parkay   2 eggs
   margarine   7 cups flour

In a large bowl, dissolve yeast in cold water. Cream butter and sugar. Add boiling water and stir occasionally to dissolve butter. When lukewarm, beat in eggs. Alternately add yeast and flour, stirring well after each addition. Mix thoroughly, cover with towel and refrigerate 4 to 8 hours (overnight). To bake, divide into 3 equal parts, shape lengthwise and place in 3 greased pans, 8½x4½x2½ or 9x5. Cover with towel and let rise 2 hours in warm place (top of stove with oven on). Dough should rise to top of pan. Bake 1 hour at 300°. Turn onto rack to cool. Slice when cool. (Slice before reheating). *Yield: 10-11 slices per loaf.*

Mrs. Roy R. Morley

ENGLISH MUFFIN BREAD

2½-3 cups flour
1 package yeast
1¼ cups warm water

1 tablespoon sugar
¾ teaspoon salt
Cornmeal

Add yeast to 1 cup of flour. Add the sugar and ¾ teaspoon of salt to water, stirring until dissolved. Add water to the flour mixture and beat with mixer ½ minute at low speed; continue beating 3 more minutes at high speed. By hand, add enough of the remaining flour to make a soft ball of dough. Place in a well-greased bowl, turning to coat, and cover and allow to rise about 1 hour. Punch down, let rest for 10 minutes and then place in a greased 1-quart baking dish which has been sprinkled with cornmeal. Cover and let rise another 30-45 minutes. Bake at 400° for 40-45 minutes.

Helen Younes

ASPHODEL BREAD

5 cups Pioneer biscuit mix
4 tablespoons sugar
½ teaspoon salt
2 envelopes yeast

2 cups warm milk
4 eggs
¼ teaspoon cream of tartar

Sift dry ingredients. Soften yeast in milk. Beat eggs and cream of tartar together. Combine dry ingredients with milk and eggs. Stir well. Cover and let rise 1 hour. Stir down, pour into oiled pans and let rise. Bake ½ hour at 350°. Serve warm.

Asphodel Plantation,
submitted by Cheryl Sullivan

MOLASSES HEALTH BREAD

3½ cups flour
1 package yeast
1¼ cups milk
¼ cup molasses
2 tablespoons margarine

1 tablespoon instant onion
   (chopped)
1 teaspoon salt
½ teaspoon oregano
1 egg

Combine 2 cups flour and the package of yeast in mixer. In pan, heat milk, molasses, margarine, onion, salt and oregano till warm (not boiling). Add the above mixture to the flour and yeast mixture. Add egg, mix well, then add rest of flour. Beat 3 minutes on high. Cover. Let rise in warm place 45 minutes. Stir down. Turn into greased 1½-quart dish. Cover, let rise for 30 minutes. Bake 350° for 35 minutes.

Sarah Aaron

A RICH WHOLE WHEAT BREAD

2 packages yeast
1¼ cups lukewarm water
1 teaspoon brown sugar
1 cup warm milk
2 teaspoons salt
¼ cup molasses
¼ cup honey

1-2 eggs, beaten
⅜ cup soft shortening
2 tablespoons orange juice
2¼ cups unbleached white flour
4 cups whole wheat flour
¼ teaspoon cumin (optional – cumin adds a peppery taste to the bread)

Proof the yeast in the warm water and the sugar. Combine the milk, salt, molasses, honey, shortening, orange juice, and eggs. Add the yeast. Add half white flour and half of whole wheat flour. Add remaining whole wheat and cumin (if using) and as much of white flour as possible. Turn out and knead — add flour as necessary. Knead until elastic and smooth. This dough is sticky so add flour to your hands, to allow ease of handling. Place in bowl. Let rise until double. Punch down and let rise again. Turn out, divide into two loaves, place in well greased pans (8½x4½x2½); let rise until double. Preheat oven to 375° during rising in pans. (Three risings of the dough are not necessary; two risings — one in bowl and one in pans works fine.) Bake for 35-45 minutes until you get the "thunk". This bread has a much darker crust than the white loaf — it may even appear burned. To soften crust, rub top of loaves with butter as soon as bread is removed from oven. THIS BREAD IS A HEAVY BREAD AND IS BETTER IF ALLOWED TO COOL. IT TENDS TO BE TOO HEAVY 'HOT FROM THE OVEN'.

Note: ½ to 1 cup cornmeal can be used for equal amount of flour for a special textured bread. Try it, you will like it.

Al Berthouex

DILLY BREAD

1 package yeast
¼ cup warm water
1 cup cottage cheese (heat to warm)
1 tablespoon butter
2 tablespoons sugar
2 tablespoons instant minced onion

2 tablespoons dill seed (or weed)
1 teaspoon salt
¼ teaspoon soda
1 egg
2 cups flour

Soften yeast in water. Set aside. Combine cottage cheese, butter, sugar, onion, dill, salt, soda, and egg. Stir in yeast. Add flour slowly, beating with a spoon. Form a stiff ball. Cover; let rise until double (about 1 hour). Punch down and put in well-greased round casserole (2-2½ quart size). Let rise 40 minutes. Pour melted butter over top and sprinkle with salt. Bake at 350° for 40-50 minutes.

Carol Thompson

Yummy served hot.

ONION-CHEESE SUPPER BREAD

½ cup onion, chopped
1 egg, beaten
½ cup milk
1½ cups packaged biscuit mix

1 cup sharp processed American cheese, shredded
2 tablespoons snipped parsley
2 tablespoons butter, melted

Cook onion in small amount hot fat till tender, but not brown. Combine egg and milk; add to biscuit mix; stir only till mix is just moistened. Add onion, half the cheese, and parsley. Spread dough in greased 8x1½-inch round cake pan. Sprinkle with remaining cheese. Drizzle melted butter over. Bake at 400° 20 minutes or till toothpick comes out clean. *Makes 6 to 8 servings.* Perfect salad go-with.

SAVORY CHEESE LOAF

½ cup margarine, softened
½ cup onion, minced
1 tablespoon prepared mustard
1 tablespoon poppy seeds

1 loaf day-old unsliced bread
8 slices Swiss cheese
2 slices bacon

Mix margarine with onions, mustard, and poppy seeds. Trim crusts from top and sides of day-old loaf of unsliced bread. Cut loaf crosswise into 1″ slices, drawing knife through bread to within 1″ of bottom crust. Insert cheese slices into cuts in loaf. Tie loaf with string to prevent slices from spreading apart. Spread the butter mixture on the top and sides. Place bacon slices on top. Bake in shallow pan at 400° for 18 minutes or until golden brown. To serve, snip or break apart.

Mrs. Ben G. Hines

POPPY-DOT CHEESE LOAF

3¾ cups packaged biscuit mix
1¼ cups sharp Cheddar cheese, shredded

1 tablespoon poppy seed
1 egg, beaten
1½ cups milk

Combine biscuit mix, cheese, and poppy seed; add egg and milk. Mix just to blend; then beat vigorously for 1 minute. Transfer dough to well-greased 9x5x3-inch loaf pan. Sprinkle with additional poppy seed. Bake at 350° for 50 to 60 minutes. Remove from pan and cool on rack.

Mrs. Ray Sturrup

MARY LANE'S BISCUITS

4   cups flour, sifted
3   teaspoons salt
2   tablespoons baking powder
¼   teaspoon soda

2   tablespoons sugar
1   cup shortening
2   cups buttermilk

Sift dry ingredients together. Add shortening and mix until coarse and mealy. Add buttermilk and mix thoroughly. Turn out on floured board and knead until you have a smooth dough that you can easily handle. Roll out to the desired thickness (about ⅓ to ½-inch thick). Cut out biscuits and place on a greased cookie sheet. Bake in a 450° oven until a golden brown.

Mary Lane Price

SOURDOUGH BISCUITS

1   package dry yeast
1   cup warm water
2   cups buttermilk
¾   cup salad oil
¼   cup sugar

4   teaspoons baking powder
¼   teaspoon soda
1½   teaspoons salt
7   cups all-purpose flour

Combine yeast and water and stir till dissolved. Add remaining ingredients and beat well. Turn out on floured surface and knead for 10 minutes. Shape into biscuits or roll and cut out. Place in greased pan and bake at 450° for 15-20 minutes. These will keep 7-10 days in refrigerator to be used as needed.

Jan Hamm

ANGEL BISCUITS

5   cups flour
1   teaspoon soda
¼   cup sugar
1½ teaspoons salt
1   teaspoon baking powder

1   cup shortening
1   yeast cake
3   tablespoons warm water
2   cups buttermilk

Sift dry ingredients together, cut in shortening. Dissolve yeast in warm water and pour into buttermilk. Add dry ingredients to liquid and work up well. This will keep in refrigerator for 1 week. When ready to use, roll out like regular biscuits. Bake on ungreased baking sheet at 425° for 10-12 minutes.

Mrs. Bobby Herndon
Mrs. Albert Waring

CRUMPETS

3 cups flour	½ teaspoon soda
1½ teaspoons yeast	½ teaspoon salt
1¾ cups warm water	¾ cup milk

Blend the flour, yeast and warm water together, cover with oiled plastic and set aside to rise about 1 hour or until light and frothy. Add soda and salt to warm milk and stir into the batter. (You may need more milk to make the batter runny). Cover and again stand until frothy, 30 minutes to 1 hour. Heat griddle, lightly grease. Grease muffin rings or tuna cans with both ends cut out. Place rings on griddle and pour about 2 tablespoons batter into each ring. Cook gently 10 minutes or until well set and bubbles have burst. Remove rings, turn, and continue cooking for 2-3 minutes until pale golden brown and thoroughly dried. Repeat until batter is used. Serve toasted with butter.

Helen Younes

CHEESE BISCUITS

½ cup butter, softened	½ teaspoon salt
½ pound American cheese, grated	1 cup all-purpose flour, presifted
¼ teaspoon cayenne pepper	Poppy seed (optional)

Mix butter and cheese together. Add dry ingredients, and work with hands until flour is worked in. Roll into balls the size of large marbles and sprinkle with poppy seed. Refrigerate at least 2 hours before baking. Bake at 400° for 15 minutes.

Mrs. Don Burnett

BEER BISCUITS

4 cups Bisquick	1 12-ounce can beer
⅓ cup sugar	

Combine in mixing bowl, and mix until smooth. Spoon into very well-greased muffin tins, and bake at 450° for 10-15 minutes. *Makes 18.*

Carol Higgins
Sue Turner

POPOVERS

1 cup flour
¼ teaspoon salt
2 eggs, well beaten

⅞ cup milk
1 tablespoon butter, melted

Preheat oven to 450°. Mix eggs, milk, and melted butter together. Stir liquid into dry mixture, then beat until well blended, no longer. Pour contents into a large measuring cup. Fill greased muffin pans ⅓ full (I prefer larger popovers and fill to ½ or ⅔.) Bake for 20 minutes. Turn the heat down to 350° and bake for 15 minutes more. DO NOT OPEN THE OVEN DURING BAKING TIME — if you open the oven you will have flat popovers —open the oven and you get no "pop".

Popover variations: use ½ whole wheat and ½ white flour and use 3 eggs. The third egg is the trick to make the whole wheat mixture pop.

Add cheese or your favorite fruit to the popover batter.

Al Berthouex

SALAD DRESSING MUFFINS

1 cup self-rising flour
½ cup milk

¼ cup salad dressing
Dash of salt

Mix all of the ingredients. Spoon into hot greased muffin tins. Bake at 350° for 10-12 minutes. *Yield 6.*

Jeanie VanVranken

Easy and delicious!

HOTEL PEABODY VANILLA MUFFINS

¾ pound sugar (2 cups)
4 eggs
1 pound flour (4 cups)
1 pint sweet milk

1 tablespoon baking powder
4 ounces melted butter (1 stick)
1 tablespoon vanilla

Beat sugar and eggs together; add flour, milk and baking powder, butter and vanilla. Mix thoroughly and bake in hot muffin pans, well greased. *Makes 36 muffins.*

Mrs. H. H. Hammer

XX CREAM ROLLS

4 tablespoons butter	1 tablespoon sugar
2 cups bisquick	¾ cup cream

Melt butter in saucepan. In mixing bowl, combine biscuit mix, sugar, and cream. Stir with fork till a soft dough is formed. Beat vigorously 20 strokes. Turn out on board lightly floured with biscuit mix. Knead 10 times and roll to an 8x12-inch rectangle. Cut with small biscuit cutter. Dip each in melted butter, coating both sides. Fold in half and place on cookie sheet. Bake at 400° till golden, about 12 minutes. Serve warm. *Makes 36.*

Barbara and Billy Mills

REFRIGERATOR ROLLS

1 package dry yeast	1 egg, beaten
2½ cups warm water	1½ teaspoons salt
½ cup sugar	8 cups flour

Dissolve yeast in ½ cup water. Cream sugar and egg. Add salt and flour, stirring well. Add yeast and remaining water and mix very well. Place in a well-greased large bowl. Grease top of dough well. Cover and store overnight in refrigerator. Shape rolls and let rise 3 hours. Bake at 400° for 15 to 20 minutes. Store unused dough in refrigerator.

Mrs. James Hunter

REFRIGERATOR ROLLS

2 yeast cakes	6 tablespoons shortening
2 teaspoons sugar	1 tablespoon salt
1 cup milk, scalded	2 eggs, beaten
1 cup boiling water	6 cups flour, sifted
6 tablespoons sugar	

Add 2 teaspoons sugar to yeast and mix until sugar is dissolved. Pour hot milk and water over remaining sugar, shortening and salt. Stir and let cool to lukewarm. Add eggs, yeast mixture and 3 cups flour. Beat thoroughly. Stir in remaining flour. The dough should be soft and sticky. Put in bowl, cover tightly and store in refrigerator 2 hours. Uncover and stir to break air bubbles. Make into rolls as needed. Let rise until double in size, 1½ to 2 hours in warm place. Bake at 400° in preheated oven for 15 to 20 minutes. Stir dough to break air bubbles every 12 hours and it will keep 7 to 10 days. If dough is allowed to rise and fall, it is ruined.

Mrs. Frank Baddour

BAKING POWDER ROLLS

2½ cups flour
½   teaspoon salt
3½ teaspoons baking powder
2   teaspoons sugar

¼ cup shortening
¾ cup milk
1 egg, beaten lightly

Sift together flour, salt, baking powder and sugar. Stir in shortening, milk and add egg. Roll to ¼" thickness, cut in rounds, brush with shortening, and bake at 375° for about 25 minutes.

Irene Paschell

This won 1st prize at Woodman's Picnic, Brush Creek, Tennessee, 1924.

ROLLS

1 cup sugar
1 cup shortening
1 quart milk
2 packages dry yeast
1 cup warm water

6 cups flour
1 teaspoon salt
1 teaspoon soda
1 teaspoon baking powder
Melted butter

Combine sugar, shortening and milk, and bring almost to a boil, melting the shortening. Let cool to lukewarm; add yeast dissolved in water and 2 cups flour. Let rise until doubled in bulk in a warm place. Combine salt, soda and baking powder with remaining flour, and gradually add to make a stiff dough. Place in covered container in refrigerator, and use as needed. Will keep for a week. Roll out dough and cut as though making biscuits. Dip in melted butter and fold in half. Let rise for 2-3 hours at room temperature. Bake at 400° for about 15 minutes.

Mary Lane Price

SPOON ROLLS

1   package dry yeast
2   cups hot tap water
1½ sticks butter, melted

½ cup sugar
1 egg
4 cups self-rising flour

Dissolve yeast in water. Add butter, sugar, egg and flour. Mix well and refrigerate. When ready to bake, put in greased muffin tins. Let sit at room temperature 25 minutes. Then bake at 425° 15 to 20 minutes or until brown.

June Spotts,
Pam Baddour

ROLLS

2 cups milk	½ teaspoon soda
1 stick margarine	1 teaspoon baking powder
½ cup sugar	1 package dry yeast
4 cups flour	¼ cup warm water
1½ teaspoons salt	

Combine the milk, margarine and sugar. Heat until blended — do not boil. Cool till lukewarm. Sift dry ingredients and add to milk mixture. Dissolve the yeast in warm water. Add to dough. Let rise in warm place till double in bulk. Add enough extra flour to make soft dough. Refrigerate and use as needed. When ready to use, shape as desired and let rise in warm place. Bake for 12-15 minutes at 450°.

Mrs. E. D. Welden

QUICK ROLLS

2 cups lukewarm water	¼ cup sugar
1 package dry yeast	¾ cup cooking oil
1 egg	4 cups self-rising flour

Combine water and yeast. Mix until yeast is dissolved. Add egg, slightly beaten, sugar, and oil and mix well. Add flour and blend well (dough will be thin.) Place without letting rise, in greased muffin tins, filling ½ to ¾ full. Let stand 10 minutes. Bake at 400° for 15 to 20 minutes. *Yields 18-24 rolls.*

Janis Lindsey

BANQUET DINNER ROLLS

4 sticks oleo	½ cup sugar
5 cups milk	1 tablespoon salt
5 pounds flour	3 packages yeast
3 eggs	½ cup lukewarm water

Melt 2 sticks oleo, add milk, cool til lukewarm. Put flour in separate bowl and add eggs, sugar and salt. Dissolve yeast in water. Add milk and butter mixture to flour and egg mixture. Add yeast. Mix well til it forms a large dough ball. Set in warm place. Let rise until it doubles amount. Knead 2 or 3 minutes. Divide into 4 parts. Take individual part of dough, pinch off dough the size of a walnut. Put three dough balls in each muffin tin. Let rise again and brush with remaining melted oleo. Bake at 350° until lightly brown.

Minnie Miller

AUNT CILE'S POCKETBOOK ROLLS

1 yeast cake
¼ cup water
½ cup sugar
2 cups milk
½ cup shortening

1 teaspoon baking powder
½ teaspoon baking soda
2 teaspoons salt
6 cups flour

Pour water over yeast and set aside. Put sugar, milk, shortening, baking powder, soda, salt and 3 cups flour in large bowl. Mix. Mix yeast and add. The mixture should be loose and gummy. Let this set at room temperature until it has doubled in size. Then add the remaining flour and knead gently. This dough can be refrigerated and kept for 4 days, sometimes longer. It is really at its best the third day. Roll out as you would biscuits and cut with biscuit cutter. Dip the cut roll into melted shortening and fold over to make the pocketbook. Cover and let the rolls double in size and bake at 400° for 20 minutes.

Mrs. Ford Turner

Have two and butter them while they're hot!

PARMESAN ROLLS

1 stick butter, softened
½ cup (heaping) mayonnaise
2 teaspoons oregano

Parmesan cheese
Paprika
Pepperidge Farm Hearth Rolls

Combine butter, mayonnaise, and oregano and place on top of hard rolls cut in half. Sprinkle Parmesan on top. Sprinkle with paprika. Bake at 350° for 15 minutes. Mixture may be made ahead and spread on rolls just prior to serving. Or rolls may be made and quick frozen. Then place rolls in freezer container for future use.

Carol Thompson

BREADS

ROLLS

2 cups milk	2 cakes yeast or 2 packages dry
½ cup Crisco	yeast
½ cup sugar	6½ cups flour or more
1 egg	1 tablespoon salt
½ cup lukewarm water	

Combine milk, Crisco and sugar. Bring to the boiling point and then cool to lukewarm. Add beaten egg and yeast softened in lukewarm water. Sift flour, measure, and resift with salt. Add to milk and mix thoroughly. Turn the stiff dough onto a floured board and knead until smooth. Place dough in greased bowl, brush top with melted butter. Cover and let rise until double in bulk (about 1 hour). Roll out on floured board and cut with desired cutter. Place rolls in greased pan, brush with melted butter, let rise until double in bulk. Bake at 400° for 15-20 minutes or until done.

Louise Westley

Or make larger for great sandwich rolls!

HOT ROLLS

1½ cups warm water	⅓ cup shortening, melted
1 package yeast	1 teaspoon salt
¾ cup sugar	5 cups flour

Dissolve yeast in water. Add sugar, shortening and salt. Add flour a little at a time, mixing as you go. Let rise to double size. Punch down. Shape to desired shape. Let rise. Bake 30 minutes at 350°.

Mrs. Jimmy Wagner

DINNER ROLLS

1 package active dry yeast	1 egg
1 cup warm water	2 tablespoons shortening
1 teaspoon salt	Butter, melted
2 tablespoons sugar	Poppy or sesame seeds
2½ cups sifted flour	

In a large mixing bowl, dissolve yeast in water. Stir in salt, sugar and half of the flour. Beat until smooth. Add egg and shortening. Beat in remaining flour until smooth. Scrape down sides of the bowl. Cover. Let rise in warm place til double in size. Grease muffin tins. Punch down dough, turn out on pastry sheet. Press dough flat; cut with shaper. Place in tins and let rise again. Brush with melted butter. Sprinkle with seeds. Bake in preheated oven at 400° for 15 to 20 minutes. *Makes 12 to 18 rolls.*

Donna Frangenberg

POTATO ROLLS

4-5	packages of dry yeast	2	tablespoons butter
1¼	cups warm water	3	cups milk, scalded (2 cups regular,
2	cups hot mashed potatoes		1 cup Pet milk)
¾	cup shortening	1	tablespoon vanilla flavoring
¾	cup white sugar	3	whole eggs + 2 more yellows (save
¼	cup brown sugar		whites)
¼-¾	cup wheat germ	12	cups Pillsbury unbleached flour
4½	teaspoons salt		

Soften yeast in warm water. Set aside. Combine potatoes, shortening, sugar, wheat germ, salt, butter, milk and vanilla. Let cool. Add eggs and yeast. Add flour a little at a time. Knead 10 minutes. Roll into ball and place in greased pan. Let rise until double, punch down and let it rest for 10 minutes. Make into rolls and let rise until double (1-1½ hours). Bake for 10-12 minutes or until brown (250-300°). Glaze with egg whites. Put in oven for 5-10 seconds, take out and put on towel until cool.

Kathy Kadell

NEVER FAIL ROLLS

2	yeast cakes, crumbled	1	teaspoon salt
1	cup warm water	1	cup boiling water
¾	cup sugar	2	eggs
¾	cup shortening	6	cups unsifted flour

Dissolve yeast in warm water. Mix sugar, shortening, salt and boiling water. When this mixture is lukewarm, add yeast mixture; then add eggs, and beat with rotary beater. Add flour, cover with greased waxed paper; put in refrigerator. Roll out and let rise when needed. Bake at 400° about 15 minutes.

Nona Ash

QUICK CORN LIGHT BREAD

2 cups buttermilk
2 packages dry yeast
¼ to ½ cup sugar
2 tablespoons shortening, melted

2 eggs
2 cups self-rising meal
1 cup self-rising flour

Slightly warm the buttermilk and dissolve yeast in it. Combine sugar, shortening and eggs. Add dry ingredients and buttermilk. Mix. Let sit for 30 minutes. Pour into hot greased bundt pan. Bake at 350° for 45 minutes.

Jessie Blackwell

CORN LIGHT BREAD

2 cups plain corn meal
½ cup sugar
1 cup flour
1 teaspoon soda

1 teaspoon salt
2 cups buttermilk
3 tablespoons bacon drippings or oil

Combine dry ingredients. Blend in milk and oil. Pour into a greased 9x5 loaf pan. Let stand in pan for 10 minutes. Bake at 375° for 35-40 minutes. Cool 5 minutes. Remove from pan and slice. Serve warm.

Bettye Mooneyhan

EASY CORNBREAD

1 package Martha White Cotton
  Pickin' Cornbread Mix
2 eggs
4 tablespoons cooking oil

1 8-ounce carton sour cream
1 8½-ounce can yellow cream style
  corn

Mix all ingredients and bake in 350° oven for 35 to 40 minutes or until golden brown.

Nell Barnes

100

MEXICAN CORNBREAD

MEXICAN CORNBREAD

1 cup cream style corn
1 cup sour cream
⅔ cup salad oil
2 eggs
1½ cups self-rising corn meal

1 teaspoon salt
1 or 2 jalapeno peppers, minced
1 tablespoon bell peppers, minced
1 cup sharp cheese, grated

Combine corn, sour cream and salad oil. Stir in eggs. Add corn meal and salt and mix well. Stir in peppers. Pour half of mixture in hot greased pan. Sprinkle half of cheese over this. Add remaining mix and cover with rest of cheese. Bake at 350° for 35 to 40 minutes.

Nora Nichols

MEXICAN CORNBREAD

1½ cups self-rising corn meal
3 eggs
1 cup cream style corn
⅔ cup salad oil
1 cup buttermilk

1 hot pepper, chopped
1 cup sharp Cheddar cheese, grated
1 small onion, chopped
Salt

Mix all ingredients. Bake in greased oblong pan at 425° for 15-20 minutes.

Jennie Yaeger

JALAPENO CORN BREAD

3 cups self-rising meal
3 eggs
½ cup oil
1 cup buttermilk
1 #2 can cream style corn

½ cup cheese, grated
1 large onion, grated
1 can jalapeno peppers, chopped
3 tablespoons sugar

Mix and cook at 450° 20 to 30 minutes, or until done.

Hazel Smith

101

HOT WATER CORN BREAD

1½ cups sifted corn meal
1   teaspoon sugar
Pinch of salt

1-2 drops bacon drippings
2   tablespoons sweet milk
Boiling water

Measure corn meal into bowl. Add sugar and salt and stir with fork. Add bacon drippings, milk, and enough boiling water to make of right consistency to drop with large spoon onto thick iron skillet or griddle greased with bacon drippings. Allow ample time for browning and turn only once. Serve at once piping hot. *Serves 4-6.*

Edna Phillips

SPOON BREAD

2 cups milk
1 cup corn meal
½ teaspoon salt

3 tablespoons oleo or butter
2 eggs
1 teaspoon baking powder

Scald milk, corn meal, salt and oleo together and stir until thick. Remove from stove. Add eggs and beat well. Add baking powder. Put in buttered baking pan and cook in 300° oven about 20 to 25 minutes.

Mrs. John Mac Smith

GEORGIA SPOONBREAD

1 cup plain corn meal
2 cups milk
3 tablespoons butter

1 teaspoon salt
3 eggs

Place corn meal in a saucepan, gradually add milk, stirring until smooth. Bring to a boil over medium heat, stirring constantly. Remove from heat; add butter and salt, stirring well after each addition. Add eggs and stir until smooth. Pour batter into well-greased 1½-quart pyrex dish. Bake at 350° for 40 to 50 minutes. Serve while hot with butter. *Yield – 6 servings.*

Virginia M. Steinek

HUSH PUPPIES – *from Pirate House, Savannah, Ga.*

1¼ pounds corn meal	¼ teaspoon salt
½ cup flour	¼ cup onion, chopped
¼ cup sugar	1 egg
2¼ teaspoons baking powder	1½ cups milk

Mix all dry ingredients thoroughly. Add onions and stir in egg. Add milk. Mixture should be stiff enough to drop from tablespoon in a solid mass. Chill. Mold dough in tablespoon and drop from spoon into moderately hot cooking oil 3 to 4 inches deep. When brown, remove from oil and drain.

Mrs. Rupple K. Dabbs

HUSH PUPPIES

2 cups corn meal	1½ cups milk
1 cup self-rising flour	1 large onion, chopped
1 tablespoon salt	1 bell pepper, chopped
2 eggs, well beaten	Hot salad oil

Combine dry ingredients. Add eggs and milk, stirring well. Add onion and bell pepper, then blend. Mixture will be thick. Dip a large spoon into hot salad oil, then into batter to spoon up each hush puppy; drop by spoonfuls into hot salad oil. Cook until golden brown on both sides. Drain well on paper towels or brown paper bag. *Yield: 3 to 4 dozen.*

Cheryl Sullivan

HUSH PUPPIES

1 cup self-rising corn meal mix	1 medium onion, chopped
½ cup milk	1 tablespoon oil
1 egg, beaten	

Gradually add milk to corn meal mix. Add beaten egg, chopped onion, and oil. Drop from teaspoon into hot, deep grease and fry until golden brown. *Serves 4 to 6.*

Linda Bell

103

QUICK COFFEE CAKE

¼ cup butter or oleo
1 cup flour
¾ cup sugar
2 teaspoons baking powder
1 egg

Milk
Cinnamon
Sugar
Butter

Melt butter and allow to cool slightly. Combine flour, sugar and baking powder. Pour butter into a measuring cup. Add egg. Add enough milk to make 1 cup of mixture. Add to flour mixture and beat until smooth. Spread in a greased and floured 9x9 pyrex dish. Mix cinnamon and sugar to taste. Sprinkle over dough. With a knife, cut through mixture so cinnamon and sugar will be marbled through cake. Dot with butter. Bake at 375° for 30 minutes. Cut in squares while warm.

Martha Whitington

Not too sweet. An old recipe.

APPLE COFFEE CAKE

¾ cup margarine
1 egg
1 tablespoon milk
2 cups flour

1 teaspoon baking powder
4 or 5 apples, peeled and sliced thin
1 small package raspberry gelatin
1 cup sugar

Cream ¼ cup margarine, egg and milk. Add 1 cup flour and baking powder. Pat dough into 10x6 pan (or 8x8). Stand apple slices into dough closely together. Sprinkle gelatin over all. Combine sugar, 1 cup flour and ½ cup margarine. Will be a crumbly mixture. Sprinkle over all. Bake at 350° for 30 minutes.

Sarah Aaron

MONKEY BREAD

3 cans biscuits
1 cup sugar
3 tablespoons cinnamon
1 cup nuts (walnuts/pecans),
  chopped

1½ sticks of oleo
1 cup brown sugar

Cut each biscuit into four pieces. Mix sugar and cinnamon. Roll biscuit pieces in sugar and cinnamon mixture. Arrange in bundt pan. Sprinkle nuts on top. Melt butter and stir in brown sugar. Pour over biscuits and nuts. Bake at 350° for 30 minutes.

Helen Robinson

BANQUET CINNAMON ROLLS

4 sticks oleo
5 cups milk
5 pounds flour
3 eggs
¾ cup sugar

1 tablespoon salt
3 packs yeast
½ cup lukewarm water
2 tablespoons cinnamon

Glaze:

3 boxes powdered sugar
1 cup milk

2 tablespoons cinnamon (more if
   desired)

Melt 2 sticks oleo, add milk, cool til lukewarm. Pour flour in separate bowl and add eggs, ½ cup sugar and salt. Dissolve yeast in water. Add milk and oleo mixture to flour and egg mixture. Add yeast. Mix well till it forms a large dough ball. Set in warm place, let rise til it doubles amount. Knead 2 or 3 minutes. Divide into 4 parts and roll out one at a time. Spread with oleo, then sprinkle ¼ cup sugar and cinnamon mixture over dough, roll and cut. Place in greased pan, brush with remaining melted oleo. Let rise again. Bake at 350° til lightly brown. Remove from oven, brush again with oleo. Let cool and then ice with the above glaze mixture.

Minnie Miller

HOT CROSS BUNS

4 cups flour
¼ cup + 1 teaspoon sugar
1 tablespoon yeast
½ cup water
¾ cup milk
1 teaspoon salt
½ teaspoon allspice

½ teaspoon cinnamon
½ teaspoon nutmeg
¼ cup butter, softened
1 egg
⅔ cup currants, chopped
⅓ cup chopped candied peel

Mix 1 cup flour, 1 teaspoon sugar, yeast, water and milk into batter. Cover and set aside about 20 minutes. Meanwhile add remaining flour to salt, sugar and spices. Add yeast mixture, butter, egg, currants and peel to batter and mix to form a soft dough. Add additional flour if dough is too sticky to work. Knead about 10 minutes until dough is smooth. Shape into ball, and place in greased bag. Let rise until doubled in bulk (2 hours at room temperature). Divide into 12 pieces, shape into buns, cover and let rise for 30 minutes. Make crosses with dough, icing, strips of candied peel or simply cut into the tops of the buns. Bake at 375° for 15-20 minutes. Transfer to baking rack and brush hot buns with sugar glaze. Served traditionally on Good Friday morning.

Helen Younes

IRISH SODA BREAD

4   cups buttermilk (1 quart)
2   eggs
¼   teaspoon soda
7   cups unbleached flour
2   cups raisins

¾   cup honey or ½ cup sugar
½   cup caraway seeds
2   teaspoons salt
2   tablespoons plus 2 teaspoons
    baking soda

Combine buttermilk, eggs, and soda in a bowl; beat well, and set aside. Combine remaining ingredients; stir in buttermilk mixture. Spoon batter into 3 greased 8½x4½x2½ loaf pans. Bake at 375° for 1 hour and 15 minutes. Let cool in pans for 15 minutes; turn out. Serve warm.

Al Berthouex

Quick bread that is super!!!

APRICOT BREAD

¾   cup dried apricots
Warm water
1   orange (juice and rind)
¾   cup honey (mild) or ⅔ cup sugar
2   tablespoons butter, melted
1   egg

2   cups flour
2   teaspoons baking powder
1   teaspoon salt
1   teaspoon soda
*½ cup nuts, chopped
1   teaspoon vanilla

*Do not use strong flavored nuts.

Cover apricots with warm water and let stand until soft. (There are several types of dried apricots available — for best results use unsulphured, Turkish variety for they are a bit sweeter and are excellent quality) use 1 cup apricots for an extra delight. (You can cut up apricots before soaking — use scissors.) Preheat oven to 350°. Grate the orange rind after juicing the orange. Save juice. When apricots are thoroughly softened, drain and save liquid. Combine orange juice and liquid from apricots, add enough water to make 1 cup. Add grated orange rind to apricots. Mix in honey (or sugar) and the butter. Stir in the beaten egg. Mix together the flour, baking powder, salt, and soda and add to apricot mixture. Mix well. Add nuts and vanilla. Stir well (batter becomes quite thick). Pour into well-greased loaf pan and bake 1 hour or until toothpick, inserted in the loaf, comes out clean. This wonderful bread is well worth the preparation. This is one recipe where the delicate blending of flavors is exciting and enticing. USE ONLY THE FINEST NATURAL INGREDIENTS. Use natural or raw sugar if the honey you have is strong flavored.

Al Berthouex

This is a moist, fruity, and delicious bread, serve with cream cheese.

BANANA MUFFINS

1 cup sugar	1 tablespoon water
½ cup butter or shortening	1¾ cups flour
1 egg	1 teaspoon vanilla
1 cup bananas, creamed	1 teaspoon nutmeg
1 teaspoon soda	½ teaspoon salt

Cream sugar and butter. Add egg and mix well. Add bananas. Dissolve soda in water and add to batter. Sift dry ingredients together and add gradually. Mix well. Spoon into greased muffin tins. Bake at 375° for 20-25 minutes. When cool, roll in powdered sugar.

Evelyn Smith

LENA'S BANANA NUT BREAD

½ cup shortening	½ teaspoon salt
1 cup sugar	3 large ripe bananas
2 eggs	4 tablespoons buttermilk
2 cups flour	½ teaspoon vanilla
1 teaspoon soda	½ cup nuts
1 teaspoon baking powder	

Cream shortening and sugar. Add eggs separately, beating well after each. Sift dry ingredients together. Mash bananas. Add bananas to buttermilk and mix alternately with flour mixture. Fold in vanilla and nuts. Pour in well-greased and floured loaf pan. Bake at 350° for 1 hour.

Mrs. John Mac Smith

CARROT BREAD

⅔ cup salad oil	1½ cups all-purpose flour
1 cup sugar	1 teaspoon cinnamon
2 eggs	1 cup carrots, grated

Cream oil and sugar. Mix eggs in well. Add flour and cinnamon and mix until smooth. Stir in carrots. Bake in a greased loaf pan for 55 minutes at 350°.

Patricia Maxwell

FIG BREAD

3½ cups sifted flour
1½ teaspoons cream of tartar
1   teaspoon salt
⅔   cup shortening (Crisco)
1½ cups sugar

4 eggs
2 cups figs, mashed, cooked and
   drained
1 cup pecans

Sift dry ingredients. Cream shortening, add sugar a little at a time until light and fluffy. Add beaten eggs and flour mixture, a little at a time until light and fluffy. Add figs — beat until smooth. Stir in pecans. Bake at 350° about 1 hour. *Makes 2 small loaves.*

Mrs. R. C. Nickle

PLUM ROLLS

2   cups cake flour, sifted
2   teaspoons baking powder
½   teaspoon salt
4   tablespoons margarine or
    butter
¾   cup milk

1½ cans purple plums, pitted
1   cup sugar
1   tablespoon flour
¼   teaspoon salt
1   tablespoon margarine or butter
1   tablespoon lemon juice

Sift flour, add baking powder and salt; cut in margarine and while stirring with a fork, add enough milk to form a soft dough. Turn out on lightly floured board and roll out about ¼-inch thick. Drain plums, reserving juice, and cut into large pieces. Cover dough with plums and roll as for jellyroll. Moisten edge of dough to seal. Cut in 1½-inch slices and place, cut side down in 13x9x2 baking pan. Combine sugar, flour and salt. Add enough water to reserved plum juice to make 2 cups. Add to dry ingredients and boil 3 minutes, stirring once or twice. Add butter and lemon juice and pour, while hot, over the rolls. Bake at 425° for 30 to 35 minutes, basting once or twice with juices in the pan. Serve warm. May be topped with whipped cream. (They will be rather sticky).

Ruby Alperin

PUMPKIN BREAD

1½ cups sugar
1⅔ cups flour
1   teaspoon soda
¾   teaspoon salt
¼   teaspoon baking powder
½   teaspoon ground cloves
½   teaspoon cinnamon

½   teaspoon nutmeg
¼   teaspoon ginger
2   eggs, slightly beaten
½   cup cooking oil
1   cup canned pumpkin
Nuts and/or raisins, as desired

Sift all dry ingredients together. Add eggs, oil, pumpkin, nuts and raisins.
Mix well. Fill greased loaf pans half full and bake at 350° for 1 hour.

Mrs. Robert A. Melhorn

PUMPKIN BREAD

3   cups sugar
1   cup Mazola oil or Crisco oil
4   eggs – one at a time
2   cups pumpkin (one average
     size can)
1½ teaspoons cinnamon

1½ teaspoons allspice
1   teaspoon nutmeg
2   teaspoons soda
1   teaspoon salt
⅔   cup warm water
3½ cups cake flour
1½-2 cups pecans, chopped

Mix in order given. Pour in 2 mini bundt pans or 3 loaf pans. Bake about 60
minutes at 325°. Test with cake tester straw.

Joy Melton

Easy recipe. I've never had a failure.

109

ZUCCHINI NUT BREAD

4   eggs
2   cups sugar
1   cup vegetable oil
3½ cups unsifted flour
1   teaspoon salt
1   teaspoon cinnamon

1½ teaspoons soda
¾   teaspoon baking powder
2   cups zucchini squash, grated
1   cup raisins
1½ teaspoons vanilla
1   cup walnuts, chopped

Use 1 loaf bread size pan or two small ones, greased and floured. Bake at 350°
55 minutes to 1 hour and 10 minutes. Allow to cool 10 minutes on rack, then
turn out. Will cut better when cool.

Orpha Robertson

ZUCCHINI BREAD

3   eggs
2   cups sugar
3   teaspoons vanilla
1   cup oil
2   heaping cups zucchini squash,
    with peeling grated
3   cups flour

1   teaspoon salt
1   teaspoon soda
¼   teaspoon baking powder
3   teaspoons cinnamon
1   cup nuts, chopped (optional)
½   cup dates, chopped (optional)

Using mixer beat eggs, add sugar, vanilla, oil and grated zucchini. Mix flour,
salt, soda, baking powder and cinnamon together. Add to egg mixture
gradually. Then add nuts and dates. (If using dates, it is best to roll them in a
little of the flour to keep them from sticking together.) Grease and flour 2 loaf
pans, approximately 8½x4½x2½. Bake at 350° for 1 hour. Test center with
toothpick.

Variations:
  Without nuts and dates.
  With coconut and nuts.
  Allspice instead of cinnamon.
  1 cup of zucchini and 1 cup of mashed bananas instead of 2 cups zucchini.

Martha Whitington
Serve sliced warm with butter, cold with cream cheese, or plain.

BRAN MUFFINS

1 cup 100% bran cereal	1 pint buttermilk
1 cup boiling water	3 cups flour
1 cup shortening	4 teaspoons soda
1 cup sugar	1¼ teaspoons salt
2 eggs	2 cups bran buds

Mix cereal and boiling water; cool. Beat shortening and sugar; add eggs and buttermilk. Add bran cereal to mixture. Sift flour, soda, and salt. Add dry ingredients to mixture until mixed well. Stir in bran buds. Pour into muffin pans. Bake in 400° oven 12 to 15 minutes. This mixture may be kept in refrigerator for 4 to 6 weeks and baked as needed.

Amy Denny

Store dough in refrigerator, and have fresh muffins every day.

PLAIN WAFFLES

2 cups flour	1 tablespoon sugar
½ teaspoon salt	¼ cup Crisco, melted
3 teaspoons baking powder	1⅔ cups sweet milk
	2 eggs, separated

Mix flour, salt, baking powder, sugar, Crisco, milk, and egg yolks in mixing bowl till well blended. Beat egg whites and fold into mixture. *Makes 7 or 8 waffles.*

Marie Hartfield

MRS. RIGGAN'S CORNBREAD

2 cups cornmeal
2 teaspoons sugar
1 teaspoon salt
2 teaspoons baking powder

1 egg
1-1½ cups buttermilk
¼-½   cup shortening or oil

Mix dry ingredients. Add egg and mix well. Gradually add buttermilk to a consistency that stirs easily. Preheat oven to 400°. Melt shortening in 8 or 9-inch iron skillet. Use enough shortening to coat inside of skillet and have enough to pour into batter. Be sure to get the shortening very hot. You can heat shortening in oven while oven is preheating. Pour hot shortening into batter and stir well, then pour into hot skillet. Bake on middle rack of oven for 20-25 minutes or until lightly browned. Move to top rack until golden brown.

Eulalee B. Dacus

An excellent recipe for crusty, old-fashioned cornbread.

A place to come together, mingle, laugh, and play: the large Recreation Center includes a game room, a conversation/grill area, and a mini-theater, which can be used for meetings as well. Shows and programs which feature the residents are regularly scheduled here. The acceptance and encouragement of friends and staff create an environment in which a mentally retarded person can confidently perform and gain applause. Self-esteem increases as residents learn and practice socialization skills and develop friendships in settings such as the Recreation Center.

"Flowers are lovely; love is flower-like;
  Friendship is a sheltering tree."
    –"Kubla Khan", Samuel Taylor Coleridge

VEGETABLES

Recreation Center

ARTICHOKE MUSHROOM VELVET

1 large onion, chopped
1 stick oleo
1 cup toasted bread crumbs
3 cans artichoke hearts

1 6-ounce can sliced mushrooms
1¼ cups Swiss cheese, grated
1 can cream of mushroom soup
2 tablespoons dry white wine

Lightly brown onions in ½ stick oleo. Set aside. In skillet, melt remaining oleo and stir in toasted bread crumbs. Drain artichoke hearts, reserving liquid. Mix artichoke hearts and mushrooms in mixing bowl. Add onions. Melt 1 cup cheese in cream of mushroom soup. Add wine and ¼ cup of artichoke liquid. Pour this over artichoke hearts and mushrooms. Mix well and put in greased 1-quart casserole. Sprinkle buttered bread crumbs and remainder of cheese over top. Bake at 350° for 45 minutes.

Sylvia Basist

STUFFED ARTICHOKES

6 artichokes
½ cup Romano cheese, grated
4 cups bread crumbs (½ white bread, ½ Italian bread)
5 garlic buds, crushed

1 tablespoon parsley
3 eggs, hard boiled (mash while hot)
1 2-ounce tin anchovies, mashed
Salt and pepper to taste
Olive oil to moisten

Wash artichokes well and clip tips. Cut bottom and stem so artichoke will stand up. Mix all dressing ingredients together and then with a teaspoon, stuff each leaf with dressing. Sprinkle generously with wine vinegar and place all 6 artichokes in a large pot with about 2 inches of water or enough to come up to the bottom leaves. Cook in covered pot for 45 minutes. Remove cover the last 10 minutes of cooking. Serve while hot.

Lee Ellis

ASPARAGUS CASSEROLE

2 cups milk	1 can asparagus
4 tablespoons flour	½ cup mild cheese, grated
4 tablespoons butter	2 eggs, hard boiled
½ teaspoon salt	Cracker crumbs
Dash of pepper	

Combine milk, flour, butter, salt and pepper in top of double boiler and cook until thick. Layer asparagus, grated cheese, sliced eggs, and white sauce. Sprinkle cracker crumbs on top. Brown in oven 20 minutes at 350° before serving.

Linda Bell

ASPARAGUS CASSEROLE

1 can asparagus, drained	1 small can sliced mushrooms
3 slices toast, cut into cubes	1 can mushroom soup
¼ cup butter	1 cup cheese, grated

Arrange asparagus in the bottom of a well-greased casserole. Cover with bread cubes. Slice butter on top of the bread cubes and add sliced mushrooms. Pour heated soup on top of mushrooms. Sprinkle on the cheese. Bread crumbs may be sprinkled on top, if desired. Bake 30 minutes at 350°. Serves 6.

Mrs. Malcolm Graham,
Mrs. Walter Scott

GLADYS' BEANS

1 can kidney beans	1 can chili
1 can pork and beans	¾ cup ketchup
1 can Mexicana corn	

Mix all together. Put in baking dish and bake at 250° for 2 hours.

Mrs. Albert Thomas

Very good for a bunch.

115

BAKED BEANS

1 quart navy beans	Pepper to taste
1 teaspoon soda	1 cup brown sugar
1 small onion, chopped	3 tablespoons molasses
½ teaspoon mustard	½ pound bacon
1 teaspoon salt	

Wash and soak beans overnight. Drain. Cover with fresh water. Heat slowly without boiling. Cook until skins burst. Add soda, cover with water. Cook 5 minutes. Drain. Place onion in bottom of bean pot or casserole. Put beans in pot and mix in mustard, salt, pepper, brown sugar, molasses, and bacon. Cover with boiling water. Cover and bake slowly 6 to 8 hours. Uncover the last hour so that beans brown. Add water, if needed.

Vera Glick

A New England recipe.

BAKED BEANS AND CHEESE CASSEROLE

½ cup ketchup	1 pound hamburger meat
¼ cup barbecue sauce	2 medium cans pork 'n beans
¼ cup brown sugar	5 slices cheese
½ cup onion, chopped	1 can of 5 biscuits

Combine ketchup, barbecue sauce, brown sugar and onion together. Set aside. Brown hamburger meat and mix it with pork 'n beans and sauce in casserole dish and bake in oven at 300° for 20 minutes. Top with cheese. Split the biscuits and lay them on top. Return to oven and bake for 15 minutes or until top crust is browned. *Serves 6.*

Bill Gurner

BAKED BEANS IN-A-HURRY

2 cans pork and beans	1 small onion, diced
1 cup brown sugar	2 teaspoons dry mustard
1 cup catsup	Bacon

Mix beans, brown sugar, catsup, onion and mustard. Place in casserole. Dot the top with sliced bacon, diced. Bake at 300°, uncovered, for about 1½ to 2 hours.

Mrs. Charles Adams, Sr.

BAKED BEANS

1 pound ground beef (or more)	1 cup catsup
½ stick butter	¼ cup mustard
3 cans pork and beans	¼ cup maple syrup
2 cans ranch style beans	2 onions, chopped fine
½ cup brown sugar	

Brown ground beef in butter. Add remaining ingredients and bake 45 minutes to one hour, or until it bubbles around edge of casserole. This makes a BIG pan of beans.

Sarah Agent

LUNCHEON GREEN BEANS

6 strips bacon	½ cup Italian dressing
3 cans sliced green beans	1 can water chestnuts, diced
2 tablespoons mayonnaise	

Fry bacon crisp and reserve drippings. Drain half of the water off green beans. Cook beans in remaining liquid with 3 tablespoons bacon drippings. Drain cooked beans thoroughly. Add remaining ingredients and toss lightly. Serve warm — not hot.

Mildred Earney

GREEN BEAN CASSEROLE

Mushrooms	2 teaspoons soy sauce
1 stick butter	1 teaspoon salt
1 onion, chopped	1 teaspoon Accent
Flour	Pepper to taste
¼ cup warm milk	3 packages frozen green beans
1 cup Half and Half	Water chestnuts, drained
¾ pound sharp Cheddar cheese	¾ cup almonds, toasted and slivered
⅛ teaspoon Tabasco	

Sauté mushrooms and onions in butter. Add flour and stir until smooth. Add milk and cream and cook in double boiler until thick. Add cheese, Tabasco, soy sauce, salt, Accent and pepper to taste. Cook until cheese melts. In a separate pan cook beans until just tender. Add water chestnuts and some almonds. Mix all ingredients together and place in a greased casserole. Top with almonds and bake at 375° for 20 minutes.

Lisa Baddour

117

GREEN BEAN CASSEROLE

1 stick oleo	Salt to taste
3 medium onions	Pepper to taste
4 tablespoons flour	12 ounces medium cheese, grated
1½ cups milk	1 can water chestnuts, sliced thinly
Dash Tabasco	1 can mushroom stems and pieces
4 teaspoons soy sauce	3 cans French style green beans

Sauté onions in oleo in heavy black skillet. Add flour, milk, Tabasco, soy sauce, salt, pepper and cheese (save some cheese for top). Drain water chestnuts, mushrooms and green beans and pour into casserole — cover with cheese. Bake at 350° for 20-30 minutes. Freezes well. *Serves 12.*

Mrs. James Robertson

GOOD NEIGHBOR CASSEROLE

1 can French style green beans, drained	1 can condensed cream of celery soup
1 tablespoon butter	1 cup canned French fried onion rings
½ cup sliced water chestnuts (optional)	

Combine in a casserole dish, beans, butter, chestnuts and soup. Cover and heat in a 350° oven for 30 minutes. Remove from oven, stir, then add onion rings on top. Return to oven and bake uncovered for about 5 minutes.

Mrs. William Sanford

GREEN BEANS, SWISS STYLE

4 cups green beans, drained	¼ teaspoon pepper
½ pound Swiss cheese, grated	1 teaspoon sugar
2 tablespoons butter	1 cup sour cream
2 tablespoons flour	1 cup corn flakes, crushed
½ teaspoon onion, grated	2 tablespoons butter, melted
1 teaspoon salt	

Place beans in greased casserole, sprinkle with cheese. Melt butter in saucepan, blend in flour. Add onion, salt, pepper, sugar and sour cream. Cook slowly for a few minutes, stirring constantly. Pour over beans and cheese. Sprinkle top with crushed corn flakes and melted butter. Bake in 400° oven for 20 minutes. *Serves 8.*

Mrs. Walter Scott

GREEN BEAN CASSEROLE

2 cans French-style green beans   ½ cup Parmesan cheese, grated
1 can cream of mushroom soup   Frozen onion rings
1 can water chestnuts, sliced

Drain juice from beans and reserve. Mix ⅓ cup bean juice with mushroom soup. Put 1 can of beans and half of the sliced water chestnuts in casserole dish. Pour half of soup mixture over layer, top with half of cheese. Repeat layer. Bake at 350° for 25 minutes. Top with onion rings and return to oven to brown.

Mrs. Albert Waring

SWEET SOUR BEANS

2 slices bacon   2 teaspoons sugar
1 small onion   ¼ cup vinegar
1 1-pound can green or wax beans   Salt and pepper

Cut bacon in pieces. Brown bacon and chopped onion lightly. Add liquid drained from beans and boil down to about ½ cup. Add beans, sugar and vinegar; season to taste. Heat. *Makes 4 servings.*

Berenice S. Clemmer

SWEET AND SOUR GREEN BEANS

4 slices bacon   3 tablespoons wine vinegar
1 pound fresh green beans or 2   2½ tablespoons cornstarch
   packages frozen green beans   1 tablespoon soy sauce
½ cup water   ¼ cup sweet pickles, chopped
3 tablespoons sugar   1 green pepper, sliced

Microwave Cooking: Cook the bacon on paper towel in dish on high until brown and crisp (3 to 4 minutes). Remove from oven, drain and crumble. Snap off ends of beans and cut in 1½-inch pieces. Place beans in a 2-quart casserole and add water. Cover and cook for 8-10 minutes or until beans are tender and firm. Drain beans and set aside, saving liquid. In same casserole, mix the sugar, vinegar, cornstarch, soy sauce and pickles. Add bean liquid and enough water to make 1½ cups. Stir into the sauce with green pepper. Cover and cook for 3 minutes, stir, cook 3 minutes more or until mixture comes to a boil. Add the beans and crumbled bacon. Cook 1 more minute to heat thoroughly. Cook frozen beans without added liquid for 10 minutes or until tender. Save liquid that results for part of sauce.

Patricia Maxwell

119

OVEN WARM STRING BEANS

2 cans string beans
8 pieces fried bacon, drained
½ cup white vinegar

½ cup sugar
Red onion, thinly sliced

Drain beans and heat for 30 minutes in salted water. Reserve hot fat from fried bacon. Mix sugar and vinegar and add to hot fat. Cook til it comes to a boil. Place beans in a casserole dish. Pour vinegar mixture over this. Then place a layer of separated rings of onion over beans and crumble bacon over top. Place this in warm oven at 150° for at least 3 hours.

Mrs. Don Burnett

BROCCOLI SUPREME

1 10-ounce package frozen
   chopped broccoli or 2 cups fresh
   chopped broccoli
1 14-ounce can artichoke hearts,
   drained and quartered
¾ can cream of mushroom soup
½ cup mayonnaise

2 eggs, slightly beaten
1 teaspoon lemon juice
1 teaspoon Worcestershire sauce
3 carrots, sliced, cooked and drained
1 cup sharp Cheddar cheese, grated
Bread crumbs
Garlic salt

Cook broccoli in small amount of boiling water until tender. Drain. Place artichokes in buttered 9-inch casserole. Combine soup, mayonnaise, eggs, lemon juice, Worcestershire, carrots and broccoli. Pour over artichokes. Sprinkle with cheese and bread crumbs and pour melted margarine over top. Sprinkle with garlic salt. Bake at 350° for 30-45 minutes.

Jessie Blackwell

BROCCOLI CASSEROLE

2 packages frozen broccoli
2 eggs
1 can mushroom soup
1 cup mayonnaise

1 small onion, grated
Salt and pepper to taste
Cheese cracker crumbs, finely rolled
Butter

Cook broccoli according to directions. Mix with egg, soup, mayonnaise, onion, salt and pepper. Put in a casserole dish. Top with cracker crumbs. Dot with butter. Bake at 350° for 45 minutes.

Mrs. Sam T. Dillahunty

BROCCOLI CASSEROLE

2　packages frozen chopped
　　broccoli
4　tablespoons oleo
2　tablespoons flour
½　cup milk

¼　cup onion, chopped
8　ounces Cheese Whiz
3　eggs, beaten
1　teaspoon salt
Buttered cracker crumbs

Thaw and drain broccoli. In saucepan, combine oleo, flour and milk and cook until slightly thickened. Stir in broccoli and onion. Mix Cheese Whiz, eggs and salt and add to broccoli mixture. Put in greased baking dish. Top with cracker crumbs. Bake at 350° for 45 minutes.

Myra T. Crowe,
Mrs. John Jenkins

RICE AND CHOPPED BROCCOLI CASSEROLE

½　cup onions, chopped
½　cup celery
Oil
1　box chopped broccoli, thawed
2　cups cooked rice

1　can cream of chicken soup
1　small jar cheese spread
1　small can evaporated milk
Potato chips, crumbled

Sauté onions and celery in oil. Add broccoli, rice, chicken soup, cheese spread and milk. Sprinkle top with crumbled potato chips. Bake at 350° for 45 minutes. *Serves 8-10.*

To make a one-dish meal, add chopped chicken, turkey or ham.

CAULIFLOWER-PEANUT POLONAISE

1　medium head cauliflower
½　cup butter
1　tablespoon fresh lemon juice

1　tablespoon chopped parsley
⅓　cup fresh bread crumbs, toasted
1　cup peanuts, coarsely chopped

Wash and separate cauliflower into flowerettes. Cook in 1-inch boiling salted water over medium heat, 8-10 minutes or until tender; drain. Melt butter; stir in lemon juice and parsley, then bread crumbs and peanuts. Pour over cooked cauliflowerettes and toss to coat. *Serves 6.*

Rose Baddour Saleeby

CABBAGE AU GRATIN

1 head cabbage	1 cup milk
2 tablespoons oleo	Bread crumbs
2 tablespoons flour	½ cup cheese, grated

Boil cabbage until tender. In saucepan, melt oleo and stir in flour. Cook slightly but do not brown. Slowly stir in milk and cook until thick. Put cabbage in flat casserole and cover with sauce. Sprinkle with bread crumbs and cheese. Bake at 350° for 30 minutes.

Mrs. Charles Adams, Jr.

FRIED GREEN CABBAGE

1 medium sized green cabbage	½ cup celery, chopped
2 tablespoons green pepper, chopped (optional)	Dash of salt
2 onions, chopped	3 tablespoons bacon drippings

Trim cabbage as needed. Remove core and slice fine on cutting board. Toss with remaining vegetables. Add bit of salt and turn into hot bacon drippings. Cover and simmer until wilted about 15 to 20 minutes, turning cabbage once or twice during this period. Serve at once. (Optional: 1 small hot pepper, chopped; red or green can be used.) *Serves 4 to 6.*

Edna Phillips

COLOSSAL CABBAGE

4 cups cabbage, shredded	½ teaspoon salt
¼ cup milk	¼ teaspoon pepper
1 tablespoon instant minced onion	2 tablespoons oleo or butter
	½ cup cheese, grated or shredded

Mix all ingredients in a 2-quart bowl. Put in microwave oven. Cook covered for 6 minutes, stirring once. Let stand for 2 minutes.

June Spotts

Turns cabbage into a gourmet's delight!

122

PENNSYLVANIA DUTCH SAUERKRAUT

1 can sauerkraut, drained
2 red apples, thinly sliced
½ cup apple brandy

1 tablespoon light brown sugar
2 tablespoons butter

Put all ingredients in heavy saucepan and simmer until apples are tender.

Mildred Earney

KRAUT

Cabbage
1 teaspoon salt

Boiling water

Chop cabbage. Bruise well. Fill jar half full of cabbage. Sift in salt on top. Fill full of boiling water. Put on cap after scalding it. Takes 60 days.

Dr. Charles Huffman
This is from the doctor that delivered all the Baddours, so you know this recipe is old!

CARROT AND ALMOND RING

2 tablespoons butter
2 tablespoons flour
½ cup milk, warmed
2 cups carrots, mashed and
   cooked
½ teaspoon salt

½ cup blanched almonds, finely
   grated
4 eggs, separated
Green peas
Parsley

In a saucepan melt the butter, add flour, and stir the roux until it is smooth. Add gradually the warm milk, bring the sauce to a boil, stirring constantly, and simmer for 5 minutes. Remove the pan from the heat and add the carrots, salt and almonds. Blend in the egg yolks, lightly beaten, and cook the mixture over very low heat for 4 to 5 minutes. Cool. Beat egg whites until they are stiff and fold them into the carrot mixture. Pour the mixture into a buttered 9-inch ring mold, set the mold in a pan of hot water, and bake the carrot ring at 350° for 50 to 60 mintues, or until it is firm. Let it stand for a minute or two and turn it out on a platter. Fill the center with buttered green peas and garnish the platter with parsley. *Serves 8.*

Nellie George Baddour

CARROT CRUNCH

1 medium bunch carrots, sliced	1 tablespoon butter, melted
1 teaspoon onion, minced	½ cup cracker crumbs
1 egg	¼ teaspoon salt
1 cup milk	¼ teaspoon seasoned salt

Cook carrots and onion together, then mash. Add egg and milk, beat thoroughly. Add remaining ingredients and put in buttered casserole. Sprinkle with additional butter and cracker crumbs. Bake at 350° for 25 minutes.

Mrs. I. R. McGraw

CELERY CASSEROLE

4 cups celery, diced	1 cup cream of chicken soup
1 can water chestnuts, drained and sliced	¼ cup butter
	⅓ cup bread crumbs
1 small can pimento, drained and chopped	1 small package sliced almonds

Cook celery in salted boiling water until tender, drain. Add water chestnuts and pimento and mix well. Stir in undiluted soup. Pour into greased casserole. Combine butter, crumbs and almonds, sprinkle over casserole. Bake 350° for 30 minutes. *Serves 6-8.*

Lynn Cravens

Cooked chicken breasts may be added for main dish.

FRESH CORN (CREAM STYLE)

1 pint fresh corn (6 or 7 ears)	¼ teaspoon black pepper
¾ stick butter or oleo	1¼ cups sweet milk
1 teaspoon salt	1 teaspoon sugar

In cutting the corn off the cob, cut half the kernel off, the next part of kernel scrape off. This is the secret to this recipe. Place all ingredients in a heavy pot, 1 or 2-quart size, on top of stove. Let come to boil, cut heat down on medium low or low and cook uncovered for 25 minutes, stirring often because it is real easy to stick and burn.

Oneida Baddour

The best cream style corn you will ever eat.

SOUTH COAST HOMINY

3 tablespoons butter
1 small onion, minced
½ cup green pepper, chopped
3 tablespoons flour
1 teaspoon salt
½ teaspoon dry mustard
Dash of cayenne pepper

1½ cups milk
1 cup sharp Cheddar cheese, grated
½ cup ripe olives, pitted and
   chopped
1 13-ounce can hominy, drained
½ cup bread crumbs, buttered

Melt butter in saucepan, add onion and green pepper and sauté 5 minutes. Blend in flour, salt, mustard and cayenne pepper. Add milk and cook, stirring constantly until mixture thickens and comes to a boil. Add grated cheese and stir until melted. Remove from heat — add olives and hominy. Put in a 6-cup baking dish — sprinkle with buttered crumbs and bake 30 minutes or until brown on top. *Serves 6-8.*

Mildred F. Fall

CORN PUDDING

2 eggs, beaten
1 tablespoon sugar
1 tablespoon cornstarch
1 cup milk
½ stick butter, melted

1 12-ounce can whole kernel corn,
   undrained
½ teaspoon salt
⅛ teaspoon pepper

Mix all the ingredients and pour into a baking dish. Cook at 325° until firm — 30 to 45 minutes. *Serves 4.*

Nellie George Baddour

FRIED CORN FRITTERS

1 17-ounce can whole kernel corn	½ cup all-purpose flour
1 teaspoon salt	2 eggs, separated
1 teaspoon sugar	Salad oil
Generous dash of pepper	

Combine corn, salt, sugar, pepper, flour and egg yolks. Beat egg whites until stiff, fold into corn mixture. Drop mixture by tablespoons into hot oil, cook until lightly browned. *Serves 8.*

Sara M. Hart

When you're looking for a new dish, try this.

EGGPLANT DRESSING

½ pound sausage or ground meat	½ cup cooked rice
¼ cup onion, chopped	1 cup cheese, shredded
½ cup celery, chopped	Toasted bread crumbs
Salt and pepper to taste	
1 medium eggplant, cooked and mashed	

Brown meat, onion and celery in skillet, stirring frequently. Salt and pepper to taste; combine with eggplant, rice and cheese. Put in a greased baking dish. Top with crumbs. Bake at 350° for 20 minutes.

Jeanie Van Vranken

EGGPLANT PUERTO RICAN

2 pounds eggplant	¼ pound cooked ham
1 pound pork, diced	1 large onion, diced
2 tablespoons oleo	1 8-ounce can tomato sauce
1 tablespoon salt	1 green pepper
Pepper	¼ cup margarine
2 teaspoons sugar	¼ pound Cheddar cheese, grated
1 tablespoon vinegar	

Cook eggplant until tender, drain and mash. Brown pork in oleo. Add salt and pepper, sugar and vinegar. Add remaining ingredients and bring to simmer. Stir in eggplant, pour into greased casserole and bake at 350° for 15 minutes.

Homazelle Ashford

SCALLOPED EGGPLANT

1 large eggplant
⅓ cup milk
1 cup condensed cream of
  mushroom soup
1 egg, slightly beaten

½ cup onions, chopped fine
1¼ cups packaged herb seasoned
  stuffing
2 tablespoons margarine, melted
1 cup sharp cheese, diced

Peel, cube and cook eggplant in salted water until tender. Drain. Stir milk into soup and add to eggplant. Blend in egg, onion and ¾ cup stuffing. Toss lightly to mix. Turn into a 10x6x1 baking dish. Crush remaining stuffing and toss with margarine. Sprinkle over casserole and top with cheese. Bake 20 minutes at 350°. Serves 6.

Mrs. John Cooper

STUFFED EGGPLANT

Eggplant
½ cup cracker crumbs
1 tablespoon olive oil
1 tablespoon butter

½ cup sweet milk
1 tablespoon onion, finely chopped
1 egg, beaten
½ cup cheese, grated

Peel eggplant and slice. Boil about 20 minutes in salt water. Drain and mash to make 2 cups of eggplant. Add crumbs, oil, butter, milk, onion and egg. Mix together and put in a casserole dish. Sprinkle with cheese. Bake in 325° oven until brown.

Mildred F. Fall

ESCALLOPED EGGPLANT

1 medium eggplant, sliced
  crosswise
1 large tomato, sliced
1 large onion, thinly sliced
¾ cup butter, melted
½ teaspoon salt

½ teaspoon dried basil leaves
¼ pound Mozzarella cheese, sliced
½ cup dried bread crumbs
2 tablespoons Parmesan cheese,
  grated

Preheat oven to 450°. On medium size heatproof platter, arrange eggplant slices, then tomato, and onion slices on top. Drizzle with ¼ cup melted butter. Sprinkle with salt and basil. Bake, covered 20 minutes. Cut Mozzarella slices in thirds; arrange over top. Stir crumbs into rest of melted butter; sprinkle over top; then sprinkle with Parmesan cheese. Bake uncovered 10 minutes.

Sue Davis

EGGPLANT SOUFFLÉ

3 pints eggplant	Salt and pepper
1½ sticks butter or oleo, melted	½ pound sharp cheese, grated
3 eggs, beaten	2 cups cracker crumbs
1 small can Pet milk	

Peel and cut eggplant into about 1-inch squares and cook until tender. Drain off most of water and add melted butter to eggplant while warm. Let cool. Add eggs, milk, salt and pepper and mix. Pour into greased casserole and top with cheese and crumbs, mixed. Dot with butter. Bake in 350° oven about 30 minutes. Top should brown slightly.

Mrs. R. O. Buck,
Marie Hartfield

EGGPLANT CASSEROLE

2 large eggplants, cubed	1 cup cracker crumbs
1 teaspoon salt	1 can oysters, drained
¼ teaspoon pepper	1 can mushroom soup
½ cup onion, chopped	1 cup Cheddar cheese, diced
2 tablespoons butter	½ cup cheese, grated
4 eggs	

Season eggplant with salt and pepper and cook until tender. Sauté onion in butter. Mash cooked eggplant in mixer. Add onion and eggs and whip. Stir in cracker crumbs, oysters, soup and diced cheese. Transfer to greased casserole and bake at 350° for 45 minutes. Add grated cheese on top and place back in oven to brown.

Mary Jane Baddour Chandler

EGGPLANT PATTY

1 cup eggplant, cooked	Pinch of black pepper
¾ cup cooked rice	Dash of red pepper sauce
1 egg	1-2 tablespoons onion, grated
2 tablespoons flour	½ cup Cheddar cheese, shredded
½ teaspoon salt	

Wash and slice or dice eggplant. No need to peel. Cook in small amount of mildly salted water until tender. Drain and measure. Mix with remaining ingredients. Cover and place in refrigerator for an hour or so. Heat bacon drippings or oil in heavy skillet but do not overheat. Drop in six patties and cook until crispy brown on both sides. Serve at once. *Makes 6 servings.*

Eulalee B. Dacus

EGGPLANT CASSEROLE

½ cup onion, chopped	1 egg, slightly beaten
¼ cup celery, chopped	1¼ cups cornbread crumbs
2 tablespoons green pepper, chopped	¼ cup milk
	Dash Tabasco
1 tablespoon oleo	Dash Worcestershire sauce
1 eggplant	Salt and pepper to taste
1 cup canned or cooked tomatoes, mashed	Sharp cheese, grated

Sauté onion, celery and green pepper in oleo. Peel, slice and soak eggplant 10 minutes in salted water. Drain. Cook in fresh salted water until tender. Drain and mash. (You should have 1½ cups eggplant.) Mix eggplant with sautéed mixture, tomatoes, egg, bread crumbs, milk, Tabasco, Worcestershire sauce and salt and pepper. Pour into a greased casserole dish and top with grated cheese. Bake in 350° oven for about 30 minutes.

Opal Deneke

DOMINO EGGPLANT CASSEROLE

2 large eggplants, peeled and cubed	2 garlic buds, chopped
	2 pounds ground chuck
¼ cup oil	Salt and pepper
1 large onion, chopped	1 cup Italian flavored bread crumbs
1 cup celery, chopped	3 eggs

Boil eggplants until tender. Drain well. In skillet, sauté in oil the onion, celery, and garlic. When tender, add ground chuck and brown lightly. Season with salt and pepper to taste. Remove from heat and add to eggplant. Add bread crumbs. Beat eggs well and add to mixture. Pour into buttered casserole and top generously with more bread crumbs. Bake at 350° for 30 minutes. Excellent with duck or roast beef.

Lee Ellis

Favorite Cajun country recipe.

CLUB MUSHROOM CASSEROLE

1½ cups fresh mushrooms, sliced	2 teaspoons Worcestershire
½ cup butter	1½ teaspoons salt
2 cups processed cheese	¼ teaspoon pepper
3 tablespoons flour	4 eggs, hard boiled
3 cups milk	4 ounces pimento

Sauté mushrooms in butter. Remove from pan, add cheese and set aside. Blend flour into pan and add milk gradually. Cook until thickened, stirring constantly. Add mushroom mixture, Worcestershire, salt, pepper, sliced eggs, and diced pimento; place in a greased casserole. Bake at 350° for 30 minutes or until bubbly. Top with shredded cheese and serve.

Dena Burns

MUSHROOM SOUFFLÉ

1 pound mushrooms, fresh or canned	Salt and pepper to taste
	Dash Tabasco
1 tablespoon onion, minced	2 tablespoons Worcestershire sauce
8 tablespoons butter	Pinch nutmeg
8 tablespoons flour	6 egg yolks, well beaten
2¼ cups milk, scalded	6 egg whites, stiffly beaten
¾ cup sharp Cheddar cheese, grated	Shrimp sauce (see page 69)

If using fresh mushrooms, wash them thoroughly. Chop caps and stems and combine with onion. Sauté in half the butter until they are light brown. Put aside. Add the remaining butter to the skillet and blend in flour and hot milk very gradually, stirring constantly until smooth. Cook until thick and add cheese, still stirring until cheese is melted. Add salt, pepper, Tabasco, Worcestershire and nutmeg. Let cool. Stir egg yolks into mixture and then gently fold in egg whites. Pour into a well greased 2½-quart baking dish and place in a pan of warm water. Bake at 325° for 1-1¼ hours or until firm. Serve immediately. Serve with shrimp sauce over top. *Serves 8.*

Mrs. William M. Forman

Versatile recipe – fits any meal.

PEAS DELICIOUS

2 tablespoons butter
2 tablespoons water
1 clove garlic
4 to 6 tiny white onions
3 large lettuce leaves, quartered

1 teaspoon sugar
¾ teaspoon salt
⅛ teaspoon pepper
2 packages frozen peas

Melt butter in large skillet. Add water, garlic, onions, lettuce, sugar, ¼ teaspoon salt and pepper. Cover and simmer 30 minutes. Stir in peas. Cover and cook over low heat 30 minutes. Remove garlic, sprinkle with remaining salt, and stir well. Serves 6.

Nellie George Baddour

MINNIE'S ENGLISH PEA CASSEROLE

2 packages frozen English peas
and onions
2 small jars pimento, chopped

2 small cans water chestnuts
2 cans cream of mushroom soup
2 cans Chinese noodles

Cook English peas and onions. Drain. Add pimento, water chestnuts, and soup in casserole dish and cook until it bubbles. Add Chinese noodles on top and cook until noodles are heated.

Minnie Miller

ENGLISH PEA AND WATER CHESTNUT CASSEROLE

1 stick oleo
1 small onion, minced
2 tablespoons green pepper,
chopped
1 cup celery, chopped
2 cans "tiny" English peas,
drained

1 can water chestnuts
2 pimentos, chopped
1 can mushroom soup
Buttered crumbs
Toasted almonds

Melt oleo in heavy skillet. Add onion, pepper and celery; sauté, stirring often until soft and lightly browned. Remove from heat and add peas and sliced water chestnuts with liquid. Fold in pimento. Arrange in 2-quart casserole a layer of vegetables. Top with undiluted soup. Add another layer of vegetables and top with remaining soup. Sprinkle top with buttered crumbs and toasted almonds. Bake at 350° until bubbling hot — about 20 minutes.

Mrs. Bill Lunsford,
Mrs. L. H. Polk

131

POTATO OMELET, COUNTRY STYLE

1½ pounds potatoes
6   slices bacon
¼   cup onion, chopped

6   eggs
Salt and pepper

Cook potatoes in boiling water until tender. Cool and cut in small slices. Fry bacon, drain and crumble. Sauté onion in bacon fat. Add potatoes, cook over medium heat until potatoes are brown. Beat eggs, add salt and pepper. Pour egg mixture over potatoes. Sprinkle with bacon. Cover and cook over low heat 5 minutes. Cut in wedges to serve. *Makes 4-6 servings.*

Mrs. Billy Dunahoo

OLIVE POTATO SCALLOP

1½ pounds Irish potatoes
1   can condensed cream of
    mushroom soup
½   cup milk
¾   cup Cheddar cheese, grated

1   can pitted ripe olives
¼   cup butter
⅛   teaspoon paprika
2   cups toasted bread cubes

Cook potatoes until tender, peel and dice — blend soup and milk until smooth. Stir in cheese — combine with potatoes and ripe olives, mix lightly. Turn into shallow buttered dish. Melt butter, add to paprika, add bread cubes and toss to coat with butter, sprinkle on top of dish. Bake at 400° for 25 minutes until topping is toasted.

Mrs. Henry Harmon

POTATO CROQUETTES

2   cups potatoes, cooked and
    mashed
2   eggs, separated
1   tablespoon butter

Pinch of salt and pepper
Flour
Cooking oil

Cook and mash potatoes. Beat egg whites. Mix potatoes, egg whites, butter, salt and pepper thoroughly. Form mixture into small balls. Dip into beaten egg yolks. Roll in flour and fry in cooking oil until browned. *Serves 6.*

Scottie Ming

POTATO CASSEROLE SUPREME

8 white potatoes	⅔ cup onion, chopped
½ cup butter	1½ cups Cheddar cheese, grated
1 can cream of chicken soup	Buttered bread crumbs
2 cups sour cream	

Cook potatoes until partially done. Cool and grate. Heat together butter, soup, sour cream, onion and cheese. Mix with potatoes. Put in greased casserole and top with bread crumbs. Bake at 350° for 45 minutes. *Serves 12.*

Doris Lanford

OREGANO POTATOES

3 large potatoes (peeled), or 1 can whole new potatoes	3 tablespoons water
	Salt and pepper to taste
2 tablespoons oil	½ teaspoon oregano

Quarter potatoes. Place in baking dish and cover with oil and water. Sprinkle on salt, pepper and oregano. Stir to coat. Bake at 375° until brown. *Serves 6.*

Jackie Edwards

Easy, flavorful and delicious.

GOURMET POTATOES

6 medium potatoes	3 green onions
2 cups Cheddar cheese, shredded	1 teaspoon salt
6 tablespoons margarine	¼ teaspoon pepper
1 cup sour cream	

Cook potatoes in skin. Cool, peel and shred on coarse grater, or potatoes may be cubed. Combine cheese and 4 tablespoons margarine in saucepan. Heat and stir until cheese is almost melted. Remove from heat and blend in sour cream, onions, salt and pepper. Fold in potatoes and spoon into 2-quart casserole. Dot with 2 tablespoons margarine. Cover and bake at 300° for about 25 minutes.

Rose Baddour Saleeby

POT LUCK POTATOES

1 2-pound package frozen hash brown potatoes, thawed	¼ teaspoon pepper
	½ cup onion, chopped
1 teaspoon salt	1 pint sour cream
1 can chicken broth	¾ cup butter, melted
2 cups Cheddar cheese, shredded	2 cups corn flakes, crushed

Combine potatoes, salt, broth, cheese, pepper, onion, sour cream and ½ cup of butter. Pour into 9x13 baking dish. Combine cornflakes with remaining butter and sprinkle on top. Bake at 350° for 45 minutes.

Mrs. John Whalen

SPINACH MOLD – LA VARENNE

1½ pounds fresh spinach	2 eggs
3 tablespoons butter	1 egg yolk
1 cup fresh bread crumbs	Pinch ground nutmeg
¾ cup hot milk	

Wash spinach well, remove stems and cook in ½ cup boiling water for 5 minutes or until tender. Drain thoroughly, squeeze to remove water and chop. Butter 3-4 cup mold well. In skillet melt the butter and add chopped spinach and cook 3-4 minutes, stirring until moisture has evaporated. Soak bread crumbs in hot milk for 5 minutes and drain. Add bread crumbs to spinach, plus the beaten eggs and nutmeg. Spoon into mold and cover with buttered foil if preparing ahead. About 1 hour before serving, preheat oven to 350° and stand mold in a pan of hot water and bring just to a boil on top of stove. Bake in the heated oven, allowing 45-55 minutes. Lift out of water bath and cool slightly before unmolding onto platter. *Serves 8.*

Lynn Cravens

SPINACH CASSEROLE

1 10-ounce package chopped, frozen spinach	1 pound small curd cottage cheese
	¼ pound Cheddar or American cheese, grated
3 eggs, beaten	
4 tablespoons flour	¼ pound Brick or Swiss cheese, grated
Salt and pepper	
¼ cup butter, melted	

Cook spinach until thawed. Beat eggs; add flour, heat; add salt and pepper, butter and spinach. Mix well. Fold in cottage cheese. Stir in other cheeses. Pour into 1½ to 2-quart casserole. Can be made the night before and baked before serving. Bake in 350° oven for 50-60 minutes. *Serves 3-4.*

Carol Thompson

SPINACH MADELEINE

2 packages frozen, chopped
   spinach
4 tablespoons butter
2 tablespoons flour
2 tablespoons onion, chopped
½ cup evaporated milk
½ teaspoon black pepper

¾ teaspoon celery salt
¾ teaspoon garlic salt
Salt to taste
1 teaspoon Worcestershire sauce
Red pepper to taste
6 ounce roll of Jalapeno cheese

Cook spinach according to directions on package. Drain and reserve liquid. Melt butter in saucepan over low heat; add flour and stir until blended and smooth, but not brown. Add onion and cook until soft but not brown. Add milk and ½ cup spinach liquid slowly, stirring constantly to avoid lumps. Cook until smooth and thick; continue stirring. Add seasonings and cheese which has been cut into small pieces. Stir until melted and combine with cooked spinach. This may be served immediately or put into a casserole and topped with buttered bread crumbs. Can be frozen and reheated. *Serves 5 to 6.*

Mrs. John Whalen

SPINACH CASSEROLE

2 packages chopped frozen
   spinach
1 package Lipton onion soup

½ stick butter or oleo, melted
1 cup sharp Cheddar cheese, grated

Cook spinach by package instructions, omitting the salt. Stir in soup and butter and pour into greased casserole. Top with cheese. Bake at 350° for 25 minutes.

Jessie Blackwell

SPINACH-ARTICHOKE CASSEROLE

3 10-ounce packages frozen
   spinach
1 can artichokes
½ cup oleo, melted

1 8-ounce package cream cheese,
   softened
4 tablespoons lemon juice
Cracker crumbs

Cook spinach and drain well. Drain artichokes and cross slice. Cover bottom of casserole with artichokes. Combine oleo, cream cheese, and lemon juice. Stir in spinach and mix well. Pour over artichokes. Top with cracker crumbs. Bake at 350° for 25 minutes. Freezes well. *Serves 8-10.*

Mrs. James Robertson

SPINACH AND EGGS

3 packages frozen spinach	1 teaspoon salt
10 eggs	1 teaspoon ground black pepper
1 tablespoon Worcestershire sauce	1 roll garlic cheese
1 teaspoon garlic salt	

Cook spinach as directed on package. Cook 6 of the eggs until hard boiled. Add remaining 4 eggs, Worcestershire, garlic salt, salt and pepper. Cook 5 minutes. Add cheese, cook until melted good. Add chopped hard boiled eggs and stir well. *Serves 12.*

Sara M. Hart

PARTY SPINACH

8 eggs, hard boiled	2 tablespoons oleo, melted
1 package spinach, cooked	Salt and pepper
½ teaspoon onion, grated	1 can mushroom soup
1 teaspoon Worcestershire sauce	1 8-ounce jar Cheese Whiz
Dash Tabasco	Parmesan cheese
2 teaspoons lemon juice	

Slice eggs in half long-ways. Remove and mash egg yolks and combine with spinach, onion, Worcestershire, Tabasco, lemon juice and oleo. Fill egg whites with this mixture and place in oblong casserole. Heat soup and Cheese Whiz in double boiler. Pour over eggs. Cover with bread crumbs, and sprinkle with Parmesan cheese. Bake at 350° until bubbly.

Charlyne Watson

CREAMED SPINACH FOR STUFFING FRESH MUSHROOMS

2 cans spinach, drained and
   chopped finely
1 cup (or more) Half and Half
½ stick butter
1 teaspoon salt (to taste)
1 teaspoon white or black pepper
   (to taste)

½ teaspoon nutmeg
Fresh mushrooms
2 tablespoons butter
¼ teaspoon salt
⅛ teaspoon paprika
½ cup milk

Heat the spinach, Half and Half, butter, salt and pepper together over medium heat, stirring almost constantly for the first 10 minutes. Add nutmeg; reduce heat to simmer, and continue to cook uncovered until the mixture becomes creamy, about 20-30 more minutes. More cream and/or butter may be added to keep the mixture liquid during beginning cooking stages. Remove stems from mushrooms and wipe caps with a cloth (washing may be necessary). Place in top of double boiler over hot water. Dot with butter. Add salt, paprika, and milk. Cover closely, steam for about 20 minutes or until tender. Stuff with creamed spinach and place in oven till hot for serving.

Nina Martin

SCALLOPED SPINACH

2 cups cooked spinach (fresh,
   frozen, or canned)
2 tablespoons chopped onion
2 eggs, beaten

½ cup milk
¼ cup American cheese, grated
Salt and pepper to taste
½ cup buttered bread crumbs

Press spinach through coarse sieve and add onion, eggs, milk, cheese, and salt and pepper. Mix and pour into 1-quart baking dish. Cover mixture with bread crumbs. Bake at 350° for 20 minutes. *Serves 4.*

Jackie Edwards

EASY SPINACH CASSEROLE

2 packages frozen chopped
   spinach

1 pint sour cream
1 envelope dry onion soup mix

Cook and drain spinach. Combine with sour cream and soup mix. Cover and bake at 350° for 30-40 minutes. *Serves 6.*

Jane Baddour,
Mary L. Hight

SPINACH CONTINENTAL

1 pound fresh spinach	¾ cup peanuts
½ cup peanut oil	2-3 tablespoons soy sauce
¼ cup onion, chopped	⅛ teaspoon cayenne pepper
1 medium tomato, cut in wedges	1-3 tablespoons peanut butter

Wash spinach, removing tough stems; drain and pat dry. In large skillet sauté onion and tomato in ¼ cup peanut oil over medium heat, until tomato is tender, yet firm. Remove tomato from skillet and keep warm. Add remaining oil to skillet. Cook spinach in skillet just until tender, pushing to one side. Stir in soy sauce and cayenne. Add 1-3 tablespoons peanut butter into liquid in pan. Heat, stirring constantly until liquid thickens. Stir in peanuts. Combine cooked tomato and onion in skillet with spinach. Season to taste. *Serves 4.*

Rose Baddour Saleeby

COCONUT SPINACH

3 10-ounce packages frozen chopped spinach	Salt
1 ⅓ cups coconut milk	Pepper

Cook spinach according to package directions. Drain completely, squeezing out all moisture with cheesecloth or paper towels. In 2-quart saucepan combine spinach with coconut milk. Season to taste with salt and pepper. Warm over low heat just before serving. *6 to 8 servings.*

SPINACH ROCKEFELLER

2 packages chopped frozen spinach	¼-½ teaspoon garlic salt
1 8-ounce package cream cheese	¼ cup buttered bread crumbs

Cook spinach as directed. Drain thoroughly. Put back in pan and add cheese, stirring, over low heat. Add garlic salt. Put in small casserole and top with crumbs. Brown in 350° oven about 20 minutes.

Diane Fair

BUTTERNUT SQUASH

1 large butternut squash	½ teaspoon vanilla
¾ cup sugar	½ teaspoon baking powder
2 tablespoons flour	2 eggs
1 stick butter	Dash of nutmeg

Peel and boil squash. Drain and put in a mixing bowl. Add the sugar, flour, butter, vanilla, baking powder, eggs and nutmeg. Mix well and put into a baking dish. Bake 1 hour at 350°.

Mrs. Malcolm Graham

PIMENTO-SQUASH CASSEROLE

1 pound squash, cut into 1-inch cubes	½ cup salad dressing
½ cup onion, chopped	½ cup pimento, chopped
¼ cup green peppers, chopped	1 egg, beaten
½ stick oleo	½ cup cheese, grated
1 teaspoon sugar	Bread crumbs

Cook squash, onions and green peppers until tender in water. Drain. Add oleo, sugar, salad dressing, pimento, egg and cheese. Pour into baking dish. Cover with bread crumbs. Bake for 35 minutes at 350°.

Elizabeth and Catherine Baddour

SQUASH DRESSING

12 small yellow squash (about 2 pounds), cooked and drained	¼ teaspoon Accent
1 cup bell pepper, chopped	1 bay leaf
1 cup celery, chopped	Dash nutmeg
1 cup onions, chopped	½ cup oil
1 teaspoon garlic salt	3 cups cornbread crumbs
1 teaspoon salt	2 eggs, beaten
1 teaspoon pepper	1 teaspoon sage
	1 cup cheese, grated

Sauté squash, bell pepper, celery, onions, garlic salt, salt, pepper, Accent, bay leaf, and nutmeg in oil over low heat. Cover pan and cook until tender. Remove bay leaf. Add cornbread crumbs, eggs, sage, and ½ cup grated cheese. Put into casserole and bake at 350° for 20 minutes. Sprinkle remaining cheese over top and return to oven for 10 more minutes. *Serves 6 to 8.*

Lisa Baddour

This is some kinda good!

SQUASH CASSEROLE

2 cups yellow squash	1 medium onion, grated
1 cup sweet milk, scalded	½ tablespoon baking powder
1 cup soft bread crumbs	1 tube Ritz crackers
2 eggs, beaten	¼ cup butter, melted
8 ounces sharp cheese, grated	

Cook, drain and mash squash. Combine milk, bread crumbs and squash. Add beaten eggs, cheese, onion and baking powder. Pour into greased 9x13 baking dish. Cover with cracker crumbs mixed with butter. Bake 30-45 minutes at 350°. Eat at once. *Serves 12-15*.

Grace Wesson

Once you've tried this recipe, you'll use it again.

SQUASH CASSEROLE

2 pounds yellow crookneck squash	1 egg, beaten
1 medium onion	1½ cups Cheddar cheese, grated
½ stick butter	Salt
¼ cup bread crumbs	Pepper
	Paprika

Cook squash and onion in small amount of water until tender. Drain. Melt butter and pour over crumbs. Mix squash, onion, crumbs and egg together. Add cheese, salt and pepper. Place in casserole dish. Sprinkle with paprika and bake at 350° for 20-25 minutes.

Lynn Cravens

SUMMER SQUASH CASSEROLE

2 pounds squash, sliced (6 cups)	1 cup dairy sour cream
¼ cup onions, chopped	1 cup carrots, shredded
1 teaspoon salt	1 8-ounce package stuffing mix
1 can condensed cream of chicken soup	½ cup butter, melted

Boil squash and onions 5 minutes in salted water. Drain. Combine soup and sour cream. Stir in carrots. Fold this into squash and onions. Combine stuffing mix and butter. Spread half of the stuffing mixture in bottom of 12x7½x2-inch baking dish. Spoon vegetable mixture on top and sprinkle remaining stuffing over vegetables and bake for 25 to 30 minutes or until thoroughly heated. *Makes 6 servings*.

Fanny Corradini

SQUASH AND CARROT CASSEROLE

8 yellow squash, cooked and
   drained
6 carrots, cooked and drained
2 eggs

½ stick butter or margarine
2 tablespoons flour
3 tablespoons onion, chopped

Beat the cooked squash and carrots together. Then beat in all other ingredients. Turn into greased shallow casserole dish. Bake at 350° for 1 hour. This can be prepared in the morning and refrigerated until time to bake. *4-5 servings.*

Rose Baddour Saleeby

STUFFED SQUASH

Whole summer squash
Butter, melted
Salt
Seasoned pepper

Onion, grated
Buttered bread crumbs
Cheddar cheese, grated

Parboil squash in salt water about 5 minutes or until tender. Cool. Scoop out squash leaving a boat. Take pulp and add butter, salt, seasoned pepper and onion. Cook until done. Spoon mixture back into squash boats. Cover with buttered bread crumbs and cheese. Bake in 400° oven until cheese is melted and topping is brown, about 25-30 minutes.

Note: Mixing Cheddar cheese with Parmesan cheese adds greater flavor. If you make these up ahead of time and let stand, the squash boats can take on seasoning from the stuffing.

Rose Baddour Saleeby

ZUCCHINI CUSTARD

1   pound zucchini squash
4   eggs, lightly beaten
1   heaping cup Cheddar cheese,
    shredded
1½ cups milk, scalded

1   tablespoon butter
1   teaspoon salt
¼   teaspoon paprika
1   heaping tablespoon green onions,
    chopped

Cook squash in boiling salted water until tender. Drain and chop. Combine eggs, cheese, milk, butter, seasonings and onions. Add squash. Pour into greased casserole. Place casserole in pan of water. Bake at 325° for 50-55 minutes. If zucchini is large, you may have to peel it as the skin will be tough. *Serves 6.*

Martha Whitington

141

SWEET POTATO CASSEROLE

3 cups sweet potatoes, cooked and mashed	1 cup brown sugar
	1 cup nuts, chopped
1 cup sugar	⅓ cup flour
½ cup butter	⅓ cup butter, melted
2 eggs	Dash of cinnamon and allspice
½ cup raisins (optional)	

Mix sweet potatoes, sugar, butter, eggs and raisins well and pour into buttered casserole. Combine brown sugar, nuts, flour, butter and spices, mix well and spread over casserole. Bake 20 minutes at 350°.

Mrs. Wayne P. Bridwell,
Mrs. Robert H. Lakey

CANDIED SWEET POTATOES

4 medium potatoes, peeled	3 tablespoons flour
1 cup sugar	2 cups cold water

Slice potatoes about ¼-inch thick. Put in pan with enough cold water to cover and cook until tender but not done. Drain; transfer potatoes to a casserole. Combine sugar and flour, add 2 cups water. Pour mixture over the potatoes. Dot with butter. Cook in 375° oven for 30 minutes or until liquid is thick.

Mrs. Toney Mobley

SWEET POTATO SOUFFLÉ

4 pounds sweet potatoes	1 teaspoon nutmeg
1 teaspoon salt	½ cup evaporated milk
1½ cups sugar	½ cup pecans, chopped
2 eggs	1 stick butter or margarine
½ cup raisins	½ cup coconut, shredded
1 lemon (grated rind and juice)	Marshmallows

Slice potatoes and boil in enough salt water to cover potatoes. Cook until tender. Mash and whip potatoes. Mix potatoes with sugar, eggs, raisins, lemon, nutmeg, milk, pecans, margarine and coconut. Pour into a greased casserole dish. Bake in oven at 350° for 30 minutes. Cover top with marshmallows just before removing from oven. Let marshmallows brown.

Nell Barnes

ORANGE AMARETTO YAMS

2 pounds yams	2 tablespoons orange juice
½ cup butter	2 teaspoons orange rind, grated
2 tablespoons sugar	½ cup Amaretto liquor

Cook yams in boiling, salted water (very little salt) until tender. Drain and peel yams. Cut into thick slices and arrange in baking dish. Cream together butter, sugar, orange juice, orange rind and Amaretto. Cover yams with this mixture. Bake at 375° until surface is nicely browned. *Makes 6 servings.*

Jackie Edwards

SWEET POTATOES FLUFF

5 cups sweet potatoes	1 cup sugar
¼ teaspoon lemon flavoring	1 small container Cool Whip
1 teaspoon orange flavoring	½ cup milk
1½ teaspoons vanilla	Marshmallows
¼ cup orange juice	

Boil sweet potatoes and whip with mixer. Add flavorings, juice, sugar, Cool Whip and milk. Pour into greased baking dish. Top with marshmallows and bake until marshmallows are brown — about 30 minutes at 350°.

Nora Nichols

FRESH VEGETABLE GOULASH IN SUMMER

1 medium onion, chopped	8-10 large tomatoes, peeled and chopped
1 quart small okra pods	
1 medium potato, chopped small	1 quart young, green butterbeans, cooked
1 pint water	
Salt and pepper	6 ears corn
4 slices salt pork	Dash red pepper

Put onion, okra, potato, water, seasonings, salt pork, tomatoes and cooked butterbeans in large pot. Cook over low heat 60-90 minutes, stirring occasionally. Scrape corn from cobs and add to goulash. Cook another 15-20 minutes. *Serves 8-10.*

Mrs. Beuford J. Wallace

With corn muffins, tea, and peach cobbler, this can't be beat!

143

VEGETABLE CASSEROLE

1 can string beans, drained
1 can shoepeg corn, drained
1 can water chestnuts, sliced and
   drained
½ cup onion, finely chopped

1 carton sour cream
1 cup Cheddar cheese, shredded
1 can celery soup
Buttered cracker crumbs

Place beans in bottom of greased casserole. Place corn over beans. Mix water chestnuts, onion, sour cream, cheese, and soup and pour over vegetables. Cover with buttered cracker crumbs. Bake at 325° until brown, or about 30 minutes.

Fonnie Mae Furness

MIXED VEGETABLES MORNAY

2 pounds frozen mixed vegetables
1 cup hot water
1 teaspoon salt
¼ teaspoon garlic salt

2 teaspoons butter
Mornay sauce (below)
2 cups buttered homemade coarse
   bread crumbs

Steam vegetables in tightly lidded pan until done; drain. Save liquid. Season vegetables with salt, garlic salt and butter. Pour into buttered baking dish. Top with Mornay sauce. Cover sauce with bread crumbs. Bake at 350° for 30 minutes. *Serves 8-10.*

Mornay Sauce:
¼ cup butter
½ cup flour
1 teaspoon salt
Garlic salt
Nutmeg

Thyme
2 tablespoons white wine
2 cups reserved liquid
½ pint whipping cream
¼ cup Parmesan cheese

Melt butter. Blend in flour, salt, garlic salt, and spices until smooth. Add warm reserved liquid and whipping cream. Cook over low heat, stirring constantly until mixture comes to a boil and thickens. Add cheese and stir until melted.

Lee Ellis

GARLIC GRIT CASSEROLE

1 cup grits	2 eggs, slightly beaten
1 stick butter	⅔ cup milk
1½ rolls garlic cheese	1 cup corn flakes, crushed

Cook grits according to package directions. Add butter, cheese and eggs and heat until melted. Stir in milk. Put in greased pyrex pan. Cover with corn flakes. Bake at 350° for about 45 minutes or 1 hour.

Rose Marie Spooner,
Jan Richardson, Betty McCallen

Good with ham.

RICE AND MUSHROOMS

2⅔ cups cooked rice	½ teaspoon salt
6 tablespoons salad oil	Green onions, chopped
2 4-ounce cans mushrooms, drained	2 tablespoons soy sauce
	2 cups beef consommé, undiluted

Mix and bake, covered, in 350° oven until water is absorbed, not more than 30-45 minutes. Do not stir.

Evelyn Spear

FLORENTINE RICE

¼ pound butter
1 cup rice
1 cup onion, minced

1 teaspoon salt
⅛ teaspoon white pepper
2 cups chicken broth

In melted butter in skillet, sauté rice, onions, salt and pepper, stirring constantly, until rice turns golden. Turn into casserole, add hot broth and bake covered at 375° for 25 minutes, or until all broth is absorbed.

Nellie George Baddour

CONSOMMÉ RICE

½ stick butter
1 cup rice
½ teaspoon salt
1 can consommé plus water to make 2 cups liquid

½ cup celery, diced
1 small bell pepper, diced
1 4-ounce can mushrooms
1 tablespoon almonds, slivered

Brown rice in butter. Place in casserole. Add salt, consommé, celery, pepper, mushrooms and almonds. Bake covered for one hour at 350°. Toss with fork before serving. *Serves 8.*

Betty McCallen

Great with wild game.

RICE AND SQUASH CASSEROLE

2 cups squash
¼ pound butter
1 cup cooked rice
½ onion, finely chopped
1 cup water

1 teaspoon salt
½ can cream of mushroom soup
Bread crumbs
Grated cheese

Cook, drain and chop squash. Melt butter in casserole and add cooked rice. Add squash and onions in layers. Mix water, salt and soup and pour over squash mixture. Top with bread crumbs and cheese. Bake 1 hour at 325°.

Jeanie Van Vranken

RICE CASSEROLE

1 cup uncooked white long grain rice	2 cups chicken bouillon
	1 teaspoon salt
1½ cups onion, chopped	White pepper to taste
3 tablespoons oil	

Brown rice and onions in the oil. Put in casserole with a cover and add chicken bouillon. Add salt and pepper. Cook 25 minutes at 375°.

Oneida Baddour

MOTHER'S RICE CASSEROLE

¾ cup rice	1 stick butter
½ cup onion, chopped	¾ can water
½ cup celery, chopped	1 can beef consommé
½ cup green pepper, chopped	Salt and pepper

Brown rice, onion, celery and pepper in butter in skillet. Mix water and consommé. Pour over rice mixture and season. Place in casserole and bake covered for 45 minutes or an hour at 325°.

Mrs. Kent Ingram

This is good and so easy.

MARSIE'S BEST

3 cups boiling water	1 package onion soup mix
½ stick oleo	1 cup rice, uncooked

Add boiling water to oleo and dissolve. Add soup mix and rice. Pour mixture into buttered casserole and cook 30 minutes at 350°.

Mrs. Wayne P. Bridwell

WILD RICE CASSEROLE

1 package wild rice
1 pound ground beef
1 medium onion, chopped

1 can pimento, chopped
1 can cream of mushroom soup

Cook rice according to package instructions. Brown ground beef and onion. Combine with rice and add pimento and soup. Mix well. Bake at 350° for 45 minutes.

Julian Neal

WILD RICE CASSEROLE

1 box Uncle Ben's Long Grain and
   Wild Rice
1 can onion soup

1 can chicken broth
1 stick butter
1 can button mushrooms

Leaving out the rice seasoning, mix rice, soup, broth, butter and mushrooms together in casserole. Cover and bake 1 hour at 350°. *Serves 6-8.*

Mary Elizabeth DeCell

WILD RICE AND PINE NUTS

¼ teaspoon rosemary
½ cup pine nuts
3 tablespoons parsley
1 teaspoon salt

2 cups wild rice
Green onions
4 cups chicken stock

Combine all ingredients in casserole. Bake 35 minutes at 350°.

Billy and Barbara Mills

FETTUCINI ALFREDO

1 pound fettucini or egg noodles	¾ cup Parmesan cheese, grated
2 tablespoons olive oil	1 egg, slightly beaten
1 stick butter or oleo	Salt and pepper
½ cup cream	

Cook noodles as directed on package. Add olive oil to prevent sticking. Melt butter in large double boiler. Add cream, cheese and beaten eggs gradually and stir until sauce is slightly thickened. Drain and wash noodles in a colander. Add to sauce. Salt and pepper to taste. Toss as a salad. Serve on a warm platter with more Parmesan on side. Serve as a side dish or meatless entree.

Jessie Blackwell

MACARONI CASSEROLE

4 ounces macaroni	6 ounces sharp cheese, shredded
1 8-ounce package sour cream	1 teaspoon paprika
1 large egg	Salt and pepper to taste
1 8-ounce package cottage cheese	

Cook macaroni in salted water. Drain. Add sour cream, egg and cheeses, reserving ½ cup sharp cheese. Stir in seasoning and mix well. Place in baking dish, sprinkle with remaining cheese, and bake at 350° for 30 minutes.

Mary L. Hight

"SPAGHETTI FACTORY" CHEESE SPAGHETTI

Spaghetti for 4	½ pound Mazithra (or Kasseri)
½ cup margarine	cheese

Cook and drain spaghetti. Add margarine and mix well to coat spaghetti. Grate cheese and sprinkle over all. Mix. Serve. *Serves 4.*

Sarah Aaron

Very rich and filling.

149

NOODLES AND WALNUTS

2 cups English walnuts
1 clove garlic, chopped
1 tablespoon parsley, finely
   chopped
1 cup milk

½ stick butter
Salt and pepper
1 5-ounce package noodles
Parmesan cheese

Grind walnuts finely. Mix chopped garlic and parsley. Heat milk till hot. Add butter, salt and pepper. Pour milk mixture gradually over nut mixture (vary milk for desired consistency) and stir thoroughly. Let nuts absorb milk for 5 to 10 minutes. Keep sauce hot. Cook noodles. Put layer of noodles and sauce and then cheese. Repeat. Sprinkle with Parmesan cheese. Serve immediately.

Billy and Barbara Mills

This is an unusually good dish.

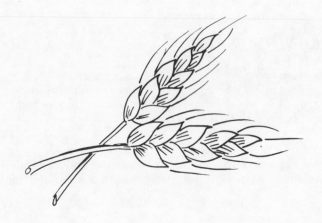

The beauty of this place surely mirrors the Hand of God, just as do these people, handicapped in some ways, reflect His glory. The residents enjoy lakes for recreation, for fishing, for study of the heaven reflected—paths to walk, trails to bicycle, and meadows to roam. The very beauty reassures the residents of their worthiness and their acceptance.

"The sun-swept spaces which the good God made"

–"City Children"
Charles Hanson Towne

SEAFOODS

Lake at Baddour Center

SHRIMP AND OYSTER GUMBO

1   large onion, chopped
2   cloves garlic, mashed
½   green pepper, chopped
2   tablespoons butter
2   tablespoons vegetable oil
1   28-ounce can okra
1   28-ounce can tomatoes
2   tablespoons butter
3   tablespoons flour
1   quart water
1   chicken bouillon cube
1   teaspoon pepper

1   teaspoon salt
1   6-ounce bottle clam juice
1   package frozen crab meat
    (optional)
1   pound fresh shrimp, shelled
1   teaspoon Tabasco
Juice of ½ lemon
1   tablespoon Worcestershire
½   pint oysters
1   tablespoon gumbo filé
2   tablespoons sherry

Sauté onion, garlic, and pepper in butter and oil until soft. Drain okra and tomatoes, reserving juice, add to sautéed onion mixture, cook for 5 minutes. In a large pot, melt 2 tablespoons butter and add flour to make a roux. Gradually add water, stir in bouillon cube, salt, pepper, clam juice, and the juice from the canned okra and tomatoes. Add sautéed vegetables, cook for 1 hour. Add crab meat, shrimp, Tabasco, lemon juice and Worcestershire. Cook for 20 minutes. Add oysters with liquid and cook 5 minutes more. Remove from heat. When cool, refrigerate for at least 12 hours. Before serving, heat, add filé and sherry.

Jane Baddour

OPAL SHRIMP CREOLE

½   cup green pepper, chopped
1   cup onion, chopped
½   cup celery, chopped
1   clove garlic, minced
3   tablespoons salad oil
2½ tablespoons flour
1   teaspoon salt

1   teaspoon sugar
1   tablespoon chili powder
1   cup water
2   cups tomato sauce
1   tablespoon vinegar
2   cups cooked shrimp
Cooked rice

Sauté pepper, onion, celery and garlic in hot oil until tender. In bowl, combine flour, salt, sugar and chili powder. Add water slowly and mix. Add to sautéed mixture and mix well. Add tomato sauce. Simmer uncovered until thick. Add vinegar and shrimp. Heat thoroughly and serve over hot cooked rice.

Mrs. John Mac Smith

SHRIMP CREOLE

4 tablespoons butter	1 teaspoon salt
1 cup onion, chopped	3 tablespoons parsley, chopped
1 cup celery, chopped	¼ teaspoon cayenne pepper
½ cup green pepper, chopped	2½ cups tomatoes, diced
2 tablespoons flour mixed in cold water	3 cups water
	3 pounds raw shrimp, cleaned

Melt butter in saucepan. Sauté onion, celery, green pepper until soft, about 5 minutes. Remove pan from direct heat and slowly stir in flour. Add salt, parsley, cayenne, tomatoes and water. Simmer 15 minutes. Add shrimp. Cover and simmer 30 minutes. Serve over cooked, fluffy rice. *Serves 4 to 6.*

Mrs. Frank Steudlein

CRAB MEAT AU GRATIN

1 small onion, diced	1 small can pimento, diced
4 tablespoons butter	Salt and pepper to taste
2 tablespoons flour, rounded	1 cup cheese, grated
1½ cups milk	Buttered bread crumbs (real fine)
2 cans crab meat	

Sauté onions in butter until soft; blend in flour and add milk, stirring constantly. Cook until thick. Add crab, pimento, salt, pepper, and cheese. Put half of mixture into greased casserole. Cover with bread crumbs; add remainder, and top with some more bread crumbs. Bake at 350° for 20 minutes.

Brenda Cole

This is out of this world.

CHESAPEAKE CASSEROLE

1 10-ounce package frozen broccoli, cooked and chopped	½ cup cream of mushroom soup
½ cup sharp cheese, grated	1 cup skim milk
1 tablespoon butter	1 tablespoon lemon juice
1 small onion, chopped	1 6-ounce package frozen king crabmeat, thawed and drained

Arrange drained broccoli on bottom of a lightly greased 1-quart casserole. Sprinkle with cheese. In saucepan, melt butter and sauté the onions until golden. Stir in soup and milk. Cook, stirring constantly until smooth. Stir in lemon juice and crabmeat. Pour over broccoli and bake for 30 minutes at 350°.

Doris Lanford

153

DEVILED CRABS

3 tablespoons butter or oleo
3 tablespoons flour
1 cup milk
½ teaspoon salt
3 tablespoons butter or oleo
½ cup onion, chopped fine

½ cup celery, chopped fine
1 pound crab meat (light or dark)
½ cup bread crumbs
Salt and pepper to taste
2 teaspoons chopped parsley

Melt 3 tablespoons butter in saucepan. Add flour and stir until smooth. Add milk and salt, and cook until thickened. Set aside. Sauté onion and celery and remaining butter for 10 minutes. Add crab meat and bread crumbs, and cook 15 minutes. Add cream sauce, salt, pepper, and parsley. Fill crab shells or small glass baking shells. Top with bread crumbs and bake at 350° for 20 minutes.

Mrs. Frank Steudlein

SEAFOOD CONCOCTION

2 cans cream of mushroom soup
½ stick butter
6 hard boiled eggs, chopped
3 small cans mushrooms, chopped

1 small can pimento, chopped
2 packages Kraft Old English cheese
4 cans crab meat

In saucepan, combine soup, butter, eggs, mushrooms, pimentos and cheese. Heat until cheese is melted. Add crab meat and cook another 10 minutes. Serve in patty shells. *Serves 12-16*.

Mary Elizabeth DeCell

CRAB CASSEROLE

3 tablespoons butter
1 medium onion, chopped
1 sweet green pepper, chopped
12 large mushrooms, sliced
¼ cup sherry

⅛ teaspoon dry mustard
1½ tablespoons flour
6 ounces crab meat (frozen or
    canned)

Sauté onions, pepper, and mushrooms in butter until tender, but not brown. Add sherry and cook 5 minutes. Add mustard and flour and cook just until thickened. Stir in crab meat and place in individual serving dishes. Sprinkle bread crumbs on top and pour small amount of melted butter over. Bake at 350° for 15 minutes.

Mrs. Hugh Dillahunty

CRABMEAT ON HOLLAND RUSK

1 8-ounce package cream cheese
1 can crabmeat
2 eggs, boiled and grated
½ cup celery, chopped fine
1 tablespoon onion juice
1 teaspoon lemon juice

¼ teaspoon cayenne pepper
6 pieces Holland Rusk rolls
6 slices Velveeta cheese
6 slices tomatoes (seeds removed)
Paprika

Blend together the cream cheese, crabmeat, eggs, and celery. Add the seasonings. Place the Holland Rusk rolls on a baking pan. Put a slice of cheese and slice of tomato on each. Top with a large spoonful of crabmeat mixture. Sprinkle top with paprika. Bake at 300° for 15-20 minutes, or until bubbly.

Mrs. Bill Lunsford

This is a delightful ladies' luncheon dish.

OVERNITE CRAB CASSEROLE

1 7½-ounce can crabmeat
1 package macaroni and cheese
    dinner
1 4½-ounce package shredded
    Cheddar cheese
2 hard boiled eggs, chopped

Pimento for color (if you like)
1 can cream of mushroom soup
1 cup milk
1 tablespoon chopped chives
½ teaspoon salt and paprika

Combine all ingredients in a deep 1-quart casserole. (Do not add anything liquid suggested on macaroni and cheese dinner. Use as is—dry uncooked macaroni and dry package cheese.) Cover and refrigerate 8 hours or longer. Bake covered one hour at 350°. *Serves 4-5.*

Sarah Aaron

DEB'S CRABMEAT QUICHE

½ stick or ½ package pie crust mix
4 eggs
2 cups light cream
½ cup onion, minced
¾ teaspoon salt

⅛ teaspoon cayenne red pepper
1 7½-ounce can crabmeat
1 cup (4 ounces) Swiss or Mozzarella cheese, shredded
½ cup parsley, snipped

Heat oven to 425°. Prepare pastry for 9-inch pie crust as directed on package. Beat eggs until well blended. Stir in cream, onion, salt and cayenne red pepper. Drain the crabmeat, remove any cartilage, and pat dry with paper towel. Sprinkle crabmeat and cheese in pastry-lined pie dish. Pour egg mixture over crabmeat and cheese. Sprinkle with the parsley. Bake 15 minutes at 425°. Reduce oven temperature to 325°. Bake 30 minutes longer or until knife inserted comes out clean. Let stand after removing from oven for 10 minutes before cutting into wedges. *Serves 6-8 people.*

Mary Alice Reed

CRABMEAT SUPREME

1 can tomato soup
½ cup beer
1 cup grated Cheddar cheese
1 tablespoon cornstarch

2 tablespoons water
2 cups canned crab meat
1 cup buttered bread crumbs
Grated cheese

In a double boiler over hot, not boiling, water heat soup and beer. Add cheese and cook, stirring constantly, until cheese melts. Blend cornstarch with water. Add and stir until thickened. Add crab meat. Mix; place in casserole. Top with buttered bread crumbs and grated cheese to cover. Broil until lightly browned. Serve over wild rice or Uncle Ben's Wild Rice and Long Grain Mixture. *Serves 4.*

Gloria O'Rourke

SCALLOPED OYSTERS

1 pint oysters
1 teaspoon salt
1 can condensed chicken gumbo
   soup

2 cups cracker crumbs
4 tablespoons butter

Drain oysters, reserving the liquid. Place one layer of oysters in baking dish. Sprinkle with salt. Pour half the soup and then half the cracker crumbs over this. Repeat with another layer of oysters, soup and crumbs. Dot with butter. Pour reserved oyster liquid over, just to the top layer of oysters. Bake in 350° oven until edges of oysters curl and top is brown. Serve hot. If desired, add 2 teaspoons of chili powder, sprinkling some over each layer of oysters.

Mrs. J. C. McCaa

ESCALLOPED OYSTER CASSEROLE

2 cups cracker crumbs
½ cup butter, melted
¼ teaspoon paprika
¼ teaspoon celery salt

1 teaspoon salt
1 pint oysters, drained
1½ cups milk

Mix crumbs, butter and seasonings. Sprinkle layer in greased casserole dish. Add half of oysters and more crumbs. Repeat layers, ending with crumbs. Pour milk over all to moisten mixture. Bake at 350° for 25 minutes. *Serves 6.*

Sally Bennett

BARBEQUED OYSTERS

1 pint oysters
Flour
3 tablespoons butter
   (do not substitute)

¼ cup butter (do not substitute)
½ cup red sherry
½ cup A-1 Steak Sauce

Wash oysters, and drain on paper towel. Dip oysters in flour and brown in 3 tablespoons melted butter. Remove oysters from skillet and add remaining butter, sherry, and A-1 sauce. Stir together. Add oysters and simmer until the oysters are tender.

Mrs. Don Burnett

OYSTERS "JOHNNY REB"

2 quarts oysters, drained	1 tablespoon Worcestershire sauce
½ cup parsley, finely chopped	2 tablespoons lemon juice
½ cup shallots or onions, finely chopped	½ cup butter, melted
	2 cups fine cracker crumbs
Salt and pepper	Paprika
Tabasco	¾ cup half milk and cream

Place a layer of oysters in bottom of shallow 2-quart baking dish. Sprinkle with half of parsley, shallots, seasonings, lemon juice, butter and crumbs. Make another layer of the same. Sprinkle with paprika. Just before baking, pour the milk into evenly spaced holes, being very careful not to moisten crumb topping all over. Bake at 375° for about 30 minutes, or until firm.

Mrs. Billy Barrett

SCALLOPED OYSTERS

1 pint oysters	¼ teaspoon pepper
½ cup butter, melted	¾ cup light cream
2 cups medium coarse cracker crumbs	¼ teaspoon Worcestershire sauce
	½ teaspoon salt

Drain oysters, reserving ¼ cup liquid. Combine crumbs and butter. Spread one-third of crumbs in well-greased baking dish. Cover with half the oysters. Sprinkle with pepper. Repeat layers. Combine cream, reserved oyster liquid, Worcestershire and salt. Pour over oysters. Top with remaining crumbs. Bake at 350° about 40 minutes. *Serves 4.*

Carol Smith

LAUNA'S SHRIMP AND WILD RICE CASSEROLE

3 tablespoons oleo
1 large onion, chopped
4-5 stalks celery, chopped
1 bell pepper, chopped
2-3 cloves garlic, minced
1 can chicken broth
1 can cream of chicken soup

1 can mushroom soup
Salt
Pepper
Lea & Perrin's Worcestershire sauce
2 ½ pounds shrimp, boiled and peeled
2 cups Uncle Ben's Wild Rice with
   Seasoning

Sauté onion, celery, pepper, and garlic in oleo. Add broth, soups, seasonings (to taste) and stir until smooth. Add shrimp and rice and put in casserole. Bake at 350° for 1 hour and 15 minutes.

Mrs. Stewart Vail

SHRIMP AND RICE DELUXE

¼ cup cooking oil
1 small onion, chopped
½ bell pepper, chopped
1 stalk of celery, chopped
3 cups of left-over cooked rice
1 can of celery creamed soup
   (diluted with ½ can water)

2 cups cooked shrimp
½ teaspoon salt
½ cup grated cheese
1 teaspoon paprika

Sauté onion, pepper, and celery in cooking oil until transparent, but not brown, stirring continuously. Remove from heat and add rice, soup, shrimp, and salt. (If canned shrimp is used, omit the salt.) Put in buttered casserole. Sprinkle with cheese and paprika. Cook at 300° for 1 hour.

Variation: Substitute 1 cup chicken for the shrimp and add 1 teaspoon salt.

Mary Lane Price

MARY LOU'S SHRIMP

5 pounds shrimp in shell
1 pound pure butter

Juice of 8 lemons
3 garlic buds

Layer shrimp in casserole, salt and pepper each layer. Melt butter and add lemon juice and garlic buds. Bake in 350° oven for 45 minutes and you have delicious peel 'em and eat 'em shrimp.

Charlyne Watson

CHICKEN AND SHRIMP JAMBALAYA

4   slices bacon, chopped
1½ cups celery, sliced
1   cup rice
1   cup onion, chopped
1   cup green pepper, chopped
1   16-ounce can tomatoes

1½ cups water
½   cup garlic flavored Bar-B-Q sauce
1   teaspoon salt
2   cups chicken, cooked and chopped
2   cups shrimp, cooked and cleaned

In 3-quart Dutch oven, fry bacon until crisp. Stir in celery, rice, onion and green pepper; cook 5 minutes, stirring frequently. Add tomatoes, water, Bar-B-Q sauce and salt; mix well. Bring to a boil. Cover and simmer 20 minutes, stirring occasionally. Add chicken and shrimp; heat thoroughly.

Mrs. Boyce Billingsley

FERNANDINA SHRIMP CASSEROLE

1   10½-ounce can cream of
    mushroom soup
½   cup Cheddar cheese, cubed
2   tablespoons butter, melted
2   tablespoons green pepper,
    chopped
2   tablespoons onion, chopped

1   tablespoon lemon juice
2   cups cooked rice
½   teaspoon Worcestershire
½   teaspoon dry mustard
1   pound raw shelled, deveined
    shrimp (not canned)
¼   teaspoon pepper

Combine all ingredients in greased casserole. Mix well. Bake uncovered 40 minutes at 375°. May be prepared a day ahead and refrigerated before baking. *Serves 4-6.* For an even fancier casserole, add cooked broccoli.

Patricia Maxwell

GRILLED SHRIMP

2   pounds large shrimp in shell
1   cup salad oil
1   cup lemon juice
2   teaspoons Italian salad
    dressing mix

2   teaspoons seasoned salt
1   teaspoon seasoned pepper
2   tablespoons brown sugar
2   tablespoons soy sauce
½   cup green onion, chopped

Mix all ingredients. Pour over washed shrimp. Refrigerate. Turn so that all marinade coats all shrimp. Grill over hot coals 10-12 minutes.

Nina Martin

BARBECUED SHRIMP

1 pound shrimp, raw and
     unpeeled
¼ pound butter
1 tablespoon lemon juice
Dash red pepper

1 ½ tablespoons pepper, coarsley
       ground
½ teaspoon salt
1 clove garlic, crushed

Wash shrimp until water is clear. Melt butter and add slightly less than 1 tablespoon of lemon juice. Add peppers, salt, garlic and shrimp. Cook in 375° oven for 20 to 30 minutes or until shrimp are pink. Place under broiler for a few minutes. Serve shrimp and sauce in a bowl, accompanied by thick slices of French bread to dunk into the sauce.

Sylvia Basist

SHRIMP IN SOUR CREAM

1 pound cooked, peeled and
     cleaned shrimp, fresh or frozen
1 4-ounce can sliced mushrooms,
     drained
2 tablespoons green onions,
     chopped
2 tablespoons butter or
     margarine, melted

1 tablespoon flour
1 10-ounce can condensed cream of
     shrimp soup
1 cup sour cream
Dash pepper
Toast points
12 drops Tabasco

Thaw frozen shrimp. Cut large shrimp in half. Cook mushrooms and onion in butter until tender. Blend in flour; add soup and cook and stir until thickened. Add sour cream, pepper, Tabasco, and shrimp. Heat, stirring constantly. Serve on toast points. *Serves 6.*

Mrs. R. L. Burns

HOT PEPPERED SHRIMP

1 pound raw headless shrimp
1 stick butter (not margarine)

4 tablespoons black pepper

Place unshelled shrimp in a baking pan. Add butter and black pepper. Bake in 375° oven 20-25 minutes. Serve with salad and French bread. Peel at the table. We cover the table with newspapers. Messy but wonderful. *Serves 2.*

Carol Higgins

SHRIMP NEWBURG

1 pound cooked shrimp, fresh or frozen
½ cup butter or margarine
2 tablespoons all-purpose flour
¾ teaspoon salt
¼ teaspoon paprika

Dash cayenne pepper
1 pint coffee cream
2 egg yolks, beaten
1½ to 2 tablespoons sherry
Toast points

Cut shrimp into ½-inch pieces. Melt butter; blend in flour, salt, paprika and pepper. Add cream gradually and cook, stirring constantly, until thick and smooth. Stir a little of the hot sauce into egg yolks; add yolks to remaining sauce, stirring constantly. Add shrimp; heat. Remove from heat and slowly stir in sherry. Serve immediately on toast points. *Makes 6 servings.*

Mrs. R. L. Burns

SALMON LOAF

1 pound can pink salmon, drained
1 can undiluted celery soup
1 cup bread crumbs

2 eggs, beaten
½ cup onions, chopped
1 tablespoon lemon juice

Mix all ingredients together. Put in greased loaf pan. Bake at 375° for 1 hour. *Serves 6.*

Mary Elizabeth DeCell

SALMON SOUFFLÉ

1 7¾-ounce can pink salmon
Milk
Oleo

2 tablespoons dry bread crumbs
3 tablespoons flour
4 eggs

Drain salmon, reserving liquid in measuring cup. To this liquid add enough milk to make 1 cup. Mash salmon with fork. Butter casserole dish and coat with bread crumbs. Melt 3 tablespoons oleo and blend in flour. Gradually add liquid mixture, stirring until thickened. Add well-beaten eggs and salmon to sauce. Pour into casserole dish and bake at 375° for 35 minutes.

Phoebe Enochs

SEVEN SEAS CASSEROLE

1   cup cream of mushroom soup
1⅛ cups water
1   teaspoon lemon juice
¼   teaspoon salt
Dash pepper
¼   cup onions, finely chopped

1⅓ cups Minute Rice
1   cup tuna, drained and flaked
1   10-ounce box Birds Eye green
    peas
½   cup grated Cheddar cheese

Combine soup, water, lemon juice, salt, pepper and onions in a saucepan.
Bring to a boil over medium heat, stirring occasionally. Pour half into a
greased 1½-quart casserole. In layers, add rice, peas, and tuna. Add remaining soup. Sprinkle with cheese. Cover and bake 15 to 20 minutes at 375°. Cut
through mixture with a knife after 10 minutes to mix well.

Mrs. James Hunter

TUNA-NOODLE CASSEROLE

1   12-ounce package egg noodles,
    cooked and drained
1   6½-ounce can tuna
1   16-ounce can peas and carrots

1   can cream of mushroom soup
Salt and pepper to taste
Cracker crumbs

Place cooked noodles in casserole. Combine rest of ingredients and pour into
casserole. Fold together. Top with cracker crumbs and dot with butter. Bake
at 350° until brown and bubbly. Serve hot. *Serves 6-8.*

Bettye Mooneyhan

TUNA OR CHICKEN CASSEROLE

3   ounces macaroni
3   ounces cream cheese
1   can condensed cream of chicken
    soup or mushroom soup
1   cup tuna or cooked chicken

1   tablespoon onion, chopped
1   tablespoon prepared mustard
¼   cup milk
Buttered bread crumbs

Cook macaroni and drain well. Soften cream cheese and blend in soup. Stir
in chicken or tuna, onion, mustard, milk and macaroni. Pour into 1¼-quart
casserole, and cover with buttered bread crumbs. Bake at 375° for 20-25
minutes. *Serves 4 to 6.*

Nancy Terry

TUNA DELIGHT

½ cup water
2 cans cream of mushroom soup
1 cup celery, chopped
2 cans tuna

1 cup cashews
2 3-ounce cans Chinese noodles
  (LaChoy Chow Mein)

Combine water and soup, and mix well. Add celery, tuna, cashews, and half the Chinese noodles. Toss lightly and put in an ungreased casserole. Top with remaining noodles and bake at 375° for 30 minutes or until bubbly. *Serves 5 or 6.*

Joy Melton

TUNA CHOW MEIN

2 tablespoons butter
1 cup onions, chopped
1 cup celery, chopped
1 can mushrooms

2 cans cream of mushroom soup
2 cans bean sprouts
2-3 cans white tuna
1 can dry Chinese noodles

Sauté onion, celery, and mushrooms in butter. Add soup, sprouts, tuna, and half the Chinese noodles, and mix well. Put in well-greased casserole dish, top with the remaining noodles, and bake at 350° for 35 minutes.

SEAFOOD CASSEROLE

1 cup fresh mushrooms, chopped	2 cups cream sauce
1 stick butter	2 tablespoons sherry
1 cup diced lobster	1 cup wine-cheese, grated
1 cup crabmeat	Cheese sauce
1 cup shrimp, boiled	

Sauté mushrooms in butter. Mix seafood, cream sauce, sherry and cheese. Pour in casserole and bake 20 minutes at 350°. Serve with cheese sauce. *Serves 8.*

Cheese Sauce:

1 cup Half and Half cream	¼ stick butter
1 tablespoon flour	½ cup cheese, grated
½ teaspoon pepper	1 egg yolk
¼ teaspoon salt	

Put all ingredients except egg yolk in top of double boiler over simmering water and cook until slightly thickened. Remove from water and blend in beaten egg yolk.

Sara M. Hart

SUSAN'S SEAFOOD NEWBURG

2 cups mushrooms, sliced	½ teaspoon dry mustard
2 cups Long Horn or Cheddar cheese, grated	½ teaspoon instant minced onions or 2 teaspoons fresh onions, grated
2 cups milk	2 egg yolks, beaten
4 tablespoons butter	2 tablespoons cream sherry
4 tablespoons flour	2-3 cups cooked shrimp, lobster or crab
½ teaspoon salt	
¼ teaspoon pepper	

Melt butter, sauté mushrooms and onions about 5 minutes or until tender. Blend in flour, salt, pepper, and dry mustard. Cook over low heat until smooth and mix well. Add milk and slowly bring to boil, stirring constantly, until consistency of thick cream. Add cheese and stir until melted. Over low heat, mix sauce and egg yolks carefully. Stir in sherry and seafood. Serve over Pepperidge Farm patty shells *(about 6 servings).*

Susan McFall

SEAFOOD CASSEROLE

4 ounces butter	3 scallions, finely chopped
3 tablespoons flour	½ cup sherry (optional)
2 cups milk	1 pound cooked crabmeat
1 teaspoon salt	1 pound cooked shrimp
White pepper to taste	½ pound Cheddar cheese, grated

Make a thick cream sauce of the butter, flour, milk and seasoning. Stir in scallions and sherry. In a greased casserole or baking dish, alternate layers of crabmeat, shrimp, cheese and cream sauce until all ingredients are used. Bake for 25 to 30 minutes in a 350° oven and serve at once over toast, rice or what have you. *Serves 8.*

Louise Westley

SEAFOOD AND WILD RICE CASSEROLE

1 package long grain wild rice mix	1 can shrimp or 1 pound fresh shrimp
½ stick oleo	1 can crab meat
1 cup onion, chopped	1 small can pimento
1 cup celery, chopped	1 small can mushrooms
1 cup bell pepper, chopped	2 cans mushroom soup

Prepare rice mix according to directions on package. While this is cooking, sauté onions, celery, and pepper in oleo in a large skillet. Add shrimp, crab, pimento, mushrooms, and rice mixture. Stir in the soup. Put in 3-quart casserole and bake at 350° for 1 or 1½ hours.

Mrs. Ray Sturrup

SEAFOOD CASSEROLE

1 small can crabmeat, drained and flaked	2 tablespoons mayonnaise
1 cup cooked shrimp	1 teaspoon lemon juice
2 tablespoons bread crumbs	Dash salt
2 tablespoons celery, chopped	Dash pepper
½ teaspoon instant minced onion	¼ cup milk

Put all ingredients in a glass casserole, mix well, and put in microwave oven. Cook uncovered until bubbly, about 2 minutes. Serve hot.

June Spotts

166

FISH COCKTAIL

1 cup onion, chopped	½ cup sweet dill pickle, chopped or
1 cup carrots, sliced	pickle relish
½ teaspoon salt	1 cup mayonnaise
Dash pepper	3 tablespoons brandy (optional)
½ cup water	2 tablespoons lemon juice
1 pound fresh fish fillets	½ cup catsup
(haddock, sole, or red snapper)	1 lemon
1 tablespoon capers	

Cook the onion, carrots, salt, pepper and water in a covered casserole in the microwave oven for 5 minutes on high. Add the fish and spoon the vegetables over it. Cover casserole with waxed paper which has been covered with margarine and cook for 5 more minutes, until fish flakes easily, and has turned white. Remove fish to a bowl and flake it with a fork. Add the cooked vegetables, the capers and pickles to flaked fish. Chill. Mix the mayonnaise, brandy, lemon juice and catsup together to make the sauce. When ready to serve, spoon sauce over each portion and garnish with a slice of lemon. Serve hot or cold. *Serves 6.*

Patricia Maxwell

BAKED FISH FILLETS

1 pound fish fillets	1 tablespoon flour
1 tablespoon lemon juice	½ cup milk
⅛ teaspoon paprika	¼ cup buttered bread crumbs
Dash salt and pepper	1 tablespoon snipped parsley
1 tablespoon butter	

Cut fillets into serving pieces. Place in greased shallow baking dish. Sprinkle with lemon juice, paprika, salt and pepper. In saucepan, melt butter; blend in flour, dash salt, and dash pepper. Add milk; cook and stir till thick and bubbly. Pour sauce over fillets. Sprinkle with bread crumbs. Bake at 350° for 35 minutes. Trim with parsley.

Sandra Jones

CREOLE GUMBO

¼ pound bacon
1 small clove garlic
6 to 8 large onions, diced
2 pounds ham, diced
2 #3 cans tomatoes
2 cans peas
2 cans tomato paste
2 cans mushrooms

1 tablespoon whole pickling
spice
25-30 whole bay leaves
1 medium sized hen
2 cans okra, washed
3 pounds fresh shrimp, halved
2 cups dry wine

Cook bacon crisp, then braise garlic and onion in bacon fat. Transfer to large stew kettle, braise diced ham and add to the braised onions. Then add tomatoes, peas, tomato paste, mushrooms, spice and bay leaves and let simmer over slow fire 5-6 hours. Boil chicken and add chicken broth to the stew kettle. Bone and dice chicken. Just before serving add diced chicken and okra and shrimp. Allow to simmer 20-30 more minutes. Remove from fire and stir in wine (preferably Port). Serve over steamed rice. *Serves 16.*

Dr. James R. Fall

The Buckman Enrichment Center is home for the older segment of Baddour Center's population. The residents of this home are provided a full, rewarding lifestyle, but at a slower pace than those involved in the regular residential program. This program was begun as the need was recognized for expanding services designed for older mentally retarded adults. The home was named in honor of Mrs. Mertie Buckman of Memphis and her family for their generous support of the Center.

"He who greets and constantly reveres the aged,
*   four things will increase to him, namely, life,*
beauty, happiness, and power."
*   –Dhammapada, c. 5th B.C.*

POULTRY & GAME

Buckman Enrichment Center

VINCENT PRICE'S CHICKEN SWEET AND HOT

½ cup butter
¼ cup Worcestershire sauce
1 large clove garlic, minced
½ cup red currant jelly
1 tablespoon Dijon mustard

1 cup orange juice
1 teaspoon powdered ginger
3 dashes Tabasco sauce
3 to 3½ pound broiler, quartered

Combine butter, Worcestershire, garlic, jelly, mustard, orange juice, ginger, and Tabasco in a pan. Heat gently, stirring, until smooth. Cool. Pour sauce over chicken and marinate for 3 hours. Cover and cook in 350° oven for 1 hour. Uncover, increase temperature to 450°. Baste frequently until brown. For better flavor, make the day ahead.

Nellie George Baddour

CHICKEN BREASTS SUZANNE

4-6 chicken breasts
Salt and pepper
1 stick of oleo
½ cup sour cream

½ cup sherry wine
1 10½-ounce can cream of mushroom
   soup

Remove skin and bones from chicken. Season chicken breasts with salt and pepper. Brown in melted oleo. Remove chicken to a greased, flat casserole pan. Add sour cream, sherry and soup to melted oleo. Mix well and pour over breasts. Cover and bake at 350° for 1-1½ hours.

Jennie Yaeger,
Doris Lanford

CHICKEN BREASTS SUPREME

4 skinned chicken breasts
½ stick butter
½ pound fresh mushrooms
2 tablespoons flour
1½ cups chicken stock
1 tablespoon tomato paste or 2
   tablespoons thick catsup

1 bay leaf
2 tablespoons chives
Salt and pepper
1 pound boiled and deveined shrimp
2 tablespoons sherry

Brown breasts in butter. Remove and wrap in foil and bake at 300° for 45 minutes. Sauté mushrooms in butter, add flour, stock, paste, bay leaf, chives, salt and pepper. Simmer until thick. Add shrimp and sherry and pour over breasts. May be served with rice or wild rice.

Martha Anne Weaver

TARRAGON CHICKEN

6 small chicken breasts
4 blades of fresh tarragon
2 tablespoons butter
6 small white onions
1 cup sour cream
½ cup red Port

3 tablespoons Madeira
½ cup rich chicken broth
Salt
Pepper
Nutmeg
Rice

In a skillet cook chicken breasts lightly in butter and set aside. Parboil tarragon and pound them to a paste with butter. Melt this flavored butter in the blazer of a chafing dish over direct heat (or in a large skillet) and add the onions, sliced thinly. Cook until the onions are delicately colored, stirring constantly. Put the top pan over hot water (if you are using the chafing dish — otherwise, just add the rest of the recipe to skillet gradually as recipe indicates); stir in sour cream and cook for 5 minutes. Stir in red Port, Madeira, and chicken broth, made by reducing 2 cups chicken broth over a hot flame to ½ cup. Bring this to a boil and simmer for 5 minutes. Place the breasts in the sauce and simmer gently. Season to taste with salt, black pepper and a dash of nutmeg. Serve with rice.

Mrs. Lowell Taylor, Jr.

QUICK CHICKEN CORDON BLEU

4 boneless chicken breasts
Salt, pepper and parsley to taste
4 strips Mozzarella cheese
4 strips ham or partly cooked
  bacon

3 tablespoons vegetable oil or ½ stick
  butter
2 cans condensed cream of chicken
  soup

Pound chicken breasts with mallet till about ⅛" thick. Salt, pepper and parsley to taste. Place on top of each chicken breast one slice of cheese and one slice of ham or bacon. Roll up jellyroll fashion and secure with toothpick. Brown chicken roll-ups in oil or butter on both sides till golden brown. Thin the cream of chicken soup with milk; pour over chicken breasts. Bring to a boil over medium heat; then simmer, covered, for 25 minutes. *Serves 4.*
Note: Cream of mushroom soup may be substituted for one or both cans of cream of chicken soup. Also for a change a little white cooking wine (about 1 tablespoon) or pea pods may be added with the soup.

Linda Stubbs

171

CRAB STUFFED CHICKEN BREASTS WITH WHITE GRAPE SAUCE

12 slices bread, toasted and diced	3 tablespoons butter
½ cup onions, minced	3 tablespoons flour
½ cup celery, chopped fine	½ teaspoon salt
½ cup cream	1½ cups chicken consommé
½ cup butter, melted	2 tablespoons lemon juice
Salt, pepper and sage to taste	2 tablespoons sugar
6 ounces frozen crab, thawed and drained	1 cup seedless grapes (fresh or canned)
6 whole chicken breasts, skinned and boned	

Combine bread cubes, onions, celery, cream, ½ cup butter, seasoning and crab meat. Mix well. Flatten chicken breasts and place 1/6 of stuffing in center of each. Roll chicken around stuffing and dust with flour. Brown in butter and place in baking dish. Bake at 375° for 25 minutes. For sauce, melt 3 tablespoons butter in saucepan. Add flour and salt and gradually add consommé, lemon juice and sugar. Cook until thickened. Add grapes just before serving. Spoon sauce over chicken. *Serves 6.*

Linda Rogus

Was grand winner of Memphis Press-Scimitar cooking contest.

CHICKEN BREAST FLORENTINE

4 chicken breast halves	¼ cup white wine
1 egg	1 package frozen leaf spinach
Flour	1 tablespoon butter
Salt	Salt
Pepper	Parmesan cheese
Paprika	Sliced Mozzarella or grated Colby cheese
¾ cup chicken broth	

Cut a pocket in breast between meat and bone. Dip in egg, then in flour seasoned with salt, pepper, and paprika. Fry in small amount of oil. Place in baking dish. In same skillet add chicken broth; let come to a boil. Add wine. Let come to a boil. Pour broth and wine mixture around chicken and bake, uncovered, in 350° oven about 1 hour. About 20 minutes before serving, cook spinach until done. Squeeze out all water and add butter and small amount salt. Mix until butter is melted. Stuff pockets of chicken breast with spinach. Sprinkle with Parmesan cheese. Add other cheese on top of breast and return to oven until cheese melts. Spoon gravy over breasts.

Mrs. Robert Homra

Makes a very good and very pretty dish.

CANTONESE BONELESS FRIED CHICKEN

3	tablespoons brandy	1	cup flour
3	tablespoons soy sauce	2	tablespoons cornstarch
½	teaspoon sugar	1	egg
12	drops ginger syrup	¾	cup water
3	deboned chicken breasts		

Mix together brandy, soy sauce, sugar, and ginger syrup. Brush mixture on all surfaces of chicken and let pieces stand 1 hour. In a bowl combine the flour, cornstarch, egg and water and beat mixture until smooth and it makes a thin batter, adding more water if needed. Coat the chicken pieces thoroughly with batter and fry in deep fat (375°) until tender and golden brown. *Serves 3 or 4.*

Oneida Baddour

BAKED CHICKEN BREASTS

½	tablespoon Worcestershire	1	cup sour cream
1	tablespoon lemon juice	5	chicken breasts, boned
1	teaspoon salt	¾	cup bread crumbs
¼	teaspoon pepper	¾	cup butter (not oleo)
1½	teaspoons celery salt		

Mix Worcestershire, lemon juice, salt, pepper, and celery salt with sour cream. Pour over chicken and marinate overnight. Roll chicken in bread crumbs, put in a well-greased shallow pan and refrigerate for 1 hour. Brush chicken with half of butter. Bake 30 minutes at 325°. Baste with remaining butter and bake 30 minutes. *Serves 5.*

Mrs. Malcolm Graham

ROLLED CHICKEN BREAST IN WINE

8	chicken breasts, deboned	1½	teaspoons butter
½	teaspoon fresh parsley,		Salt and pepper
	chopped	8	bouillon cubes
	Little garlic, pressed	7 or 8	cups water
	Flour	¾	cup wine

Roll chicken in parsley and garlic. Sprinkle with salt and pepper and coat with flour. Brown in butter in skillet. Place in baking dish. Dissolve bouillon cubes in water. Combine with wine and pour over chicken. Bake uncovered for 2 hours at 350°.

Billy and Barbara Mills

SESAME BAKED CHICKEN

2 eggs, slightly beaten
1 tablespoon water
1 tablespoon soy sauce
1 teaspoon salt
¼ teaspoon pepper
¼ cup flour

6 large chicken breasts, boned and
   skinned
½ cup sesame seeds
¼ cup butter, melted
Mushroom sauce

Combine eggs, water, soy sauce, salt and pepper. Mix well. Coat chicken with flour, dip in egg mixture, then sesame seeds. Pour butter in shallow pan, add chicken, turning to coat. Bake 400° for 40 to 50 minutes, til golden brown and tender. Serve with mushroom sauce. *Serves 6.*

Mushroom Sauce:

1½ cups mushrooms, sliced
¼   cup butter
1   cup water, divided
2   tablespoons cornstarch

1 teaspoon Worcestershire sauce
1 teaspoon salt
Dash pepper

Sauté mushrooms in butter, add ¾ cup water. Make paste of ¼ cup water and cornstarch. Blend in mushrooms and liquid. Stir til thick. Add Worcestershire sauce, salt and pepper.

Mary Virginia Southwell

CHICKEN CHABLIS

5 tablespoons butter
3-ounce can mushrooms
Flour
Salt and pepper to taste

4 chicken breasts (halves)
⅔ cup dry white wine (Chablis or
   Vermouth)
Sliced Swiss cheese

Melt 2 tablespoons butter in a skillet, stir in drained mushrooms and cook for 5 minutes over low heat. Remove mushrooms from skillet; lightly flour, salt, and pepper chicken breasts. Add remaining butter to skillet and brown chicken. Remove chicken from skillet, add wine to skillet and bring to boil while scraping bottom and sides of pan. Stir mushrooms in and remove from heat. Place chicken breasts skin down in a casserole dish. Pour wine and mushrooms over and bake uncovered for 35 minutes in 350° oven. Turn chicken up, spoon mushrooms over and top with thin slices of cheese. Bake 15 minutes longer, basting frequently. *Serves 4.*

Mrs. W. K. Ingram

CHICKEN MARSALA

4 chicken breasts	Pinch oregano
3 tablespoons flour	3 tablespoons olive oil
½ teaspoon seasoned salt	3 tablespoons butter
Dash pepper	½ cup California Marsala wine

Remove skin from chicken breasts; dredge in flour; season with salt and pepper. Sprinkle oregano over breasts. Heat oil and butter in big skillet. Brown chicken, cavity side first. After browning, add wine. Cover and simmer ½ hour or till tender. Serve with risotto. *Serves 2-4.*

Mary Farrago

BREAST OF CHICKEN

6 chicken breasts	2 cans cream of chicken soup
Pepper	1½ cups sour cream
6 slices bacon	8 ounces cream cheese
1 package dried beef	Rice

Pepper, do not salt, chicken breasts. Wrap slice of bacon around each. Place layer of dried beef in bottom of baking dish. Place bacon-wrapped breasts in dish and cover with mixture of soup, sour cream and cheese. Cover lightly with foil. Place in 325° oven for 2 hours. Remove foil and brown slightly. Serve on bed of rice. *Serves 6.*

Mrs. John Jenkins

CREAMED CHICKEN

1 cup mushrooms, sliced	Salt and pepper
¼ cup green pepper, chopped	1 egg yolk, beaten
¼ cup butter or margarine	2½ cups chicken, cooked and diced
3 tablespoons flour	2 tablespoons pimento, finely cut
1 small carton Half and Half	1 small can tiny English peas

Lightly brown mushrooms and green peppers in butter. Add flour and blend. Add milk and seasonings, and cook until thick, stirring constantly. Stir some of the hot mixture into the egg yolk and add to remaining hot mixture. Cook a minute or two, stirring constantly. Add chicken, pimento, and peas. Serve in Pepperidge Farm patty shells or on hot toast points. *Serves 6.*

Minnie Miller

BREAST OF CHICKEN A 'LA KING

6 frying chicken breasts	Flour
¼ pound butter	1 egg
1 teaspoon chopped chives or parsley	Bread crumbs
	Shortening

Have butcher debone chicken, leaving half of upper wing bone in. Soften butter and blend in chives or parsley. Shape into 6 rolls, 2 inches long. Chill until firm. Pound out chicken to flatten. Place a butter roll on each breast, fold meat over, and cover butter completely. Chill thoroughly. Flour chicken and dip in slightly beaten egg, and then in bread crumbs. Brown on both sides in ½ inch of hot shortening. Place in baking pan in 350° oven for 20 minutes.

Mrs. J. C. McCaa

CHICKEN A LA KING

1 can mushrooms	1 tablespoon capers
5 tablespoons salad oil	Dash paprika
2 cups chicken, diced (white preferred)	½ teaspoon salt
3 tablespoons pimento, chopped	1 tablespoon oleo
6 tablespoons green pepper, chopped	2½ tablespoons flour
	3 cups rich cream
	2 egg yolks

Cook mushrooms in salad oil about 5 minutes. Mix chicken, pimento, green pepper and capers. Season with paprika and salt. Add mushrooms to this mixture. Make white sauce of oleo, flour and cream. Gradually add beaten egg yolks to sauce. Mix chicken mixture and white sauce and beat thoroughly. May be served in patty shells or on toast. *Serves 8.*

Mrs. R. C. Nickle

BARBEQUED CHICKEN (EASY)

⅔ stick oleo	1 king size Coca-Cola
1 small onion	1 chicken, cut up
1 cup catsup	

Mix oleo, onion, catsup, and Coca-Cola in large skillet. Add salted and peppered chicken pieces and cook on low heat for about an hour (covered).

Josie Baddour

CHICKEN STROGANOFF

4 cups chicken, diced and cooked
1 carton sour cream
1 envelope onion soup mix
1 can cream of mushroom soup,
  undiluted

1 4-ounce can sliced mushrooms,
  drained
Hot cooked rice

Combine chicken, sour cream, soup mix, soup, and mushrooms. Mix well. Spoon into lightly greased casserole. Bake at 350° for 30 minutes. Serve over rice.

Mary L. Hight

PRESSED CHICKEN LOAF

4 cups chicken breasts, boiled
2 tablespoons Knox gelatin
2½ cups chicken broth
¾ cup celery, finely chopped

1 can small green peas, drained
1 large jar pimentos, chopped
3 eggs, hard boiled

Dissolve gelatin into ½ cup of chicken broth; add 2 cups of boiling broth to the gelatin mixture. In separate bowl, mix chopped chicken, celery, peas, and pimentos, season well. Press into a pan and place sliced eggs on top. Pour the chicken broth with the gelatin mixture over top of all. Let harden. Slice and serve on lettuce with mayonnaise.

Mrs. Hugh Dillahunty

Great for ladies' luncheon with a fruit salad and vegetable.

SOUTHERN CHICKEN HASH

4-5 pound hen
1 cup celery, finely chopped
Cayenne pepper
2 small onions, finely chopped
½ cup bell pepper, finely chopped
1 stick butter
½ cup chicken broth

2 tablespoons cornstarch
1 6-ounce can whole mushrooms
¼ cup parsley, finely chopped
Salt and pepper to taste
Tabasco
3 eggs, hard boiled

Cook hen until very tender with tops of celery and a little cayenne pepper. Sauté onions and pepper in butter and ¼ cup chicken broth. Add cornstarch made into a paste with remaining ¼ cup chicken broth. Add celery, mushrooms, parsley, and cut-up chicken. Season and add a few dashes of Tabasco. Slice hard boiled eggs and serve on top of hash. *Serves 8.*

Mrs. William Forman

Handed down several generations from old Vicksburg, Miss. family.

CURRIED CHICKEN FROM IMPERIAL HOTEL, TOKYO

½ cup butter or oleo	2 teaspoons curry powder
1 medium onion, chopped	2½ cups chicken broth
1 clove garlic	3 cups chicken, cooked and cut in
1 stalk celery, diced	large pieces
½ teaspoon dry mustard	½ teaspoon caraway seed
1 bay leaf	1 small can tomato sauce
Parsley	½ cup chutney
1 tart apple, chopped	Condiments
2 tablespoons flour	

Cook onions in butter, add garlic, celery, mustard, bay leaf, parsley, and apple. Cook 8 minutes. Add flour, curry powder, chicken broth and other ingredients. Simmer until tender. Serve over hot rice and condiments.

Condiments: Chopped bell pepper, chopped tomatoes, chopped hard boiled eggs, toasted coconut, etc.

Mary Jane Baddour Chandler

CHICKEN CURRY

2 tablespoons butter or oleo	2½ teaspoons curry powder
1½ cups apple, finely chopped	1 teaspoon salt
½ cup onion, chopped	1½ cups chicken broth
½ cup celery, chopped	1 can tomato paste
1 clove garlic, minced	1 bay leaf
2 tablespoons flour	2 cups chicken, cooked and cubed

Melt butter; add apple, onion, celery and garlic. Cook 5 minutes. Stir in flour, curry powder and salt, and slowly stir in chicken broth, tomato paste and bay leaf. Cook and stir until thick. Add chicken and heat thoroughly. Serve over rice. *Serves 5 to 6.* Condiments suggested are raisins, coconut, chopped eggs, chutney, chopped bacon and chopped peanuts.

Jane Baddour

CHICKEN CASHEW

½ cup onion, chopped
¼ cup pepper, chopped
1 cup celery chunks
1 stick butter
1 can cream of chicken soup

1 can sliced water chestnuts
1 cup chicken, cooked and diced
1 small can mushroom pieces, drained
½ cup salted cashew nuts

Sauté onion, pepper, and celery in butter. Add soup, water chestnuts, chicken and mushrooms, and cook until heated. Stir in cashews. Serve over rice or Chinese noodles.

June Spotts

SOY SAUCE CHICKEN

5 pounds chicken
1 cup soy sauce
¾ cup sugar
2 tablespoons onion, minced

¼ teaspoon ground ginger
¼ teaspoon Accent
½ teaspoon garlic salt

To use for chicken dinner, use about 5 pounds of your favorite chicken parts. To use for a party food, use about 5 pounds chicken wings. Cut off bony ends and discard. Cut wing at the joint. To make sauce, combine soy sauce, sugar, onion, ginger, Accent, and garlic salt. Pour over chicken. Simmer about 2 hours.

Rosemond Deeb

INDONESIAN CHICKEN

8 halves chicken breasts
1 small onion, chopped
1½-pound can tomatoes, mashed
Salt and pepper
1 cup chicken bouillon

½ cup sherry
½ teaspoon salt
½ teaspoon paprika
1 tablespoon parsley, chopped
2 rounded tablespoons cornstarch

Brown chicken in ½ cup oil. Add onion, tomatoes, salt and pepper. Cover and cook 1 hour. Remove chicken, and place skin side up on serving dish. Mix bouillon, sherry, salt, paprika, and parsley together and add to skillet containing the tomatoes and onion. Bring to a slow boil. Thicken with cornstarch and boil, stirring, about 5 minutes. Pour over chicken. Serve on a bed of rice and sprinkle with a few green peas for color. Side dishes of grated coconut, fried Chinese noodles and chopped peanuts accompany this, to be sprinkled over each portion as served.

Ruby Alperin
Nice for buffet. Can make ahead of time and put together at the last minute.

179

GREEK CHICKEN

2 chicken breasts
4 chicken thighs
½ cup lemon juice
½ cup olive oil

½ teaspoon oregano
¼ teaspoon thyme
Salt and coarsely ground pepper

Place chicken in a covered baking dish. Cover chicken with lemon juice, olive oil, oregano, thyme, and salt and pepper, adding 1 ingredient at a time (do not mix). Marinate for 4 hours, or refrigerate overnight. Remove lid and bake at 375° for approximately 30 minutes. *Serves 3 to 4.*

Jackie Edwards

ERNESTINE'S FRIED CHICKEN

6-8 pieces chicken
Salt and pepper
2 cups milk

2 eggs
Flour

Salt and pepper the chicken. In a mixing bowl, mix the milk and eggs. Add chicken and let set 1 hour. Remove chicken from liquid and roll in flour. Fry until golden brown. While the chicken is cooking, pierce with a fork in several places twice during the cooking time. When brown, remove from grease and drain well.

Ernestine Goodall

OVEN FRIED CHICKEN

¼ cup shortening
¼ cup oleo
1 cup Bisquick

1 teaspoon paprika
Salt and pepper
1 frying chicken, cut up

Place shortening and oleo in large baking pan. Place in oven to melt. In plastic bag, mix Bisquick, paprika, salt and pepper. Coat each piece of chicken by shaking in plastic bag. Arrange in pan of melted shortening and oleo. Bake at 450° for 45 minutes. Turn each piece and continue to bake for 15 minutes more.

Helen Robinson

CHICKEN PIE

3-4 pound hen
3½ cups flour
1 cup milk
3 eggs, hard boiled
½ cup onion, chopped

Pepper
1 teaspoon salt
½ cup shortening
½ cup water

Boil chicken until tender. Remove bones and place meat in large baking dish. Reheat 4 cups of remaining broth, season to taste, and add 1 cup flour, milk, finely chopped eggs, onion and pepper. Pour over chicken. In separate bowl, place remaining flour, salt and shortening. Cut shortening in until it resembles cornmeal. Add water and mix until dough holds together. Roll dough out on floured board. Cut half of dough into squares. Drop in remaining chicken broth and cook 10 minutes. Add to chicken. Place remaining dough over top of pan sealing the edges. Cut 4 or 5 slits in crust and dot with butter. Bake at 450° for 15 to 20 minutes or until brown.

Connie Banks

CHICKEN PIE

1 hen or large fryer
3 eggs, hard boiled
2 cups flour
2 heaping tablespoons Crisco

1 teaspoon baking powder
1½ cups sweet milk
1 teaspoon salt

Cook chicken until tender. Bone and cut up in bite size pieces, reserving broth. Add eggs, sliced thin. Mix flour, Crisco, baking powder, ½ cup milk and salt to make pastry. Roll out on floured board. Use half of pastry to line bottom of pan. Add chicken and eggs. Cut remaining pastry into strips and use them to make lattice-work on top of pie. Between strips, sprinkle salt and pepper to taste; dot with butter, sprinkle with flour. Add broth and remaining milk. Bake at 350° for 1 hour.

Mrs. Johnson Barrett

CROCK POT CHICKEN ENCHILADA

6-8 half chicken breasts
½ cup onion, chopped
½ cup celery, chopped
½ cup bell pepper, chopped
1 garlic clove, minced

1 10-ounce can enchilada sauce
1 teaspoon salt
¼ teaspoon black pepper
¼ cup water

Put all ingredients in a crock pot. Cook on high for 2 hours, then low for 4 hours. Serve over yellow rice. *Serves 6-8.*

Mrs. William M. Forman

CHICKEN AND TOMATOES
(CHI TING CH'AO HSI HUNG SHIH)

1 pound chicken meat, uncooked	1 cup onions, cubed
2½ tablespoons soy sauce	¼ teaspoon salt
1 tablespoon sherry	1 teaspoon sugar
2 tablespoons cornstarch	½ cup soup stock or water
½ cup oil	2 tomatoes, peeled and cubed

Cut chicken meat in 1-inch squares. Dredge it with a mixture of 1 tablespoon soy sauce, sherry, and 1 tablespoon cornstarch. Heat pan, add oil; sauté dredged chicken until tender. Add onions and fry a few seconds. Drain chicken and onion. Reheat pan and add 2 tablespoons of the drained oil, remaining 1 tablespoon cornstarch, remaining 1½ tablespoons soy sauce, salt, sugar, and soup stock or water. Boil a few seconds. To the boiling sauce, add chicken, onions, and tomatoes. Heat thoroughly and serve hot. May be made in advance to the point before adding chicken, onions, and tomatoes.

Billy and Barbara Mills

MARIE'S CHICKEN CASSEROLE

1 can cream of chicken soup	1 3-ounce can sliced mushrooms,
½ cup mayonnaise	drained
2½ cups chicken, cooked and diced	¼ cup pimento, chopped
1 cup celery, chopped	½ cup slivered almonds
2 teaspoons onion, chopped	1 cup potato chips
3 hard cooked eggs, chopped	

In casserole, mix soup and mayonnaise. Add chicken, celery, onion, eggs, mushrooms, pimento, and ¼ cup of the almonds. Mix well. Sprinkle top with remaining almonds and potato chips. Bake at 350° for 20-25 minutes.

Mrs. L. H. Polk

CHICKEN SOUFFLÉ

1 fryer	1 cup mushroom soup
Celery, onions, pimentos, green	2 cups milk
pepper	2 eggs, beaten
6 slices bread, buttered	Grated cheese

Cut up and bone chicken. Place in bottom of casserole. Add vegetables to taste. Cut bread into bite-size pieces and add. Combine soup, milk and eggs. Pour over bread. Sprinkle with grated cheese. Refrigerate overnight. Bake at 325° for 50 minutes.

Ruth Barbat

CHICKEN CASSEROLE

1   stick oleo, melted
¼   teaspoon salt
4   tablespoons flour
2   cups milk
4   ounces Velveeta cheese, diced

2   cups cooked chicken, chopped
3   hard boiled eggs, chopped
Dash Tabasco
Onion salt (optional)

Add salt and flour to oleo, and stir together until bubbly. Add milk, stirring well. Add cheese and cook, stirring often, until thickened. Stir in chicken, eggs, Tabasco, and onion salt. Place in greased casserole and bake at 350° for 30 minutes.

Dottie Schoettle

BROCCOLI AND CHICKEN CASSEROLE

2   boxes frozen cut broccoli, cooked
     as on package
5   chicken breasts
2   cans of cream of chicken soup,
     undiluted
1   cup Hellman's mayonnaise

4   tablespoons lemon juice
1   cup sharp Cheddar cheese, grated
½   teaspoon curry powder
Croutons
Almonds

Boil chicken until tender in salted water. Remove from bone; cut in bite size pieces. Layer chicken and cooked broccoli pieces. Top with mixture of soup, mayonnaise, lemon juice, cheese, curry powder. Top with croutons and almonds. Bake until mixture bubbles. *Serves 12.*

Mrs. Donald Foster, Nellie Baddour Pike,
Betty McCallen, Pat Keen

FRYER STUFFED WITH RICE

2½ or 3 pound fryer
2   cups cooked rice
½   cup celery, chopped
½   cup onion, chopped

1   teaspoon salt
½   teaspoon black pepper
1   teaspoon poultry seasoning

Mix rice, celery, onion, salt, pepper and poultry seasoning together. Spoon this mixture into the fryer. If any left over, place outside of fryer under wings and between legs and body of fowl. Bake in covered dish for one hour at 350°.

Oneida Baddour

183

KING RANCH CHICKEN

1 fryer or hen	2 cups American cheese, grated
½ cup celery, chopped	1 can mushroom soup
1 small onion	1 small can Rotel
Salt and pepper	1 medium onion, minced
10-12 tortillas	

Cook chicken in water with celery, onion, salt and pepper. Reserve broth. Debone chicken and cut into pieces. Pour 2 cups chicken broth into 6x15 baking dish. Place half the tortillas in bottom of pan, and in layers, add the chicken, cheese, soup, Rotel, onion and rest of tortillas. Pour 2 cups chicken broth over casserole. Bake at 325° for 45 minutes. If it comes out too dry, pour more broth over, and cover with foil.

Mrs. Carlton Stubbs

CHICKEN BREASTS

1⅓ cups Minute Rice	⅓ cup sherry (optional)
½ envelope onion soup mix	4 chicken breasts
1 can mushroom soup	½ stick oleo, melted
1¼ cups boiling water	Salt and pepper
2 tablespoons pimento, chopped	Paprika

Combine rice, soups, water, pimento and sherry in casserole. Roll chicken in oleo, sprinkle with salt and pepper and paprika. Place chicken on top of rice mixture. Cover and bake 1 hour and 15 minutes at 375° or for 2 hours at 300°.

Mrs. Albert L. Waring

HOT CHICKEN SALAD CASSEROLE

1½ cups rice	½ cup almonds, chopped
⅔ cup mayonnaise	1 cup celery, diced
1 can cream of chicken soup	¼ cup green peppers, diced or
½ can cream of mushroom soup	pimentos or stuffed olives
1 small can mushrooms, drained	3 hard cooked eggs, chopped
3 cups chicken, cooked and diced	2 tablespoons lemon juice
3 tablespoons onion, grated	1 tablespoon soy or Worcestershire sauce

Cook rice according to package directions. Combine all ingredients together. Put in greased casserole — top with crushed potato chips. Bake at 350° for 30 minutes. Can freeze and bake later.

Mrs. Harold Redfearn

BONED CHICKEN BREAST WITH PROSCUITTO AND CHEESE

4 individual chicken breasts, skinned and boned	Flour
	1 egg
Salt and red pepper	Bread crumbs
8 thin slices proscuitto (ham can be substituted)	¼ cup oil
	1 cup chicken stock
8 thin slices Swiss cheese	¼ cup sherry wine

With a sharp knife, carefully slice chicken breast horizontally to make 8 thin slices. Pound chicken slices lightly with flat cleaver. Season the slices with salt and red pepper. On each slice of chicken, put proscuitto or ham, and cheese. Roll and pin with toothpick. Roll in flour, dip in egg, then roll in bread crumbs. Preheat oil in skillet and brown chicken til golden. *Do not overcook.* Transfer chicken to shallow baking dish, pour stock over chicken and bake at 325-350° for 20 minutes. Add sherry 10 minutes before cooking time is up.

Fanny Corrodini

CHICKEN AND GREEN NOODLE CASSEROLE

2 large fryers	½ cup Cheddar cheese, grated
6 ounces spinach noodles	1 6-ounce can mushrooms
1 cup onions, chopped	¾ cup stuffed olives
1 cup celery, chopped	1 teaspoon soy sauce
1 cup green pepper, chopped	Dash Tabasco
4 tablespoons oleo	Salt and pepper to taste
1 can cream of mushroom soup	1 2-ounce package slivered almonds

Simmer fryers in water until tender, remove meat from bones and cut into bite size pieces, reserving stock. Cook noodles according to package directions in chicken stock and drain. Sauté onion, celery, and bell pepper lightly in oleo. Blend in soup, heat, add cheese, and stir until melted. Add mushrooms, olives, chicken, noodles and seasonings. Place in greased casserole, and sprinkle with almonds. Bake at 350° for 30 minutes. Makes two 1½-quart casseroles. *Serves 8 or 10.*

Syble Bollinger

CHICKEN, RICE AND SPINACH CASSEROLE

4 tablespoons onion, chopped
4 tablespoons celery, chopped
4 tablespoons oleo
2 cups chicken broth
1 can beef bouillon
1 can mushroom soup
1 package frozen chopped
 spinach, cooked and drained

4 cups chicken, cooked and chopped
1 cup rice, uncooked
Salt and pepper
1 cup medium Cheddar cheese,
 grated

Sauté onion and celery in oleo. Add broth, bouillon, soup, spinach and chicken, and stir. Add rice and stir well. Salt and pepper to taste. Pour into 3-quart casserole. Bake covered at 375° for 1 hour. Remove from oven, top with cheese, return uncovered long enough to melt cheese.

Mrs. Charles Adams, Jr.

CHICKEN CASSEROLE

1 can cream of celery soup
½ cup mayonnaise
2 cups water
2 cups chicken, cooked
 and diced
1 package white and wild rice

1 pound can French style green
 beans, not drained
1 medium onion, chopped
1 medium jar pimento, chopped
1 can water chestnuts, sliced
Salt and pepper to taste

Combine soup, mayonnaise, and water and mix well. Stir in chicken, rice, green beans, onion, pimento, water chestnuts, and salt and pepper. Place in greased casserole and bake at 350° for 1 hour.

Mrs. Ray Sturrup

CHICKEN CASSEROLE

2 cups chicken, diced
¼ cup mayonnaise
1 cup cooked rice
½ teaspoon salt
4-ounce can mushrooms
2 tablespoons butter

2 cans cream of chicken soup
1 cup celery, diced
1 tablespoon lemon juice
1 tablespoon onion, finely chopped
½ cup shredded almonds
Corn flakes or bread crumbs

Combine above ingredients and place in 9x13 casserole. Dot with butter, and top with corn flakes or bread crumbs. Bake at 350° for 30 to 40 minutes. Serves 6.

Mrs. Walter Scott

CHICKEN SPAGHETTI

1 large hen
2 onions, chopped
2 tablespoons flour
2 tablespoons bacon drippings
2 #3 cans tomatoes
1 bell pepper
2 buttons garlic

2 tablespoons sugar
1 can tomato paste
1 pound spaghetti, boiled
Grated Hoop or Parmesan cheese
  (optional)
Mushrooms (optional)

Cook hen until tender. Cool, bone and chop. Brown onion with flour in bacon drippings. Add tomatoes, bell pepper, garlic and sugar. Cook until thick. Add tomato paste and chicken. Mix in boiled spaghetti. Let simmer. Keep moist with chicken broth. Serve hot with cheese, if desired. Mushrooms may also be added to the sauce, if the family likes them.

Mrs. L. L. Riggan

CHICKEN SPAGHETTI

1 pound onions, chopped fine
1 stalk celery, chopped
1 large bell pepper, chopped
1 large jar pimento, chopped
1 cup chicken stock
1 can tomato soup
1 can cream of mushroom soup
1 small jar stuffed olives or
  5 or 6 ounces salad olives

1 can mushroom pieces (more if
  desired)
6 pound chicken, cooked and
  chopped
1½ boxes spaghetti or vermicelli
Red pepper (optional)

Cook onions and celery in small amount of butter until golden brown. Add pepper, pimento and chicken stock. Cook until all ingredients are well done. Add tomato soup, mushroom soup, olives, mushrooms and chicken. Cook spaghetti as directed on box. Add to above sauce. Salt and pepper to taste. Add extra chicken stock if needed. *Serves 12-15.*

Variation: Use 1 pound of Cheddar cheese with other ingredients, holding out 1 cup to sprinkle over top.

Amanda Wise

CHICKEN SPAGHETTI

1 large fryer
1 large onion, chopped
1 cup bell pepper, chopped
1 can cream of mushroom soup

1 can cream of celery soup
2 cups grated cheese
1 package vermicelli

Boil chicken; cool. Debone and chop. Add to sautéed onion and pepper. Simmer 5 minutes. Add soups and cheese. Cook for 30 to 45 minutes. If needed, add water. Cook vermicelli according to package directions, and mix in.

Wyeth Chandler
Mayor of Memphis

CHICKEN CASSEROLE

1 chicken
2 cups cooked rice
2 pounds canned peas and carrots
2 cans cream of mushroom soup
½ cup grated cheese

2 tablespoons curry powder
1 can refrigerated biscuits
1 cup sour cream
1 egg
½ cup salad dressing

Boil chicken in salted water until tender. Line casserole dish with rice. Pour peas and carrots over rice. Remove chicken from bones, cut into small pieces, and place over peas and carrots. Pour mushroom soup over all. Sprinkle with cheese and curry powder. Split each biscuit in half, and place biscuits on top of casserole. In separate bowl, beat sour cream and egg together. Add salad dressing, mix, and spread over biscuits. Bake at 350° for 1 hour and 45 minutes.

Marie Hartfield

CHICKEN AND RICE CASSEROLE

1 cut up chicken
1 cup uncooked rice
1 can cream of celery soup

½ soup can milk
¼ cup water
1 package onion soup mix

In a buttered casserole dish, place chicken. Add rice, soup, milk, water and onion soup. Cover dish with foil. Cook for 2 hours at 350°.

Gladys Jones

188

TEXAS RANCH CASSEROLE

1 can cream of chicken soup
1 can cream of mushroom soup
½ can Rotel tomatoes
½ can chicken broth
1 dozen tortillas, torn in small
   pieces

2 cups chicken, cooked and chopped
1 onion, chopped
2 cups cheese, grated

Combine soups, add Rotel and chicken broth. Arrange alternate layers of tortillas, chicken, onion, sauce and cheese in baking dish. Bake in preheated oven at 350° for 45 minutes to 1 hour.

Donna Poteet

SWISS CHICKEN

8 chicken breast halves, deboned
1 can cream of chicken soup
½ soup can water
1 package Swiss cheese slices,
   without holes

1 stick butter
1 package Pepperidge Farm Herb
   Dressing

Place chicken in casserole. Combine soup and water and pour over chicken. Place a slice of cheese on each chicken breast. Melt butter and combine with dressing; sprinkle on casserole. Cover and cook at 375° for 30-40 minutes.

Joy Melton

CHICKEN AND YELLOW RICE

2 chickens, boiled and deboned
1 can tomatoes, stewed
2 onions, chopped
1 bell pepper, chopped
1 pod garlic, chopped

½ cup oil
2 cups yellow rice, uncooked
2 teaspoons turmeric
3 bay leaves
6 cups broth

Put chicken in large Dutch oven. Add tomatoes. Cook onions, bell pepper, and garlic in oil. Pour this over tomatoes. Sprinkle rice on top. Add turmeric and bay leaves to broth and pour over rice. Bake at 350° for 1 hour and 10 minutes. First 35 minutes without lid, second 35 minutes with lid.

Mrs. Steve McDoniel

189

CHICKEN TETRAZZINI

1 4-pound hen	1½ cups cream
3 tablespoons butter	2 large cans mushrooms
3 tablespoons celery, chopped	4 eggs, hard boiled
1 tablespoon bell pepper	8-ounce package small egg noodles,
4 cups chicken broth	cooked and drained
½ cup flour	½ cup Parmesan cheese
¼ teaspoon cayenne pepper	½ cup bread crumbs
¼ teaspoon black pepper	

Boil hen in salt water until tender. Remove bones and skin. Cut meat in bite size pieces. Melt butter in large skillet. Add celery and bell peppers and cook until tender. Add broth. Stir in flour and peppers and mix well. Add cream, mushrooms, eggs, and chicken that has been drained. Add noodles and mix. Pour into 3-quart casserole. Top with cheese and bread crumbs. Bake at 400° for 30 minutes. You can use mushroom soup in place of cream sauce.

Barbara Petty

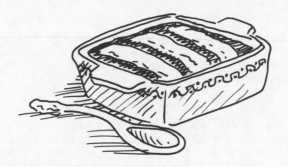

ARROZ CON POLLO

1 chicken, cut up	½ teaspoon pepper
3 cups boiling water	1 teaspoon paprika
¼ cup oil (not olive oil)	2 bay leaves
4 onions, chopped	Minced parsley, to taste
1 clove garlic, minced	¼ teaspoon saffron
1 cup rice, rinsed	2-4 chopped pimentos
1½ teaspoons salt	

Put chicken in boiling water. Cover and boil gently for 20-30 minutes. Heat oil, and stir in onions, garlic, and rice. Sauté for 10 minutes, being careful not to brown the rice. To cooked chicken and broth, add salt, pepper, paprika, bay leaves, and saffron. Spread the rice mixture evenly over the chicken. Cover and boil gently about 40-60 minutes or until rice is soft and chicken is tender. Add pimento just before serving. Better if prepared the day before and reheated just before serving. *Serves 4.*

Charles MacCracken

CAJUN CHICKEN

1 chicken, cut up
Several stalks celery
1 bay leaf
½ pound sausage
1 onion, chopped
5 cups chicken broth
1 can sliced mushrooms

1 cup raw rice (may be instant)
2 packages dried chicken noodle
  soup
1 can cream of mushroom soup,
  undiluted
Almonds

Cook chicken in salt water with 1 stalk celery and bay leaf until tender. Remove from bone and save broth. Brown sausage and drain off grease. Add onion, chicken broth (if not enough, add water to make 5 cups), mushrooms, rice and soups. Cook for 40 minutes. Transfer to casserole, top with almonds, and bake at 350° for 30 minutes.

CHICKEN 'N NOODLES

1 4-5 pound chicken
1 12-ounce package noodles
6 eggs, hard boiled
2 cans cream of mushroom soup
1 small can pimento

½ pound sharp Cheddar cheese,
  grated
Worcestershire sauce
Salt
Pepper

Cook chicken and cut into bite size pieces. Cook noodles in the chicken broth. Place half of noodles in baking dish. Top with half the chicken. Slice 3 of the hard boiled eggs over chicken. Add 1 can of undiluted soup. Sprinkle with half the pimento and cheese. Add a dash of Worcestershire and salt and pepper. Repeat, ending with cheese. Heat at 300° for 30 minutes. *Serves 12.* If prepared the day before, add 15 minutes to cooking time.

Mrs. Beuford J. Wallace

SUPER EASY CHICKEN AND RICE

1 cut-up chicken
Salt
1 cup rice
1 can cream of chicken soup
1 can onion soup
½ cup green pepper, chopped

½ cup celery, chopped
½ cup water
1 teaspoon Accent
1 tablespoon Lea and Perrin's
  Worcestershire sauce

Line pan with chicken, salted. Sprinkle with rice. Mix remaining ingredients in large bowl and pour over chicken and rice. Bake at 375° covered with foil, until rice is tender.

Mrs. Boyce Billingsley

CHICKEN LIVERS WITH RICE

¼ cup butter or margarine	1 can cream of chicken soup,
3 tablespoons onion, minced	undiluted
1 ⅓ cups cooked Minute Rice	½ cup milk
½ pound chicken livers, cut in	1 tablespoon chopped parsley
1-inch pieces	Pinch of dried basil

Melt 1 tablespoon butter in pan, add onion and cook till tender. Add to rice and cook as package directs. Meanwhile roll livers in seasoned flour. Sauté in remaining butter until brown. Combine in 1½-quart casserole the livers, rice, soup and rest of ingredients. Bake until hot and bubbly about 30 minutes at 375°. Plain or yellow rice may be used. Cook first and then measure right amount and mix with other ingredients.

Dena Burns

CORNISH HENS

1 cup cooked wild and white rice	¼ teaspoon poultry seasoning
1 stalk celery, chopped	1 small can chopped mushrooms
4 tablespoons margarine	4 Cornish hens
1 teaspoon salt	

Cook rice as directed. Add celery, margarine, salt, poultry seasoning and mushrooms. Stuff in hens and bake at 350° for 1 hour, basting occasionally.

Mary Jane Baddour Chandler

TURKEY CASSEROLE

2 cups celery, chopped	3 cups milk
½ cup onion, chopped	6 cups noodles, cooked
¼ cup butter	7 cups turkey, cooked and diced
3 cans cream of celery soup	½ cup pimento
3 cans cream of mushroom soup	½ cup bread crumbs

Sauté celery and onion in butter. Blend in soups and milk. Add noodles, turkey and pimento. Put into two 3-quart casseroles. Sprinkle bread crumbs on top. Bake at 350° for 30 minutes. *Serves 20.*

Mrs. John Jenkins

BERNICE'S CORNBREAD DRESSING

6 cups self-rising cornmeal
½ cup plain flour
¼ cup sugar
4 cups sweet milk
4 eggs
¾ cup oleo, melted

1 heaping tablespoon sage
1 tablespoon black pepper
4 cups onion, chopped
4 tablespoons oleo
1 teaspoon salt
8 cups chicken broth

Mix meal, flour and sugar together. Add milk and eggs, and then oleo. Work up to a smooth mixture. Bake for 30 minutes at 400°. Crumble cornbread up while still warm. Add sage and black pepper. Sauté onions in skillet with oleo and salt until transparent. Then pour onions and chicken broth into cornbread. Mix together and pour into a 9x13″ pan. Bake at 400° for approximately 25-30 minutes or until done.

Bernice Alexander

STRIP DUMPLINGS

1½ cups flour, sifted
Dash salt
½ teaspoon baking powder
1½ tablespoons Crisco
1 egg

Dash celery salt
Warm chicken broth
Dash black pepper
1 chicken bouillon cube

Mix flour, salt, baking powder and shortening. Beat egg in cup. Put egg in flour and mix. Then mix bouillon cube and dash of celery salt in broth. Mix flour mixture with broth. Must be pretty dry or stiff. Roll out very thin. Cut into pieces 1½ by 1 inches. Drop in one at a time and cook about 10 minutes in covered pot.

Margarite Cotton

BERNICE'S OLD-FASHIONED DUMPLINGS

2½ cups flour
2 eggs
1 teaspoon salt

½ stick oleo
½ cup milk
Chicken broth

Mix flour, eggs, salt, oleo and milk together. Knead until stiff. Roll out to thickness of pie crust. Cut in 1-2 inch strips. Use reserved broth from cooked chicken. Bring broth to a boil and drop dumpling strips in one at a time. Cook about 10 minutes, or until dumplings are firm.

Bernice Alexander

DEER STEAKS

Deer steaks
Olive oil
Lemon Juice
Whiskey

Flour
Salt
Pepper

Marinate steaks in olive oil, lemon juice, and whiskey. Leave out overnight and put in refrigerator all day. Roll in flour, salt to taste and lots of pepper; and fry.

Grace Knolton

GRILLED DOVE BREASTS – STUFFED

Dove breasts
3 parts apple, chopped or grated

1 part hot cherry pepper, chopped
Bacon

Combine apple and cherry pepper to make stuffing. Place small amount of stuffing between two dove breasts. Wrap with bacon. Secure with toothpicks. Grill 2½″ from charcoal fire which has turned white. Grill 45 minutes to 1 hour, turning frequently.

Reesa Graham

BARBEQUED DUCK

Ducks
Salt and pepper

Olive oil
Sauce (recipe below)

Split ducks, salt and pepper. Place on grill, bone side down over low to medium coals. Baste with olive oil and turn frequently. Leave on bone side ⅔ of time. After approximately 45 minutes, begin to baste with sauce and turn until tender. (Approximately 1½ hours total cooking time.)

Sauce for Barbequed Duck:

1½ sticks butter
1 cup catsup
1 cup vinegar
1 lemon
1 garlic clove or purée
2 tablespoons Worcestershire
   sauce

2 teaspoons season salt
1 tablespoon chili powder
1 teaspoon celery salt
Tabasco to taste
Salt and pepper to taste
1 teaspoon onion purée

Melt margarine and add catsup, vinegar and lemon juice. Add other ingredients and simmer 15 minutes.

Lisa Baddour

PETER'S ISLAND WILD DUCK

4 wild ducks
1 7-ounce package wild rice
1 medium size onion

¾ stick butter
1 large can mushrooms or 1 small
   package fresh mushrooms

Cook ducks in oven until tender (4 or 5 hours at 350°) with strip of bacon on top. I also stuff my ducks with whatever is available — apples, oranges, celery, potatoes, onions, peppers, cabbage, etc. Cook package of wild rice as directed (for extra flavor, use some chicken broth instead of water). When ducks are done, take meat off duck breast and legs. Melt butter, sauté onions and mushrooms. Mix rice, duck, onions and mushrooms together. Add more butter to get consistency desired. Salt and pepper to taste.

Sally Saig

Use as a main course or serve in a chafing dish with melba rounds.

ROAST DUCK

1 duck
¼ apple
¼ onion
½ stick margarine

1 cup water
Seasoning salt
Poultry seasoning

If duck is frozen, thaw at room temperature. Stuff duck with apple and onion. In baking pan, melt margarine and water. Add 1 teaspoon seasoning salt. Place duck in pan, and cover. Bake at 350° for 3½ hours. Every 30 minutes, baste with drippings, and sprinkle duck with seasoning salt and poultry seasoning. Remove top from pan, increase heat to 450°, and brown for 15 minutes. Make gravy with broth. Serve with wild rice.

William Sanford

SMOKED DUCKS

Large mallard ducks
Water
Plain or pickling salt

Red pepper
Currant jelly
Port wine

Soak ducks in brine made by adding to cold water enough salt to float a raw egg (in the shell). Use a brick or weight to hold ducks down. Keep temperature below 40° by adding ice. Soak for 18 hours. Then coat outside of ducks with red pepper. Cold smoke for 18-24 hours, or smoke in cajun cooker with chips of green hickory about 6 hours, or until done. Slice thin and serve at room temperature with sauce made by combining 2 parts jelly to 1 part wine.

Mrs. Lowell Taylor, Jr.

POULTRY AND GAME

195

ROAST DUCK WITH SAUERKRAUT

½ cup salt pork, finely diced
1 onion, finely chopped
1 apple, peeled and finely chopped
Salt
Pepper
¼ teaspoon thyme

1 teaspoon caraway seed
3 cups sauerkraut, well drained
4-5 pound duck
Lemon juice
1 cup red wine

Fry salt pork in a large skillet. Add onion and apple, and sauté until lightly colored. Add salt and pepper to taste, thyme, caraway seed, and sauerkraut. Mix thoroughly. Rub inside of duck with lemon juice, and stuff with sauerkraut mixture. Sew up the opening. Place duck on a rack in a roasting pan, and roast at 350° for 2½ hours, basting often with wine.

Mrs. C. S. Sanders, Jr.

DUCK WITH ORANGE

1 duck
Salt and pepper
½ cup sugar
1 tablespoon wine vinegar

Juice of 2 oranges
¼ cup Grand Marnier
Rind of 1 orange, grated
Strips of orange peel

Salt and pepper duck and roast in 325° oven for 1 hour and 15 minutes. Skim off the fat. In a heavy pan, combine sugar and vinegar. Cook over low heat until sugar caramelizes. Add orange juice, Grand Marnier, and orange rind. Blend well. Add pan juices from duck and bring to a boil. Add orange peel strips and pour over duck.

Billy and Barbara Mills

BUCK'S WILD DUCK

1 duck breast (2 halves)
1 cup Wondra flour
2 tablespoons seasoning salt
¼ teaspoon pepper

1 egg
1 small can Pet milk
Cooking oil

Mix dry ingredients in plastic bag. Slice duck breast (across grain) into ½" strips. Mix egg and milk. Dip strips into egg mixture, then shake in flour mixture. Pour oil into skillet until about ½" deep, then heat to 400°. Drop duck into skillet, making sure oil stays hot and continues to bubble. Fry until light brown on both sides, about 5-8 minutes. *Do Not Over-Cook* – centers should be slightly pink. Drain on paper towels or brown paper bag. Excellent when served with rice and gravy made from the drippings. *Serves 3.*

Mary Simpson

RICE STUFFING FOR DUCK

14-ounce package precooked
   long-grain rice
2 13¾-ounce cans chicken broth
1 cup water
½ teaspoon salt
⅛ teaspoon pepper

1½ teaspoons celery salt
¼ cup butter or margarine
⅔ cup onion, chopped
½ cup parsley, minced
8½-ounce can water chestnuts,
   drained and sliced

In a large saucepan, bring the rice, chicken broth, water, salt, pepper, and celery salt to a boil; simmer, covered, until liquid is absorbed — 5 to 7 minutes. In a medium skillet in the hot butter, gently cook the onion until softened; add to rice with parsley and water chestnuts; toss well. Use as a stuffing for two 4- to 5-pound ducks or chickens. Roast by your favorite method.

BAKED RABBIT

2 2-pound ready-to-cook rabbits,
   cut up
¼ cup flour
2 teaspoons salt
⅛ teaspoon pepper

¼ cup fat or salad oil
¼ cup onion, sliced
2 bouillon cubes
2 cups boiling water

Start heating oven to 350°. Roll rabbit pieces in ¼ cup flour combined with salt, pepper. In fat in Dutch oven, cook onion until tender. Remove onion; brown rabbit in same fat. Arrange onion over rabbit; add bouillon cubes, boiling water; stir till cubes dissolve. Bake covered, 1½ hours or till tender. *Makes 5 or 6 servings.*

RED HOT AND BLACK CHICKEN STRIPS (BITS)

3 pounds boned chicken breasts	½ teaspoon black pepper
⅛ cup garlic salt	1 cup all purpose flour
2 tablespoons ground red pepper (do not use cayenne pepper)	

Cut chicken breast lengthwise in 1-inch pieces. Sprinkle garlic salt freely over chicken, turning pieces so they are evenly coated. Continue with the red pepper and then the black pepper in the same manner. Set aside for about 1 hour to let chicken absorb flavor. Dust chicken pieces with flour, then deep fry in vegetable oil at 375° to 400° for 3 minutes. Place chicken on a paper towel to drain. Serve warm or cold. *Serves 6.*

Charles Baddour

This recipe has won national acclaim. For small amounts, a mini-fryer is ideal.

The Shed and Jane Caffey Clinic meets many health needs of the residents. Staffed by a Registered Nurse and aides, the Clinic provides screening, supervision of residents' medication programs, and first aid treatment for those on campus. They act as liaison between residents and their doctors when appropriate. In addition to treatment rooms, there are patient rooms for extended clinic care. Bricks, with names of friends of the Caffeys and of the Center etched in them, pave the Clinic entrance.

"The health of the people is really the foundation
upon which all their happiness and all their
powers depend."
–Speech by Benjamin Disraeli, 1877

MEATS

Shed & Jane Caffey Clinic

PRIME RIB ROAST

7 pound rib roast
½ cup Worcestershire sauce
Ground peppercorns
2 cloves garlic
½ cup prepared mustard

Flour
Potatoes
Carrots
Onions
Green peppers

With ice pick, make small holes all over the roast. Rub in the Worcestershire sauce, then the pepper, then garlic and mustard. Marinate at least overnight. When ready for oven, rub with flour and arrange vegetables sliced 1½-2 inches thick on top, securing with toothpicks where necessary. Cook in 300° oven for 18 minutes per pound for a rare roast (about 2 hours and 6 minutes.)

Mrs. Rupple K. Dabbs

Delicious!!

EYE OF ROUND (Roast Beef)

Eye of Round roast
Black pepper

Seasoning

Have roast at room temperature. Sprinkle with coarse black pepper or other seasoning. Preheat oven to 500° and bake 5 minutes per pound. Turn off and do not open oven for 2 hours. Roast will be pink.

Mrs. Donald Foster

SEVEN BLADE POT ROAST

1 7-blade chuck roast
1 package dry onion soup

1 can mushroom soup
Stew vegetables

Trim and wipe dry the roast and brown it. Prepare an aluminum foil container for the meat. Sprinkle the dry onion soup over the meat and empty the mushroom soup on top of that (two onion soups may be used if you prefer stronger flavor). Seal the aluminum container and cook at 300° for about 4 hours. The meat should be falling off the bone. This cut of meat can be greasy, so about 20 minutes before the meat is done make horizontal cuts in the foil at about the top of the gravy level. The grease can then drain. Stew vegetables can be added for the last 1½ to 2 hours of cooking.

Charles MacCracken

SHISH-KA-BOB – MARINATED

1 ½ pounds boneless beef cut in
     1 ½" cubes
2   medium onions, quartered
2   tomatoes, cut in eighths
2   medium green peppers,
     quartered
¼   cup olive oil

¼   cup lemon juice or vinegar
1   teaspoon salt
½   teaspoon pepper
1   clove garlic, minced
½   cup onion, chopped
¼   cup fresh parsley, chopped

Mix the olive oil, lemon juice, salt, pepper, garlic, onion, and parsley. Marinate the beef cubes in this sauce for 2 to 3 hours or refrigerate overnight. Fill the skewers, alternating the meat with the cubed vegetables. Broil over hot coals to medium rare, rotating skewers often. Makes 30 beef cubes.

SHISH-KA-BOB

1 ½ pounds boneless beef, cut into
     1 ½" cubes
2   medium onions, quartered
2   medium green peppers,
     quartered

2   tomatoes, cut in eighths
     Other vegetables to taste
½   teaspoon salt
¼   teaspoon black pepper

Salt and pepper the beef cubes. Fill the skewers, alternating the beef cubes and the vegetables. Broil over hot coals to medium rare, rotating skewers often. Makes 30 beef cubes.

Variation: Omit the quartered vegetables. Combine 1 chopped onion, 1 chopped green pepper, 1 cut up tomato, ¼ cup chopped parsley. Mix with ¼ cup olive oil, ¼ cup vinegar. When Ka-bobs are cooked, slide skewers over on these vegetables so that the meat juices soak into the vegetables.

BEEF SHORT RIBS

6   pounds lean beef short ribs
1   tablespoon salt
1   tablespoon Accent
8   peppercorns

2   onions, sliced
1   carrot, diced
½   cup parsley
     Horseradish

(If you can get ribs not cut, they are a little better.) Place ribs in kettle and cover with cold water. Cook on high til it begins to boil. Lower heat and cook 2 hours. Add vegetables and seasonings and cook 2 more hours. Serve with horseradish.

Mrs. William F. Ledsinger

Makes a delicious start for vegetable soup the next day.

MARINATED BEEF TENDERLOIN

1 beef tenderloin	¼ cup oil or Italian Wishbone Salad
1 small bottle soy sauce	Dressing

Combine soy sauce and oil or dressing. Marinate meat 2-3 hours, turning often. Do not drain. Cook 20-25 minutes at 400° for medium rare.

Mrs. W. K. Ingram

Always pink and delicious.

BRISKET

3 or 5 pounds brisket (may use other type of pot roast)	1 package Lipton onion soup
Garlic salt to taste	½ cup brown sugar
	⅔ cup catsup

Place meat in pan lined with heavy duty foil. Season with garlic salt. Sprinkle soup mix and brown sugar over top of meat. Spread with catsup. Seal foil. Bake at 325° for 3 hours.

Mrs. Harold Tannen

ROUND STEAK WITH LEMON JUICE

1 pound round steak, sliced thin	2 teaspoons instant beef bouillon
1 tablespoon butter	Black pepper
⅓ cup lemon juice	½ lemon, sliced paper thin

Cut steak into small pieces, trimming away fat and pound until thin. Melt butter in skillet and sauté meat over medium heat. Turn only one time. After turning, pour lemon juice directly onto each piece of steak. Then add bouillon, pepper and lemon to meat. After meat has cooked on the second side (it does not need to brown), cover and cook over low heat until tender. If more juice is desired, ⅓ cup water may be added.

Mrs. H. E. Manning

STEAK AND CHEESE BAKE

¼ cup Crisco oil
4-6 minute steaks
½ cup flour
½ teaspoon salt

Pepper
1 cup Mozzarella cheese (or Swiss),
   grated
2 cups tomato juice

Preheat oven to 325°. In skillet, put oil and heat until hot. Flour the steak, and salt and pepper to taste. Brown on each side, but do not overcook. When browned, remove and put in 9x13 baking dish. Layer the meat with cheese and cover with tomato juice. Bake for about 30 minutes. Ready to serve.

SPANISH STEAK

1 round steak, 2-inches thick
4 tablespoons flour
Salt and pepper
1 onion, sliced
1 green pepper, sliced

1 small jar pimentos
1 small bottle stuffed olives
2 cans tomato soup
1 soup can water

Dredge steak in flour and salt and pepper. Place in a large baking dish, cover with sliced onions, layer of green pepper rings, pimentos and a small bottle of stuffed olives with brine. Over this mixture pour soup and water. Cover and bake in moderate oven for 2 hours. This dish is really great with rice.

Mrs. Hugh Dillahunty

CHUCK WAGON STEAK

1 ½ pounds round steak
⅓ cup flour
1 teaspoon salt
¼ teaspoon pepper
3 tablespoons oil
2 bouillon cubes

2 ½ cups hot water
½ cup barbeque sauce
1 tablespoon chili powder
1 bell pepper, diced
½ cup stuffed olives, sliced

Mix flour, salt and pepper. Pound into meat. Brown in hot oil. Blend bouillon cubes in 2 cups hot water. Add ½ cup water, barbeque sauce, chili powder, bell pepper, and olives. Simmer 1½ to 2 hours until meat is tender.

Brenda Cole

Best way to cook is in electric skillet.

HAMBURGER STROGANOFF

1 cup onion, chopped	2 tablespoons Worcestershire
1 tablespoon Wesson oil	1 teaspoon pepper
1 pound ground beef	¼ cup green pepper, chopped
3 cups tomato juice	1 cup sour cream
1 teaspoon salt	1 small can mushrooms
1½ tablespoons celery salt	

Sauté onions in oil. Add ground beef, tomato juice, and seasonings. Bring to a rapid boil. Cover and simmer for 20 minutes. Add green pepper and cook 10 more minutes. Stir in sour cream slowly, add mushrooms, and bring to a boil. *Serves 6.*

Barbara Petty

JIFFY BEEF STROGANOFF

1 pound ground chuck or ground beef	1 3-ounce can sliced mushrooms
1 tablespoon shortening	3½ cups hot water
1 envelope dry onion soup	2 tablespoons flour
½ teaspoon ginger	1 cup sour cream
3 cups uncooked medium-wide noodles	2 tablespoons sherry (optional)

Brown beef in shortening in 10" skillet. Drain off fat and sprinkle onion soup and ginger over meat and then arrange noodles in a layer over this. Add mushrooms with its liquid and pour the hot water over noodles. Cover and cook 20 minutes at a low temperature til noodles are done. Blend flour into sour cream and stir into stroganoff. Cook 3 minutes longer. May add sherry just before serving. *Makes 6 servings.*

Martha Anne Weaver

HAMBURGER STROGANOFF

3 or 4 potatoes, sliced	2 onions, sliced
1 pound hamburger	1 can tomato soup
Carrots	1 can water
1 can English peas, drained	Salt

Place a layer of potatoes on bottom of casserole dish. Add a layer of carrots, a layer of peas and a layer of onion. Brown hamburger meat and place on top of onions. Combine soup and water and pour over the top. Sprinkle with salt. Stir occasionally. Cook on stove 1½ hours. (This is an ideal recipe for a crock pot.)

Debbie West

BEEF STROGANOFF

2 pounds round steak, cut
   ½ inch thick
Flour to dredge meat
¼ cup butter and oil mixed
½ cup onion, chopped
1-2 cloves garlic, minced
1 can sliced mushrooms
2 tablespoons butter

3-5 tablespoons flour
1 tablespoon tomato paste
1 can beef consommé
½ teaspoon Worcestershire sauce
2 teaspoons salt
¼ teaspoon pepper
2 tablespoons cooking sherry
1 cup sour cream

Cut meat into 2-inch strips, ¼ inch wide and ¼ inch thick. Dredge and pound in flour. Brown in butter and oil. Brown onions, garlic, and mushrooms in last meat browning. Remove from pan. Add additional butter and blend in flour as in making cream sauce. Add tomato paste. Slowly pour in consommé, Worcestershire, salt and pepper. Cook over low heat and stir until thickened. Add water to thin if necessary. Return meat to pan and sauce. Add cooking sherry. Cook over low heat with tight fitting cover for 25 minutes or more, stirring occasionally. (May be frozen at this point). Stir in sour cream at end of cooking time and simmer for a short while.

Mrs. Ben G. Hines

PEPPER STEAK

1 ½ pounds sirloin (½" thick),
   bite size
½ teaspoon salt
1 cup onion, diced
1 cup beef bouillon
3 tablespoons soy sauce
1 clove garlic, minced

2 green peppers, cut in 1" pieces
2 tablespoons cornstarch
¼ cup cold water
2 tomatoes, peeled and cut into
   eighths
3-4 cups hot cooked rice

Trim fat and bone from meat. Use fat for grease. Brown thoroughly on one side. Turn and sprinkle with salt. Brown other side and sprinkle with remaining salt. Push meat to side and brown onion. Cook and stir until tender. Add bouillon, soy sauce and garlic. Cover and simmer 10 minutes. Add green pepper, cover and simmer 5 minutes. Blend cornstarch with water. Gradually stir into skillet, stirring until mixture boils. Add tomatoes and heat thoroughly. Serve immediately over rice.

Rose Marie Spooner

ORIENTAL BEEF

6 breakfast steaks
Meat tenderizer
3 tablespoons cooking oil
1 green pepper
1 red pepper

2 ribs celery
2 small onions, sliced thin
1 cup mushrooms
1 cup water chestnuts

Sauce:

1½ cups water
¾ teaspoon powdered ginger
3 tablespoons soy sauce

1 beef bouillon cube
2 teaspoons sugar
2 tablespoons cornstarch

Sprinkle meat with tenderizer. Cut into ½-inch strips (Note: steaks ⅛-inch thick may be partially frozen and easily cut with kitchen shears). Brown beef in hot oil for 3 minutes. Remove meat to dish. Cut vegetables in diagonal strips; cook for few minutes in the oil. Combine water, ginger, soy sauce, bouillon, sugar and cornstarch to make sauce. Return meat to skillet. Pour sauce over vegetables and meat. Reduce heat and cook slowly, approximately 30 minutes. Liquid may be added to achieve desired consistency of sauce. Serve over rice or Chinese noodles.

Mrs. Robert A. Melhorn

CHINESE PEPPER STEAK

2 pounds round or sirloin steak
1 tablespoon oil or shortening
1 large onion, thinly sliced
2 cloves garlic, chopped
3 teaspoons instant bouillon
  or 3 bouillon cubes
1½ cups water

3 tablespoons cornstarch
3 tablespoons soy sauce
½ pound fresh mushrooms, sautéed
1 can water chestnuts, thinly sliced
¼ cup dry sherry (optional)
2 bell peppers, sliced into strips

Slice meat into 1-inch strips. Heat oil in Dutch oven and brown meat. Remove meat and sauté onion and garlic. Return meat to pan. Add bouillon and water. Cover and simmer until meat is tender, about 20 minutes. Mix cornstarch and soy sauce. Add to pan with mushrooms and water chestnuts and sherry. Cook until thickened. Add bell peppers the last few minutes. Peppers should be tender crisp. Serve over rice.

Mrs. H. E. Manning

GREEN PEPPER STEAK

1 pound top round steak	½ teaspoon curry powder
1 tablespoon oil	1 cup dry red wine
1 clove garlic, crushed	1 large green pepper
2 onions, coarsely chopped	1 6-ounce can mushroom slices
Salt and pepper	Tomato slices for garnish

Trim fat from meat. Cut into ½-inch strips. Brown well in oil with garlic. Add half of chopped onion, salt, pepper, curry powder and wine. Simmer, covered, 1 hour. Add more liquid if needed. Cut green pepper in thin strips. Brown with remaining onion in small amount of oil. Add to steak. Stir in mushrooms. Simmer 20 minutes more. Serve with tomato slices on top.

Ann Basore

FLANK STEAK

⅔ cup soy sauce	2 teaspoons dry mustard
⅓ cup salad oil	6 garlic cloves, crushed
2 teaspoons Accent	2 flank steaks
2 teaspoons ginger	

Prepare marinade by combining soy sauce, oil, Accent, ginger, mustard, and garlic. Marinate steaks in this mixture for 24 hours in the refrigerator in a tightly sealed container, turning frequently. Broil 3-5 minutes on each side and slice in ¾" strips on a diagonal to the grain. Plan on ⅓ to ½ pound per person.

Charles MacCracken

FLANK STEAK (with Teriyaki Sauce)

¼ cup soy sauce	1½ teaspoons ginger
3 tablespoons honey	¾ cup salad oil
2 tablespoons vinegar	1 onion, finely chopped
1 teaspoon garlic salt	2 flank steaks

Mix all ingredients together and marinate steaks 24-48 hours. Cook over charcoal fire 5 minutes on each side. Slice thinly diagonally.

Mary Virginia Gaines

BEEF BURGUNDY

10 small onions, sliced
2 tablespoons bacon grease
2 pounds round steak, cut
   into ¼" cubes
2 tablespoons flour
Pinch of salt

Pinch of pepper
Pinch of marjoram
Pinch of thyme
½ cup canned beef bouillon
1 cup Burgundy wine
½ pound fresh mushrooms, sliced

Sauté onions until soft in bacon grease. Remove from pan. Brown beef cubes in same pan. Sprinkle flour over beef and add the other seasonings, bouillon and wine. Stir and let simmer slowly for 3¼ hours. If liquid boils away, add more bouillon and wine. Return onions to pan and add mushrooms. Cook ¾ hour more, barely simmering.

Lee Ellis

MEAT WITH WINE

4 pounds beef
Garlic cloves
1 stick oleo

2 cups Burgundy wine
¼ cup water
Salt and pepper

Cut meat in 2-inch cubes. Insert a clove of garlic in each piece of meat. Brown in oleo in skillet. Transfer to casserole and add 1 cup wine and the water. Salt and pepper to taste. Bake in 350° oven about 45 minutes. Add remaining wine and cook another 15-20 minutes, or until tender. Serve on a bed of rice. Freezes well. *Serves 6-8.*

Mrs. M. D. Baddour

This was always served when "special" company came to dinner.

BEEF BURGUNDY

2 pound chuck or round beef
Garlic
Flour
2 tablespoons cooking oil
Burgundy and water

1 can mushrooms and broth
1 cup onion, chopped and sautéed
⅛ teaspoon marjoram
⅛ teaspoon thyme

Trim fat from meat and cut in 1½" or 2" cubes. Cut a slit in each piece and insert clove of garlic into meat. Roll meat in flour. Heat oil in oven-proof skillet or pan with cover. Brown meat on all sides. Cover with mixture of half Burgundy and half water. Add mushrooms, sautéed onions, marjoram, and thyme. Cover and bake in slow oven 2 hours.

Mrs. H. E. Manning

STATUS STEW

2 pounds rump steak or sirloin, cubed
½ stick butter
2 large onions, chopped
1 clove garlic or ⅛ teaspoon garlic powder
1 tablespoon flour
½ pound bacon, browned and chopped

2 teaspoons Bouquet Garni
1 teaspoon salt
1 teaspoon ground pepper
1 bottle Beaujolais red wine
1 cup mushroom caps
2 teaspoons chopped parsley

Brown steak, onions, and garlic in butter. Add flour. Add bacon, seasonings, and wine. Simmer 2 hours. Add mushroom caps and parsley. Serve over wild rice (or Uncle Ben's wild rice and long grain mixture). *Serves 4.*

Serve with garlic bread, favorite tossed green salad and cream cheese pie. And, of course, a bottle of Beaujolais red wine.

Gloria O'Rourke

BRUNSWICK STEW

2 fryers
2 pounds stew meat
½ pound boiling meat
2 onions, chopped
3 carrots, chopped
4 potatoes, chopped
½ stalk celery, chopped
Chicken broth
Salt and pepper
Red pepper

1 tablespoon diced parsley
1 tablespoon Worcestershire
1 can (1 pound 12 ounce) tomatoes
1 large can tomato paste
1 large package frozen okra
1 small package frozen string beans
1 small package frozen lima beans
1 small package frozen corn, creamed or whole kernel
1 small package frozen English peas

Boil and bone fryers, reserving broth. Cut meat into small pieces. Brown stew meat and boiling meat, and put meat, chicken and broth in a big pot. Add onions, carrots, potatoes and celery with salt, peppers, parsley, and Worcestershire. Bring to boil. Add tomatoes, tomato paste, okra and string beans, and continue cooking slowly. Cook lima beans, corn and peas in small amount of water, and add to stew the last 30-40 minutes. This can simmer all day. *Serves 12-15.*

Mrs. Beuford J. Wallace

FORGOTTEN STEW

1 pound lean stew meat	1 tablespoon sugar
2 potatoes, quartered	1 tablespoon tapioca
2 carrots, sliced	8 ounces tomato sauce
2 onions, quartered	½ cup water
¼ cup celery, chopped	

Put in casserole dish the stew meat, potatoes, carrots, onions, and celery. Sprinkle with sugar and tapioca. Combine tomato sauce with water and pour over top. Cover tightly. Put in 250° oven and do not peek for 4 hours.

June Spotts

SIX HOUR STEW

3 pounds stew meat or cubed chuck roast	4 large potatoes, quartered
1 can cream of mushroom soup	1 envelope dry onion soup
1 soup can water	3 onions, quartered
3 stalks celery	1 #2 can tomatoes
8 carrots, thickly sliced	1 teaspoon basil
	4 tablespoons tapioca

Place all ingredients in a heavy roaster with a tight fitting lid and bake at 275° for 6 hours. *DO NOT OPEN OVEN DOOR!!*

Martha Ann Weaver

FLIGHT "257" – MEATBALLS AND SAUERKRAUT

1 pound ground beef chuck	2 tablespoons oil
1 pound ground lean pork	2 tart green apples, peeled and cut into eighths
1 teaspoon salt	
½ cup thick applesauce	1 large onion, finely chopped
½ cup dry bread crumbs	2 pounds drained sauerkraut
2 tablespoons chili sauce	¾ cup dry white wine – or apple cider
⅛ teaspoon ground allspice	
⅛ teaspoon freshly ground black pepper	

In a bowl combine the beef, pork, salt, applesauce, bread crumbs, chili sauce, allspice and pepper. Mix lightly and form into ¾″ balls. In a large skillet heat the oil and brown the meat balls a few at a time. Sauté the apple and onion in the drippings remaining in the skillet until tender. Stir in the sauerkraut, wine or apple cider and bring to a boil. Place meat balls on top of sauerkraut, cover and simmer for 30 minutes. *Yield: 6-8 servings.*

ITALIAN RED WINE MEAT BALLS

2 ½ pounds ground chuck
1   package onion soup mix
½   cup grated Parmesan cheese
1   tablespoon parsley, minced
¼   cup plus 2 tablespoons
   cracker crumbs

½   cup water
2   eggs
½   teaspoon garlic salt
Salt and pepper to taste

Mix all ingredients together and shape into bite-size meat balls. Place on greased cookie sheet and bake at 350° about 15 minutes or until brown. Serve in chafing dish with sauce below.

Sauce:

1   large can tomato juice
3   tablespoons onion flakes

1   small pod garlic, crushed
½   cup Italian red wine

Mix all together and heat with meat balls in chafing dish.

EASY SWEDISH MEAT BALLS

3   slices bread
1   cup light cream
2   pounds ground round steak
¼   cup onion, chopped
1   egg
1   teaspoon salt

½   teaspoon pepper
1   teaspoon dried parsley flakes
¼   teaspoon ginger
1   can Campbell's Cream of
   Mushroom With Wine soup

Soak bread in cream and combine with the meat, onion, egg and spices. Shape into bite-size balls and brown in small amount of vegetable shortening over low heat. Place in serving dish and cover with heated soup.

June Smith

PORCUPINE MEAT BALLS

1 ½ pounds ground beef
½   cup uncooked rice
1   teaspoon salt
¼   teaspoon pepper

¼   cup onion, chopped
1   can condensed tomato soup
½   cup water

Combine meat, rice, salt, pepper and onion. Shape into small balls. Blend soup and water till mixture begins to simmer. Add meat balls. Cook about 30 minutes. *Makes 6 to 8 servings.*

Sue Turner

PORCUPINE MEATBALLS

1 package beef Rice-a-Roni
1 pound ground beef
1 egg, beaten

Dash salt and pepper
2 ½ cups hot water

Combine Rice-a-Roni ingredients with ground beef, egg, salt and pepper. Shape into meatballs (approximately 20). Brown on all sides in skillet. Combine contents of beef seasonings packet with hot water. Pour over meat. Cover and simmer 30 minutes. Thicken gravy if desired.

Debbi Allday

ALFRED'S MEAT BALLS

4 slices bacon, chopped
½ Spanish onion, chopped
1 pound ground lean beef, chuck,
    flank, round, bottom round, or
    sirloin
½ cup parsley, chopped
4 scallions with green, chopped

2 egg yolks
Dash of cumin
Dash of powdered thyme
Dash of oregano
Salt and pepper to taste
Meat sauce (see page 218)

Cook the bacon with the onions for a few minutes and add other ingredients. Make meat balls the size as desired and roll them in flour. Heat butter or good olive oil in frying pan and fry the meat balls in it for a few minutes to give some color and taste to them. Prepare meat sauce and put the meat balls in it and bring it to a boil and let simmer for 5 minutes. Ready to serve over spaghetti or noodles as desired.

Palm Beach Kennel Club Chef

BARBEQUED MEATBALLS

1 pound ground lean chuck (beef)
1 cup bread crumbs
½ cup sweet milk
1 cup tomato ketchup
½ cup water
½ cup onion, chopped

½ cup green peppers, chopped
1 teaspoon salt
½ teaspoon black pepper
1 ½ teaspoons sugar
1 tablespoon Worcestershire sauce

Combine meat, bread crumbs and mix well. Make into balls. Place in baking dish. Make sauce of remaining ingredients. Pour sauce over meatballs. Bake uncovered in 325° oven for 1 hour. *Serves 4-5.*

Mrs. J. E. Craig

POTATO MEAT LOAF

2   large Irish potatoes
1½ pounds ground beef or chuck
Salt
Garlic salt
½ cup celery, chopped

½ cup onion, chopped
⅓ cup green pepper, chopped
1   egg
Barbecue sauce or catsup

Grate potatoes. Season meat with salt and little garlic salt. Mix with grated potatoes. Add vegetables and egg. Make 2 loaves, brush with barbecue sauce or catsup or both. Cover and bake at 350° for 45 to 60 minutes.

Rebecca Barrett

INDIVIDUAL APPLESAUCE MEAT LOAVES

½ cup onion, minced
1   pound ground beef or chuck
½ pound ground lean pork
1½ teaspoons sage

1   tablespoon Worcestershire sauce
1   teaspoon salt
1½ cups canned applesauce
1   cup dry bread crumbs

Combine onion, beef, pork, sage, Worcestershire sauce and salt; mix well. Add applesauce and crumbs; mix well. Pack into large greased muffin pans. Bake in moderate oven at 350° for 30-40 minutes. *Yields 6 servings.* Serve with seasoned rice, carrots, and peas.

Marguerite Baddour

MINI MEAT LOAVES

1   10¾-ounce can tomato soup
1   pound ground beef
¼ cup fine dry bread crumbs
1   egg, slightly beaten
¼ cup onion, finely chopped
1   teaspoon salt

¼ teaspoon crushed thyme leaves
2   tablespoons shortening
2-4 tablespoons water
¼ teaspoon pepper
¼ teaspoon sage

Mix thoroughly ¼ cup soup, beef, bread crumbs, egg, onion, salt, and thyme. Shape firmly into 6 mini meat loaves. In skillet brown loaves in shortening; pour off fat. Stir in remaining soup and seasonings and water. Cover, cook over low heat 20 minutes. Stir occasionally. *Makes 6 servings.*

Debbi Allday

MY FAVORITE MEAT LOAF

2 pounds ground beef
1 pound ground pork
2 garlic cloves, pressed
1 large onion, finely chopped
1 teaspoon salt
1 teaspoon pepper

1 crumbled bay leaf
½ teaspoon thyme
1 teaspoon green pepper, chopped
½ cup dry bread crumbs
2 eggs
Bacon or salt pork

Mix all ingredients but bacon. Knead with hands til well blended. Make long loaf and press firmly. Arrange bacon (or salt pork) on bottom of baking dish. Brush loaf with butter (optional). Put 2 or 3 slices of bacon across top of loaf and bake at 325° 1½ to 1¾ hours, basting frequently. Let stand 15 minutes before serving.

Mrs. William F. Ledsinger

Fantastic as cold meat loaf sandwiches.

MEAT LOAF STUFFING

1 can mushrooms
Butter

Sour cream
Favorite meat loaf

Drain mushrooms. Sauté in small amount of butter. Mix with commercial sour cream. Place half of your favorite meat loaf in loaf pan and make long trench in center. Fill trench with sour cream and mushroom mixture. Place rest of meat loaf on top and bake like regular recipe.

Mrs. William F. Ledsinger

SANDERS' CHILI CON CARNE FOR A CROWD

3 to 4 pounds of ground chuck or
  round (lean meat)
3 large yellow onions, sliced
  thin
1 package chili seasoning
1 Owens chili log
1-2 large cans of mushrooms
1 can tomato soup

1 can ripe olives, drained and
  chopped
½ teaspoon garlic, minced
2 cans whole tomatoes
2 small cans tomato sauce
3 tablespoons chili powder, or to taste
¼ teaspoon cayenne, if desired
Parmesan cheese

In large soup pot: lightly brown ground meat with onions and chili seasoning. Pour off grease. Add remaining ingredients with sliced chili log. Do not drain any of the canned ingredients, as the liquid enhances the flavor. Simmer at least 3 hours, and serve hot. Sprinkle Parmesan over top of chili, amply. Serve with garlic bread and tossed salad.

Mrs. C. S. Sanders, Jr.

CHILI SUPREME *(Party Portion of 12)*

4	green peppers, chopped
6	tablespoons vegetable oil
1½	pounds onions, chopped
2½	pounds ground beef
1	pound mild pork sausage
½	pound butter or margarine
3	16-ounce cans tomatoes, undrained
3	heaping tablespoons dry parsley flakes
3	heaping tablespoons chili powder
3	heaping tablespoons cumin powder
2	tablespoons salt
1½	teaspoons pepper
1½	teaspoons monosodium glutamate
1½	teaspoons powdered garlic or 2 cloves, peeled and chopped
2	16-ounce cans pinto beans

In small skillet sauté peppers in vegetable oil for about 5 minutes. Add onions and cook till tender. In large skillet or Dutch oven fry the ground beef and pork sausage until slightly brown, ladle off excess fat. Then add the margarine or butter. In a large pot, cut up the tomatoes. Add the parsley and spices and simmer for about 30 minutes. Add the peppers, onions, meat and butter and continue cooking for 10 minutes. Add the beans and heat for an additional 4 to 5 minutes.

Bernice Wienstroer

DIET CHILI

2½	pounds ground lean chuck
3	cloves of garlic, crushed
2½	tablespoons chili powder
½	medium onion, chopped
½	teaspoon black pepper
1	drop Sweeta
1	teaspoon salt
2½	teaspoons Accent
1	cup water
3	cups tomato juice

Combine meat, garlic, chili powder, onion, pepper, Sweeta, salt and Accent in skillet. Brown well. Add water and juice and simmer for 45 minutes or until tender. Freezes extra well. When heating frozen chili add 4-ounce can of tomato juice and dash of Tabasco. Let simmer 15 minutes.

Charles Baddour

LESPEDESA POINT CHILI

1   pound ground chuck
1 ½ teaspoons onion powder
1 ½ teaspoons garlic salt
2   packages chili seasoning mix
1   can (1 pound 13 ounce)
    tomatoes

2   bay leaves, crushed
3   tablespoons chili powder
1   can (1 pound 4 ounce) kidney
    beans

Brown meat with onion powder, garlic salt, and chili seasoning. Add tomatoes, bay leaves and chili powder. Cook all day on low heat; 1 hour before serving add beans. *Makes 4 servings.* Delicious to serve on rice.

Marilyn Baddour Aaron

Grand! Men love it.

CHILI

Bacon grease
1   large onion, chopped
1   medium green pepper, chopped
1 ½ pounds ground hamburger or
    chuck
1   medium can tomatoes,
    chopped in blender

1   can tomato paste
2   big pimentos, chopped
1   large can mushrooms
Salt and pepper
4   tablespoons chili powder
2   cans kidney beans, drained

Sauté onion and green pepper in bacon grease. Add meat and brown. Place in a large container and add tomatoes, paste, pimentos, mushrooms, salt and pepper, chili powder and 1¼ cans beans. Mash up remaining beans and add to mixture. Simmer about 3 hours.

Joy Melton

CHILIA MANANA

1   pound ground chuck, seared
1   can cream of mushroom soup
1   can green chilies, chopped
1   large can evaporated milk
½   teaspoon oregano
¼   teaspoon cumin, ground

Garlic to taste
1   onion, chopped
Salt and pepper
Cheese, grated
6   corn tortillas, browned

Mix together browned meat, soup, chilies, milk, oregano, cumin, garlic, onion and salt and pepper. In bottom of dish, place a layer of browned tortillas, over this a layer of sauce, top with layer of cheese, and so on. Bake at 350° til bubbly, and cheese is melted.

Mrs. Steve McDoniel

216

CHILI

2½	cups dry pinto beans	1½	cups water
2	pounds ground chuck	1	can Rotel
1	pound sirloin steak, cubed	5	tablespoons flour
3	medium onions, chopped	4	tablespoons salt
1-2	cloves garlic, crushed	1	teaspoon pepper
1-3	jalapeno peppers	2	cups tomato juice
3	tablespoons chili powder	½	teaspoon ground cumin
4	tablespoons cornmeal	½	teaspoon red pepper

Cook pinto beans. Brown ground chuck and drain off grease. Brown steak cubes. Sauté onion and garlic. Combine all ingredients and simmer for several hours.

CHILI

1	pound ground beef	Pepper
2	medium onions, chopped	1-2 tablespoons chili powder
6	buttons garlic	1 quart boiling water
3	small cans tomato sauce	1 #2 can red kidney beans
Salt		

Sauté beef. Add beef, onions, garlic, tomato sauce, and seasonings to boiling water. Cook slowly for 1½ hours with top off. Add beans and cook another half hour slowly. Serve on rice, if desired. *Serves 4.*

Mrs. James Robertson

HURRY UP CHILI CASSEROLE

4	ounces lasagna noodles	⅛ teaspoon pepper
2	15-ounce cans chili con carne without beans	1 8-ounce package Mozzarella cheese, sliced
½	cup dry red wine	1 cup cream style cottage cheese
½	cup chili sauce	⅓ cup grated Parmesan cheese

Heat oven to 350°. Cook lasagna noodles according to package instructions. Drain. Combine chili, wine, chili sauce and pepper in saucepan. Heat. Layer ⅓ of the noodles into shallow baking pan. Add layer of ⅓ chili mixture and ⅓ each kind of cheese. Repeat layers twice. Baked covered 25 minutes, then 5 minutes uncovered. *Serves 6.*

Mrs. W. K. Ingram

BEEF

ITALIAN SPAGHETTI

2-3 bags dried mushrooms
¾ quart water
1 large onion, sliced
1 small green pepper, chopped
1 stalk celery, chopped
2 cloves garlic

1 large can Italian tomatoes
1 can Italian tomato paste
Dash red pepper
Dash paprika
1 pound spaghetti
Romano cheese

Wash mushrooms thoroughly. Put in water and let soak 20 or 30 minutes. Do not drain this water off; use in sauce. Tenderize sliced onion, pepper and celery in bacon drippings. (Can also use stock from beef roast.) Add undrained mushrooms, garlic, tomatoes, tomato paste, red pepper and paprika. Put into Dutch oven. Let boil, then let simmer 3 hours with pan tightly covered. Boil spaghetti until tender. Put in casserole — one layer of spaghetti, then layer of sauce. Over top, sprinkle heavily with grated cheese. (Use salt and pepper to taste.)

Mrs. Claude B. Senhausen

Been in the family over a century.

ALFRED'S MEAT SAUCE

4 slices bacon, diced
3 ounces butter or good olive oil
1 medium size Spanish or red onion, chopped
5 fresh mushrooms, chopped or 2 ounces dried Italian mushrooms, chopped
4 garlic cloves, chopped
8 ounces ground pork (lean shoulder or other part)
8 ounces ground beef (lean chuck)
1 ounce Accent or glutamate
8 ounces dry white wine
1 can (about 1 ½ pound) tomato puree
1 4-ounce can tomato paste

1 #5 can or ½ gallon whole tomatoes
1 quart chicken or beef stock (or tomato juice)
½ cup parsley, chopped
1 branch celery, chopped
2 bay leaves
Pinch of thyme leaves
Pinch of rosemary leaves
Pinch of oregano
Pinch of grated nutmeg
1 clove, to be removed when sauce is done
Few leaves of fresh basil or salt and pepper

In saucepan, cook bacon. Add butter or oil and onions. When lightly browned, add mushrooms and garlic, then pork and beef. After a few minutes add wine and then the rest of spices, tomatoes and liquid. Cook slowly for about 2 hours. Before serving, add parsley.

Palm Beach Kennel Club Chef

218

MEAT BALLS AND SPAGHETTI SAUCE

3 6-ounce cans tomato paste (Contadina)
9 tomato paste cans of water
1 #2 can whole tomatoes
1 medium onion, chopped
8 cloves garlic, chopped fine
1 teaspoon dried mint (or 2 or 3 sprigs fresh mint)
1 teaspoon parsley

1 teaspoon basil leaves
1 teaspoon oregano
1 teaspoon rosemary
3 bay leaves
½ cup sugar
1 7-ounce can mushrooms
2 teaspoons hot sauce
Salt and pepper
2 tablespoons Worcestershire sauce

Meat Balls:

1½ pounds ground beef
1 onion, finely chopped
4 tablespoons bell pepper, chopped
2 eggs

1 cup bread crumbs
3 tablespoons Parmesan cheese
3 medium garlic cloves, pressed
Salt and pepper

Combine all sauce ingredients in saucepan and cook for 3 hours, adding more water if necessary.

For meat balls, combine remaining ingredients and shape into balls. Fry quickly until outside browns. Add to sauce and cook together 3 more hours.

Mrs. Frank Steudlein

Copies of this recipe have been requested 30 to 40 times.

THE BEST SPAGHETTI SAUCE

1 cup onion, diced
4 cloves garlic, diced
1 cup parsley, chopped
2 bay leaves
¾ cup olive oil
7 cups tomatoes
2 peppercorns
2 whole cloves
1 teaspoon oregano (optional)

¼ teaspoon nutmeg
¼ teaspoon red pepper
3 teaspoons salt
½ teaspoon black pepper
3-pound English cut roast
2 cups mushroom slices
1 pound ground beef, browned
1 small can tomato paste

Sauté onion, garlic, parsley and bay leaf in hot oil. Add tomatoes, peppercorns, cloves, oregano, nutmeg, red pepper, salt and pepper. Add roast and simmer 2 or 3 hours. About 30 minutes before ready, add mushrooms, ground beef and tomato paste.

Billy and Barbara Mills

SPAGHETTI SAUCE

1 pound ground chuck	1 can (1 pound, 13 ounce) tomatoes
2 teaspoons garlic salt	or tomato sauce
2 packages French's spaghetti	1 6-ounce can tomato paste
seasoning mix	1½ teaspoons cinnamon
Onion powder or finely chopped	1½ teaspoons chili powder
onion	1 teaspoon salt
1 can tomato soup (do not dilute)	⅛ teaspoon pepper

Brown ground chuck. Drain, leaving 2 tablespoons of oil. Add garlic salt, spaghetti seasoning and onion powder while browning. Add soup, tomatoes, and tomato paste. Add cinnamon, chili powder, salt and pepper. Cook all day on low heat. *Yields 6 cups.*

Marilyn Baddour Aaron

GREEK SPAGHETTI

2 small onions, chopped	1 small can tomato sauce
2 cloves garlic, diced	1 tomato sauce can of water
½ teaspoon rosemary leaves	16 ounces spaghetti
½ stick oleo	1 can cream of mushroom soup
2 pounds ground meat	1 pound Velveeta cheese, grated
½ cup sherry or cooking wine	Black olives, sliced (optional)
1 #303 can stewed tomatoes	

Cook onions, garlic, and rosemary in oleo until clear. In separate pan, brown meat. Add to onions. Add sherry, tomatoes, tomato sauce and water. Cook uncovered about 2 hours on low. Cook spaghetti. Grease two 2-quart casseroles. In each, place a layer of spaghetti, layer of sauce, layer of soup, and layer of cheese. Top with olives. Bake at 325° for 20 minutes.

Mrs. George Moore, Jr.

SPAGHETTI CASSEROLE

2 tablespoons oil	1 teaspoon salt
1 onion, chopped	1 pound noodles, cooked and
2 pounds ground chuck	drained
3 pints meatless mushroom	Seasoned salt
spaghetti (I use Ragu)	1 pound Cheddar cheese, grated

In oil, brown onion and meat, drain, add spaghetti sauce and salt. In baking dish, arrange half of noodles, half of sauce and half of cheese, sprinkle with seasoned salt. Make another layer of noodles and sauce. Top with cheese. Bake at 350° until hot and bubbly. *Serves 8 to 10.*

Syble Bollinger

LASAGNE

4	tablespoons vegetable oil	2	28-ounce cans tomatoes
1½	cups onion, chopped	1	15-ounce can tomato sauce
1	tablespoon garlic, chopped	1	6-ounce can tomato paste
1½	pounds ground chuck	1	cup water
1	teaspoon oregano leaves	1	pound Ricotta cheese
1	teaspoon basil leaves	2	eggs
1	bay leaf	½	cup parsley
2	teaspoons sugar	12	ounces Mozzarella cheese
2	teaspoons salt	8	tablespoons Parmesan cheese
1¼	teaspoons pepper	1	1-pound box lasagne noodles

Heat oil, add onion and garlic. Sauté over medium heat 5 minutes. Add meat and cook until brown. Break up large clumps of meat. Stir in oregano, basil, bay leaf, sugar, 1 teaspoon salt and ½ teaspoon pepper. Add tomatoes, tomato sauce, tomato paste, and water. (Break up tomatoes in blender.) Heat to boiling, reduce heat and simmer uncovered 60 minutes. Stir occasionally. Meanwhile, make Ricotta filling: In a large bowl, combine Ricotta, eggs, 1¼ teaspoons salt and ¾ teaspoon pepper. Beat with spoon until smooth. Stir in parsley, 8 ounces of Mozzarella, diced, and 4 tablespoons Parmesan. Set aside. Cook lasagne noodles and drain. Preheat oven to 350°. Lightly grease two 7x11x2 baking dishes. Spoon a little meat sauce in the bottom of each. Layer noodles, cheese mixture, sauce in pan, ending with sauce. Sprinkle with remaining cheese and top with remaining Mozzarella cheese, sliced. Bake 45-60 minutes. Remove from oven and set 5 minutes. You may prepare ahead and refrigerate before baking. When you do, add 15 minutes to baking time.

Sue Presley

LASAGNA WITH SPINACH

2	pounds pork and beef, ground	1	package lasagna noodles
2	envelopes Lowry's spaghetti mix	1	package frozen spinach, thawed
2	small onions, chopped		and drained
1	tablespoon salt	3	large eggs, beaten
	Garlic salt to taste	2	cups small curd cottage cheese
1	large can tomatoes	½	pound Mozzarella cheese
1	large can tomato paste	½	cup Parmesan cheese

Brown meat in skillet. Add spaghetti mix, onions, salt, garlic salt, tomatoes, and tomato paste. Cook 30 minutes. Cook lasagna noodles according to package instructions. Combine spinach with eggs and cottage cheese. In baking dish layer sauce, noodles, cottage cheese mixture and cheeses. Bake at 350° for 30 minutes. Let set 10 minutes before cutting.

Joyce T. Ferguson

MEXICAN PLATE

Fritos or tortillas
1 cup ground chuck
Celery
1 teaspoon salt
Pepper
Whole onions

Bay leaves
Oregano
3 tablespoons onions, finely chopped
4 tablespoons lettuce, chopped
1 medium tomato, chopped
2 tablespoons sharp cheese, grated

Sauce:

1 package enchilada sauce mix
1 can enchilada sauce

1 can chili (no beans)

Cover dinner plate with thin layer of fritos or tortillas. Cook ground chuck with celery, salt, pepper, whole onions, bay leaves and oregano. Spread over chips. Sprinkle with onions. Cover with lettuce and then with tomato. Sprinkle with cheese. Heat enchilada sauce mix, chili, and enchilada sauce in double boiler. Pour one cup over plate. *Makes one serving.*

Mrs. John Cooper

MEXICAN CASSEROLE

1 cup rice
1 pound ground beef
1 medium onion, chopped
2 tablespoons shortening

1 large can or jar of taco sauce
1 can pinto beans
1 can tomato soup
Slices of cheese

Cook rice. Brown beef and onion in shortening. Remove from heat and add taco sauce, beans, soup, and cooked rice. Mix well. Transfer to baking dish and cover with slices of chese. Bake at 350° until cheese melts.

Debbie West

FRIED RICE AND MEAT

1 medium onion, chopped
2 tablespoons oil
½ pound beef, finely chopped

4 cups cooked rice, cooled
2 tablespoons soy sauce
1 egg, beaten

Heat oil in large fry pan. Add onion and meat. Cook and stir over medium heat until onion is tender. Add rice and soy sauce. Lower heat and cook 10 minutes. Stir egg into rice mixture. Cook and stir 5 minutes. *Serves 4.*

Charles Baddour

MOCK FILET MIGNON

1 ½ pounds ground beef
2   cups cooked rice
1   cup onion, minced
1   clove garlic, crushed
2   tablespoons Worcestershire
     sauce

1 ½ teaspoons salt
¼   teaspoon pepper
8   slices bacon
Mushroom sauce (recipe below)

Combine meat with rice and seasonings. Divide into eight parts and form into patties, about three-quarter inch thick. Wrap bacon around each and fasten with toothpicks. Place on ungreased baking sheet and bake at 450° for 15 minutes. Serve with sauce.

Mushroom Sauce:

1 can cream of mushroom soup   ¼ cup milk

In saucepan, combine soup and milk. Heat thoroughly, stirring often. Makes 1½ cups sauce.

Sarah Smith

GETWELL ROAD MOO-GOO

1 pound round steak or rump
   roast, cubed
2 teaspoons garlic salt
2 tablespoons vegetable oil
3 medium size onions, chopped or
   quartered and sliced
2 bouillon cubes
1 4-ounce can sliced (or pieces and
   stems) mushrooms

2 ½ cups hot water
1   tablespoon cinnamon
1   teaspoon black pepper
1   10-ounce package Chinese style
     vegetables, Birds Eye brand
1   10-ounce package Japanese style
     stir fry vegetables, Birds Eye
     brand (discard package of
     seasoning)

Sprinkle meat with garlic salt and let set for 3-5 minutes. Put oil, onions, bouillon cubes, mushrooms, and meat in large skillet or Dutch oven and cook until onions are in a transparent state. Add water. Blend in cinnamon and pepper and cook for 5 minutes. Add vegetables and cook on medium heat for approximately 15 minutes or until vegetables are nearly done. Cover and simmer for 5 minutes. Serve over Uncle Bens long grain rice. Use 1 cup uncooked rice using directions on box for cooking. Steak can be substituted with chicken or veal.

Charles Baddour

A dieter's delight!

MEAT CROQUETTES

2 cups cooked meat (any kind)
1 teaspoon chopped parsley
½ teaspoon salt
⅛ teaspoon pepper
2 tablespoons butter
2 tablespoons flour

½ cup stock or water
½ cup mushrooms, chopped
1 egg yolk
1 egg beaten with 2 tablespoons oil
Bread crumbs

Grind meat, add parsley, salt and pepper. Melt butter in large skillet, stir in flour and add stock or water. Blend well. Add meat and mushrooms. Simmer 10 minutes or until very thick. Cool and add egg yolk. Form into balls or ovals. Dip in the egg and oil mixture and roll in bread crumbs. Fry in deep fat until golden brown.

Billy and Barbara Mills

STUFFED GREEN PEPPERS

4 medium size green peppers
1 pound ground beef
1 medium onion, chopped

⅓ cup cooked rice
¼ cup steak sauce (best is Heinz 57)
¼ cup tomato ketchup

Slice stem ends from peppers; scoop out seeds. Blanch in boiling salted water 5 minutes; drain well. Combine ground beef, onion, rice, steak sauce and ketchup. Stuff peppers. Arrange in greased baking dish. Top with extra sauce, if desired. Bake in 350° oven 45-50 minutes or until meat is cooked. *Makes 4 servings.*

Cheryl Grace

HAMBURGER CHEESE NOODLE CASSEROLE

1 8-ounce package noodles
1½ pounds ground chuck
1 tablespoon butter
Salt and pepper
2 8-ounce cans tomato sauce
1 cup cottage cheese

1 8-ounce package cream cheese
½ cup sour cream
⅓ cup onion, chopped
1 tablespoon green pepper, chopped
2 tablespoons butter, melted

Cook noodles. Brown ground chuck in 1 tablespoon butter; add salt and pepper to taste. Stir in tomato sauce. In a bowl combine cottage cheese, cream cheese, sour cream, onion, and green pepper. Grease a 2-quart casserole. Put half the noodles in the bottom. Cover with cheese mixture. Spread remaining noodles over. Pour melted butter over, then meat mixture. Cook for 20 minutes at 350°. If prepared early and refrigerated, bring to room temperature before cooking.

Doris Lanford

VEGETABLE-MEAT CASSEROLE

1   pound ground steak
1   onion, sliced
¼   cup butter
3-4 raw carrots, thinly sliced

2-3 potatoes, thinly sliced
2   cans tomato juice
Salt and pepper
Dash of butter

Brown meat and onions in butter. Place in greased casserole. Add in layers, the carrots and potatoes. Pour tomato juice on top. Season with salt and pepper. Dot generously with butter. Bake at 350° for 1 hour.

Vera Glick

GRANDMOTHER'S CASSEROLE

1   pound ground chuck
2   tablespoons shortening
1   medium onion, chopped
¼   cup green peppers, chopped
2   medium cans tomatoes
1   tablespoon ketchup

1   tablespoon steak sauce
5   ounces elbow macaroni
Salt and pepper
1   can cream of mushroom soup
1   cup grated cheese

Brown ground chuck in shortening in heavy skillet, add onion and peppers and let simmer for about 5 minutes. Add tomatoes, ketchup and steak sauce and simmer for 3 minutes. Cook macaroni according to package directions. Combine macaroni and ground beef mixture in baking dish, season to taste, gently spoon in soup and mix lightly. Sprinkle cheese on top and bake at 350° for 30 minutes. *Serves 6.*

Mary Simpson

CASSEROLE ITALIANO

4   cups elbow macaroni
2   medium onions, chopped
2   tablespoons butter
1   pound ground beef
1   teaspoon salt

¼   teaspoon pepper
¼   teaspoon garlic salt
2   cups sharp Cheddar cheese,
     shredded
2   8-ounce cans tomato sauce

Cook and drain macaroni. Sauté onion in butter, then add ground beef, salt, pepper, and garlic salt. Cook until browned. Mix all ingredients together. Put in a 4-quart casserole dish. Bake at 325° for 30 minutes.

Gloria Riley

225

CANTONESE CASSEROLE

1½ pounds ground beef	1 16-ounce can bean sprouts (or
1 10-ounce package green peas,	fresh)
thawed	1 4-ounce can mushroom bits and
2½ cups celery, thinly sliced	pieces, drained
1 large onion, diced	1 4-ounce can shoestring potatoes or
1 green pepper, diced	5-ounce can chow mein noodles
1 can cream of mushroom soup	
1 8½-ounce can water chestnuts,	
sliced	

Brown ground beef. Put beef in 3-quart casserole and add green peas, celery, onion, green pepper, soup, water chestnuts, bean sprouts and mushrooms. Mix and bake uncovered for 30-40 minutes at 375°. Top with shoestring potatoes or chow mein noodles. *Serves 4-6.*

Charles MacCracken

This is a pseudo Chinese dish that is easy to throw together.

ROUND STEAK CASSEROLE *(For Crock Pot)*

2 pounds round steak, ½ inch thick	1 can French-style green beans,
Garlic salt	drained
Salt and pepper	1 10-ounce can tomato soup
1 onion, thinly sliced	1 pound can tomatoes, peeled and
3-4 potatoes, peeled and quartered	whole
(optional)	

Season round steak lightly with garlic salt, and salt and pepper. Cut in serving pieces and place in crock pot with onion which has been separated into rings. Add potatoes and green beans. Top with soup and tomatoes. Cover and cook on low for 8 hours. Remove cover during last half hour if too liquid. To cook in 2-quart crock pot, reduce ingredients slightly. Serve over rice.

Betty Highfill

CORN PONE PIE

2 pounds ground beef	1 pint tomato juice
1 onion	cornbread batter
2 cans great northern beans	

Brown meat and onion. Add beans and juice. Bake at 350° for 30 minutes or until firm. Put cornbread batter on top and put back in oven for 30-35 minutes until cornbread is done.

Mrs. Jimmy Wagner

7-RIB PARTY PORK

1 7-rib pork loin roast,
   boned
Garlic salt

$10,000 Bar-B-Q sauce (see
   page 73)
Kraft Bar-B-Q sauce

Ask your butcher to bone the roast and cut away all but the loin. Sprinkle generously with garlic salt. Place roast, fat side up, on a rack in 9x13 pan. Add water to top of rack. Roast at 375° for 1 hour and 15 minutes. Baste with $10,000 Bar-B-Q sauce every 15 minutes, turning roast over each time. Remove from heat and cool for 1 hour. Slice in ¼" slices and baste well with Kraft Bar-B-Q sauce. Stack the sliced meat in a baking pan, cover with foil and place in 150° oven 1 hour. Can be cooked on the grill using the same method.

Charles Baddour

Also good for sandwiches.

APPLE STUFFED PORK ROAST

4-4½ pound pork rib roast
¾ cup celery, chopped
½ cup onion, chopped
6 tablespoons butter or margarine
3 cups herb-seasoned stuffing mix

1½ cups apple, pared and chopped
¾ cup water
½ teaspoon salt
½ teaspoon dried rosemary, crushed

Rib roast should have backbone loosened and 8 pockets cut. Cook celery and onion in butter until tender but not brown. In mixing bowl, toss together stuffing mix, apple, water, salt, rosemary, and celery mixture. Stuff about ⅓ cup mixture into each pocket of the roast. Place roast, fat side up, in an open roasting pan. Roast in 325° oven 2½ hours, until meat thermometer registers 170°. Bake the remaining stuffing in a small casserole for the last 30 minutes of the roasting time. Remove backbone from the roast and serve. Serves 8.

Mrs. James H. Wright

BARBEQUED RIBS

3-4 pounds ribs
2 onions, chopped
2 tablespoons vinegar
2 tablespoons Worcestershire
1 tablespoon salt
½ teaspoon red pepper

¾ cup catsup
¾ cup water (more if needed)
1 teaspoon paprika
½ teaspoon black pepper
1 teaspoon chili powder

Sprinkle ribs with salt. Brown ribs. Mix remaining ingredients to make sauce. Pour sauce over browned ribs and cook until tender on top of stove at low heat. Can use pork chops instead of ribs.

Earline Whitfield

SAUCY SPARERIBS

2 ½-3 pounds spareribs
¼ cup oil
½ cup onions, sliced
½ cup water
½ cup catsup
¼ cup vinegar

2 tablespoons brown sugar
1 teaspoon salt
1 tablespoon Worcestershire sauce
1 teaspoon dry mustard
½ teaspoon paprika

Cut spareribs into serving pieces. Brown on all sides in oil in Corningware or oven-proof pan. Remove from heat. Add onions. Combine remaining ingredients and pour over spareribs. Cover. Marinate in refrigerator at least 2 hours, or overnight. Place covered skillet in preheated 350° oven and bake 1¾ hours. Spoon sauce over ribs 2 or 3 times during baking. Remove cover, wipe off edges of dish with a damp paper towel. Turn on broiler and crisp for 5 minutes. *Serves 6.*

Mrs. Jimmy Lemons

CHARLES' RIBS

4 sides of ribs
Garlic salt

$10,000 Bar-B-Q sauce (page 73)

Choose small ribs for best flavor. Rub both sides of ribs generously with garlic salt. Place ribs, bone side down, over a glowing fire on the grill. Turn often, basting each time with $10,000 Bar-B-Q sauce. When the meat has pulled away from the bone, move to cooler side of the grill. Stack them on top of each other, continue to baste, and let them absorb the smoke for 30 minutes. Baste again and place ribs in baking dish. Cover tightly with aluminum foil, and place in 150° oven for 1 hour.

Charles Baddour

PORK AND SAUERKRAUT

6 large shoulder pork chops
2 quarts sauerkraut
2 tablespoons caraway seeds

½ cup catsup
½ cup brown sugar
Pork rind (optional)

Brown pork chops. In saucepan, combine sauerkraut, caraway seeds, catsup, brown sugar and pork rind. Simmer slowly for 1 hour. Add the pork and simmer another hour. Serves 6. (Flavor is better the second day.)

Charles MacCracken

Many find sauerkraut too bitter – this sweetens it up some.

MARY'S PORK CHOPS

4 extra thick pork chops (center
    cut – ½ to ¾ inch thick)

½ cup soy sauce
Pepper

Marinate pork chops in soy sauce at least four hours. Remove and place on broiler. Sprinkle pepper on both sides (no salt as soy sauce is quite salty). Broil until nice and brown (6-8 minutes). Turn and broil for another 6-8 minutes or until brown. Serves 4.

Mary Simpson

PORK CHOPS

6 pork chops
Salt and pepper
2 tablespoons shortening
1 cup uncooked rice

4 cups beef bouillon
½ cup onion, diced
½ cup green pepper, chopped
¼ teaspoon thyme

Sprinkle pork chops with salt and pepper. Brown in shortening. Remove pork chops and place them in baking pan. Add rice to the grease, and brown, stirring often. Spoon off excess grease and add bouillon, onion, green pepper, and thyme. Stir, and add to pork chops. Cover, and bake at 350° for 1½ hours. Check occasionally to see if more water should be added.

Brenda Cole
Jessie Morgan

PORK CHOPS ITALIAN

4-6 pork chops
1   can cream style corn
2   tablespoons green peppers,
     cut into small pieces
1   tablespoon onion, chopped

1   cup soft bread crumbs
1   egg, beaten
2   tablespoons butter, melted
Salt and pepper

Brown pork chops lightly. Salt and pepper to taste. Place pork chops in baking pan and cover with combined corn, peppers, onion, bread crumbs, egg, butter, and salt and pepper. Add just enough water to cover bottom of pan. Bake 45 minutes to 1 hour in 350° oven.

Phoebe Enochs

BAKED PORK CHOPS

4   lean pork chops, cut ¾ inch
     thick
Salt and pepper
Flour
½ cup cooking oil

1   green pepper, sliced in rings
1   cup cooked rice
4   slices Velveeta cheese
4   slices onion
1   can tomato paste

Salt, pepper and flour pork chops on both sides. Brown in hot oil, and lay in large baking dish. Place a slice of green pepper on each and fill with 4 tablespoons rice for each chop. Top with cheese slices and onion rings. Spread tomato paste on top. Cover dish with foil, and bake at 375° until tender, about 1 hour.

Nona Ash

SCALLOPED POTATOES/PORK CHOPS

6   pork chops
1   teaspoon salt
Pepper
2   tablespoons oleo

2   tablespoons flour
2½ cups milk
6   medium potatoes, sliced
2   medium onions, sliced

Season pork chops with salt and pepper. Brown in frying pan. Remove from pan. Melt butter. Add flour and blend well. Add milk slowly. Cook until thick, stirring constantly. Alternately place potatoes, onions, cream sauce and pork chops in greased casserole. Cover. Bake 1½ hours at 350° until tender. Uncover the last 15 minutes to brown. *Serves 6.*

Helen Robinson

CANTONESE SWEET AND SOUR PORK

2   pounds pork, cooked and cut
    into 2-inch cubes
3   tablespoons soy sauce
2   tablespoons cornstarch
2   cups cooking oil
1   medium onion, sliced very thin

4   carrots, sliced in rings
1   large bell pepper, cut in 1-inch
    squares
1   20-ounce can pineapple chunks
    Sweet and Sour sauce (recipe below)

Dredge pork with mixture of soy sauce and cornstarch. Heat oil until very hot and cook meat until brown. Remove meat from oil and drain. Reheat pan and add onion, carrots, bell pepper and pineapple. Sauté until onion is limp. Add sweet and sour sauce and pork, and heat thoroughly. Serve with rice. *Serves 4-6.*

Sweet and Sour Sauce:

¾   cup granulated sugar
¼   cup soy sauce
4   tablespoons cornstarch

⅔   cup water
½   cup vinegar
⅛   teaspoon ginger

In a saucepan, blend all ingredients together and cook until thick.

Mrs. William M. Forman

SWEET AND SOUR PORK

1½ pounds pork, cubed
    Salt and pepper
½   cup barbecue sauce
½   cup pineapple syrup
¼   cup vinegar

1   tablespoon cornstarch
1   20-ounce can pineapple chunks
1   green pepper
    Cooked rice

Brown meat in a small amount of oil and season. Stir in combined barbecue sauce, pineapple syrup, vinegar, and cornstarch; cover and simmer 35 minutes. Add pineapple and sliced green pepper. Simmer 10 minutes. Serve over rice. *Serves 4.*

Carol Higgins

Make plenty – they'll want seconds.

OVEN KALUA PORK

1 tablespoon rock salt	1 teaspoon minced garlic
1 teaspoon monosodium glutamate (msg)	1 tablespoon grated fresh ginger (or 1 teaspoon grated dried ginger)
3 tablespoons soy sauce	3 to 4 pounds pork butt, slashed

Combine first five ingredients. Rub over pork. Line 9x13 pan with aluminum foil, allowing foil to extend generously over one end. Place pork on foil. Fold foil over the pork, sealing well. Roast in 325° oven 4 hours. To serve: Shred with 2 forks or with fingers instead of carving.

Mildred Earney

We ate this in Hawaii, only they cook theirs in an open pit.

CREOLE PORK AND SPAGHETTI

4 onions, minced	2 cups cheese, grated
2 pounds pork shoulder, ground	1 teaspoon salt
1 quart cooked spaghetti	1 cup dry bread crumbs
1½ cups cooked tomatoes	¼ cup oleo

Brown onions and meat in skillet; mix with spaghetti, tomatoes, cheese and salt. Place in greased baking dish. Sprinkle crumbs on top; dot with oleo and bake at 350° for 30 minutes. *Serves 8 to 10.*

William Sanford

HAM ROYALE

5-pound ham
¾ cup orange juice
½ cup sherry
1 cup brown sugar

Dash ground cloves
2 tablespoons prepared mustard
Cornstarch
Water

Prick holes in ham. Combine orange juice, sherry, brown sugar, cloves, and mustard and make marinade. Marinate for several hours or overnight, turning occasionally. Bake ham at 325° for 1¼ hours, basting with marinade. Remove ham to warm platter. Make sauce as follows: Degrease pan juices and measure. For each cup of juice, thicken with 1 tablespoon cornstarch mixed with 1 tablespoon water. Heat and stir while sauce thickens.

Rosemond Deeb

TOMATO-HAM BUFFET RING

2 envelopes plain gelatin
1¼ cups water
1 can tomato soup
8-ounce package cream cheese
2 tablespoons lemon juice

1 tablespoon onion, grated
½ cup mayonnaise
2 teaspoons prepared mustard
2 cups ham (or chicken or crab),
cooked and ground

Soften gelatin in ¼ cup water. Combine soup and 1 cup water, heat to boil, remove from heat. Add gelatin and cream cheese, blend thoroughly, cool. Add lemon juice, onion, mayonnaise, mustard and meat. Pour in mold and chill til firm. Serve on lettuce, garnish with stuffed olives. *Makes 10-12 servings.*

William B. Gill

233

HAM LOAF

¾ pound cured ham, ground
¾ pound fresh pork, ground
1 egg, beaten
¼ cup milk
½ cup bread crumbs
¼ can tomato soup

¼ teaspoon paprika
¼ teaspoon salt
1 cup water
½ onion, chopped
Mustard sauce (recipe below)

Combine ham, pork, egg, milk, bread crumbs, soup, paprika, and salt. Shape into loaf. Place in greased pan. Add onions and water. Bake at 350° for 1½ hours. Serve with mustard sauce. *Serves 6.*

Mustard Sauce:

¼ cup tomato soup
¼ cup prepared mustard
¼ cup vinegar

¼ cup sugar
¼ cup shortening
2 egg yolks

Combine in top of double boiler. Cook until thick. Serve with ham loaf.

Phoebe Enochs

CRÊPES FILLED WITH HAM & SWISS CHEESE

1 cup flour
1 teaspoon salt
2 eggs

1 cup milk
2 tablespoons vegetable oil
1 tablespoon butter

Beat all ingredients except butter in blender. Chill one hour or longer. Mix again. Add milk if batter is too thick. Turn stove burner on high for a few minutes. Reduce heat to medium and cook crêpes. *Makes about 20.*

Ham and Cheese Filling:

1 cup minus 1 tablespoon butter
1 cup minus 1 tablespoon flour
5 cups milk

Dash of salt
1½ cups shredded Swiss cheese
1½ cups diced cooked ham

Melt butter. Stir in flour when foamy, add milk and cook, while stirring, til very thick. Do not boil. Add salt, cheese and ham, while hot. Spoon filling onto crêpes and roll. Arrange in baking dish and spoon some filling over top. Cook in 400° oven til very hot, 15-20 minutes.

Mrs. William F. Ledsinger

SAUSAGE BUFFET CASSEROLE

2 cups rice
2 envelopes chicken noodle
   soup mix
9 cups boiling water
2 pounds bulk sausage

1 bunch celery, chopped
1 green pepper, chopped
2 onions, chopped
1¼ cups whole blanched almonds
   (halved or slivered)

Add rice and soup mix to boiling water. Cover and boil for 30 minutes. Brown the sausage. Drain off the grease and add celery, green pepper, and onions. Sauté with the sausage until soft. Add rice mixture. Stir in 1 cup of almonds. Place in casserole and top with remaining almonds. Bake at 350° for 30 minutes. *Makes 16 generous servings.*

Dena Burns

SAUERKRAUT AND SAUSAGE

1 quart freshly cut kraut
1 bay leaf
2 pounds of pork / beef sausage
   (Ekrich, Hillshire or Polish)

1 medium onion, chopped
¾ stick butter or margarine
1½ tablespoons flour

Rinse kraut in colander, boil ½ hour with bay leaf and sausage in stainless steel utensil or 12 minutes in pressure cooker. In small skillet, sauté onions in butter until brown, stirring often. When brown, add the flour and brown. Add the mixture to the kraut, stir and heat a few more minutes. Serve with mashed potatoes.

Bernice Wienstroer
Good the second day, so don't be afraid to increase the quantity.

RICE-SAUSAGE CASSEROLE

1 package long grain and
   wild rice
1 pound pork sausage
1 can mushroom soup

½ cup milk
1 3-ounce can mushrooms
2 tablespoons Worcestershire sauce

Cook rice according to instructions on box. Meanwhile, fry sausage and drain. To sausage, add the mushroom soup, milk, mushrooms and Worcestershire sauce. Stir all together, then add rice. Bake at 350° for 40 minutes.

Mrs. Harold Riggan

DACUS SAUSAGE

6 pounds Boston Butt pork,
    ground

2 ounces Old Fashion Pork Sausage
    Seasoning

Mix well. Refrigerate at least 2 hours before using. For each additional 3 pounds of meat, add 1 ounce of seasoning. (Seasoning can be bought at Liberty Cash Grocery in Collierville, Tn and at Liberty Cash Grocery #88 at 2178 S. Third St. in Memphis, Tn.)

This sausage was made for many years at the old Dacus Lumber Company store – West Memphis, Ark.

CALIFORNIA BEANS & WEINERS

¾ cup apple, chopped into large
    chunks
½ cup onion, chopped
1 #303 can pork and beans
¼ teaspoon Tabasco

¼ cup catsup
1 teaspoon dry mustard
1 tablespoon Worcestershire sauce
4 smoked sausage links (about 1
    cup), thinly sliced

Mix all ingredients in 1½-quart casserole or bean pot. Bake uncovered at 375° for 1 hour.

June Spotts

"REUBEN" CASSEROLE

1 14- or 16-ounce can sauerkraut
    (about 2¼ cups)
⅓ cup bottled Thousand Island
    dressing
1 12-ounce can luncheon meat or
    hot dogs, thinly sliced

1 8-ounce package Swiss or
    Muenster cheese slices
About ½ 8-ounce loaf party rye bread
    slices
1 tablespoon butter or margarine,
    melted

About 45 minutes before serving, preheat oven to 400°. In 13" by 9" baking dish, with fork, stir sauerkraut with its liquid and Thousand Island dressing; top with a layer of luncheon meat. Bake 15 minutes until bubbly hot. Remove dish from oven. Place cheese on top of meat in a single layer; top with a layer of bread. Lightly brush bread with butter or margarine. Bake 10 minutes longer or until bread is crisp. *Makes 8 servings.*

Amy Denny

Great for teenagers!

MARSALA SCALLOPINI OF VEAL

2 pounds veal steak, cut in 1½-inch pieces	2 tablespoons flour
1 small onion, finely chopped	2 teaspoons salt
1 clove garlic, minced	¼ teaspoon pepper
2 tablespoons butter	½ cup Marsala wine
	½ pound fresh mushrooms, sliced

Brown veal, onion and garlic in butter. Sprinkle with flour, salt and pepper. Add wine, cover and simmer about 20 minutes. Add mushrooms and continue to cook about 10 minutes. Serve with Risotto.

Risotto:

1 small onion, finely chopped	2½ cups chicken broth (made from Spice Islands stock)
4 tablespoons butter	
1 cup rice	Grated Parmesan cheese
½ teaspoon salt	

Sauté onion in butter until golden brown. Add uncooked rice and continue heating until rice is slightly browned, stirring constantly. Add salt to boiling chicken broth, then add rice. Cover and reduce heat to low and cook 18 minutes, or until rice is tender and excess liquid has evaporated. Serve hot, topped or mixed with grated Parmesan cheese.

Lee Ellis

VEAL POCKETBOOKS

6 thin veal steaks (about 1½ pounds)	2 tablespoons cooking oil
	1 can cream of mushroom soup
6 slices boiled ham	¾ cup light cream
6 slices Swiss cheese	½ cup Sauterne wine
2 tablespoons flour	3 tablespoons onion, finely chopped
¼ teaspoon paprika	Hot cooked rice

Trim cheese and ham slices to fit lower half of veal steaks. Fold veal over to enclose cheese and ham, and carefully dip each piece in flour mixed with paprika. Brown slowly until crusty in heated oil, being very careful to keep meat and filling intact. Drain off excess fat in pan. Combine soup, cream, wine and onions. Pour over meat. Cover and cook over low heat for 30 minutes. Serve with hot rice.

Lee Ellis

VEAL DE VERMOUTH

3 pounds veal rump roast,
  boneless
Thin slices pork fat or bacon
Salt

Pepper
1 cup Vermouth
Small baby carrots
2 dozen small white onions

The roast should be rolled and tied. Wrap roast in thin slices of pork fat or bacon slices and salt and pepper to taste. Place roast in a heavy Dutch oven and place in a preheated 350° oven. Baste every 10 minutes or so, each time adding a little dry Vermouth. After about 1 hour, the roast should be sufficiently browned. Add lots of small baby carrots, scraped and cut into thin rounds, and white onions. Spoon some of the sauce over the vegetables, cover with aluminum foil *and* the cover of the Dutch oven. In another 45 minutes, the roast will be ready, juicy and aromatic and the carrots and onions will be lightly caramelized. Can be served very hot or well chilled. If you prefer it hot, let it cool a bit before slicing.

Lee Ellis

STUFFED LEG OF LAMB

1 large leg of lamb
1 pound ground veal
1 pound seasoned pork sausage
½ pound fresh mushrooms
Bread crumbs
Onion
Salt

Pepper
Rosemary
Thyme
¼ cup flour
½ bottle Heinz 57 sauce
½ bottle A-1 Steak sauce
1 jar mint jelly

Have butcher remove bone from meat. Combine veal, sausage, and mushrooms and sauté until lightly browned. Spoon off grease, and drain on paper towel. Mix with bread crumbs, onion, salt, pepper, rosemary and thyme to taste. Stuff in lamb, roll and tie closed. On large piece of heavy foil, sprinkle the flour. Place the lamb on the foil and roll in the flour, covering well. Combine sauces and jelly, mix with a beater, pour over the lamb, and seal foil. Bake at 350° for 3 hours. Pour juices off to make gravy. Spoon off fat, and thicken if needed. Keep lamb warm until ready to serve.

Gloria O'Rourke

GLAZED CORNED BEEF

5 pounds corned beef, brisket or
   rump
1 10-ounce jar apple jelly
1 lemon, rind and juice
1 orange, rind and juice

1 can (1 pound, 13 ounce) apricot
   halves, drained
1 can (1 pound, 4 ounce) pineapple
   chunks, drained

Place corned beef in large kettle. Cover with water and simmer, 3 to 4 hours or until tender. Combine jelly, lemon rind and juice, orange rind and juice in saucepan. Heat until jelly melts. Remove corned beef from water to shallow pan. Arrange apricot halves and pineapple chunks around meat. Baste meat and fruit with half the jelly glaze. Bake at 375° for 25 minutes. Baste again with remaining glaze. Bake 30 minutes longer. Remove all to heated platter and garnish with parsley.

Lee Ellis

CORN BEEF QUICKIE

6-8 English muffins (bakery or
   frozen)
½ cup onion, minced
¼ cup bell pepper, minced
1 can corned beef

Mayonnaise
8 slices American cheese
1 can Campbell's vegetable soup (or
   mushroom, cream of chicken)

Place English muffin halves open face in pyrex dish; toast in oven until brown; remove. Mix together onion, pepper, corned beef and enough mayonnaise to mix well. Shape into patties and brown on both sides in Wesson oil, using a black skillet. Remove and place on the toasted muffins. Make a criss-cross of cheese over each patty. Pour soup over top. Heat in 350° oven until hot.

Fran Hilliard

CHITTERLINGS

10 pounds chitterlings
1 ½ tablespoons salt
½   tablespoon crushed red
    peppers

½ tablespoon black pepper
3 garlic pieces

Wash chitterlings thoroughly. Trim fat, leaving small amount on chitterlings for seasoning. In large saucepan, cover chitterlings with water. Boil chitterlings 10 minutes. Then add all seasoning above. Cook until tender, about 3 to 5 hours. Drain and cut in serving-size pieces. *Makes 6 to 8 servings.*

Pan-Fried Chitterlings:

Dip boiled chitterlings in cornmeal. In skillet, pan-fry chitterlings in hot shortening until brown.

Deep-Fried Chitterlings:

Dip boiled chitterlings in egg, then crushed saltine crackers. Fry in deep hot fat (375°) till brown.

Marion Cox

ARKANSAS CHICKEN

"Streak o' lean" salt pork
Cold water
3 tablespoons honey

Buttermilk
Flour

Have your butcher slice your "streak o' lean" salt pork allowing at least 2 pieces per person. Rinse off in cold water, then put in mixing bowl. Cover with cold water, adding honey. Let set at least 1 hour. Remove one piece at a time and coat with buttermilk, roll in flour and fry in shallow amount of oil until crisp. Delicious with homemade vegetable soup and corn sticks or with just vegetables.

Mrs. Bill Lunsford
My mother used this before she was married; she will be 100 years old this year.

TURNIP GREEN SANDWICH

½ cup turnip greens, cooked
Mustard

2 pieces of dry toast

Put well drained hot turnip greens on toast spread with mustard to make sandwich.

Johnny Veglio

KRAUT KRUGER

Cool Rise White Bread:

5½-6½ cups all purpose flour
2 pkgs. active dry yeast
2 tablespoons sugar
1 tablespoon salt

¼ cup softened margarine or
   shortening
2¼ cups very hot tap water
Cooking oil

Spoon or pour flour into dry measuring cup. Level off and pour measured flour onto wax paper. Combine 2 cups flour, undissolved yeast, sugar and salt in large bowl. Stir well to blend. Add softened margarine. Add hot water to dry ingredients all at once. Beat with electric mixer at medium speed for 2 minutes. Scrape bowl occasionally. Add 1 cup more flour. Beat with electric mixer at high speed for 1 minute or until thick and elastic. Scrape bowl occasionally. Stir in remaining flour gradually with wooden spoon. Use just enough flour to make a soft dough which leaves sides of bowl. Turn out onto floured board. Round up into a ball. Knead 5-10 minutes or until dough is smooth and elastic. Cover with plastic wrap then a towel. Let rest for 20 minutes on board. Punch down. Roll small pieces of dough and fill with kraut mixture. Fold and seal edges. Brush with cooking oil. Cover with plastic wrap and let rise until double in size. Bake at 350 degrees until golden brown approximately 25 minutes. Brush with butter.

Kraut Mixture:

1 or 2 onions
2 lbs. ground chuck or round steak

1 lb. hot sausage
Approximately 2 lb. head cabbage

Brown and drain meat and chopped onion. Add salt and pepper to taste. Chop and steam cabbage. Drain and combine with meat mixture. One onion can be steamed with cabbage. This should be cooled to a comfortable warm before filling buns.

This recipe can be changed to taste, more or less of any ingredient does not change the end results.

Johnnie Mowry

BARBEQUED POT ROAST

4-5 pounds beef pot roast
2 teaspoons salt
¼ teaspoon pepper
2 tablespoons butter
½ cup water
1 8-ounce can tomato sauce
3 medium onions

2 cloves garlic
2 tablespoons brown sugar
½ teaspoon dry mustard
¼ cup vinegar
¼ cup catsup
¼ cup lemon juice
1 tablespoon Worcestershire sauce

Rub pot roast with salt and pepper. Brown all sides in melted butter. Add water, tomato sauce, sliced onions, finely chopped garlic. Cover and cook over low heat for 1½ hours. Mix remaining ingredients together and pour over pot roast. Cook slowly for another 1½ hours or until meat is very tender. Great when served with buttered noodles, asparagus spears, garlic bread and tossed salad.

Lee Ellis

Favorite for all ages.

An expansive greenhouse operation at Baddour Center, which employs many of the residents, produces and/or distributes plants and shrubs. Seasonal and maintenance landscaping of the Center grounds provides employment for those who love the outdoors. Potting soil is made and packaged for wholesale and retail sales. A Lawn and Garden Center complements the retail greenhouse sales on campus and creates even more jobs for the residents.

"There is no unbelief;
Whoever plants a seed beneath the sod
And waits to see it push away the clod,
He trusts in God."
–"There Is No Unbelief," Lizzie York Case

SWEETS

Greenhouse

MY GRANDCHILDREN'S FAVORITE APPLE CAKE

3 cups flour
2 cups sugar
1 cup oil
4 eggs
¼ cup orange juice

2 ½ teaspoons vanilla
2 ½ teaspoons baking powder
2 or 3 apples
Cinnamon

Mix the flour, sugar, oil, eggs, juice, vanilla and baking powder together and beat with mixer at medium speed for 2 minutes. Grease a tube pan and put half the batter in; arrange thin slices of apples around the pan; sprinkle with cinnamon and a little sugar. Put the rest of the batter on top and repeat apples, cinnamon and sugar. Bake about 1½ hours at 325°. When almost cool, put a powdered sugar glaze on top. Do not cover. This has a cookie-like crunchy crust. Freezes well. Is very good with no icing.

Irma Jo Williams

FRESH APPLE CAKE

3 cups apples, chopped
2 cups sugar
1 ½ cups oil
3 eggs, beaten

1 teaspoon soda
1 teaspoon salt
3 cups plain flour, sifted
2 teaspoons vanilla

Mix or fold together apples, sugar and oil. Then add eggs, soda, salt, flour and vanilla. Put in a large greased rectangular pan. Put in cold oven and turn to 325°. Bake 1 hour.

Icing:

1 cup light brown sugar
1 stick butter

¼ cup canned cream
1 teaspoon vanilla

Combine sugar, butter and cream in saucepan and heat until smooth. Remove from heat and stir in vanilla. Stick holes in top of cake and spread with icing.

Patricia Maxwell

JEWISH APPLE CAKE

5 apples, sliced	½ teaspoon salt
1¼ cups sugar	1 cup salad oil
½ teaspoon cinnamon	⅓ cup juice of orange
3 cups all purpose flour	2 teaspoons vanilla
1⅓ cups sugar	4 eggs
3 teaspoons baking powder	

Combine apples, sugar and cinnamon. Set aside. Mix flour, sugar and baking powder. Make a well, place remaining ingredients into it. Stir until batter is smooth. Pour half of batter into greased tube pan. Pat apples onto batter. Pour remaining batter over apples. Bake 50-60 minutes at 350°.

Pat Wheeler

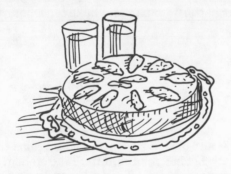

OLD FASHIONED STACK CAKE

2½ cups dried apples	1 teaspoon baking powder
Sugar and cinnamon to taste	¼ teaspoon soda
½ cup shortening	½ teaspoon salt
1 cup sugar	½ cup milk
1 egg	¼ cup buttermilk
1 teaspoon vanilla	4 tablespoons butter, melted
4 cups flour	

Soak apples overnight and cook until tender. Add sugar and cinnamon, then mash. Cream shortening and sugar, add beaten egg and vanilla. Sift dry ingredients together and add alternately with milk to creamed mixture until soft dough is formed. Divide dough into 6 equal parts putting each in bottom of greased 9-inch pie pan. (This will be a very thin crust.) Bake at 400° for 12 minutes or until dough is light brown. Remove from pan immediately and brush with melted butter. Put hot fruit between each layer, on top and sides. Keep in tight container for 12 to 24 hours before serving. Keep refrigerated. This is good cold or hot, plain or with ice cream.

Adele Baddour Lykens

WET WALNUT BANANA CAKE

1½ boxes Duncan Hines Deluxe II banana cake mix	¾ cup oil
	1 cup pear nectar
1 3¾-ounce package instant banana pudding	½ cup water
	6 eggs
1 3¾-ounce package instant French vanilla pudding	2 medium to large bananas, mashed
	1 cup walnuts, chopped

NOTE: ½ box cake mix equals to 2¼ cups

Preheat oven to 325°. Blend cake mix and puddings with oil, nectar and water for 2 minutes at medium speed. Add eggs one at a time, beating well after each addition. Add banana and beat at medium to high speed for 1 minute. Fold in walnuts. Grease and flour a large tube pan and line bottom with wax paper. Pour batter into pan and bake for 1 hour and 15 minutes or until done.

Caramel Icing:

¼ cup milk	2 cups confectioners sugar
½ cup light brown sugar	1 teaspoon vanilla
4 tablespoons oleo	Dash of salt

Put milk, brown sugar and oleo in saucepan and let come to a boil over low heat stirring constantly. Let boil for 1 minute. Take off heat and add confectioner's sugar and beat until smooth. Then add vanilla and dash of salt. Stir well and ice warm cake. If too thick, add more milk. NOTE: If you prefer a darker color, add 1 tablespoon brown sugar.

Charles Baddour

Due to great demand, I'm forced to give out this secret recipe.

BANANA CAKE

¼ pound butter	3 cups flour
½ cup oil	2½ teaspoons cinnamon
2 cups sugar	1½ teaspoons cloves
4 eggs	2 teaspoons soda
2 cups nuts, chopped	½ teaspoon salt
2 cups seedless raisins	6 ripe bananas, creamed

Cream butter and oil and add sugar; cream well. Add well-beaten eggs, and stir in nuts and raisins. Mix flour with spices, soda and salt and add to mixture. Last add creamed bananas. Bake in 250 to 300° oven for 2 hours or more.

Marie Hartfield

Everbody loves this cake.

BANANA SPLIT CAKE

1 stick butter, melted
1 ½ cups graham cracker crumbs
2 egg whites
2 cups confectioners sugar
8-ounce package cream cheese, softeneed

3 or 4 bananas
1 large can crushed pineapple
1 cup chopped nuts
9-ounce carton Cool Whip
½ cup cherries, halved
Chocolate syrup

Combine butter with crumbs and pat in bottom of 9x13" pan. Beat egg whites and sugar til blended. Add cream cheese and beat until smooth. Spread over graham cracker crust. Slice bananas and put a layer on cream cheese mixture. Drain pineapple. Spread evenly over bananas. Sprinkle about ½ to ¾ of the chopped nuts over the pineapple. Spread the Cool Whip evenly over this. Garnish with the rest of the chopped nuts and cherries and drizzle with chocolate syrup. Refrigerate.

Sandra Jones, Rosemond Deeb,
Mrs. R. L. Burns, Mrs. Toney Mobley

BANANA CAKE

¾ cup butter
2 cups sugar
2 eggs
3 cups flour
1 ½ teaspoons baking soda

½ teaspoon salt
1 ⅛ cups buttermilk
½ teaspoon vanilla
1 ½ cups banana (mashed, but not mushy)

Cream butter, add sugar gradually. Beat in eggs one at a time. Sift flour, soda and salt together. Add alternately with buttermilk. Stir in vanilla and bananas. Makes 3 layers. Cook at 350° until light touch of cake springs back. Cool and frost with Crisco Icing.

Crisco Icing:

1 box confectioners sugar
¼ cup Karo light syrup
½ cup Crisco shortening

1 egg
2 teaspoons flavoring
½ teaspoon salt

Beat until creamy. Spread on cool cake.

Mrs. Harold Ashley

STRAWBERRY BANANA CAKE

1 Duncan Hines strawberry cake mix
4 heaping tablespoons Pillsbury butter recipe cake mix
1 package instant banana pudding
1 package Dream Whip

1⅛ cups of water
½ cup + 1 tablespoon Crisco oil
1 teaspoon banana flavoring
4 eggs
1 medium or large banana, mashed to a mushy state

Preheat oven to 300°. Put dry ingredients in large mixing bowl. Add water, oil and flavoring. Mix well. Add eggs one at a time, beating well after each addition. Then add the banana and beat on high speed for 2 minutes. Pour into a well-greased and floured bundt pan and bake at 300° for 65 minutes.

Drizzle:

1 cup confectioners sugar
1½ tablespoons milk
2 teaspoons butter flavoring

1 teaspoon strawberry flavoring
1 drop of red food coloring

Blend together by hand in a mixing bowl and put over slightly warm or cold cake. If you want the drizzle light, use more milk; or if you want it heavier, use less milk.

Charles Baddour

CARROT CAKE

2 cups sugar
1½ cups oil
4 eggs
2¼ cups self-rising flour, sifted

2 teaspoons cinnamon
3 cups carrots, grated
½ cup pecans (optional)

Combine sugar, oil and eggs. Beat at medium speed for 2 minutes. Sift dry ingredients together. Add to mixture and beat at low speed for 1 minute. Add grated carrots and nuts. Spread batter in a greased and floured 13x9½x2 inch pan. Bake at 300° for about 1 hour — until cake tests done with a toothpick. When cool, spread with Cream Cheese Frosting.

Cream Cheese Frosting:

1 8-ounce package cream cheese
1¼ cups butter or margarine

2 teaspoons vanilla
1 pound confectioners sugar

Let cream cheese and butter warm to room temperature. Beat them together and add the vanilla. Gradually beat in sugar. Blend well.

Mrs. E. H. Clarke
Mrs. Jack Atkins, Jr.

CARROT PECAN CAKE

1¼ cups salad oil	2 teaspoons cinnamon
2 cups sugar	1 teaspoon salt
2 cups sifted flour	4 eggs
1 teaspoon baking soda	3 cups carrots, grated
2 teaspoons baking powder	1 cup pecans, finely chopped

Combine oil and sugar, mix well. Sift together dry ingredients. Sift half of dry ingredients into sugar mixture. Blend. Sift in remaining dry ingredients alternately with eggs, one at a time, mixing well after each addition. Add carrots and mix well, then mix in pecans. Pour in three 9″ cake pans. Bake at 325° for 25-30 minutes, or until done.

Coconut Pecan Frosting:

1 cup evaporated milk	1 teaspoon vanilla
1 cup sugar	1⅓ cups coconut
3 egg yolks, slightly beaten	1 cup pecans, chopped
½ cup butter or margarine	

Combine milk, sugar, egg yolks, butter and vanilla in saucepan. Cook and stir over medium heat until thickened — about 12 minutes. Add coconut and pecans. Cool until thick enough to spread — beat occasionally. *Makes 2½ cups.* (If you like a lot of frosting, double this recipe.)

Hazel Smith

MIDGET CHEESECAKE

3 8-ounce packages cream cheese, softened	1 cup sour cream
	¼ cup sugar
5 eggs	½ teaspoon vanilla
1 cup sugar	Strawberry or blueberry preserves
½ teaspoon vanilla	

Midget aluminum foil baking cups "Baker's Choice" brand may be purchased at grocery.

Combine cream cheese, eggs, sugar and vanilla, mixing well and making sure there are no lumps. Drop into baking cups (¾ full) and bake for 30 to 40 minutes at 300°. Do not brown. Allow to cool. Combine sour cream, sugar and vanilla. Top each "midget" with ½ teaspoon mixture, then ½ teaspoon preserves. Bake at 300° for 5 minutes. Cool. These freeze great. To serve, remove from freezer and allow to reach room temperature.

Barbara Petty

HELEN DENEKA'S CHEESE CAKE

Crust:

1 cup enriched flour, sifted	½ cup butter or oleo
¾ cup sugar	1 egg yolk, slightly beaten
1 teaspoon lemon peel, grated	¼ teaspoon vanilla

Combine flour, sugar and lemon peel. Cut in butter until mixture is crumbly. Add egg yolk and vanilla. Blend thoroughly with mixer. Pat ⅓ of dough on bottom of 9-inch spring form pan with sides removed. Bake at 400° for about 6 minutes or until golden. Cool. Butter sides of pan and attach to bottom part. Pat remaining dough evenly on sides to height of about 2 inches.

Cake:

5 8-ounce packages cream cheese	3 tablespoons enriched flour
¼ teaspoon vanilla	¼ teaspoon salt
¾ teaspoon lemon peel, grated	5 eggs plus 2 egg yolks
1¾ cups sugar	¼ cup XX cream

Stir cream cheese to soften. Beat until fluffy. Add vanilla and lemon peel. Mix sugar, flour and salt together. Gradually blend into cheese. Add eggs and yolks, one at a time, beating well after each one. Gently stir in cream. Pour into crust. Bake at 500° for 5 to 8 minutes or until top edge of crust is golden. Reduce oven heat to 200° and bake for 1 hour longer. Remove from oven and cool in the pan for about 3 hours. Remove sides of pan and glaze.

Strawberry Glaze:

2 to 3 cups fresh strawberries	½ to ¾ cup sugar (depending on
1 cup water	amount and the sweetness of
1½ tablespoons cornstarch	berries)

Crush 1 cup strawberries, add the water and cook 2 minutes. Put through sieve. Mix cornstarch with sugar and stir into hot berry mixture. Bring to boiling, stirring constantly. Cook and stir until thick and clear. Cool to room temperature. Place remaining berries on top of cooled cheese cake. Pour glaze over strawberries. Chill about 2 hours.

Variation: Pineapple Glaze:

Mix 3 tablespoons of sugar and 1 tablespoon cornstarch. Stir in 1 cup unsweetened pineapple juice and ¼ teaspoon grated lemon peel. Heat, stirring until comes to boil. Cool to room temperature. Trim dessert with canned crushed pineapple. Spoon glaze over and chill 2 hours.

Special hints for this recipe continued on next page.

Hints:

1. Pat crust over bottom of a spring form pan with sides removed. Bake. When cool, assemble pan and hold onto edge of sides of pan to pat side crust.
2. When pouring cream cheese filling into pan, break any surface bubbles.
3. When the baked cheese cake is thoroughly cool, run spatula around sides to loosen. Open clasp of pan and gently lift off upper part of pan.
4. Border with a swirl of ½ pineapple rings and center with rosy spring strawberries. Spoon glaze over and chill.
5. Be sure after cooling to keep in refrigerator.

Helen Baddour Deneka

MOM'S CHEESECAKE

1 cup chocolate wafers, finely crushed	3 eggs
2 tablespoons sugar	2 tablespoons butter, melted
3 tablespoons butter, melted	2 tablespoons brown sugar, packed
3 8-ounce packages cream cheese	⅓ cup evaporated milk
¾ cup sugar	1 egg, beaten
¼ cup cocoa	½ teaspoon vanilla
2 teaspoons vanilla	½ cup pecans, chopped
	½ cup flaked coconut

Combine crumbs, sugar and butter. Press into bottom of 9-inch spring form pan. Bake at 325° for 10 minutes. Combine cream cheese, sugar, cocoa and vanilla. Add eggs, one at a time, mixing well after each addition. Pour over crumbs. Bake at 350° for 35 minutes. Cool. Remove rim of pan and chill well. Combine butter, brown sugar, milk, egg and vanilla. Cook over low heat, stirring constantly until thickened. Add pecans and coconut. Cool. Spread on top of cheese cake.

Lee Ellis

Handed down from my Pennsylvania grandmother.

CHEESECAKE

Graham cracker crust
3   pounds cream cheese (use
    Philadelphia brand only)
2¼ cups sugar
4½ tablespoons flour

½   teaspoon salt
2   teaspoons vanilla
8   eggs
3   cups whipping cream with 2½ cups
    milk or 5½ cups single x cream

Have largest spring form pan lined with graham cracker crust and refrigerate overnight before baking cake. Cream cheese and sugar by hand with spoon or on very lowest speed on mixer. *Do not over-mix.* Add flour, salt and vanilla. Using mixer on low speed, drop eggs in one at a time and stir until well mixed into the batter. Then add liquids. Strain batter and pour into lined spring form. Bake in pre-heated oven at 275° for 2 hours. Turn off oven and allow cake to stay in oven until cold. (Put cookie sheet under spring form and bake on lower rack, about ⅓ up.)

ONEIDA'S CHEESE CAKE

1½ cups fine Zwieback crumbs
2   tablespoons butter or oleo
2   tablespoons sugar
½   cup sugar
2   tablespoons enriched flour
¼   teaspoon salt
2   8-ounce packages cream
    cheese, softened

1   teaspoon vanilla
1   teaspoon lemon flavoring
¾   teaspoon lemon peel
4   eggs, separated
1   cup whipping cream

Blend Zwieback crumbs with butter and 2 tablespoons sugar. Press onto bottom and sides of buttered 9-inch spring form pan. Blend ½ cup sugar with flour, salt, and cream cheese. Add vanilla, lemon flavoring and lemon peel. Stir in egg yolks and mix well. Add cream and blend. Fold in stiffly beaten egg whites. Pour mixture on top of crumbs. Bake in slow oven (325°) 1¼ hours. Crack the oven door and leave cake to cool for 1 hour. Remove from oven and cool completely before topping with blueberry pie filling or your favorite fruit. This also can be served plain.

Oneida Baddour

15 MINUTE LEMON CHEESECAKE

1 8-ounce package cream cheese
2 cups milk

1 package lemon instant pudding
8-inch graham cracker crust

Stir cream cheese until soft. Blend in ½ cup milk until creamy. Add remaining milk and then pudding mix. Beat slowly with egg beater 1 minute. Pour into cooled crumb crust. Sprinkle graham cracker crumbs on top to make extra crunchy. Chill.

CHESS CAKE

2 sticks butter
1 box light brown sugar
¾ cup white sugar
4 eggs

2 cups self-rising flour
1 cup pecans, chopped
1 ½ teaspoons vanilla

Preheat oven to 350°. Melt butter, add sugars and mix. Add eggs 1 at a time, beating after each. Fold in flour and nuts, add vanilla. Bake in 2 greased 8-inch pans about 40 minutes. (Can be baked in 1 oblong pan). Cut in squares.

Mrs. R. O. Buck
Lilly Baddour Icenhour

CHESS CAKE

1 Duncan Hines butter cake mix
1 stick butter, softened
1 egg, slightly beaten

1 box of confectioners sugar
3 eggs, slightly beaten
8 ounces cream cheese

Combine cake mix, butter and egg and pat into 9x13″ pan. Mix sugar, eggs and cream cheese, and pour on other mixture. Bake at 350° for 40 minutes until brown. *Serves 12.*

Betty McCallen

253

CHOCOLATE VELVET CAKE

1½ cups chocolate wafer crumbs
⅓ cup margarine, melted
1 8-ounce package cream cheese, softened
½ cup sugar
1 teaspoon vanilla

2 eggs, separated
1 6-ounce package semi-sweet chocolate pieces, melted
1 cup heavy cream
¾ cup nuts, chopped
Whipped cream or shaved chocolate

Preheat oven to 325°. Combine crumbs and margarine. Press into 9" square pan. Bake 10 minutes. Cool. Combine cream cheese, ¼ cup sugar and vanilla. Mix until well blended. Stir in beaten egg yolks and chocolate pieces. Blend well. Beat egg whites and gradually add remaining ¼ cup sugar. Beat until soft peaks form. Fold into chocolate mixture. Whip cream and fold into mixture. Add nuts. Pour mixture over crumbs. Freeze. Garnish with whipped cream or shaved chocolate before serving. Remove from freezer about 10 minutes before serving for easier slicing into wedges. Serves 10-12.

Amy Denny

PRIDE OF THE SOUTHLAND CAKE

1 stick butter
2 cups sugar
8 ounces cream cheese
2 cups thick sour cream
4 eggs, separated

3 cups flour, sifted
2 teaspoons soda
1 teaspoon salt
¼ pound German sweet chocolate
2 teaspoons vanilla

Cream butter, 1½ cups sugar, cream cheese, sour cream and egg yolks together. Gradually add flour, soda, and salt. Melt chocolate in double boiler and stir into batter. Beat egg whites with remaining ½ cup sugar until they form firm peaks. Add vanilla and fold gently into batter. Pour into well-greased and floured 9x12" cake pan. Bake at 350° for 1 hour.

Glaze:

1 cup sugar
½ cup buttermilk
1 tablespoon white Karo syrup
¾ stick butter

1 cup pecans, toasted and chopped
15 maraschino cherries, sliced
1 teaspoon vanilla

Bring sugar, buttermilk, syrup and butter to boil. Add pecans, cherries and vanilla. Boil for 5 minutes and pour over hot cake.

Berenice S. Clemmer

MINNIE'S GOOD CHOCOLATE CAKE

1 cup granulated sugar	½ cup hot water
½ cup packed brown sugar	1¾ cups all purpose flour
½ cup shortening	1 teaspoon baking soda
3 eggs	¼ teaspoon salt
1 teaspoon vanilla	⅔ cup buttermilk
3 1-ounce squares unsweetened chocolate	Mocha frosting
	Chopped walnuts

Cream sugars and shortening till light and fluffy. Add eggs, one at a time, beating well after each. Add vanilla. Melt chocolate in the hot water over low heat; blend thoroughly and cool slightly. Add to creamed mixture. Stir flour, soda and salt together. Beat into creamed mixture alternately with milk, beating well after each addition. Pour into 3 greased and floured 8" round baking pans. Bake at 350° for 20 to 25 minutes. Cool 10 minutes; remove from pans. Cool. Fill and frost with mocha frosting. Sprinkle nuts on cake.

Mocha Frosting:

16-ounce package powdered sugar	6 tablespoons butter
½ cup unsweetened cocoa powder	1 teaspoon vanilla
½ teaspoon instant coffee powder	2 tablespoons milk

Sift together powdered sugar, cocoa and instant coffee. Beat 2 cups of the mixture into butter and vanilla. Add remaining sugar mixture alternately with milk to make spreading consistency. Beat well.

Minnie Miller

PISTACHIO CAKE

1 box Duncan Hines yellow cake mix	1 cup water
	1 teaspoon vanilla
1 box pistachio instant pudding mix	5 eggs
	5½-ounce can Hershey syrup
½ cup oil	½ cup nuts, chopped
½ cup sugar	½ cup semi-sweet chocolate chips

Combine cake mix, pudding mix, oil, sugar, water, vanilla and eggs, and beat well for 2 minutes. Take out 1 cup batter and mix with Hershey syrup. Grease and flour bundt pan. Sprinkle nuts and chocolate chips on bottom of pan. Pour batter on top of nuts and chips. Swirl batter with syrup on top. Bake 1 hour at 350°. Cool 10 minutes, then remove from pan.

Beverly Reeves

DEVILS FOOD CAKE

2 ounces chocolate squares
½ cup boiling water
2 cups sugar
½ cup butter

2 eggs
1 cup buttermilk
1 teaspoon soda
2 cups flour

Melt chocolate in boiling water. Cream sugar and butter. Add eggs and mix well. Stir in melted chocolate. Alternately add buttermilk and dry ingredients. Bake in two 9" cake pans at 350° for about 30 minutes.

Mrs. Charlie Williams
This recipe is over 100 years old, and originally called for baking in a heavy iron skillet.

WALDORF ASTORIA RED CHOCOLATE CAKE

½ cup butter (no substitute)
1 ½ cups sugar
1 teaspoon vanilla
2 eggs
2 heaping teaspoons cocoa
1 ½ ounces red food coloring

2 ½ cups cake flour
1 teaspoon salt
1 cup buttermilk
1 teaspoon soda
1 tablespoon vinegar

Cream butter, sugar and vanilla. Add eggs one at a time. Mix well. Make a thin paste of cocoa and food colorings. Add to the creamed mixture. Sift flour and salt together. Add flour mixture and buttermilk to creamed mixture one tablespoon at a time, beginning and ending with flour. Mix soda and vinegar and blend into the mixture last. Grease and flour two 8-inch pans. Bake in preheated 350° oven for 20 to 30 minutes. Remove and allow to cool.

Frosting:

6 tablespoons flour
2 cups milk
2 cups sugar

2 cups butter (no substitute)
2 teaspoons vanilla

Make a thick paste of flour and milk and gradually add remaining milk. Cook in double boiler, beating constantly until thick. Then cool. Cream butter and sugar. Add vanilla and beat until fluffy. Then add the cooled milk mixture and continue beating until like whipped cream. Cool before icing cake. CAKE AND ICING MUST BE COOL.

Veronica Troutt
Makes a beautiful holiday cake. The recipe came from the famous New York Hotel.

"MELT IN YOUR MOUTH" CHOCOLATE CAKE

1 ½ cups cake flour	⅔ cup buttermilk
¼ cup cocoa	⅔ cup shortening
1 ½ teaspoons soda	½ cup buttermilk
1 ¼ cups sugar	2 eggs
¾ teaspoon salt	1 teaspoon vanilla

Sift flour, cocoa, soda, sugar and salt together. Put in mixer bowl. Add buttermilk, shortening and beat 2 minutes. Add ½ cup more buttermilk, eggs and vanilla. Continue beating until well mixed. Line two 8" cake pans with waxed paper. Divide into pans. Bake at 350° for 25 minutes.

Icing:

½ cup butter or oleo	1 box powdered sugar
3 tablespoons cocoa	1 cup nuts, chopped
6 tablespoons Coca-Cola	

Combine butter, cocoa, and Coca-Cola in small pan. Let come to a boil. Put sugar in mixer bowl. Pour cola mixture over sugar, beat until spreading consistency, add nuts.

Mrs. Robert Homra

Everyone loves this.

SPUMONI CAKE

Chocolate cake, baked in 2 layers	*10-ounce package frozen strawberries,*
4 *cups whipping cream*	*thawed and drained well*
½ *cup confectioners sugar, sifted*	*Few drops yellow food coloring*
Few drops green food coloring	½ *teaspoon rum flavoring*
½ *teaspoon vanilla*	5 *tablespoons cocoa, sifted*
¼ *cup pistachio nuts, chopped*	½ *teaspoon cinnamon*
Few drops red food coloring	

Split each layer in half so you have 4 thin layers. Whip half of the whipping cream with half of the sugar until soft peaks form. Divide into 3 parts. Add green coloring, vanilla and nuts to first third of whipped cream, and spread over one layer of cake. Add second cake layer. Combine red coloring and strawberries with next part of whipped cream and spread over cake. Add third layer of cake. Combine yellow coloring and rum with remaining whipped cream. Spread on cake and top with last cake. Whip remaining 2 cups whipped cream with ¼ cup confectioners sugar. Add cocoa and cinnamon. Frost entire cake. Refrigerate.

Lee Ellis

COCA-COLA CAKE

2 cups flour	2 eggs, beaten
2 cups sugar	1 teaspoon soda
2 sticks oleo	1 teaspoon vanilla
1 cup Coca-Cola	3 tablespoons cocoa
½ cup buttermilk	1 ⅓ cups miniature marshmallows

Combine flour and sugar. Heat oleo and Coca-Cola to boiling point; pour over flour mixture. Mix well. Add buttermilk, eggs, soda, vanilla, cocoa and marshmallows. Pour into greased pan. Bake at 350° for 35 minutes.

Coca Cola Icing:

½ cup oleo	1 box powdered sugar
6 tablespoons Coca-Cola	1 cup pecans, chopped
3 tablespoons cocoa	

Combine oleo, Coca-Cola and cocoa. Heat mixture. Pour over powdered sugar. Beat well. Ice cake while cake is still hot. Sprinkle chopped nuts over cake.

Sylvia Basist

CHOCOLATE CAKE

½ cup butter	2 teaspoons baking powder
2 cups sugar	1 ½ cups milk
4 chocolate squares	2 teaspoons vanilla
2 eggs, beaten	1 cup chopped nuts
2 cups flour	

Cream butter and sugar. Add melted chocolate. Then add eggs and mix well. Sift flour and baking powder together. Add flour to butter mixture, alternating with milk. Add vanilla and beat for 3-4 minutes. Then add nuts and pour into two greased and floured 9-inch layer pans. Bake at 350° for 25 minutes or until done.

Chocolate Icing:

1 pound powdered sugar	1 egg, beaten
½ cup butter	1 teaspoon vanilla
2 chocolate squares	1 cup chopped nuts
2 teaspoons lemon juice	

Cream sugar and butter. Add melted chocolate and lemon juice, egg, vanilla and chopped nuts. Blend well.

Mrs. Gabe Enochs

GERMAN CHOCOLATE COCONUT PUDDING CAKE

1 package Duncan Hines yellow cake mix
1 small package Jello vanilla instant pudding
1 4-ounce bar of German sweet chocolate, melted

4 eggs
1¼ cups buttermilk
¼ cup oil
1 cup Bakers angel flake coconut

Combine all ingredients except coconut in a large mixing bowl and blend about 4 minutes at medium speed. Fold in coconut. Pour in a large (12-cup) greased and floured bundt pan. Bake at 350° for 50 to 60 minutes. Check at 45 minutes to make sure it is not overcooking.

Icing:

1 4-ounce bar of German chocolate
¼ cup water
1 tablespoon oleo

1 cup confectioners sugar
1 teaspoon vanilla
Dash salt

Melt the chocolate, water and oleo in a saucepan. Add the sugar and heat until it dissolves. Take off heat and add vanilla and salt. Blend until smooth. Drizzle over slightly warm cake.

Charles Baddour

CHOCOLATE CHERRY BRANDY CAKE

1 box Duncan Hines Swiss Chocolate cake mix
1 box Jello instant chocolate pudding
1 cup sour cream
1 teaspoon brandy flavoring
¼ cup wild cherry brandy
½ cup + 1 tablespoon Crisco oil

¼ cup maraschino cherry syrup
5 eggs
½ cup maraschino cherries, diced
¾ cup chopped dates
½ cup pecans, chopped
1 tablespoon flour to coat nuts and dates

Preheat oven to 325°. Blend cake mix and pudding in large bowl with sour cream, flavoring, brandy, oil and cherry juice for 2 minutes at medium speed. Add eggs one at a time, beating well after each addition. Stir in cherries. Coat dates and pecans with flour. Fold into batter. Put in large bundt pan and bake at 325° for 55-60 minutes, or until done.

Charles Baddour

MISSISSIPPI MUD CAKE

1 cup butter	Pinch salt
½ cup cocoa	1½ cups nuts, chopped
2 cups sugar	1 teaspoon vanilla
4 eggs, slightly beaten	Miniature marshmallows
1½ cups self-rising flour	Chocolate frosting

Melt butter and cocoa together on low heat. Remove from heat and stir in sugar and beaten eggs. Mix well. Add flour, salt, nuts and vanilla. Mix well. Spoon batter into a greased and floured 13x9x2" pan. Bake at 350° for 35-45 minutes. Sprinkle marshmallows on top of hot cake. Cover with chocolate frosting.

Frosting:

1-pound box confectioners sugar	⅓ cup cocoa
½ cup whole milk	½ stick butter

Combine sugar, milk, cocoa and soft butter. Mix until smooth and spread on hot cake.

Cheryl Grace,
Veronica Troutt

CHOCOLATE FUDGE SHEET CAKE

1 cup water	½ teaspoon salt
½ cup oil	2 eggs
1 stick oleo	½ cup buttermilk
3 tablespoons cocoa	1 teaspoon soda
2 cups sugar	1 teaspoon vanilla
2 cups flour	

Bring water, oil, oleo and cocoa to a boil. Put sugar, flour and salt in bowl. Pour in the boiling liquid and beat well. Add eggs, buttermilk, soda and vanilla. Beat well. Pour into greased and floured sheet cake pan and bake at 350° for 20-25 minutes.

Icing:

1 stick oleo	1 teaspoon vanilla
3 tablespoons cocoa	½ to 1 cup pecans, chopped
6 tablespoons cream or milk	1-pound box confectioners sugar

Combine oleo, cocoa and milk and heat until oleo melts. Beat in rest of ingredients. Spread on hot cake. Cool and cut.

Joyce T. Ferguson

GERMAN SWEET CHOCOLATE CAKE

1 package German sweet chocolate	2 cups sugar
2 ½ cups cake flour (sift, then measure)	4 eggs, separated
½ teaspoon salt	3 tablespoons pure vanilla
1 cup butter or oleo	1 teaspoon soda
	1 cup buttermilk

Have all at room temperature. Melt chocolate in top of double boiler. Cool to lukewarm. Sift together 3 times the flour and salt. Set aside. Cream butter. Add sugar, 2 tablespoons at a time. Add 4 egg yolks, one at a time. With mixer at blending speed, add vanilla and cooled chocolate, beating well after each addition. Dissolve soda in buttermilk. Add flour and milk alternately, beginning and ending with flour. Fold in beaten egg whites last. Bake for 28 to 30 minutes at 325° in 3 greased and floured cake pans.

Filling for German Sweet Chocolate Cake:

½ pint whipping cream	¼ cup butter
3 egg yolks	1 cup flaked coconut
1 cup sugar	1 cup nuts, chopped

Mix cream, egg yolks, sugar, and butter in saucepan. Cook over moderate heat until thick, stirring constantly. Remove from heat. Add coconut and nuts and mix well. Cool. As you stack the cake, spread the filling almost to the edge of each layer. Use your favorite chocolate icing to cover the side and edge of top layer.

Nellie George Baddour

Won a prize at the Mid-South Fair in Memphis.

HOT FUDGE CAKE

1 German chocolate cake mix	1 teaspoon vanilla
3 cups sugar	1 large can Pet milk
1 stick oleo	Vanilla ice cream
2 squares chocolate	

Bake cake according to directions using 13x9" pan. Let cool completely. Make fudge in double boiler by combining sugar, oleo, chocolate, vanilla. Add a small amount of Pet milk every few minutes until all gone. This takes about one hour. DO NOT ADD MILK ALL AT ONCE OR IT WILL BE SUGARY. Cut cake in squares and split into layers. Place a square of ice cream in middle and top with hot fudge.

Sarah Agent

Can also use hot fudge for ice cream topping. It is out of this world.

261

SELF-ICE CAKE

1 cup chopped dates	1 teaspoon vanilla
1 cup boiling water	1¾ cups flour
1 teaspoon soda	½ teaspoon salt
½ cup shortening	½ teaspoon cream of tartar
1 cup sugar	1 6-ounce package of chocolate morsels
2 eggs	¾ cup nuts, chopped
2 teaspoons or 2 tablespoons cocoa	

Combine dates, water and soda, let stand until cool. Cream shortening and sugar. Add eggs and beat well. Add cocoa and vanilla. Blend well. Slowly add flour, salt and cream of tartar. Stir until well blended. Carefully fold in date mixture. Pour in 13x9x2-inch pan. Sprinkle chocolate morsels and nuts over cake. Bake 350° for 30 minutes.

Mary Virginia Southwell

TUNNEL OF FUDGE

1½ cups oleo or butter	1 package Pillsbury 2-layer size
6 eggs	double Dutch butter-cream
1½ cups sugar	chocolate frosting mix or fudge
2 cups all-purpose flour	frosting mix
2 cups chopped walnuts or pecans	

Leave oleo and eggs out overnight to get to room temperature. Cream butter at high speed. Add eggs, one at a time, beating well after each. Gradually add sugar and continue creaming at high speed until light and fluffy. Fold in flour on slow speed. Also fold in nuts and frosting mix until well blended. Pour batter in greased bundt pan. Bake at 350° for 54-60 minutes. Cool 2 hours. Remove from pan and cool completely. The secret to this cake is the cooking time. Remember the center is supposed to be soft.

Marilyn Baddour Aaron

Always a hit!

CHOCOLATE CHIP CAKE

1 box yellow cake mix
1 box instant vanilla pudding
4 eggs
1 cup milk
1 cup cooking oil

1 4-ounce bar cooking chocolate, grated
1 6-ounce package chocolate chips
¼ cup confectioners sugar

Combine cake mix, pudding, eggs, milk and oil. Beat 2 minutes. Stir in grated chocolate and chocolate chips. Pour into well-oiled and floured bundt or tube pan. (Cocoa may be used instead of flour.) Bake at 350° about 1 hour. Test for doneness and cook longer, if necessary. Sprinkle with confectioners sugar.

Sara Patrick

PINEAPPLE COCONUT CAKE

3 cups flour
2 teaspoons baking powder
⅛ teaspoon salt
¾ cup shortening

1¼ cups sugar
4 eggs, separated
1 cup milk
1 teaspoon vanilla

Sift flour and measure. Add baking powder and salt, and sift together. Cream shortening and sugar gradually, then egg yolks, milk and flour. Blend thoroughly. Add flavoring and fold in stiffly beaten egg whites. Pour into two 9″ pans and bake at 350° for 25 minutes.

Filling:

2 cups sugar
1 #2 can crushed pineapple

2 egg yolks
2 tablespoons flour

Dissolve sugar with pineapple juice and cook until it spins a thread. Mix egg yolks and flour into a paste. Mix with pineapple thoroughly. Gradually add the syrup. Return to stove and cook until thick. Spread between layers of cake.

Icing:

1½ cups sugar
4 tablespoons white corn syrup
1 cup water

2 egg whites, beaten stiff
1 teaspoon vanilla

Boil sugar, syrup and water together until it forms a soft ball in cold water. Pour slowly over egg whites, beating constantly. Spread on top and sides of cake before it becomes firm. Sometimes for variety cover with coconut.

Mrs. J. E. Eubanks

CAKES

FRESH COCONUT CAKE

2 fresh coconuts	2 teaspoons salt
4 cups flour, sifted	6 egg whites
2⅔ cups sugar	2 cups xx cream, beaten stiffly
5½ teaspoons baking powder	3 teaspoons vanilla

Grate coconuts, reserving milk. Sift flour 2 times with sugar, baking powder and 1½ teaspoons salt. Beat egg whites with remaining ½ teaspoon salt until stiff peaks form. Combine cream and egg whites lightly with a wire whisk. Fold in 1 cup coconut milk and vanilla. Fold dry ingredients in, one third at a time. Pour into 4 greased and floured cake pans. Bake at 350° for 20-25 minutes.

Icing:

4½ cups sugar	6 egg whites
1 cup water	⅓ cup powdered sugar
6 tablespoons white Karo	Grated coconut

Combine sugar, water, and Karo and boil until it makes a soft ball in cold water. Beat egg whites stiff. Add syrup to egg whites. Fold in sugar. Spread icing over cooled cake. Sprinkle coconut over each layer and on top and sides of cake.

Joyce T. Ferguson

LUSCIOUS COCONUT CAKE

1 package butter cake mix	2 6-ounce packages frozen coconut, thawed
1¾ cups sugar	
2 8-ounce cartons commercial sour cream	1 9-ounce carton frozen whipped topping, thawed

Prepare cake mix according to package directions, making two 8-inch layers. When completely cool, split both layers. Combine sugar, sour cream and coconut, blending well, and chill. Reserve 1 cup sour cream mixture for frosting and spread remainder between layers of cake. Combine reserved sour cream mixture with whipped topping. Blend until smooth. Spread on top and sides of cake. Seal cake in an airtight container and refrigerate for 3 days before serving. This will keep many days longer if it has the chance.

Nora Nichols

JAM CAKE

3 cups flour	2 sticks butter or oleo
1 teaspoon nutmeg	2 cups sugar
1 teaspoon cinnamon	4 eggs, separated
1 teaspoon allspice	1¼ cups buttermilk
½ teaspoon salt	1 heaping cup jam

Sift dry ingredients together. Cream butter and sugar. Add flour mixture alternately with buttermilk. Add yolks and jam. Beat well. Beat egg whites very stiff and fold into batter. Bake in three 9″ cake pans about 35 minutes in 350° oven or until cake pulls away from pan. Cool on wire rack.

Mrs. W. Paul Pennebaker

Makes a very moist cake.

JAM CAKE

2 cups sugar	1 teaspoon soda
1 cup butter	1 cup pecans
3 eggs	1 cup chopped dates
1 cup buttermilk	1 cup raisins
1 cup jam (seedless)	1 large apple, grated
3 cups plain flour	

Cream butter and sugar. Add eggs. Combine buttermilk and jam, and add alternately with dry ingredients. Add nuts and fruit. Mix well. Bake in three 9″ cake pans at 350° for 30 minutes. Cool before icing.

Filling:

2 cups sugar	1 cup flaked coconut
2 tablespoons flour	1 cup chopped dates (optional)
1½ cups sweet milk	1 cup raisins
1 cup butter	1 large apple, grated
1 cup nuts, chopped	

Mix sugar and flour, add milk and butter. Cook until mixture thickens, stirring. Remove from heat. Stir in nuts, coconut, dates, raisins and apple.

Mrs. Eugene Walters,
Nora Nichols

JAM CAKE

1½ cups margarine	2 teaspoons allspice
2 cups sugar	2 teaspoons cinnamon
6 eggs	2 teaspoons nutmeg
3½ cups flour	6 tablespoons buttermilk
2 teaspoons soda	2 cups strawberry jam

Cream soft margarine. Add sugar slowly, beating until creamy. Add eggs one at a time. Sift flour and measure. Then sift again with soda and spices. Add flour mixture alternately with buttermilk. Mix well. Fold in strawberry jam. Grease pans and sprinkle with flour. Pour into 4 square 8-inch cake pans. Bake at 375° about 30-40 minutes or until done. Cool and turn out. Use Uncooked Caramel Icing to cover cake.

Uncooked Caramel Icing:

1½ sticks oleo	2 teaspoons vanilla
½ cup cream	½ teaspoon salt
2 cups dark brown sugar	Confectioners sugar

Melt oleo in cream. While hot, stir in the brown sugar. Cool and stir in vanilla. Stir in salt and enough confectioners sugar to right consistency to spread.

Mrs. J. E. Price

BLACKBERRY JAM CAKE

1 cup butter	1 teaspoon nutmeg
2 cups sugar	1 teaspoon allspice
2 cups jam	4 cups flour
6 eggs, separated	2 teaspoons soda
1 teaspoon cinnamon	½ cup sour cream

Cream butter and sugar. Add jam and mix. Add beaten egg yolks and spices; sift and measure flour, resift with soda added; stir in alternately flour and sour cream. Fold in well beaten egg whites. Bake at 350° for 30-35 minutes in three 9-inch layers and put together with choice of icing. Other jams or preserves may be substituted (rename the cake).

Mrs. Johnson Barrett

EASY JAM CAKE

1 cup butter	1 teaspoon cloves
1 ½ cups sugar	½ teaspoon nutmeg
3 eggs	½ teaspoon salt
3 cups sifted flour	1 cup sour milk
1 teaspoon soda	1 large cup jam
1 teaspoon cinnamon	

Cream butter and sugar, add eggs and beat. Alternate sifted dry ingredients with milk, then add jam and beat. Bake in greased and floured tube pan in 350° oven for 30 to 40 minutes. Leave plain or frost with favorite icing.

Mrs. Bernard High

CALIFORNIA ORCHARD CAKE

1 box orange cake mix	¾ cup oil
½ box pineapple cake mix	¾ cup pear nectar
(2¼ cups)	¾ cup water
1 small package peach Jello	6 eggs
1 box pineapple instant pudding	1 package Dream Whip

Mix cake mixes, Jello and pudding in large mixing bowl with oil, nectar, and water. Add eggs one at a time, beating well after each addition. Fold in Dream Whip and mix well. Grease and flour a large tube pan and line the bottom with wax paper. Pour batter into pan and bake at 325° for 1 hour and 10 minutes or until tested done.

Icing for California Orchard Pound Cake:

1 pound of confectioners sugar	½ teaspoon coconut flavoring
1 stick butter	½ cup coconut
¼ cup milk	1 drop red coloring
½ teaspoon orange flavoring	1 drop yellow coloring

Put sugar in mixing bowl and make a well. Pour melted butter into well and mix together until it forms a ball. Add milk until it reaches a spreadable consistency. Then add flavoring, coconut, and coloring to form an apricot color. Spread over cake while still warm. Let icing run down the sides while spreading with a knife.

Charles Baddour

ORANGE CHIFFON CAKE DELIGHT

1 bakery orange chiffon cake
1 can sweetened condensed milk
8 tablespoons lemon juice
4 tablespoons orange juice
4 teaspoons lemon rind, grated
4 teaspoons orange rind, grated
½ pint whipping cream, whipped

Slice cake in two layers. Mix juices and rind with milk until thick. Fold whipped cream into orange-lemon mixture. Spread on layers of cake. Refrigerate. This cake freezes beautifully; can be sliced while frozen, and thaws quickly. *Serves 10-12*.

Amy Denny

ORANGE-RAISIN CAKE

1 orange
1 cup raisins
⅓ cup walnuts
2 cups flour
1 teaspoon soda
1 teaspoon salt
1 cup sugar
½ cup shortening
1 cup milk
2 eggs

Topping:

⅓ cup orange juice
⅓ cup sugar
1 teaspoon cinnamon
¼ cup walnuts, chopped

Grind entire orange, raisins and walnuts together. Sift together the flour, soda, salt and sugar. Add shortening and ¾ cup milk and beat for 2 minutes. Add eggs and remaining milk and beat for another 2 minutes. Fold in orange and raisin mixture. Pour into well-greased and lightly-floured 9x13-inch pan. Bake 40-50 minutes at 350°. Drip orange juice over warm cake. Combine sugar, cinnamon and walnuts for topping. Sprinkle over cake.

Irma Jo Williams

Very old and very good.

BOB BURNS' GOOD CAKE

1 box Duncan Hines Deluxe II
yellow cake mix
4 eggs

¾ cup oil
1 11-ounce can mandarin oranges

Mix all together with beater. Bake in three 9-inch round cake pans for 20 minutes at 350°.

Icing:

3-ounce package instant French
vanilla pudding mix
1 9-ounce carton Cool Whip

1 16-ounce can crushed pineapple
(with heavy syrup)

Stir with spoon and spread between each layer and on top. Sprinkle top with pecans. Cake must be kept refrigerated.

Bob Burns

ORANGE SLICE CAKE

1 cup oleo
2 cups sugar
4 eggs
1 teaspoon soda
½ cup buttermilk
3½ cups flour

1 pound dates, chopped
1 pound orange slice candy,
chopped
2 cups nuts
1 cup coconut

Cream oleo and sugar. Add eggs one at a time. Beat well. Dissolve soda in buttermilk. Place flour in large bowl. Add dates, orange slices and nuts. Stir to coat each piece. Add this and coconut to creamed mixture. This makes a stiff dough that should be mixed with hands. Place in greased 13x9x3 pan. Bake 2½-3 hours at 250°.

Icing:

1 cup fresh orange juice

2 cups powdered sugar

Pour icing on hot cake. Let stand in pan overnight. Cut in squares.

Mrs. Rupple K. Dabbs,
Martha Anne Weaver

This is a moist "fruit cake" type cake.

BUTTERMILK CAKE

1 cup Crisco shortening
3 cups sugar
6 eggs
¼ teaspoon salt

1 teaspoon vanilla
3 cups flour
1 cup buttermilk
¼ teaspoon soda

Cream shortening and sugar; add one egg at a time, beating after each addition. Add salt and vanilla. Alternate flour and buttermilk, starting and ending with flour. Dissolve soda in last addition of buttermilk. Bake in a greased and floured tube pan at 325° for 1 hour. Cool for 5 minutes before removing from pan.

This is a versatile cake. You can make the delicious Buttermilk Cake, or use it as the basic recipe to make other cakes. Four variations are given below.

Chocolate Cake:

To Buttermilk Cake, add 16 ounces of Hershey Syrup as last ingredient. An optional ingredient is 1 cup of chopped nuts. Bake as usual.

Orange Cake:

Make Buttermilk Cake according to above recipe. While it's baking, combine 1 cup sugar, ¾ cup orange juice, and 1 tablespoon butter in a saucepan, and heat until dissolved. When cake is done, poke the top with holes with a long-pronged fork. Spoon the warm juice mixture over the cake. Let set 5 minutes before removing from pan.

Coconut-Pineapple Cake:

Add to Buttermilk Cake batter 8 ounces of crushed pineapple, drained very well, and 3½ ounces of Angel Flake coconut. Bake as usual.

Date Nut Cake:

To Buttermilk cake batter add 8-ounce package of chopped dates and 1 cup chopped nuts as last ingredients. Bake as usual. When cake is done, add the orange juice sauce in recipe for Orange Cake.

Mrs. W. K. Ingram

SOUR CREAM CAKE

1 box Duncan Hines butter cake mix
½ cup sugar
¾ cup buttery Wesson oil

1 8-ounce carton sour cream
4 eggs
1 box Betty Crocker coconut pecan frosting mix

Mix cake mix, sugar, oil, sour cream and eggs. Mix well and pour half of batter into greased tube pan. Prepare icing according to package directions and spoon into pan. Add rest of the batter. Bake at 350° for 1 hour or until done.

Gloria Riley

AUNT TINA'S POUND CAKE

½ pound butter
1¾ cups sugar

5 eggs
2 cups flour

Cream butter and sugar until creamy. Add eggs one at a time beating at high speed. Turn speed to low on mixer and add flour. Bake in loaf or stem pan 1 hour and 15 minutes at 325°.

Helen Baddour Deneka

You will be surprised at how good this cake is – especially if you use real butter.

COCONUT POUND CAKE

2 sticks oleo
⅔ cup shortening
3 cups sugar
5 eggs
3 cups cake flour

1 cup milk
1 can angel flake coconut
1 teaspoon coconut flavoring
1 teaspoon vanilla flavoring

Mix in order given and bake in tube pan at 325° for 1½ hours.

June Smith

GERMAN CHOCOLATE POUND CAKE

2 cups sugar	1 cup buttermilk
1 cup shortening	3 cups sifted flour
4 eggs	½ teaspoon soda
2 teaspoons vanilla	1 teaspoon salt
2 teaspoons butter flavor	1 ½ packages German sweet chocolate

Cream sugar and shortening. Add eggs, flavors and buttermilk. Sift together flour, soda and salt and add. Mix well. Add softened chocolate and blend together. Bake in well-greased and floured 9" stem pan for 1½ hours at 300°. Serve hot or cold. May be served with German chocolate sauce and whipped cream, if desired.

German Chocolate Sauce:

1 bar German chocolate	1 cup powdered sugar
1 tablespoon butter	Dash of salt
¼ cup strong coffee	½ teaspoon vanilla

Over low heat melt chocolate and butter in the coffee. When melted add sugar, salt and vanilla. Beat with mixer.

Doris Lanford

ITALIAN CREAM CHEESE CAKE

1 stick margarine	1 cup buttermilk
½ cup oil	1 teaspoon vanilla
2 cups sugar	1 small can coconut
5 eggs, separated	1 cup nuts
2 cups flour	

Beat margarine and oil until smooth. Add sugar and beat until smooth. Add egg yolks and beat well. Add flour alternately with buttermilk. Stir in vanilla, coconut and nuts, then fold in beaten egg whites. Bake in 3 layers at 350° for 25 minutes.

Frosting:

8 ounces cream cheese, softened	1 teaspoon vanilla
½ stick butter, softened	1 cup nuts, chopped
1 box powdered sugar	

Beat cream cheese and butter until smooth. Add sugar and beat well. Add vanilla. Sprinkle top of cake with nuts.

Linda Long, Mrs. Bobby Herndon,
Brenda Cole, Jeanie Van Vranken

SOUR CREAM POUND CAKE

1 cup butter	⅛ teaspoon salt
3 cups sugar	6 eggs
3 cups cake flour, sifted	1 cup sour cream
¼ teaspoon soda	1 teaspoon vanilla

Cream butter and sugar until light and fluffy. Sift dry ingredients together. Add eggs alternately with sour cream and flour, beating well after each addition. Add vanilla. Pour into tube pan (greased and floured on bottom). Cut circle 1 inch deep around center of cake. Place in *cold* oven. Turn oven to 300° and bake 1½ hours. When done, remove from oven and turn out of pan.

Lemon Glaze:

1½ cups sugar	1 tablespoon corn syrup
1 cup water	Juice and grated rind of 1 lemon

Mix sugar, water, syrup and boil fast, uncovered, for 10 minutes. Remove and stir in lemon juice and rind. Spoon on cake while hot.

Jennie Yaeger

5-FLAVOR POUND CAKE

1 cup milk	5 eggs
2 sticks butter	1 teaspoon rum flavoring
1 cup vegetable oil	1 teaspoon coconut flavoring
3 cups sugar	1 teaspoon butter flavoring
3 cups all-purpose flour	1 teaspoon lemon flavoring
½ teaspoon baking powder	1 teaspoon vanilla flavoring

Cream butter, vegetable oil and sugar to light and fluffy. Add beaten eggs. Combine flour and baking powder and add to creamed mixture alternately with milk. (Put flavoring in milk.) Spoon into greased bundt pan or 2 small loaf pans. Bake at 350° for about 1 hour.

Glaze:

1 cup sugar	1 teaspoon each of all flavorings plus
½ cup water	almond

Combine in saucepan. Melt and pour over cake.

Using this recipe in September, 1980, Rita Bryant won first prize in bundt cakes and first prize for "Best in Show" over-all cakes in the Alabama State Fair in Birmingham.

Mrs. John Wilson,
Mrs. George Moore, Jr.

COCONUT-BLACK WALNUT POUND CAKE

2 cups sugar	½ teaspoon baking powder
1 cup salad oil	1 cup buttermilk
4 eggs, beaten	1 cup black walnuts, chopped
3 cups flour	1 cup flaked coconut
½ teaspoon salt	2 teaspoons coconut extract
½ teaspoon soda	Coconut Syrup

Combine sugar, salad oil, and eggs; beat well. Combine dry ingredients; add to sugar mixture alternately with buttermilk, beating well after each addition. Stir in nuts, coconut, and flavoring. Pour batter into a well-greased and floured 10-inch tube pan. Bake at 325° for 1 hour and 5 minutes, or until tests done. Pour hot Coconut Syrup over hot cake. Allow cake to remain in pan 4 hours to absorb syrup. Wrap well. (Cake will be very moist.)

Coconut Syrup:

1 cup sugar	½ cup water
2 tablespoons butter or margarine	1 teaspoon coconut extract

Combine sugar, butter, and water in a saucepan. Bring to a boil; boil 5 minutes. Remove from heat; stir in flavoring.

Mrs. Bennie Cox

PECAN POUND CAKE

½ cup butter	1 teaspoon cream of tartar
2 cups sugar	½ teaspoon soda
10 eggs, separated	1 cup pecan halves
4 cups flour	1 teaspoon vanilla (optional)

Cream the butter and sugar. Add the yolks of the eggs, beaten lightly. Add flour and beaten egg whites alternately, saving 1 cup of flour. Sift the cream of tartar and soda in the last cup of flour and dust the pecan halves with this mixture. Add vanilla and pecans. Bake for 1 hour at 350° in a well-buttered and floured tube pan. Cut the cake in thin slices and serve with coffee, tea or as a dessert.

Mrs. J. C. McCaa

ORANGE POUND CAKE

2 sticks oleo
½ cup Wesson oil
2 cups sugar
5 eggs
¼ teaspoon salt

1 teaspoon vanilla flavoring
1 teaspoon orange flavoring
3 cups cake flour
7 ounces orange juice

Cream oleo, oil and sugar together. Add beaten eggs and mix well. Add salt and flavorings. Add flour and orange juice alternately and mix well. Bake in tube pan at 325° for 1 hour and 20 minutes.

Mary Greer

"MISS PET'S" POUND CAKE

1 pound butter
3 cups sugar
9 or 10 eggs (room temperature)
4 cups flour

3 teaspoons baking powder
½ to 1 cup milk
1 teaspoon vanilla extract
1 teaspoon lemon extract

Cream butter, gradually add sugar. Beat egg yolks to lemon yellow, add to butter and sugar. Alternate dry ingredients and milk. Add the extracts. Beat very well. Fold in stiffly beaten egg white. Bake for 1 hour and 30 minutes at 325° in a large, well-greased and floured tube pan. Let cool for 5 minutes in pan. Turn out on cooling rack for complete cooling.

Mrs. L. H. Polk

HARVEY WALLBANGER CAKE

1 box pound cake mix
1 small package vanilla instant
   pudding
½ cup salad oil

4 eggs
½ cup orange juice
½ cup Galiano liqueur
1 teaspoon vodka

Put all ingredients in mixing bowl and mix 5 minutes on medium speed. Grease and flour cake pan (bundt or pound). Bake at 325° for 45 minutes to 1 hour.

Icing:

1 cup confectioners sugar, sifted
1 tablespoon orange juice

1 tablespoon Galiano
1 teaspoon vodka

Mix all ingredients together and drizzle over cake while warm.

Nancy Terry

275

CAKES

COCONUT-POUND CAKE

2 cups sugar
1 cup shortening
5 eggs
2 cups self-rising flour

1 cup buttermilk
1½ teaspoons coconut flavoring
1 cup coconut

Cream sugar and shortening together. Add eggs, beating mixture after each egg. Add flour and buttermilk alternately. Add coconut flavoring and coconut. Bake in well-greased and floured tube pan at 325° for 1 hour and 15 minutes. Note: Line bottom of tube pan with waxed paper cut 1 inch larger than pan bottom.

Glaze:

1 cup sugar
½ cup water

1½ teaspoons coconut flavoring

Combine, bring to boil. Pour over warm cake. Let cake cool in pan.

Mrs. Robert A. Melhorne

NO BAKE RUM CAKE

1 package pistachio instant pudding
1 package chocolate instant pudding
3 packages Stella Doro toasted almond biscuits

1 cup milk
3-4 ounces white rum
1 large carton Cool Whip
½ cup nuts

Make instant puddings according to directions. Dip 1 side of biscuits quickly into dish of milk, and place in bottom of 9x13" pan. Pour half of rum over biscuits, then spread pistachio pudding over layer. Spread some Cool Whip over pudding. Again dip biscuits in milk and make second layer. Pour rest of rum over this layer. Spread chocolate pudding over and the rest of the Cool Whip. Sprinkle with nuts. Cover with foil and refrigerate for 2 days.

Helen Younes

Absolutely delicious.

276

RUM CAKE

½ cup pecans, chopped	5 eggs
2 cups cake flour	1 teaspoon rum flavoring
½ teaspoon baking powder	1 teaspoon butter flavoring
½ pound butter	1 teaspoon vanilla
1¾ cups sugar	2 tablespoons white rum

Grease bundt pan with butter. Sprinkle with pecans. Sift cake flour and measure. Resift with baking powder. Cream butter with sugar. Add eggs one at a time, beating well after each. Fold in rum flavoring, butter flavoring, vanilla, and white rum. Add flour mixture. Fold in with gentle up-and-over motion. Bake at 325° for more than 1 hour. Let cake stand 10 minutes. Add half of rum syrup; let stand 15 minutes. Remove cake from pan; add other half of syrup.

Rum Syrup:

1 cup sugar	1 teaspoon rum flavoring
½ cup water	1 tablespoon white rum

Bring sugar and water to boil. Remove from heat and add flavoring and rum.

Mrs. C. D. Williams

QUICK RUM CAKE

1 cup pecans, chopped	½ cup rum
1 package yellow cake mix	4 eggs
1 package French vanilla instant pudding	1 stick butter
	1 cup sugar
½ cup water	¼ cup water
½ cup Wesson oil	2 ounces rum

Sprinkle chopped pecans on bottom of greased tube or bundt pan. Mix together cake mix, pudding, water, Wesson oil and rum. Beat in eggs one at a time. Pour batter into pan and bake 1 hour at 325°. Let cool.

Sauce: Boil butter, sugar, water and rum together in saucepan. Pour over cake while in pan. This will soak into cake. Let cake completely cool before removing from pan. This freezes beautifully.

ITALIAN BUCHELATO CAKE

½ cup margarine
1 cup sugar
3 eggs, separated
3 cups flour
3 teaspoons baking powder

1 cup milk
2 tablespoons aniseed
2 teaspoons aniseed extract
2 teaspoons rum

Have eggs, milk and margarine at room temperature. Cream margarine and sugar, then add egg yolks. Cream together. Alternately add flour, baking powder, and milk, ending with flour. Beat egg whites and add to batter. Add aniseed and extract, and rum. Use 10″ round pan, greased and floured. Bake at 350° for 1 hour. Check doneness with toothpick. Top with powdered sugar when cool.

Fanny Corradini

SHERRY CAKE

1 angel food cake
4 eggs, separated
1 cup sugar
⅓ cup sherry

1 envelope gelatin
½ cup milk
1 pint heavy cream

Tear cake into bite-size pieces. In top of double boiler make custard of beaten egg yolks, ½ cup sugar and sherry. Cook until thickened and remove from heat. Add gelatin dissolved in milk. Beat egg whites, add ¼ cup sugar while beating, until stiff. Add to custard. Beat cream with ¼ cup sugar. Add ⅔ of this to custard mixture, saving ⅓ to ice cake. Flavor this ⅓ with sherry to taste. Rinse tube pan with cold water. Put in layers of cake alternately with custard, ending with custard. Refrigerate. Several hours before serving, run knife around pan and shake cake out. Ice with remaining ⅓ of cream.

Mrs. Walter Scott

PUMPKIN CAKE

2 cups all purpose flour	4 eggs
2 teaspoons soda	2 cups sugar
2 teaspoons cinnamon	1 cup Wesson oil
½ teaspoon salt	2 cups pumpkin

Combine flour, soda, cinnamon and salt in one bowl. In second bowl mix eggs and sugar, beating well. Add oil and beat. Beat in flour mixture gradually. Add pumpkin. Beat well again. Cook at 350° for 40-50 minutes.

Icing:

1 stick butter	1 teaspoon vanilla
8 ounces cream cheese	1 box confectioners sugar

Soften butter and cream cheese. Mix well. Add vanilla. Add confectioners sugar and beat until smooth.

Connie Banks

YAM CROWN CAKE

2 cups sifted flour	2 cups sugar
1 teaspoon salt	4 eggs
1½ teaspoons soda	2 teaspoons vanilla
1¼ teaspoons cinnamon	2 cups sweet potatoes, mashed
1 teaspoon nutmeg	½ cup nuts, chopped
1¼ cups oil	

Mix flour and spices. In mixing bowl combine oil and sugar and mix thoroughly. Add eggs, one at a time, mixing after each addition. Add vanilla. Add dry ingredients and mashed sweet potatoes. Add nuts. Mix thoroughly. Put into greased bundt pan and bake at 350° for 1 hour and 15 minutes. Let stand 5 or 10 minutes. Invert on rack and cool. Split cooled cake and spread frosting. Put top back on cake. Powdered sugar may be sprinkled over top if desired.

Cream Cheese Frosting:

½ stick oleo	½ teaspoon vanilla
3 ounces cream cheese	½ cup nuts, chopped
½ box confectioners sugar	

Mix well. Spread between layers of cake.

Myrtle Burks

GINGERBREAD

½ cup shortening	1 teaspoon baking powder
½ cup sugar	1½ teaspoons soda
2 eggs	¼ teaspoon salt
1 cup molasses	1 teaspoon cinnamon
1 cap butter flavoring	1 teaspoon nutmeg
1 cup boiling water	2 teaspoons ginger
3 cups flour	

Cream together shortening and sugar. Add eggs, one at a time, beating well after each one. Add molasses, butter flavoring, and boiling water. Fold in sifted dry ingredients. Bake 45 minutes in greased and floured 9x13″ pan at 325°.

Mrs. Carlton Stubbs

GINGERBREAD

1 egg	¼ teaspoon soda
¼ cup shortening	½ teaspoon ginger
¼ cup sugar	½ teaspoon cloves
¼ cup sorghum molasses	½ teaspoon allspice
1 cup flour	⅛ teaspoon nutmeg
1 teaspoon baking powder	⅓ cup milk
¼ teaspoon salt	

Mix together by hand, the egg, shortening, sugar and molasses. Sift dry ingredients together and add alternately with milk. Prepare loaf pan with greased brown or wax paper in bottom and bake at 325° for 30 minutes.

Louise Grandstaff

This recipe won a prize for four years at Wilson County Fair, the years being 1923 to 1927. Also was used by county demonstrating agents.

MOLASSES CAKE

2 eggs, beaten
¾ cup sugar
¾ cup molasses
¾ cup shortening, melted
1 teaspoon soda

1 teaspoon vanilla
½ teaspoon cinnamon
2 ½ cups self-rising flour
1 cup boiling water

Combine eggs, sugar, molasses, and shortening together. Add remaining ingredients, adding boiling water last. Whip. Bake at 300° in tube pan for 60 minutes or until done.

Mary Riley

APPLESAUCE PINEAPPLE CAKE

3 ½ cups cake flour
2 teaspoons baking powder
½ teaspoon soda
1 teaspoon salt
2 teaspoons cinnamon
½ teaspoon cloves
2 cups sugar

½ cup Crisco
1 egg
2 cups applesauce
1 9-ounce can crushed pineapple,
     drained
1 cup nuts, chopped

Place flour, baking powder, soda, salt, cinnamon, cloves, sugar, Crisco, and egg in mixing bowl. Add 1 cup applesauce and mix thoroughly. Add remaining applesauce and pineapple and mix. Stir in nuts. Pour into greased and floured 10-inch tube pan. Bake in 350° oven 1 hour and 30 minutes or until done. Cool in pan. Leave plain or frost with caramel frosting.

Mrs. Bernard High

PRUNE CAKE

2 cups sugar
1 cup Wesson oil
3 eggs, well beaten
1 cup buttermilk
1 cup unsweetened prunes, cooked
     and diced
2 cups flour

1 teaspoon soda
1 teaspoon salt
1 teaspoon cinnamon
1 teaspoon ground cloves
1 teaspoon nutmeg
1 teaspoon vanilla
1 cup pecans, broken

Mix sugar and oil together. Add beaten eggs and mix well. Blend in buttermilk and prunes. Sift flour with all dry indredients and add, mixing well. Add vanilla and pecans. Bake in greased and floured tube or bundt pan for 55-60 minutes at 325°.

Mattie Jones,
Laura Thorne

PLUM CAKE

2 cups sugar
2 cups sifted self-rising flour
1 teaspoon cinnamon
1 teaspoon nutmeg
1 cup Wesson oil

3 eggs, beaten well
2 small jars baby strained plums
1 teaspoon vanilla
1 cup nuts, chopped

Combine all ingredients and beat well. Bake in tube pan at 350° for 1 hour.

Icing:

1 cup confectioners sugar

Juice of 1 lemon

Mix well. Put on cake while warm.

Mrs. Jimmy Lemons,
Helen Robinson

TOMATO SOUP CAKE

1 cup sugar
2 tablespoons shortening
1 teaspoon baking soda
1 can tomato soup
1¾ cups flour

½ teaspoon cloves
½ teaspoon cinnamon
½ teaspoon nutmeg
1 cup raisins
1 cup nuts

Cream sugar and shortening. Dissolve soda in soup and add combined dry ingredients. Add to batter and mix well. Stir in raisins and nuts. Pour into greased and floured 9x13 pan and bake at 350° for 60 minutes. Cool.

Icing:

1 package Philadelphia cream
   cheese

1 cup confectioners sugar
½ teaspoon vanilla

Whip together and spread over cooled cake.

Vera Glick

A family favorite.

MINNIE MAXEY'S EGGLESS, MILKLESS, BUTTERLESS CAKE

2 cups brown sugar	2 teaspoons cinnamon
1 cup shortening or oleo	1 teaspoon nutmeg
2 cups raisins	2 teaspoons baking soda
1 teaspoon cloves	3 tablespoons warm water
2 cups boiling water	3½ cups flour
¼ teaspoon salt	

Bring sugar, shortening, raisins, cloves, water, salt, cinnamon and nutmeg to boiling. Boil for 2 minutes, stirring constantly. Cool. Dissolve baking soda in water and add to cooled batter. Stir in flour. Bake in three 9-inch pans at 325-350° for 30-40 minutes. Serve plain or with Caramel Frosting below.

Caramel Frosting:

1½ cups brown sugar	¾ cup light cream
½ teaspoon butter	

Boil together about 45 minutes until it reaches a soft ball stage. Beat until it reaches a spreading consistency.

Mrs. Don Burnett

STRAWBERRY DATE CAKE

1 box strawberry cake mix	½ cup oil
1 envelope Dream Whip	1 10-ounce package frozen
1 small package Jello instant	strawberries, thawed
vanilla pudding	4 eggs
½ cup water	½ cup chopped sugared dates
1 teaspoon strawberry flavoring	½ cup coconut

Combine dry ingredients. Add water, flavoring, oil, and strawberries and mix at medium speed for 2 minutes. Add eggs one at at time, beating well after each addition. Beat for 2 more minutes after adding eggs. Fold in remaining ingredients and place in large (12-cup) greased and floured bundt pan. Bake at 350° for 45 to 55 minutes or until done.

Charles Baddour

CHOCOLATE COVERED STRAWBERRY CAKE

1 Swiss chocolate Duncan Hines
  cake mix
1 small package strawberry Jello
1 small package instant vanilla
  pudding
½ cup oil
1 10-ounce box frozen
  strawberries, thawed

¼ cup water
1 teaspoon strawberry flavoring
4 eggs
1 cup dates, chopped
1 tablespoon flour
16 pecan halves (optional)

Preheat oven to 350°. Blend cake mix, Jello and pudding in a large bowl with oil, strawberries, water and flavoring at medium speed for 2 minutes. Add eggs one at a time, beating well after each addition. Beat for 2 minutes more. Fold in dates that have been floured. Place pecan halves in the bottom of a well greased and floured bundt pan before adding batter to keep dates from sticking to bottom of pan. Bake 45-50 minutes, or until tested done.

Charles Baddour

STRAWBERRY CAKE

4 eggs
¾ cup Wesson oil
¾ cup water
½ cup frozen strawberries

1 package white cake mix
3 tablespoons cake flour
1 small box strawberry gelatin

Mix eggs, oil, water and strawberries together. Stir in combined cake mix, cake flour and gelatin. Mix well. Bake in two 9-inch pans (lined with waxed paper) at 350° for about 20 minutes or until center springs back to touch. Cool and ice.

Icing:

1 box confectioners sugar
1 stick butter

½ cup strawberries
Red food coloring (optional)

Combine all ingredients, adding enough strawberries for spreading consistency. If deeper color is desired, add several drops of red food coloring. Decorate top with fresh strawberries. *Serves 12.*

Brenda Vick

1-2-3-4-5 WHITE CAKE

1 cup butter, softened	5 egg whites, beaten til stiff
2 cups sugar	½ teaspoon salt
3 cups flour	1 cup milk
4 teaspoons baking powder	1 teaspoon vanilla

Cream butter, adding sugar a little at a time til well blended. Add baking powder and salt to flour. Alternate flour and milk til smooth. Fold in beaten egg whites. Add vanilla. Pour into three 9″ pans (line bottoms with waxed paper and grease). Bake at 350° for 30 minutes or until done.

Randy Caldwell

Makes a rather large and very good cake.

GOLD CAKE

4½ cups flour	2 cups sugar
4½ teaspoons baking powder	8 eggs, separated
½ teaspoon salt	1½ cups milk
1 cup butter	2 teaspoons vanilla

Sift flour. Add baking powder and salt. Sift together 3 times. Cream butter, sugar and egg yolks until light and fluffy. Add flour, milk and flavoring. Beat egg whites until stiff and fold in. *Makes 3 layers.* Bake at 350° about 30 minutes.

Marion Cox

PLAIN CAKE

½ cup shortening	½ teaspoon baking powder
2 sticks butter or oleo	½ cup Pet milk
3 cups sugar	½ cup plain milk
5 eggs	1 teaspoon coconut flavoring
3 cups flour	1 teaspoon almond extract

Cream shortening, butter and sugar. Add eggs, one at a time, beating after each egg. Sift flour and baking powder together. Add alternately with milk. Beat well. Add flavorings and bake at 325° for 1½ hours. May substitute 2 teaspoons vanilla for coconut flavoring and almond extract.

Gertrude Dacus

CAKES

BUTTER CAKE

1 ¾ cups sugar	1 teaspoon vanilla extract
1 cup shortening	1 teaspoon butter extract
5 eggs	¼ teaspoon salt
1 ⅔ cups flour	

Grease and flour a 10″ tube pan. Cream sugar and shortening 5 minutes. Drop in one egg at a time; beat each egg 2 minutes. Fold in flour at low speed. Add flavorings and salt; blend. Bake at 350° for 45 minutes. Turn off oven and leave cake in 15 minutes longer. Set cake on wet cloth; go around cake pan with a knife. Turn cake out on a cake rack.

Linda Stubbs

NEIMAN MARCUS COFFEE ANGEL FOOD CAKE

1 ½ cups sugar, sifted	1 ¼ teaspoons cream of tartar
1 cup cake flour, sifted	½ teaspoon vanilla
½ teaspoon salt	1 tablespoon powdered instant
1 ¼ cups egg whites (10-12)	coffee

Add ½ cup of the sugar to flour. Sift together 4 times. Add salt to egg white and beat with flat wire whisk or rotary egg beater until foamy. Sprinkle cream of tartar over eggs and continue beating to soft-peak stage. Add remaining cup of sugar by sprinkling ¼ cup at a time over egg whites and blending carefully into, about 20 strokes each time. Fold in vanilla and instant coffee. (Be sure coffee is powdered). Sift flour mixture over egg whites about ¼ at a time and fold in lightly, about 10 strokes each time. Pour into ungreased 10-inch round tube pan. Bake in 350° oven for 35-45 minutes. Remove from oven and invert pan on cooling rack.

Butter Icing:

½ cup butter	1 teaspoon vanilla
¼ teaspoon salt	2 tablespoons powdered coffee
2 ½ cups confectioners sugar	1 small package slivered almonds
3 to 4 tablespoons milk	

Cream butter, add salt and sugar, a small amount at a time, beating all the while. Add milk as needed and flavoring. Beat until light and fluffy. Add coffee. Toast almonds. After applying icing to cake, place almonds, one at a time on icing for tasteful results.

Mrs. Frank Steudlein

This is the most delicious cake I have ever eaten.

286

APRICOT NECTAR CAKE

1 box Duncan Hines lemon
supreme cake mix
1 package lemon Jello
¾ cup apricot nectar

½ cup Wesson oil
½ teaspoon salt
1 teaspoon vanilla
4 eggs

Mix cake mix, Jello, nectar, oil, salt and vanilla. Add eggs, one at a time, mixing well after each one. Bake in well-greased and floured tube pan at 325° for 50 minutes. While cake is still hot, punch holes with toothpick and pour glaze over and let stand overnight.

Glaze:

3 cups powdered sugar
¼ cup lemon juice

¾ cup orange juice
2 tablespoons dried lemon peel

Jan Richardson,
Mrs. James Hunter

CARAMEL CAKE

¾ cup shortening
1¾ cups sugar
¾ cup milk
3 cups flour

3 teaspoons baking powder
4 egg whites
1 teaspoon vanilla

Cream shortening and sugar together. Then add milk alternately with the sifted dry ingredients. Fold in the stiffly beaten egg whites to which vanilla has been added. Stir well, but never beat. Bake at 350° for 25-30 minutes.

Icing:

2 cups light brown sugar
1 cup granulated sugar
½ teaspoon salt

½ cup milk
2 tablespoons shortening or butter
1 teaspoon vanilla

Cook sugar, salt, and milk together. Stir until all lumps are dissolved, then remove from heat. Add the shortening and cook to 110°. Beat hard until it will hold shape on cake. Add vanilla. If desired decorate with halves of English walnuts or pecans.

Mrs. H. H. Hagen

This recipe won a prize at the Wilson County Fair at Lebanon, Tenn, also Tennessee State Fair at Nashville in 1927.

FROSTED CHERRY-DATE CAKE

1 box Pillsbury cherry cake mix	½ cup Crisco oil
1 package Dream Whip	4 eggs
1 package French vanilla pudding mix	½ cup maraschino cherries, sliced
	½ cup dates, chopped
1 cup water or part water and part cherry juice to make 1 cup	½ cup (or more) coconut

Mix cake mix, Dream Whip, pudding mix, water and oil for about 3 minutes. Add eggs one at a time. Mix well. Add cherries, dates and coconut. Pour in greased, floured bundt pan. Bake 45-50 minutes at 350°.

Drizzle for Top:

1 cup xx powdered sugar	1 or 2 or 3 tablespoons milk
1 teaspoon butter flavoring	1 drop red food coloring (optional)
1 teaspoon vanilla (or cherry) flavoring	

Mix until stiff to pour. Pour over warm cake.

Charles Baddour

TOASTED BUTTER PECAN CAKE

3 tablespoons butter	2 eggs
1 ⅓ cups pecans, chopped	2 cups flour
¾ cup butter	2 teaspoons baking powder
1 ⅓ cups sugar	¼ teaspoon salt
1 ½ teaspoons vanilla	⅔ cup milk

In baking pan dot 3 tablespoons butter over pecans. Toast at 350° for 15 minutes. Cream ¾ cup butter, gradually adding sugar; beat until fluffy. Add vanilla. Beat in eggs, one at a time. Sift together flour, baking powder and salt. Add to creamed mixture alternately with milk. Beat after each addition. Fold in 1 cup pecans. Set aside remaining ⅓ cup pecans for top of cake. Bake at 350° in two floured pans for 30-35 minutes. Cool completely before icing.

Frosting:

4 tablespoons butter	1 teaspoon vanilla
3 cups powdered sugar	2 ½ to 3 tablespoons light cream

Combine all ingredients in mixing bowl. Beat until smooth. Spread frosting on cake and between layers. Sprinkle remaining pecans in wreath atop cake.

Mrs. Ben G. Hines

FIG CAKE

2 cups all purpose flour	1 cup oil
1 teaspoon cinnamon	3 eggs
1 teaspoon cloves	1 cup buttermilk
1 teaspoon nutmeg	1 cup fig preserves
1 teaspoon salt	1 teaspoon vanilla
1 teaspoon soda	1 cup pecans, chopped (optional)
1½ cups sugar	

Mix all dry ingredients. Add oil and beat well. Add eggs one at a time alternately with milk. Stir in figs, vanilla, and pecans. Bake in bundt pan about 1 hour at 325°.

Mrs. Roy B. Morley

LADY BALTIMORE CAKE

3 cups flour	2 cups sugar
3 teaspoons baking powder	1 cup milk
½ teaspoon salt	1 teaspoon vanilla flavoring
1 cup shortening	5 egg whites

Sift flour once, measure, add baking powder and salt and sift 3 times. Cream shortening, add sugar, cream thoroughly. Add flour alternately with milk, adding flour last. Stir in vanilla. Beat egg whites and fold in. Bake in three 9-inch layers at 375° for 20-30 minutes or until done. Use Maltimation cake filling.

Maltimation Cake Filling:

1 tablespoon flour	1 pound white raisins
Pinch salt	1 pound candied cherries, chopped
1 cup sugar	1 pound coconut
8 egg yolks, beaten	1 pound English walnuts, chopped
1 cup milk	1 pound pecans, chopped
½ pound butter	

Mix flour, salt, sugar and egg yolks. Add milk and cook in a double boiler until thick. Beat in butter and add fruit and nuts. Spread between layers and on top of Lady Baltimore Cake.

Sarah Smith

Given to me by my mother about thirty years ago.

DUMP CAKE

2 cans cherry pie filling	1 can walnuts
1 small can crushed pineapple	1 cup coconut
1 yellow cake mix	1 stick margarine

Grease pan thoroughly. Pour cherry filling in pan, add pineapple on top of filling, add dry cake mix. Add walnuts and coconut on top of cake mix. Melt butter and pour onto cake. Bake at 350° until brown.

Debbie West

Easy and good.

POPPY SEED LOAF CAKE

3 cups flour, unsifted	1 ½ cups milk
1 ½ teaspoons salt	1 ½ teaspoons almond flavoring
1 ½ teaspoons baking powder	1 ½ tablespoons poppy seed
3 eggs	1 ½ teaspoons vanilla
1 ⅛ cups oil	1 ½ teaspoons butter flavoring
2 ½ cups sugar	

Mix well for 2 minutes with mixer. Pour into 2 wax paper-lined loaf pans. Bake 1 hour at 350°.

Glaze:

1 ¼ cups orange juice	½ teaspoon butter flavoring
¾ cup sugar	½ teaspoon vanilla
½ teaspoon almond flavoring	

Pour over hot cake.

Mrs. Malcolm Graham

PINEAPPLE CAKE

1 package yellow cake mix, prepared	1 package vanilla pudding, prepared
1 15 ½-ounce can crushed pineapple	Whipped cream

Prepare cake according to package directions. Bake in 13x9x2″ pan. While still hot from oven, pour undrained pineapple over cake in pan. Refrigerate overnight. Prepare pudding and spread over all. Just before serving, spread a layer of whipped cream.

Sarah Aaron

FROSTED LEMON CAKE

1 box lemon cake mix	2 teaspoons lemon flavoring
½ box lemon cake mix (2¼ cups)	1 teaspoon coconut flavoring
1 box lemon Jello instant	6 eggs
pudding	1 package Dream Whip
¾ cup oil	1 cup coconut
1½ cups water	

Blend cake mix and pudding in large bowl with oil, water, and flavoring for 2 minutes at medium speed. Add eggs one at a time, beating well after each addition. Beat for 2 more minutes. Fold in Dream Whip and coconut. Pour in large tube pan which has been greased and floured. Cook at 325° for 1 hour and 10 minutes or until done.

Icing for Frosted Lemon Cake:

1 pound of confectioners sugar	1 teaspoon lemon flavoring
1 stick butter	½ cup coconut
¼ cup milk	2 drops yellow food coloring
½ teaspoon coconut flavoring	

Put sugar in mixing bowl and make a well. Pour melted butter into well and mix together until it forms a ball. Add milk until it reaches a spreadable consistency. Then add flavoring, coconut, and coloring. Spread over cake while still warm. Let icing run down the sides while spreading with a knife.

Charles Baddour

GRANDMOTHER JORDAN'S FRESH PEACH CAKE

2 cups sugar	1 teaspoon salt
1¼ cups Wesson oil	1 teaspoon vanilla
3 large eggs	3 cups raw peaches
3 cups plain flour	1 cup pecans, chopped
1 teaspoon soda	

Cream sugar, oil and eggs. Add flour, soda, salt and vanilla. Mix well. Add peaches and pecans. Bake in greased and floured tube pan at 325° for 1 hour. Let cool about 20 minutes. Turn out and spread with topping while warm.

Topping:

½ cup light brown sugar	¼ cup canned milk
½ stick oleo	1 teaspoon vanilla

Beat until smooth and spread on top of cake.

Mrs. Kent Ingram

This is a delicious cake.

291

PLAINS GEORGIA CAKE

1 box yellow cake mix
1 package French vanilla
   pudding mix
½ teaspoon nutmeg
½ cup oil
1 teaspoon butter flavoring

2 teaspoons vanilla butter and nut
   flavoring
1 cup water
4 eggs
¾ cup nuts, chopped
½ cup Reeses peanut butter chips

Mix cake mix, pudding mix, nutmeg, oil, flavorings and water until well blended. Add eggs one at a time, beating well after each addition. Fold in nuts and peanut butter chips. Pour in a greased and floured large bundt pan. Bake at 350° for 45 to 55 minutes or until done. Turn out with top side up, drizzle cake while slightly warm with the Plains Georgia Icing.

Plains Georgia Icing:

4 ounces peanut butter chips
1 tablespoon butter or oleo
¼ cup water

1 cup xx sugar
1 teaspoon vanilla
Dash of salt

Over slow heat, melt chips, butter and water. Add sugar, vanilla and salt. Beat until smooth. Pour over warm cake.

Charles Baddour

SEVEN-UP CAKE

1 box Duncan Hines pineapple
   supreme (or lemon) cake mix
1 box instant vanilla (or lemon)
   pudding
¾ cup oil
10-ounce bottle 7-up

6 eggs
1½ cups sugar
1 11-ounce can crushed pineapple
¾ stick margarine
2 tablespoons flour
1 cup coconut (optional)

Combine cake mix, pudding, oil and 7-up. Mix well. Add 4 eggs, one at a time, mixing well after each egg. Pour into 9x13" pan and bake at 350° for 30-40 minutes. Make filling by combining sugar, remaining 2 eggs, undrained pineapple, margarine and flour and cooking until thick, stirring constantly. Stir in coconut and spread on hot cake.

Jennie Yaeger,
Veronica Troutt, Linda Long

CARAMEL FROSTING

½ cup butter or Parkay oleo
1 cup firmly packed light brown
   sugar

¼ cup milk
1 teaspoon vanilla
1¾ cups confectioners sugar, sifted

Melt butter; add brown sugar and bring to a boil over low heat. Boil 2 minutes, stirring constantly. Add milk; return to boil, stirring constantly. Remove from heat. Cool to lukewarm. Add vanilla. Gradually beat in confectioners sugar until spreading consistency.

Charles Baddour

EASY CARAMEL ICING OR CANDY

1 stick oleo
2 cups sugar
⅔ cup sweet milk

Dash salt
30 Kraft caramel candies
1 cup nuts

Mix oleo, sugar, milk and salt in heavy saucepan and cook over low heat to the soft ball stage. Add caramels. Stir until melted. Add nuts and beat until thick. Spread on cake.

Mrs. John Sanders

CARAMEL ICING

2 cups white sugar
2 sticks oleo or butter
2 tablespoons white Karo syrup

1 teaspoon soda
1 cup buttermilk
2 teaspoons vanilla

Put sugar, oleo and syrup in top of double boiler. Dissolve soda in buttermilk and add. Bring to hard boil until forms soft balls in cold water. Remove from stove. Add flavoring and beat lightly until cool and thick enough to spread.

Mrs. Hershel Christian

NEVER-FAIL CHOCOLATE ICING

2 cups sugar
½ cup milk
¼ cup white Karo syrup

2 squares baking chocolate
½ cup shortening
1 teaspoon vanilla

Mix sugar, milk, syrup, chocolate and shortening in saucepan. Let come to boil, scraping sides till well dissolved. Boil 3 minutes or 220° on candy thermometer. Remove from heat. Let cool about 10 minutes. Add vanilla and beat till spreading consistency. (Can be thinned with milk or cream if allowed to get too thick). Will ice two 9" layers 1½ times. Will ice three 9" layers. Will be creamy and good.

Randy Caldwell

FILLING FOR GERMAN CHOCOLATE CAKE

3 egg yolks
1 cup sugar
1 cup Pet milk
1 stick oleo

1 tablespoon flour
1 cup coconut
1 cup pecans
1 teaspoon vanilla

Beat egg yolks. Add sugar, milk, oleo and flour. Cook in double boiler or heavy saucepan until thick. Cool. Add coconut, pecans, and vanilla.

Grace Knolton

DRIZZLE

1 cup confectioners sugar
2 teaspoons butter flavoring

1 teaspoon vanilla
1-2 tablespoons milk

Mix well and drizzle over any cake. Flavoring can be changed and food coloring added to suit cake.

Charles Baddour

LADY BALTIMORE FILLING

1 cup sweet milk
1 tablespoon butter
6 egg yolks
1 cup sugar
3 tablespoons flour

1 cup raisins
1 cup figs
1 cup dates
3 cups nuts, chopped

Put milk on in double boiler and let start boiling. Then add butter, egg yolks, sugar and flour. Cook until thick. Remove from stove and add fruit and nuts. Use on white cake.

Mrs. T. R. Vance

From a World War II cookbook.

LEMON GLAZE

2 cups unsifted confectioners
    sugar
2 tablespoons light cream

2 tablespoons lemon juice
Coarsely grated lemon peel

Mix all ingredients and beat until smooth.

BOILED ICING

1 cup water
1 teaspoon vinegar
4 cups sugar

4 egg whites
1 teaspoon lemon juice

Boil together water, vinegar, sugar until it spins a thread. Pour slowly over stiffly beaten egg whites and beat until creamy. Add lemon juice.

Mrs. Earl Ellis

A World War II recipe.

ORANGE ICING

½ stick butter
1 pound box confectioners sugar

⅓ cup orange juice
Grated rind of one orange

Cream butter and sugar. Add juice and rind of orange and beat until creamy consistency for spreading is reached.

FLUFFY 7 MINUTE ICING

2 egg whites
1 ½ cups light corn syrup
Dash of salt

1 teaspoon vanilla
½ tablespoon lemon juice (optional)

Combine egg whites, syrup and salt in top of double boiler, beating with egg beater until thoroughly mixed. Place over rapidly boiling water. Beat constantly for 7 minutes, or until it stands in peaks. Remove from heat, add vanilla and beat until thick enough to spread. Lemon juice may be added to make it less sweet.

WHITE FROSTING

½ cup butter or margarine
1 cup granulated sugar
¼ cup milk
1 ¾ to 2 cups sifted confectioners sugar

1 teaspoon vanilla extract or ½ teaspoon almond extract

Melt butter in small saucepan, over medium heat. Remove from heat. Add granulated sugar and milk, stirring until well blended. Over medium heat, bring to boiling, stirring. Remove from heat; let cool slightly. With portable electric mixer at medium speed, or wooden spoon, gradually beat 1¾ cups confectioners sugar into warm mixture, beating well after each addition, until frosting is thick enough to spread and barely holds its shape. If frosting seems too thin to spread, gradually beat in a little more confectioners' sugar. Add vanilla.

MAMA'S CHOCOLATE PIE

1 cup sugar	2 cups milk
2 tablespoons flour or cornstarch	5 egg yolks, beaten
¼ teaspoon salt	3 tablespoons butter
4 tablespoons cocoa	1 ½ teaspoons vanilla

In saucepan, combine sugar, flour, salt, and cocoa. Gradually stir in milk. Cook and stir over medium heat until bubbly. Cook and stir 2 minutes. Remove from heat. Stir small amount of hot mixture into egg yolks, then add yolks to remaining hot mixture. Cook for about 2 minutes, stirring constantly. Remove from heat. Add butter and vanilla. Pour into cooled, baked 10-inch pastry shell. Spread meringue over pie and bake at 350° for 12 to 15 minutes.

Meringue:

4 egg whites	¼ teaspoon cream of tartar
½ teaspoon vanilla	6 tablespoons sugar

Beat egg whites (which are at room temperature) with vanilla and cream of tartar until soft peaks form. Gradually add sugar, beating until stiff and glossy peaks form. Spread meringue over hot filling, sealing to edge of pastry. Bake at 350° for 12-15 minutes or until golden brown. Note: before cutting a meringue-topped pie, dip knife in water.

Mrs. M. D. Baddour

CAROLE'S CHOCOLATE ICE BOX PIE

1 cup sugar	1 cup milk
2 tablespoons flour	1 ½ tablespoons butter
2 tablespoons cocoa	1 teaspoon vanilla
3 egg yolks	

Mix sugar, flour, cocoa. Add well-beaten egg yolks. Add milk and cook until thick. Then add butter and vanilla. Mix and pour into baked pie shell. Refrigerate.

Topping: XX whipping cream is the best; if you prefer meringue, that is good also.

Carole McCallum

CHOCOLATE PIE

2 eggs, separated	1 tablespoon flour
1 pint sweet milk	2½ tablespoons cocoa
½ cup sugar	¼ teaspoon salt
1 tablespoon cornstarch	1 teaspoon vanilla

Beat egg yolks and add milk. Sift all dry ingredients together. Add to milk and egg. Cook in double boiler until thick. Add vanilla. Put in baked pie shell, add meringue made of reserved egg whites and bake at 350° for 15 minutes until light brown.

Mrs. R. O. Buck, Sr.

GRACE'S CHOCOLATE PIE

1½ cups sugar	4 tablespoons cocoa
½ cup butter	1 teaspoon vanilla
5 eggs	Pie crust
1 cup sweet milk	3 tablespoons sugar

Cream sugar and butter. Add 2 eggs and 3 egg yolks (reserving 3 egg whites), and mix well. Add milk, cocoa and vanilla. Pour into 9-inch unbaked pie shell. Bake at 350° for 30-35 minutes. Make meringue from reserved egg whites and 3 tablespoons sugar. Cover top of pie with meringue and brown for 15 minutes at 350°.

Grace Wesson

INSTANT CHOCOLATE PIE

1 8-inch graham cracker ready crust pie shell	1 cup milk
	2 cups non-dairy whipped topping
1 4½-ounce package instant chocolate pudding mix	¼ cup chopped pecans
	Chopped pecans

Prepare pudding mix according to directions, using only 1 cup milk. Blend in 1½ cups whipped topping and ¼ cup pecans. Spoon into baked pie shell. Decorate with remaining ½ cup whipped topping and additional nuts. Chill at least 1 hour. *Serves 6.*

Variation: Use banana pudding mix instead of chocolate and 2 bananas instead of pecans.

Pam Baddour

So simple anyone can make to please their man.

BLACK BOTTOM PIE

3 cups crushed chocolate wafers
6 tablespoons soft butter or
    margarine
2 envelopes unflavored gelatin
½ cup cold water
3 cups milk
6 egg yolks, beaten
½ cup granulated sugar

¼ teaspoon salt
4 teaspoons cornstarch
2 teaspoons vanilla
3 squares unsweetened chocolate,
    melted
6 egg whites
½ cup granulated sugar
2 tablespoons white rum

Using fork, mix wafer crumbs with butter until crumbly. With back of spoon, press to bottom and sides of two 9-inch pie plates. Bake at 375° for 8 minutes. Cool. Add gelatin to water; set aside. Scald milk in double boiler. Combine eggs, sugar, salt, and cornstarch and slowly stir into milk. Cook, stirring, over boiling water, until custard coats on spoon. Remove from heat, add gelatin and stir until melted. To half of custard, add vanilla and chocolate. Beat until smooth. Cool until mixture mounds. Divide between two crusts. Chill. Chill other half of custard until it just begins to set. Meanwhile, beat egg whites until they form peaks when beater is raised. Slowly add ½ cup sugar and rum. Fold into custard. Spoon on top of chocolate mixture in shells. Freeze or refrigerate. Makes 2 pies. Top with whipped cream and shaved chocolate before serving.

Joyce T. Ferguson

Specialty of my house.

CHOCOLATE SUNDAE PIE

½ pound graham crackers,
    crushed
1 stick butter, melted
1 package plain gelatin
½ cup cold water

3 eggs, separated
1 cup sugar
1½ cups milk
½ pint XX cream
1 almond chocolate bar, grated

For crust, line pie pan with graham cracker crumbs. Pour melted butter over. In small bowl, dissolve gelatin in water; set aside. Beat egg yolks, adding sugar and milk. Mix in double boiler and cook until mixture begins to thicken or coats a spoon. Remove from heat and add gelatin. Cool. Beat egg whites until stiff and fold into custard. Pour into crust, and refrigerate until congealed. Whip cream and pile on pie. Sprinkle with grated chocolate bar.

Mrs. James H. Wright

CHOCOLATE BAVARIAN PIE

1   9-inch pie shell made with
    Famous (Nabisco) chocolate
    wafers
½   stick oleo, melted
1   envelope plain gelatin
¼   cup water
1   cup milk

3   eggs
½   cup sugar
½   teaspoon salt
1   cup xx cream
1   teaspoon vanilla
Grated chocolate

Crush wafers with rolling pin or blender. Add melted oleo and mix. Put in pie pan and press into shape. Cook 5 minutes at 350°. Cool. Dissolve gelatin in water. Put milk, eggs, sugar and salt in double boiler and cook until coats spoon (5 minutes). Add gelatin and cool until partially set. Fold in whipped cream and vanilla. Pour into chocolate shell. Grate chocolate over top, chill several hours. Serves 6.

Randy Caldwell

FRENCH CHOCOLATE PIE

½   cup egg whites (3 or 4 eggs)
½   cup sugar
¼   teaspoon cream of tartar
½   cup sugar

½   cup sliced almonds
¼   cup cocoa
½   pint heavy cream

Beat egg whites until stiff. Add sugar and cream of tartar, beating well. In separate bowl, mix sugar, almonds, and cocoa. Fold into egg whites. Pour into ungreased 9″ pie pan. Bake at 350° for 30 minutes. Whip cream. Pour into pie.

Sue Turner

CHOCOLATE-COCONUT PIE

3   cups sugar
Pinch salt
7   tablespoons cocoa
4   eggs
1   teaspoon vanilla

1   large can Pet milk
1   stick margarine, melted
2   cups coconut
2   cups nuts (optional)

Mix sugar, salt and cocoa together. Add eggs and mix well. Stir in vanilla, milk, margarine, coconut, and nuts. Pour into 2 unbaked pie shells. Bake at 350° about 40 minutes or until firm.

Mrs. Robert Lakey

GRANNY'S CHOCOLATE FUDGE PIE

1 cup sugar
3 tablespoons cocoa
2 tablespoons Nestle's Quik
3 tablespoons flour
3 egg yolks, beaten
1 cup milk

3 tablespoons butter or margarine
1 teaspoon vanilla extract
½ cup chopped pecans (optional)
1 9-inch baked pie shell
Meringue (recipe follows)

Combine sugar, cocoa, Quik and flour in a saucepan. Combine egg yolks and milk, blending well; add to dry ingredients. Cook slowly over low heat, stirring constantly, until very thick. Remove from heat; add butter, vanilla and nuts; blend well. Pour into pie shell; top with meringue. Bake at 325° for 20 to 30 minutes until meringue is slightly browned. Chill 6 hours before serving.

Meringue:

3 egg whites
¼ teaspoon cream of tartar

6 tablespoons sugar
½ teaspoon vanilla extract

Combine egg whites and cream of tartar; beat until frothy. Add sugar, a small amount at a time, and continue beating until mixture is thick and glossy. Fold in flavoring.

Linda Stubbs

SALLY'S FUDGE PIE

1½ sticks oleo, melted
1½ cups sugar
3   eggs, beaten
¾   cup flour

3 tablespoons cocoa
1 teaspoon vanilla
⅛ teaspoon salt
¾ cup pecans

Cream oleo and sugar. Stir in beaten eggs, mixing well. Sift flour and cocoa together and add. Stir in vanilla, salt, and pecans. Grease a pie plate with oleo. Dust with flour. Pour in mixture and bake at 350° for 30-40 minutes. Top of pie will crack. Don't overcook. Serve topped with ice cream or whipped cream.

Beth Vail

BROWNIE PIE

3 egg whites
Pinch salt
¾ cup sugar
¾ cup chocolate wafer crumbs

½ cup nuts, chopped
1 teaspoon vanilla
1 cup whipping cream
Sugar

Beat egg whites with salt until soft peaks form; gradually add sugar, beating until stiff. Fold in crumbs, nuts and ½ teaspoon vanilla. Spread mixture in a buttered 9-inch pie plate, bringing up on side as crust. Bake in 325° oven about 30 minutes. Remove from oven and cool thoroughly. Beat cream stiff and sweeten to taste, add remaining vanilla. Spread on cool pie and chill for about 4 hours.

Homazelle Ashford

FUDGE PIE

1 cup sugar
2 whole eggs
2 heaping tablespoons flour
3 tablespoons cocoa

½ cup milk
1 teaspoon vanilla
3 tablespoons butter, melted

Mix above ingredients and pour into unbaked pie shell. Bake at 350° for 30 minutes. Serve with whipped cream or vanilla ice cream if desired.

Betty Highfill

HELEN'S BROWNIE PIE

1 cup sugar
½ cup flour
2 eggs, beaten
1 stick butter, melted and cooled

1 cup English walnuts
1 cup chocolate chips
1 teaspoon vanilla

Mix sugar and flour. Add eggs and then butter. Add English walnuts and chocolate chips and vanilla. Pour into unbaked pie shell and bake 30 minutes at 350°. You may have to bake longer because ovens vary. Test with a toothpick. It should be chewy, but not runny.

Helen Baddour Deneka

The easiest and best chocolate pie you've ever tasted!

CHOCOLATE CHEESE PIE

1 8-ounce package cream cheese,
   softened
¼ cup sugar
1 teaspoon vanilla
2 eggs, separated
1 6-ounce package semi-sweet
   chocolate morsels

¼ cup sugar
1 cup heavy cream, whipped
½ cup pecans, chopped
9-inch graham cracker crust

Combine cream cheese, sugar and vanilla and blend thoroughly. Stir in beaten egg yolks. In top of double boiler, melt chocolate morsels over hot, not boiling water. Add this to the cream cheese mixture. Beat egg whites until foamy. Add sugar and continue beating until stiff peaks form. Fold into chocolate mixture. Fold whipped cream into the chocolate mixture. Fold in pecans. Spread into graham cracker crust and freeze.

Mary Virginia Gaines

CHOCOLATE CHESS PIE

1 unbaked 10" pie crust
1¼ cups granulated sugar
3 tablespoons cocoa
2 beaten eggs

1 small can evaporated milk
½ stick oleo, melted
1 teaspoon vanilla

Combine sugar and cocoa. Add eggs, milk, oleo, and vanilla. Pour into pie shell and bake at 350° for 40 minutes.

Donna Frangenberg

CHESS PIE

2 whole eggs, beaten
1 cup sugar
½ cup brown sugar
1 tablespoon plain corn meal
1 tablespoon flour

¼ cup sweet milk
1 stick butter, melted
½ teaspoon vinegar
1 tablespoon vanilla

Beat all ingredients with mixer for 5 minutes. Place in uncooked pie shell. Bake at 325° for 45 minutes. Cool before cutting.

Mrs. Frank Baddour

CHESS PIE

¼ cup butter
1 cup sugar
1 tablespoon flour
3 egg yolks
1 tablespoon water

1¼ teaspoons vinegar
1 teaspoon vanilla
Pie shell
3 tablespoons sugar

Cream butter and 1 cup sugar. Add flour. Add egg yolks, water, vinegar, and vanilla. Bake at 325° for 45 minutes in uncooked pie shell. Cover with meringue made with whites of egg and remaining sugar.

Harriett Manning

CREAM CHESS PIE

1½ cups sugar
⅓ cup shortening
1 tablespoon flour
3 eggs

1 cup evaporated milk
⅛ teaspoon nutmeg
⅛ teaspoon salt
9-inch unbaked pastry

Place sugar, shortening and flour in bowl; cream. Add eggs, one at a time, beating thoroughly after each. Add milk, nutmeg and salt, mix. Pour into pastry. Bake in 400° oven 15 minutes; reduce heat to 350° and bake 30 minutes longer.

Sarah Smith

LEMON CHESS PIE

2 cups sugar
1 tablespoon flour
1 tablespoon corn meal
4 unbeaten eggs

¼ cup oleo, melted
¼ cup sweet milk
¼ cup lemon juice
Pinch of salt

Combine all ingredients and stir just enough to mix. Pour into unbaked pie shell and bake at 375° about 35 minutes or until filling is set.

Mary Riley

FRESH COCONUT PIE

¾ cup sugar
2 tablespoons cornstarch
4 eggs, separated
1 ½ cups milk
1 tablespoon butter

½ teaspoon pure vanilla
2 cups freshly grated coconut
Baked pie shell
3 tablespoons sugar

Mix sugar and cornstarch until smooth. Add egg yolks, stirring until mixed. Add milk, butter and vanilla. Cook over double boiler until thick. Add coconut, leaving ¼ cup for meringue. Pour into precooked pie shell. Beat egg whites until they hold a peak; add 3 tablespoons sugar to meringue. Cover pie, sealing it well and sprinkle remaining coconut on top. Brown in oven at 350°.

Mrs. R. K. Baddour
(submitted by Nellie B. Pike)

COCONUT PIE

3 eggs
1 stick oleo, melted
1 ½ cups sugar
½ teaspoon vanilla

1 tablespoon vinegar
Pinch salt
1 ⅓ cups coconut
9-inch unbaked pie shell

Beat eggs slightly and add oleo and sugar. Cream well. Add vanilla, vinegar, and salt. Stir in coconut and pour into unbaked shell. Bake in 350° oven for about 45 minutes, or until set.

Opal Deneke

BLENDER PIE

2 cups milk
4 eggs
1 ½ teaspoons vanilla
½ cup Bisquick mix

½ stick butter
¾ cup sugar
1 cup coconut

Put all ingredients in blender. Blend for 3 minutes. Pour into pie pan and allow to set for 5 minutes. Bake at 350° for 40 minutes. Makes its own crust.

Debbie West, Connie Banks,
Pat Wheeler, Sandra Jones

COCONUT PIE

½ cup sugar
⅓ cup flour
3 eggs, separated
2 cups milk
¾ cup coconut

¼ cup butter (optional)
1 9-inch pastry shell, baked
¼ teaspoon cream of tartar
6 tablespoons sugar

Combine sugar and flour in top of double boiler. Beat egg yolks in small bowl and add ¼ cup of milk. Heat remaining milk and add to sugar and flour mixture. Cook in double boiler, stirring until it thickens. Slowly add eggs and milk to mixture, stirring constantly. Add coconut. For a richer pie, add ¼ cup butter. Pour into pastry shell. Make meringue by beating egg whites and cream of tartar until stiff. Add sugar gradually and continue beating until it holds a peak. Spread on pie and bake at 400° until brown, about 10 minutes.

Mrs. Jimmy Lemons

FRENCH COCONUT PIE

3 eggs
1 stick oleo, melted
1½ cups sugar

6 tablespoons buttermilk
1 cup coconut
1 unbaked 9-inch pie shell

Mix all ingredients. Put in unbaked pie shell and bake at 350° for 30 to 40 minutes or until golden brown. *Serves 6.*

Barbara Petty

FRENCH COCONUT PIE

1 stick butter, melted
1½ cups sugar
3 eggs

1 tablespoon vinegar
1 cup coconut

Mix all ingredients. Pour into unbaked pie shell. Bake for 1 hour at 350°.

Mrs. Jimmy Wagner

LEMON PIE

1   cup sugar
2 ½ tablespoons cornstarch
3   eggs
¼   teaspoon salt

1 ½ cups hot water
2   lemons, juiced, or ⅓ cup juice
Grated rind of one lemon
2   tablespoons butter

Sift sugar and cornstarch together. Beat 2 egg yolks and 1 whole egg. Stir in salt, sugar, and cornstarch and mix well. Add hot water and mix. Add lemon juice and rind. Cook in double boiler until thick. Add butter. Pour into pie shell, add meringue made from remaining egg whites, and bake at 350° for 15 minutes, until meringue is brown.

Mrs. R. O. Buck, Sr.

LEMON ICE BOX PIE

½ cup lemon juice
1 can Eagle Brand milk
1 teaspoon grated lemon rind

2 eggs, separated
1 graham cracker crumb pie shell
Vanilla wafers

Mix lemon juice, Eagle Brand milk, rind, and egg yolks together. Line pie shell with vanilla wafers. Pour mixture into pie shell and top with meringue made from reserved egg whites. Cook at 350° for 12-15 minutes or until topping is golden brown.

Carolyn Chalk

LEMON TARTS

1   cup sugar
¼   cup cornstarch
1 ¼ cups milk
3   egg yolks, slightly beaten
⅓   cup lemon juice

1   teaspoon lemon rind, grated
¼   cup margarine
1   cup sour cream
6-8 3-inch tart shells, baked

Mix sugar and cornstarch in a saucepan. Gradually add milk, stirring until smooth. Stir in egg yolks, lemon juice and lemon rind until blended. Add margarine and cook over medium heat, stirring constantly, until mixture comes to a boil. Boil for one minute. Pour into bowl and cover with plastic. Chill. Fold in sour cream. Turn into baked pastry shells. Serve at once or chill until serving time. Garnish with whipped cream. *Serves 6-8.*

Marie Baddour Albertson

ANGEL PIE

4 eggs, separated	4 tablespoons lemon juice
¼ teaspoon cream of tartar	1 tablespoon grated lemon rind
1 ½ cups sugar	1 carton whipping cream

Beat egg whites until frothy. Add cream of tartar and beat until stiff. Gradually add 1 cup sugar and beat until very stiff and glossy. Butter a 9-inch pie plate. Shape meringue to plate. Bake at 250-275° for 1 hour. Let cool overnight. Beat egg yolks, add remaining sugar and mix well. Add lemon juice and rind, and mix. Cook in top of double boiler until very thick, stirring. Cool. Whip cream and fold into cooled egg yolk mixture. Pour into meringue shell. Decorate top of pie with some reserved whipped cream. Refrigerate until firm.

Mrs. Robert Homra

APRICOT PIE

2 cups mixed cookie crumbs (use ½ macaroons and ½ vanilla wafers or graham crackers)	¾ cup sugar
	¼ teaspoon salt
	3 eggs, well beaten
¼ cup brown sugar	2 cups milk, scalded
½ cup butter, melted	½ stick butter
1 box dried apricots (or 2 6-ounce bags)	½ teaspoon vanilla
	½ pint whipped cream
3 tablespoons sugar	Nutmeg
¼ cup cornstarch	

Mix cookie crumbs with brown sugar and melted butter. Press into 9-inch pie plate or 7½x11¾ pyrex and bake 10 minutes at 300°. Chill. Stew apricots and sugar according to directions on box. Mash well. Cool. Pour into crust. Mix cornstarch, sugar and salt to well beaten eggs. Beat until fluffy. Add milk and butter. Cook until thickens. Add vanilla. Let cool and pour over apricots. Top with whipped cream and sprinkle with nutmeg.

Janie Barton

BLUEBERRY PIE

2 eggs, beaten	1 graham cracker pie crust, partly cooked
½ cup sugar	
1 teaspoon vanilla	1 blueberry pie mix
8 ounces cream cheese	Whip cream (optional)

Combine eggs, sugar, vanilla and cream cheese. Blend well, put in pie crust and bake 20 minutes at 375°. Cool and add berry mix. Top with whip cream if desired. Chill thoroughly before serving.

Mrs. Frank Baddour

BLUEBERRY PIE

1   unbaked pie shell
4   cups fresh blueberries
1   cup sugar
2   tablespoons cornstarch
1   tablespoon lemon juice
½   teaspoon salt

2   tablespoons butter
¼   cup unsifted all purpose flour
2   tablespoons brown sugar
¼   teaspoon cinnamon
¼   teaspoon nutmeg
½   cup angel flake coconut

Mix blueberries, sugar, cornstarch, lemon juice, and salt and pour into un-baked pie shell. Cut together butter, flour, brown sugar, cinnamon, and nut-meg and sprinkle over blueberry mixture. Bake for 30 minutes in 425° oven. Sprinkle coconut on top of pie and bake 8 to 10 minutes longer.

Amy Denny

CHERRY FRUIT PIES

1   large can cherry pie filling
1   8-ounce can crushed pineapple
1   cup confectioners sugar
3   tablespoons flour
1   box orange Jello
1   teaspoon vanilla

¼   teaspoon red food color
3   bananas, chopped fine
1   cup pecans, chopped
2   graham cracker crusts, baked
Dream Whip

Mix pie filling, undrained pineapple, sugar, flour. Cook until thickened (about 5 minutes). Remove from heat, add Jello, vanilla, food color, bananas and pecans. Pour into pie shells. Chill. Add topping of Dream Whip when ready to serve. *Makes 2 pies.*

Mrs. Robert Lakey

MISS NELLIE'S ENGLISH APPLE PIE

4   large apples
¾   cup sugar
1   teaspoon cinnamon
½   cup butter
½   cup brown sugar

1   teaspoon cinnamon
1   cup flour
3   tablespoons water
½   cup pecans

Peel and dice apples into buttered baking dish. Sprinkle with sugar and cinnamon. In mixing bowl, cream butter and sugar. Add cinnamon, flour and water. Mix well. Stir in pecans. Roll into crust and cover apple mixture. Bake for 1 hour at 350°.

Variation: Substitute peaches and nutmeg for apples and cinnamon. Sprinkle peaches with a few drops of lemon juice and vanilla.

Nellie George Baddour

KARO PECAN PIE

1 cup red Karo	½ teaspoon salt
½ cup sugar	1 cup pecans
2 tablespoons flour	3 eggs
1 ½ teaspoons vanilla flavoring	1 unbaked pie shell
2 tablespoons butter	

Combine Karo, sugar, flour, vanilla, butter and salt. Add slightly beaten eggs and mix well. Stir in pecans, and pour into pie shell. Bake in oven at 350° for about 45 minutes or until set.

Mrs. J. R. Collier, Sr.

DEAR ABBY'S PECAN PIE

1 cup white corn syrup	1 teaspoon vanilla
1 cup dark brown sugar	3 eggs
⅓ teaspoon salt	1 9-inch pie shell
⅓ cup butter or margarine, melted	1 heaping cup shelled whole pecans

Combine syrup, sugar, salt, butter, vanilla and mix well. Add slightly beaten eggs. Pour into unbaked pie shell. Sprinkle pecans over all. Bake in pre-heated 350° oven for approximately 45 minutes. When cool, you may top with whipped cream or ice cream, but nothing tops this.

Abigail Van Buren

PECAN PIE

2 9-inch pie shells	½ teaspoon lemon extract
4 eggs, separated	¼ teaspoon salt
2 cups granulated sugar	2 cups brown sugar
2 cups sour cream	2 cups broken pecan meats
½ cup sifted flour	

Bake pie shells until half done, about 5-8 minutes. In double boiler, mix egg yolks, sugar, and sour cream. Stir in flour, lemon, and salt. Cook until thickened, about 45 minutes. Spoon into pie shells. In a bowl, beat egg whites and brown sugar. Stir in pecans. Spread over pie and bake at 325° for 15 minutes, or until brown.

Berenice S. Clemmer

A different, highly appealing pecan pie.

SWEET POTATO PIE

2 cups mashed cooked potatoes
1 cup sugar
½ stick oleo
1 egg

1 tsp. nutmeg
½ tsp. cinnamon
1 tsp. vanilla

Mix together and pour in unbaked 9 inch pie crust and bake for 1 hour at 350 degrees.

SOUTHERN COMFORT PEACH PIE

Filling:

10 to 12 fresh peaches, peeled and
    quartered, or 2 cans (1-pound
    13-ounce) waterpacked peaches,
    well drained
½ cup Southern Comfort

⅔ cup sugar
⅓ cup ground almonds
3 tablespoons butter
2 tablespoons flour
Dash of salt

Crust:

1   cup sifted flour
½ teaspoon salt
½ cup shortening or butter
2½ tablespoons ice water

2 tablespoons whipping cream
Whipped cream, sour cream, crème
    fraiche or vanilla ice cream

Fill a deep 10-inch pie pan with peaches. Pour Southern Comfort evenly over top. Combine sugar, almonds, butter, flour and salt in bowl and mix together, cutting in butter with pastry blender or fork. Sprinkle evenly over peaches. Prepare top crust by combining flour and salt in bowl; work in shortening with pastry blender or fingers, or use food processor. Sprinkle with water, a little at a time, until mixture can be pressed into ball. Chill 10 minutes before rolling out. Preheat oven to 450°. Cut a small hole in center of pastry (use a small decorative cutter such as a truffle cutter, if you have one) and arrange pastry on top of pie dish. Crimp edge; use any extra dough to make cutouts for top, if desired. Brush pastry with cream. Bake 10 minutes. Reduce heat to 350° and continue baking until peaches are tender and crust is rich golden brown, about 15 to 20 minutes. Serve warm with your favorite accompaniment.

PIES

EASY CRUST PEACH PIE

1 stick oleo, melted
1½ cups sugar
1 cup self-rising flour

½ cup milk
1 15-ounce can sliced cling peaches

Combine butter, sugar, flour, and milk in mixing bowl and mix well. Pour half of dough mixture into 1½-quart casserole dish. Pour entire can of peaches over this and add rest of dough mixture. Bake 10 minutes at 350°, then turn oven to 400° and bake for another 35 minutes or until done. Makes its own crust!

Debbi Allday

PEACH COBBLER

1 quart sliced peaches, with syrup
½ stick butter, melted
½ cup flour
½ cup yellow cake mix

2 cups sugar
2 teaspoons vanilla flavoring
1 teaspoon nutmeg

Mix peaches, butter, flour, cake mix, and sugar. Then add flavoring and nutmeg. Pour into a 9 x 13 pyrex baking dish. Make pie crust and criss-cross across the top. Bake at 350° for 45 minutes.

Bernice Alexander

QUICK FRUIT COBBLER

1 cup flour
1 tablespoon baking powder
1 cup sugar
1 cup milk

1 can of desired fruit (apples, peaches, apricots, etc.)
½ cup butter
Cinnamon

Sift dry ingredients, mix sugar and milk with dry ingredients, pour the well mixed batter in a well-buttered baking dish. Add one can of any desired fruit; dot with butter and sprinkle cinnamon on top to taste. Bake at 350° for 30 minutes. This is a good weekday dessert. Serve hot with ice cream on top.

Mrs. Hugh Dillahunty

STRAWBERRY PIE

¾ cup flour
6 tablespoons margarine
⅓ cup nuts
3 tablespoons brown sugar
1 cup strawberries, sliced

1 cup whipping cream
1 tablespoon sugar
1 cup cold milk
1 package instant vanilla pudding
  mix

Heat oven to 425°. Combine flour, margarine, nuts, and brown sugar. Mix with hands til crumbly. Press mixture into 9″ pie pan. Place 8″ cake pan on top. Bake 15 mintues. Remove cake pan for cooling. Whip cream and sugar until soft peaks form. Set aside. Pour milk into bowl. Add pudding, beat well — about 1 minute. Immediately fold whipped cream and strawberries into pudding, pour into shell. Chill til firm.

Fanny Corradini

STRAWBERRY PIE

1 3-ounce package strawberry
  Jello
1 cup hot water
1 box frozen strawberries

1 pint vanilla ice cream
1 baked pie crust
Whipped cream (optional)

Dissolve Jello in hot water. Stir in partly thawed box of strawberries. Add softened ice cream. Stir until smooth. Pour into baked pie crust. Serve with Cool Whip or whipped cream, if desired. Good just plain.

Mrs. Charles Adams

MILLION DOLLAR PIE

14-ounce can Eagle Brand milk
9-ounce container Cool Whip
1 small can crushed pineapple,
  drained

2 bananas, sliced (optional)
1 cup pecans, chopped
1 cup coconut
6 tablespoons lemon juice

Blend Eagle Brand and Cool Whip well, then add the rest of ingredients. Make 2 graham cracker crusts. Sprinkle small amount of sugar on crusts and warm in oven. Pour pie filling into crusts and chill. *Makes 2 pies.*

Mary Maxey,
Mrs. William Sanford

FRIED PIES

5 cups plain flour	1 teaspoon salt
1 teaspoon baking soda	1 cup Crisco
1 heaping teaspoon baking powder	2½ cups buttermilk
	Filling (see note below)

Sift flour, soda, baking powder and salt together. Gently blend in Crisco with fingertips until thoroughly mixed. Stir in buttermilk. (Use more if necessary to make a stiff sticky dough). Place heaping tablespoons of dough onto floured sheet. Sprinkle top with flour. Lightly roll and press into round balls between hands. With rolling pin, roll flat about ½ inch thick. Drop in center of dough, one heaping tablespoon filling, fold over and press ends together with fingertip. Roll out all dough and fill all pies before starting to fry. Deep fry in hot skillet of ½ Crisco and ½ Crisco oil (some bacon grease can be used) until golden brown, turning once.

Filling: Dried apples, peaches or apricots may be used as pie filling, cooked according to directions on package, or use pudding mix of any kind. Filling should be cold.

Mrs. Henrie Robbins

FRENCH RAISIN NUT PIE

½ cup butter, softened	½ teaspoon cinnamon
1½ cups sugar	½ teaspoon allspice
3 eggs	½ teaspoon cloves
1 cup seedless raisins	2 tablespoons vinegar
1 cup nuts, chopped	9-inch unbaked pie shell

Cream butter and add sugar slowly while beating. Add 1 egg at a time and beat only until blended. Add raisins and nuts. Mix well. Stir in spices and vinegar. Pour into pie shell and bake in 350° oven for 30 minutes. Remove from oven and cool.

Jan Richardson

ALL-GOOD PIE

1 cup sugar	1 cup pecans, chopped
½ cup butter	1 tablespoon vanilla
2 eggs, separated	1 tablespoon vinegar
1 cup seedless raisins	Pie crust

Mix sugar, butter and yolks of eggs thoroughly. Add raisins, nuts, vanilla and vinegar. Fold in stiffly beaten egg whites. Bake slowly in a rich crust at 300° for about 40 minutes or until light brown. Serve with whipped cream or a small scoop of vanilla ice cream.

Mrs. W. O. Byler

BUTTERMILK PIE

½   cup butter
1½ cups sugar
3   whole eggs
1   tablespoon cornstarch

1   teaspoon vanilla
½   cup buttermilk
Pie shell

Cream butter and sugar. Add well-beaten eggs. Add cornstarch and vanilla; beat until well blended before adding buttermilk. Put in unbaked pie shell. Bake at 350° for 35 minutes.

Harriett Manning

MARTHA WASHINGTON NUTMEG CUSTARD PIE

Pastry for 9-inch pie
3   cups milk
1   bay leaf
1   3-inch cinnamon stick
3   eggs

3   egg yolks
½   cup sugar
1   teaspoon pure vanilla extract
¾   teaspoon ground nutmeg
⅛   teaspoon salt

Line pan with pastry; flute edge and prick bottom and sides with fork tines. Bake in preheated 425° oven for 7 minutes. Remove pie shell from stove and lower heat to 325°. Scald milk and bay leaf and cinnamon. Mix eggs with egg yolks, sugar, vanilla, nutmeg, and salt. Strain milk and add to egg mixture. Mix well. Pour into pie shell. Bake at 325° until a knife inserted in center comes out clean, about 55 minutes. Cool on wire rack. Serve at room temperature with whipped cream. Sprinkle with nutmeg if desired.

White House Cook Book of President's Wives

BUTTERSCOTCH PIE

¼   cup cornstarch or ⅓ cup flour
1   cup light brown sugar
¼   teaspoon salt
2   cups milk, scalded

3   egg yolks, slightly beaten
½   teaspoon vanilla
3   tablespoons butter or oleo

Mix flour and brown sugar and salt, add milk slowly. Cook stirring constantly until mixture thickens. Add small amount to egg yolks and stir. Add egg yolks to sauce and cook to boil. Remove from heat, add flavoring and oleo and cool 10 minutes before putting in pie crust. Top with meringue.

Minnie Miller

RICE KRISPIE PIE

2 full cups Rice Krispies
1 3 ½-ounce can coconut
½ cup oleo
½ cup pecans, chopped

½ cup brown sugar, packed
½ gallon vanilla ice cream
Butterscotch sauce

Mix Krispies, coconut, pecans and oleo. Put in 350° oven on cookie sheet and let brown, stirring occasionally. Stir in brown sugar and mix until slightly melted. Line baking pan with wax paper. Cover with half the Rice Krispie crumbs. Spoon in softened ice cream and sprinkle remaining crumbs on top. Cover with foil and freeze. Cut in squares and serve with butterscotch sauce.

Grace Wesson

Snap, crackle and good!

RUM CREAM PIE

1 ½ packages unflavored gelatin
½ cup cold water
6 egg yolks
1 scant cup sugar

1 package whipped cream
⅓ cup light rum
2 graham cracker crusts
Grated chocolate

Put gelatin in cold water and melt over hot water. Beat egg yolks and sugar well. Add gelatin mixture. Add whipped cream and fold in rum. Pour into crusts and grate chocolate on top.

Louise Pearson

STRAWBERRY SUNDAE PIE

⅓ cup butter
⅔ cup flour
⅓ cup brown sugar
¾ cup chopped almonds
1 pint vanilla ice cream

1 10-ounce package strawberry
   halves, thawed
½ teaspoon almond extract
2 teaspoons cornstarch

Melt butter in skillet over low heat; add flour, brown sugar and ½ cup almonds. Stir over low heat until crumbs are golden brown, about 3 minutes. Turn into 9" pie plate and press with fork against bottom and sides. Bake 5 minutes at 375°. Cool. Soften ice cream slightly and pack gently into cooled pie shell. Freeze. Combine strawberry halves, almond extract, and cornstarch in saucepan. Heat, stirring until mixture comes to a boil and is thickened. Cool. Spoon over pie just before serving. Sprinkle pie with remaining ¼ cup almonds. *Makes 6 to 8 servings.*

Doris Lanford

HEATH BAR PIE

1 cooled graham cracker crust	¼ cup butter
7 Heath bars	¼ cup white syrup
1½ quarts butter pecan ice cream	1 cup evaporated milk
1 cup sugar	1 cup chocolate chips

Crush Heath bars and place on cooled crust. Top with ice cream. Freeze. For sauce, boil sugar, butter, syrup, evaporated milk for one minute. Add chips. Remove pie from freezer about 20 minutes before serving and top with hot fudge sauce.

Anita M. Slaughter

LEMON ICE CREAM PIE

⅓ cup oleo	3 eggs
2 teaspoons lemon rind	1 quart vanilla ice cream, softened
½ cup lemon juice	1 9-inch pie shell
¼ teaspoon salt	3 egg whites
1 cup sugar	½ cup sugar

Combine oleo, lemon rind, lemon juice, salt, sugar and eggs in double boiler until thick. Cool. Place half of custard in baked pie shell. Top with half of the ice cream. Freeze. Then add rest of custard and ice cream. Refreeze. Make meringue by beating egg whites until stiff, and add ½ cup sugar. Cover top of pie with meringue and brown at 475° for 4 or 5 minutes. (Place frozen pie on cookie sheet so not to break.) Freeze.

Mary Jane Baddour Chandler

MINT ICE CREAM PIE

2 cups Nabisco chocolate wafer crumbs	3 pints vanilla ice cream, softened
⅓ cup butter, softened	5 tablespoons green Crème de Menthe

Make pie crust of chocolate wafer crumbs and butter. Freeze 1½ hours. Swirl ice cream and Crème de Menthe together. Pour into crust. Freeze. When serving, pour fudge sauce on top of each piece.

Fudge Sauce:

3 ounces unsweetened chocolate	⅛ teaspoon salt
½ cup water	4½ tablespoons butter
¾ cup sugar	¾ teaspoon vanilla

Combine and heat chocolate and water. Add sugar and salt; cook 10 minutes. Remove from heat and stir in butter and vanilla.

Mary Farrago

CHERRY CHEESE PIE

2 cups all-purpose flour
1 cup pecans, chopped
2 sticks butter or margarine,
   softened

½ box confectioners sugar
2 8-ounce packages cream cheese
13½-ounce container Cool Whip
1 can cherry pie filling

Combine flour, pecans, and butter. Press into pie pan to make a shell. Bake at 350° for 25-30 minutes. Cool. With hands, mix together sugar and cream cheese. Fold in the Cool Whip and pour into cooled crust. Top with pie filling. Refrigerate.

Bob Burns

FROZEN GRASSHOPPER PIE

2 tablespoons oleo, melted
14 chocolate wafers, crushed
Pinch of mace
24 marshmallows

½ cup milk
4 tablespoons crème de menthe
2 tablespoons crème de cocoa *
1 cup XX cream, whipped

Combine oleo, chocolate wafers and mace. Press into a 9-inch pie pan to make shell. In top of double boiler, melt marshmallows in milk. Add crème de menthe and crème de cocoa. Cool. Fold in whipped cream. Freeze.

Sara M. Hart

RITZ CRACKER PIE

20 Ritz crackers, crushed
4 egg whites, beaten stiff

1 cup sugar
1 cup nuts, chopped

Mix together. Pour into greased pan. Cook 25 minutes at 350°. *Serves 6.*

Lynda Akil

PEANUT BUTTER ICE CREAM PIE

1 quart vanilla ice cream,
   softened
½ cup whipping cream, whipped
   and slightly sweetened

½ cup chunky peanut butter
1 9-inch graham cracker pie crust
¼ cup graham cracker crumb
   mixture

Fold whipped cream and peanut butter into ice cream. Pour into pie crust. Sprinkle crumb mixture around outer edge. Freeze. *Serves 6-8.*

Amy Denny,
Eulalee B. Dacus

PIE CRUST TID BITS

Left over pie dough   Cheese, grated

Roll left-over pie dough, then sprinkle with grated cheese. Cut in fancy shapes. Bake — serve with salads or tea.

Mrs. R. C. Nickle

NEVER FAIL PIE PASTRY

1¼ cups shortening
3 cups flour
1 teaspoon salt

1 egg, well beaten
5 tablespoons water
1 tablespoon vinegar

Cut shortening into flour and salt. Combine egg, water and vinegar. Pour liquid into flour mixture all at once. Blend with spoon just until flour is all moistened. Roll out on floured board. *Makes 2 double crusts.* This is an easy crust to handle and can be rerolled without toughening. Keep in refrigerator up to two weeks. To store divide into 4 equal balls and wrap in foil.

Mrs. Burton W. Renager

NO ROLL PIE CRUST

1½ cups self-rising flour
1 teaspoon salt
1½ teaspoons sugar

2 tablespoons milk
½ cup cooking oil

Put flour, salt and sugar in pie pan. Mix milk with cooking oil and pour over flour. Mix with fork. Pat out as thin as desired for crust with hands. Bake at 375° until brown if recipe calls for already baked crust.

Nell Barnes

319

HAZEL SMITH'S FRESH APPLE COOKIES

1¼ cups brown sugar
½ cup butter
2 eggs
¼ cup milk
2 cups flour
1 teaspoon baking powder
½ teaspoon salt
1 teaspoon cinnamon

½ teaspoon cloves
½ teaspoon nutmeg
1½ cups fresh apples, diced
1 cup walnuts, chopped
1 cup raisins
1 16-ounce package butterscotch pieces

Cream brown sugar and butter. Add beaten eggs and milk. Gradually add dry ingredients. Stir in apples, walnuts, raisins, and butterscotch. Drop on pan, and bake in center of oven for 10-12 minutes at 400°. *Makes 4 dozen.*

Hazel Smith

APPLE BALLS

1 cup butter
2 cups sugar
2 tablespoons cocoa
1 cup apples (yellow or tart), grated

Dash salt
3 cups rolled quick oats
1 teaspoon vanilla
1 cup nuts, chopped
Confectioners sugar

Cook butter, sugar, cocoa, apples and salt in saucepan until it hard boils for one minute. Remove from heat. Add the oats, vanilla, and nuts. Mix well. You may add more oats if necessary. Drop by teaspoonful on wax paper (the smaller the ball, the better). Let cool. Roll balls in confectioners sugar. *Makes about 110 balls.* Stays fresh up to a year in the icebox.

DATE NUT BALLS

½ cup sugar
½ cup brown sugar
1 stick oleo
Pinch salt
1 8-ounce package dates, chopped

1 teaspoon vanilla
2 cups Rice Krispies
1 cup nuts
1 cup coconut (optional)

In saucepan combine sugars, oleo, salt and dates. Allow to boil for 5 minutes, stirring constantly. Remove from heat; add vanilla. Fold in Rice Krispies, nuts and coconut. While warm, roll into balls and let dry on waxed paper. *Makes 5 dozen.*

Jan Richardson,
Brenda Vick

FRUIT COOKIES

1 cup brown sugar	⅓ cup bourbon
½ cup butter	1 teaspoon vanilla
4 eggs	1 pound cherries
3 tablespoons buttermilk	1 pound pineapple
1 teaspoon soda	1 cup dark raisins, chopped
3 cups flour	1 pound nuts, chopped
½ teaspoon nutmeg	1 pound dates, chopped

Cream sugar and butter. Add well-beaten eggs and buttermilk. Gradually add dry ingredients and mix well. Mix in bourbon and vanilla. Stir in fruits and nuts. Drop by teaspoon on greased cookie sheet. Bake 15 to 20 minutes at 350°. *Makes 70-100 cookies.*

Mrs. James Newman

FRUIT COOKIES

1 can Eagle Brand milk	2 cups coconut
1 cup nuts, chopped	

Combine Eagle Brand and nuts. Mix well and roll into balls. Roll balls in coconut. Place on a well-greased pan and bake at 400° for 15-20 minutes or until light brown.

Mrs. Hugh Dillahunty

LEMON COOKIES

¾ cup margarine	½ teaspoon soda
¾ cup sugar	½ teaspoon cream of tartar
1 egg, slightly beaten	½ teaspoon salt
1 teaspoon lemon flavoring	Sugar
2 cups all-purpose flour	

Cream margarine and sugar; add egg and lemon flavoring, sift dry ingredients together and add to creamed mixture. Roll in balls and dip in sugar. Place balls on a cookie sheet. Press each cookie with a fork. Bake at 350° for 10 minutes.

Jan Hamm

WILLIAMSBURG COOKIES

1 can Eagle Brand milk
1 can coconut

1 package dried apricots
Pecans

Mix all ingredients and drop by teaspoonful on greased cookie sheet. Cook until lightly brown.

Grace Wesson

ORANGE SLICE COOKIES

1 pound orange slice candy,
   chopped
1-2 cups coconut

2 cans Eagle Brand milk
2 cups pecans, chopped

Mix all ingredients together. Pour into a flat pan and bake for 30-40 minutes at 350°. While still warm, dip out of pan and roll into balls, and dip into confectioners sugar.

Josie Baddour
Helen Robinson

ORANGE BALLS

1 12-ounce package vanilla wafer
   crumbs
1 16-ounce box powdered sugar
½ cup butter, softened

1 6-ounce can frozen, unsweetened
   orange juice, thawed
1 cup nuts, finely chopped
Flaked coconut (optional)

Combine crumbs, powdered sugar, butter, juice and nuts. Mixing well with hands, form into bite-size balls. If desired, roll in flaked coconut. Chill until firm. *Makes about 60 balls.* May store in refrigerator for up to 2 weeks and they are ready in minutes at room temperature.

Mrs. Charles Carr

Ready in minutes for unexpected guests.

ALMOND DELIGHTS

1 cup flour
1 teaspoon baking powder
¼ teaspoon salt
¼ teaspoon cinnamon
½ cup white sugar
½ cup brown sugar

½ cup shortening
2 egg yolks
1 tablespoon water
½ cup chopped almonds or pecans
1 cup oats (uncooked)

Sift flour, baking powder, salt, cinnamon and white sugar into bowl. Add brown sugar, shortening, egg yolks and water. Beat until smooth. Fold in almonds and oats. Shape into balls. Place on greased baking sheet and bake at 375° for 10 minutes.

Frosting:

2½ cups confectioners sugar
½ cup nonfat dry milk
6 tablespoons butter

1½ teaspoons vanilla
2 tablespoons water

Sift sugar with dry milk. Cream butter until fluffy, then gradually beat in half sugar-milk mixture. Blend in vanilla and add 1 tablespoon water, add remaining half of sugar-milk mixture. Beat in remaining water to bring to spreading consistency.

Brenda Vick

EASY SAND TARTS

1 cup butter, softened
½ cup powdered sugar
2 teaspoons vanilla
½ teaspoon salt

2 cups flour (unsifted)
2 cups nuts, chopped
Powdered sugar

Cream butter and powdered sugar. Stir in vanilla. Add salt and flour, and mix well. Stir in nuts. Shape in small balls. Bake on ungreased cookie sheet at 325° for 20 to 25 minutes. Roll in additional powdered sugar after cooking.

Mrs. Charles Adams, Sr.

OATMEAL COOKIES

1 cup butter	1 cup nuts, chopped
1 cup sugar	1 cup raisins
3 eggs	1 teaspoon cinnamon
1 teaspoon soda	½ teaspoon nutmeg
½ cup buttermilk	¼ teaspoon salt
2 cups flour (use ½ cup flour for nuts and raisins)	2 ½ cups oatmeal (old fashioned)

Cream butter and sugar and add beaten eggs. Dissolve soda in buttermilk and add to batter. Mix ½ cup flour with the nuts and raisins in a separate bowl. Sift spices with flour and stir into batter. Stir in nuts, raisins and oatmeal. (For a nutty flavor, toast the oatmeal on a shallow pan in the oven, being careful not to burn it.) Drop by spoonful on greased cookie sheet and bake at 400°. *Makes about 5 dozen.*

Mrs. R. O. Buck, Sr.

QUAKER OATMEAL COOKIES

½ cup butter	1 teaspoon soda
½ cup bacon drippings	5 tablespoons raisin juice
1 cup sugar	2 cups oatmeal, uncooked
1 egg	2 cups flour, sifted
1 cup raisins, stewed	¼ teaspoon salt

Cream butter and drippings. Add sugar and cream again. Add beaten egg, raisins, then soda dissolved in raisin juice. Add dry ingredients, and beat well. Add more flour if mixture is not thick enough. Drop on greased pan by the teaspoon. Bake for 10-12 minutes at 400°. *Makes about 3 dozen large cookies.*

Marie Colling

Used by the Quakers more than one hundred years ago.

PEANUT BUTTER OATMEAL COOKIES

½ cup milk	½ cup peanut butter
½ stick butter	1 teaspoon vanilla
2 cups sugar	3 cups oats
3 tablespoons cocoa	

In saucepan, mix milk, butter, sugar, and cocoa. Boil 1 minute. Remove from heat and stir in peanut butter and vanilla. Gradually stir in oats, mixing well. Drop on wax paper and allow to cool. *Makes 2 dozen.*

Bill Gurner

ICE BOX COOKIES

2 cups brown sugar	1 teaspoon soda
1 cup butter	½ teaspoon nutmeg
2 eggs	1 teaspoon vanilla
3 ½ cups sifted flour	1 cup nuts, chopped fine

Cream sugar and butter. Add eggs, beating well. Add dry ingredients and mix well. Stir in vanilla and nuts. Mold into long roll. Wrap with wax paper. Chill in refrigerator overnight. Slice and bake. This lasts in the refrigerator for at least 2 weeks. Especially nice during the holidays when company drops by *unexpectedly.*

Vera Glick

GINGER ICE BOX COOKIES

1 cup shortening	1 teaspoon soda
1 cup sugar	4 ½ cups flour
2 eggs	1 teaspoon salt
2 teaspoons ginger	½ cup molasses

Cream shortening and sugar. Add eggs, and mix well. Stir in dry ingredients until moistened. Add molasses and mix well. Shape into 2 long rolls. Chill. Slice thin and bake in 350° oven for 10 to 12 minutes. *Makes about 4 dozen cookies.*

Orpha Robertson

REFRIGERATOR COOKIES

¾ cup butter or Crisco (or ½ butter and ½ Crisco making ¾ cup)	½ teaspoon soda
	½ teaspoon cream of tartar
1 cup sugar	1 teaspoon vanilla
1 egg	½ cup nuts (optional)
2 cups flour	

Cream shortening and sugar. Add egg. Add sifted dry ingredients and vanilla. Mix well. Mold into rolls. Wrap in wax paper and refrigerate. Slice and bake on middle rack at 375° 8 to 10 minutes, or until brown.

Mrs. R. A. Caldwell, Sr.

TEA CAKES

1 ½ cups sugar	½ teaspoon salt
2 sticks oleo or butter	3 teaspoons vanilla flavoring
3 eggs + 1 egg white	2 teaspoons orange flavoring
6 cups flour	2 teaspoons butter flavoring
3 heaping teaspoons baking powder	

Cream sugar and oleo, add eggs. Sift 4 cups flour, baking powder, and salt together and add slowly to egg mixture. Add flavorings. Do this with mixer. Stir in by hand about 2 more cups of flour so the mixture will look like biscuit dough. Roll out on floured board about ¼ inch thick, and cut with a 2-inch biscuit cutter or any size you want. Place on greased pan and bake on bottom of oven for 6 minutes then middle of oven for 6 minutes at 400°.

Oneida Baddour

SUGAR COOKIES

2 cups flour	1 cup + 2 tablespoons sugar
3 teaspoons baking powder	2 large eggs
Pinch salt	1 teaspoon vanilla
¾ cup butter	

Blend dry ingredients. Set aside. Cream butter and sugar. Add eggs and vanilla, beating well. Add dry ingredients and blend. Drop by teaspoon on cookie sheet. Bake 10-12 minutes at 375°. Chocolate chips or coconut may be added.

Lillie Bryant

BUTTER DROP COOKIES

1 cup butter	2 ¼ cups sifted flour
⅔ cup firmly packed brown sugar	¼ teaspoon salt
1 egg	1 package Bakers Coconut
2 teaspoons vanilla	(optional)

Cream butter and sugar until light. Blend in egg and vanilla. Blend in flour, salt, and coconut. Drop from teaspoon onto ungreased cookie sheet. Bake in 400° oven 8 to 10 minutes. *Makes 4 dozen cookies.*

Mrs. James Hunter

CHIP SURPRISE

1 pound oleo	1 cup potato chips, crushed
3 ¾ cups flour	3 teaspoons any flavoring (vanilla,
1 ½ cups sugar	almond, coconut, etc.)

Mix well. Drop on ungreased pans. Bake 15 minutes at 350°. *Yield: 150*

Rebecca Barrett

COWBOY COOKIES

2 cups self-rising flour	1 teaspoon soda
2 cups quick rolled oats	1 teaspoon baking powder
1 cup shortening	Salt
1 cup white sugar	1 cup nuts
1 cup dark brown sugar	1 cup raisins
1 teaspoon apple pie spice	1 package chocolate or butterscotch
⅓ cup buttermilk	chips
2 eggs	

Mix, drop by teaspoonfuls on greased sheet. Bake at 350° until done (very crisp).

Mrs. William B. Gill

FORGOTTEN COOKIES

2 egg whites	1 teaspoon vanilla extract
⅔ cup sugar	1 cup chopped pecans
Pinch salt	1 cup Rice Krispies

Beat egg whites until foamy (be sure that eggs are at room temperature before using.) Gradually add sugar and continue beating until stiff. Add salt and vanilla. Mix well, then add nuts and Rice Krispies. Preheat oven to 350°. Drop cookies by teaspoonfuls onto ungreased, foil-covered cookie sheet. Place cookies in oven and immediately turn oven off. Leave cookies in closed oven overnight or until oven is completely cool. *Yields approximately 2 dozen cookies.*

Mrs. John Wilson

HELEN'S NO BAKE GINGER COOKIE BALLS

2 cups finely crushed gingersnaps (about 40)
¾ cup pecans, coarsely chopped
¼ cup orange flavored liqueur or brandy

2 tablespoons orange rind, grated
2 tablespoons honey
½ cup pecans, ground

In a large bowl, mix gingersnaps, chopped pecans, liqueur, orange rind and honey. Shape the mixture into balls about 1 inch in size. (If you stir the mixture well, there is ample liquid in this recipe.) Then coat the balls in the ground pecans. Store in a tightly covered container to mellow. They may be stored for at least two weeks. *This makes from 40-50 cookies.*

NUTMEG BUTTERBALLS

1 cup butter, softened
½ cup sugar
1 ⅓ cups blanched almonds, chopped

2 teaspoons nutmeg
1 teaspoon vanilla
2 cups flour
½ cup confectioners sugar

Cream butter and sugar. Add almonds and vanilla. Work flour in with fingers. Shape in balls the size of a quarter. Chill until cold. Bake on greased cookie sheets 15-20 minutes at 300°. Mix confectioners sugar and nutmeg. Roll cookies while hot in this mixture. *Makes 6 dozen.*

Mrs. Ford Turner

COOKIE DOUGH FOR COOKIE PRESS

1 pound butter
2 cups sugar
5 cups flour

2 eggs, beaten
2 teaspoons vanilla
Food coloring (Optional)

Place ingredients in bowl and mix. The dough will be stiff. Place in a cookie press and create. Bake at 375° for 10 minutes.

Tip: Have several cookie sheets ready and turn the oven on when you are finished pushing the cookies out. This way you can color the dough, decorate the cookies without rushing. Also, your dough will remain stiff and you will have better formed cookies. These cookies will keep 3 weeks in a tin and they freeze well. I use them at Christmas time.

Mrs. Ford Turner

MARGUERITE'S CHOCOLATE FUDGE

3   cups sugar
⅔ to 1 cup cocoa
Dash salt
1 ½ cups milk

1 ½ tablespoons Karo
1   stick butter
1   teaspoon vanilla
1   cup nuts

Mix sugar, cocoa, salt, and milk. Add Karo, cook on high and stir until it boils, then turn heat down to medium high and quit stirring. When it makes a soft ball, take off stove and add butter and beat well. Add vanilla and nuts.

Marguerite Baddour

Good beating makes this candy extra smooth.

PECAN FUDGE

¾   cup cocoa
3   cups sugar
3   tablespoons white corn syrup
1 ⅛ cups Pet milk

6   tablespoons water
1   cup pecans
⅛   teaspoon salt
1 ½ teaspoons vanilla

In saucepan, combine cocoa, sugar and syrup. Dilute milk with water and add. Stir in pecans. When well blended, cook over low heat stirring constantly until sugar dissolves. Boil slowly, stirring occasionally or until a few drops form a soft ball in cold water. Cool to room temperature. Beat and add salt and vanilla. Pour into buttered pan and cut when firm enough.

BUTTERSCOTCH FUDGE

1 cup sugar	½ cup cream
½ cup brown sugar	⅓ cup butter
⅓ cup white corn syrup	¾ cup pecans, chopped
Few grains salt	1 teaspoon vanilla

Mix sugars, corn syrup, salt and cream in saucepan. Cook to boiling point, stirring constantly to 238° or until a few drops form a soft ball in cold water. Remove from heat. Add butter. Cool at room temperature. Add pecans and vanilla. Beat until candy will hold its shape. Drop from a teaspoon onto waxed paper. *Makes about 3 dozen.*

PEANUT BUTTER FUDGE

12-ounce jar peanut butter	2½ cups sugar
2 teaspoons vanilla	¾ cup milk
½ stick oleo	4 tablespoons Karo
2 cups nuts, chopped	½ cup sugar, browned in saucepan

In a bowl, combine the peanut butter, vanilla, oleo and nuts. Mix sugar, milk and Karo in saucepan, bring to a boil. Pour in browned sugar, stirring until dissolved. Cook until soft ball stage. Pour into peanut butter mixture and beat until it holds shape. Spread on buttered plate.

Janie Barton

EASY DIVINITY CANDY

1 ½ cups sugar
½ cup water
Pinch of salt

1 jar marshmallow creme
1 tablespoon vanilla
1 cup nuts, chopped (optional)

Cook sugar and water to soft ball stage. Turn off heat and stir in marshmallow creme, add vanilla and nuts and stir until well mixed. Turn out in greased pan and let cool and set up.

Mrs. John Wilson

NEVER FAIL DIVINITY

3 cups sugar
½ cup water
½ cup white Karo

2 large egg whites
1 teaspoon vanilla
1 or more cups of nuts

Combine sugar, water and Karo in saucepan over high heat. Stir only until sugar dissolves. While syrup is cooking, beat egg whites in large mixer bowl until stiff on high speed. (Be sure bowl and beaters are free of grease.) Cook syrup to 240°. Pour about ½ of syrup over egg whites, beating constantly with mixer. Return syrup to high heat and cook to 265°. Pour over mixture in bowl beating constantly. (Do not scrape syrup pan.) Add vanilla and beat to mix. Remove bowl from mixer and beat with wooden spoon until candy starts to lose gloss. Stir in nuts and continue to beat until candy holds shape when dropped from spoon. Drop on waxed paper. (Do not store in tightly covered container as candy will become sticky. If this happens, expose to air to let dry out.)

Opal Deneke

BUTTER DIVINITY

4 cups white sugar
⅛ teaspoon salt
1 cup light corn syrup
1 cup water

4 egg whites, stiffly beaten
½ cup butter
1 teaspoon vanilla
1 cup nuts, chopped

Combine sugar, salt, syrup and water, bring to a boil, stirring constantly, until sugar is dissolved. Boil to 262° on candy thermometer. Remove from heat, pour slowly over egg whites, beating with electric mixer. Continue beating for 5 minutes. Mixture will be very stiff. Add butter, vanilla and nuts. Beat by hand until firm. Drop by teaspoonfuls on waxed paper. Let stand until firm. Store in airtight container.

Sarah Edwards

PRALINES

1   cup granulated sugar
1   cup packed light brown sugar
⅛ teaspoon salt
½ teaspoon soda

1   cup buttermilk
2   tablespoons butter
1   teaspoon vanilla
1   cup pecans, broken

Use heavy 4-quart pan. Mix sugars, salt, soda, and buttermilk. Stir til sugar dissolves over low heat. Boil over moderate heat without stirring to 230°. Remove from heat. Add butter, vanilla and nuts. Beat with wooden spoon until it begins to look sugary. Quickly spoon onto waxed paper. *Yields about 30 pieces.*

Nancy Webb

EASY NEVER-FAIL PRALINES

1   pound light brown sugar
7 or 8 tablespoons water

1   or more cups pecans
½ stick of butter

Let sugar and water boil hard, then add pecans. Cook until mixture reaches soft ball stage. Add butter and remove from fire. Beat until creamy, but of consistency that will spread. Drop by spoonfuls onto sheet of waxed paper and let harden. Make certain there are sufficient nuts in each spoonful.

June Smith

DOROTHY JEAN'S PRALINES

1   cup canned milk
2   cups sugar
Dash of salt

1   teaspoon vanilla extract
1 to 1 ½ cups pecans

Bring sugar and milk to a foaming boil, stirring constantly. Let boil for 10 minutes over medium heat, being very careful not to let it burn. Remove from heat and beat slightly. Add salt, vanilla and nuts. Let cool until chalky substance appears on side of pan. Drop by teaspoonfuls onto waxed paper.

Linda Stubbs

CHOCOLATE LOGS

1 pound confectioners sugar
1 cup flaked coconut
1 cup pecans or peanuts, chopped
1 teaspoon vanilla
1 cup graham cracker crumbs

½ cup crunchy peanut butter
1 cup butter or oleo
½ block paraffin
1 6-ounce package semi-sweet
   chocolate chips

Mix sugar, coconut, nuts, vanilla and graham cracker crumbs into peanut butter. Pour melted butter over this and blend well. Shape into 2 logs (or small bite size balls) and chill. In double boiler melt together chocolate chips and paraffin. After candy chills, dip it into the melted chocolate and paraffin and place on waxed paper til dried (or in refrigerator). This candy freezes well, which allows you to make a large batch and save some.

Scottie Ming

BUTTERMILK PECAN CANDY

1 cup buttermilk
2 cups sugar
1 teaspoon soda

1 teaspoon vanilla
1 teaspoon oleo
2½ cups pecans

Cook milk, sugar, soda, vanilla and oleo until it forms a hard ball in water. Add pecans. Beat until it is creamy and drop on waxed paper.

ENGLISH ALMOND TOFFEE

⅔ cup oleo
½ cup sugar
⅓ cup water

⅔ cup almonds, chopped
¼ teaspoon baking soda
2 small Hershey bars

Combine oleo, sugar and water in heavy pan over high heat, stirring constantly until mixture boils. Cook without stirring to 236° over medium heat. Add almonds. Cook, stirring constantly to 290°. Remove from heat and add baking soda. Mix well and spread on buttered sheet about ¼ inch thick. Place Hershey bars on top. Heat from candy will melt bars. Spread over top of toffee. Cool and break into pieces of desired size. Store in tightly closed container. (This may be easily tripled but do not triple the amount of soda).

Opal Deneke

DATE NUT ROLL

2 cups granulated sugar
1 cup whipping cream
1 cup dates, chopped
2 tablespoons butter

1 teaspoon vanilla
⅛ teaspoon salt
1 cup pecans, broken

Mix sugar and cream in double boiler. Cook on medium heat, stirring constantly, about 10 minutes or until mixture forms a medium ball when dropped in cold water. Add dates. Cook additional 5 minutes. Remove from heat. Add butter, vanilla and salt. Beat vigorously until thick. Stir in nuts. Pour mixture on a very damp linen towel. Roll. Refrigerate. Cut in slices. *Yield 20 slices.*

Virginia M. Steinek

Everybody's favorite.

DATE LOAF

4 cups sugar
2 tablespoons butter or oleo
1½ cups milk

1 8-ounce package dates
1½ cups nuts

Mix sugar, butter, milk and dates and allow to boil fast, stirring constantly. Test by dropping in cup of water. When a hard ball is formed, take off stove and let set a few minutes. Beat hard and add nuts until it begins hardening. Make a loaf on a wet towel. Wrap in towel in loaf shape and allow to cool. When cool, cut with hot knife.

Mrs. Woods C. Eastland

PEANUT BRITTLE

2 cups sugar
½ cup water
½ cup white Karo syrup

2 cups raw peanuts
½ stick oleo
1 teaspoon soda

Cook sugar, water and syrup until it comes to a boil. Add raw peanuts and cook until mixture becomes a dark caramel. Remove from stove; quickly add oleo and soda, and pour into greased pan. When hard, break into pieces.

Mrs. E. H. Clarke

NOUGAT

1 cup blanched filberts
2 4½-ounce cans blanched
    almonds
2 cups sugar
1 cup light corn syrup

½ cup honey
¼ teaspoon salt
2 egg whites
2 teaspoons vanilla
¼ cup butter or margarine

Preheat oven to 350°. Spread filberts and almonds on cookie sheet. Toast in oven 10 minutes or until golden. Butter 11x7x1¼-inch pan. In heavy straight sided 3-quart pan, combine sugar, corn syrup, honey, salt and ¼ cup water. Stir over medium heat until sugar is dissolved. Continue cooking without stirring to 252° on candy thermometer or until small amount in cold water forms a hard ball. Meanwhile, in large bowl of electric mixer, at high speed, beat egg whites until stiff peaks form. In thin stream, pour about ¼ of hot syrup over egg whites, beating constantly at high speed 5 minutes, or until mixture is stiff enough to hold its shape. Cook rest of syrup to 315-318° on candy thermometer, or until a small amount in cold water forms brittle threads. In thin stream pour hot syrup over meringue, beating constantly at high speed, until stiff enough to hold its shape. Add vanilla and butter, beating until thickened again —about 5 minutes. With wooden spoon, stir in toasted nuts. Turn mixture into prepared pan. Smooth top with spatula. Refrigerate until firm (about 1 hour). Loosen edge of candy all around; turn out in large block. With sharp knife, cut into 1½x1-inch pieces. Wrap each piece in waxed paper. Refrigerate until solid. Makes 2½ pounds.

M. J. Brogan

BAKED FUDGE

4 eggs
2 cups sugar
½ cup cocoa
½ cup flour

½ teaspoon salt
1 cup butter, melted
1 cup pecans, broken
1 teaspoon vanilla

Beat eggs, add all dry ingredients. Mix well. Stir in melted butter, pecans and vanilla. Pour into 11x7" metal pan and set in another pan of boiling water. Bake in 350° oven for 45 minutes or until set like custard. Do not overbake. Cool and cut into squares. Serve with whipped cream or ice cream. Serve warm.

Mrs. John Cooper,
Mrs. Boyce Billingsley

BOSTON BROWNIES

4 squares unsweetened chocolate	4 eggs
½ pound butter	2 teaspoons vanilla
2 cups sugar	1 cup nuts
1 cup flour	1 cup milk chocolate chips

Melt chocolate and butter together. In a large bowl, mix sugar, flour, eggs and vanilla. Add melted chocolate and mix well. Stir in nuts and chocolate chips. Pour into greased 9x13 pan. Bake at 350° for 30 minutes. Test corners to see if done, as center should still seem gooey. Cool 30 minutes. Refrigerate for 1½ hours to 2 hours. *Cut into 16-18 squares.*

Dorrie Weiner

Using this recipe in December, 1981, Charles Baddour won the Mid-South Best Brownie Contest sponsored by the Memphis Press Scimitar...a Memphis, Tennessee newspaper.

BUTTERSCOTCH BROWNIES

¼ cup butter	1 teaspoon baking powder
1 cup brown sugar	½ teaspoon salt
1 egg	½ cup pecans, chopped
1 teaspoon vanilla	Confectioners sugar
½ cup all-purpose flour	

Melt butter in saucepan. Stir brown sugar into it until dissolved. Cool these ingredients slightly. Add egg and vanilla and beat well. Sift, then measure flour. Resift it with baking powder and salt. Stir these ingredients into the butter mixture. Add pecans. Pour the batter into a greased and floured 8x8″ pan. Bake at 350° for about 30 minutes. When cool, dust with confectioners sugar and cut into bars.

Mrs. Donald Foster

CUP CAKE BROWNIES

4 squares semi-sweet chocolate	4 eggs
2 sticks butter	2 cups pecans
1 cup flour	1 teaspoon vanilla
1¾ cups sugar	

Melt together chocolate squares and butter. Then mix flour, sugar and eggs (one at a time and stirring as little as possible). Add this to the chocolate mixture; add pecans and vanilla. Put in cup cake papers, filling ½ full. Bake at 350° until a straw (cake tester) comes out clean (about 25 minutes).

Joy Melton

BROWNIES

1   stick butter
1   cup sugar
4   eggs
1   can chocolate syrup

1   cup flour
Nuts
1   teaspoon baking powder

Cream butter, sugar and eggs. Mix in remaining ingredients. Bake in a greased and floured pan for 25 minutes at 350°.

Frosting:

1   stick butter
1 ½ cups sugar

⅓ cup evaporated milk
½ cup chocolate chips

Place butter, sugar and milk in a saucepan and bring to a boil. Boil 1 minute and stir in chocolate chips. Beat until stiff.

Bob Burns

BROWNIES

4   eggs
2   cups sugar
1   cup oil
1 ½ cups flour
¼   cup cocoa

1   teaspoon baking powder
1   teaspoon salt
2   teaspoons vanilla
2   cups nuts, chopped

Beat eggs until light; add sugar and oil, beating well after each addition. Sift flour, measure, then sift again with cocoa, baking powder, and salt. Add to first mixture, mix well, add vanilla and nuts. Bake at 350° 30 to 35 minutes. Do not over-bake. *Makes 32.*

Syble Bollinger

CHEWY CARAMEL BROWNIES

2   cups packed light brown sugar
1   cup all-purpose flour
1   cup nuts, chopped (optional)
½   cup shortening
2   eggs

2   teaspoons double-acting baking
    powder
2   teaspoons vanilla extract
¾   teaspoon salt

Preheat oven to 350°. Grease and flour pan (15½x10½). Mix all ingredients well with mixer on medium speed; evenly spread in pan. Bake 25 minutes or until golden brown. Cool and then cut into squares.

CARAMEL FUDGE BROWNIES

1 14-ounce package light Kraft
   caramels
1 small can evaporated milk
1 package German chocolate cake
   mix

¾ cup margarine
1 cup nuts, chopped
1 6-ounce package chocolate chips

In a double boiler combine caramels and ⅓ cup evaporated milk until caramels are melted. Set aside, grease and flour a 9x13″ pan. Combine cake mix, margarine, ⅓ cup evaporated milk and nuts. Stir by hand. Press ½ of dough mixture in pan. Bake at 350° for 6 minutes then sprinkle chocolate chips over baked crust. Immediately drizzle caramel mixture over top and spoon remaining dough mixture over this. Return to oven and bake 15 to 18 minutes at 350°.

Carol Thompson
Beverly Reeves

FUDGE SQUARES

½ cup butter, melted
2 tablespoons cocoa
1 cup sugar
2 eggs, well beaten
¾ cup flour
1 cup nuts, chopped
¾ package marshmallows

2 tablespoons butter, softened
3 tablespoons cocoa
4 tablespoons Pet milk
1 teaspoon vanilla
2 cups powdered sugar
Pecan halves

Mix butter, cocoa, sugar and eggs together. Add flour and nuts. Pour into greased and floured 9-inch square pan. Bake at 350° for 20 minutes. Arrange marshmallows on top and return to oven until melted and lightly browned. Make icing of butter, cocoa, milk, vanilla and powdered sugar. Spread on cake and arrange pecan halves on top, so each piece will have a pecan half.

Mattie Jones

RUTH'S HONEY GRAHAMS

1 cup butter
1 cup brown sugar

Graham crackers
1 cup pecans, chopped

Boil butter and sugar together for 2 minutes. Lay whole graham crackers flat on cookie sheet. Add pecans to the butter-sugar mixture and pour over the crackers. Bake at 350° for 10 minutes.

Mrs. L. H. Polk

CHOCOLATE CHERRY BARS

1 package Pillsbury Plus devils
  food or chocolate fudge cake
  mix

1 21-ounce can cherry pie filling
1 teaspoon almond or vanilla extract
2 eggs, beaten

Mix and stir by hand until well mixed. Bake 25 to 30 minutes at 350° in 12x19 greased and floured pan.

Frosting:

1 cup sugar
5 tablespoons butter or margarine
⅓ cup milk

1 cup (6-ounce package) semi-sweet
  chocolate pieces

Combine sugar, butter and milk. Boil. Stir constantly for 1 minute. Remove from heat. Stir in chocolate pieces until smooth. Pour over warm cake.

Mrs. E. D. Welden,
Mrs. Bernard High

STIR-ME-NOTS

½ cup butter or margarine,
  melted
1½ cups graham cracker crumbs
1 cup coconut, shredded
1 12-ounce package semi-sweet
  chocolate pieces

1 14-ounce can sweetened condensed
  milk
1 cup walnuts, chopped

Preheat oven to 350°. Pour butter in 13x9-inch baking dish. Sprinkle graham cracker crumbs evenly over melted butter; then the coconut. Sprinkle on the chocolate pieces. Pour the condensed milk evenly over all ingredients in the dish. Top with nuts. Do not stir. Bake 35 to 40 minutes. Cool completely. *Cut into 32 pieces.*

Mrs. Bobby Herndon,
Dottie Lawyer, Carol Smith

LUCILLE'S COOKIES

1 cup sugar
½ pound butter
½ teaspoon vanilla

1 egg, separated
2 cups flour
1 cup nuts, chopped

Mix sugar and butter. Stir in vanilla and egg yolk. Sift flour into mixture and mix well. Spread in thin layer in baking pan. Paint with egg white. Pour nuts over top. Bake at 350° for 25-27 minutes. Cut and remove from pan while hot.

Billy and Barbara Mills

PECAN SHORT BREAD

1 cup butter, softened
⅔ cup sugar
¾ cup pecans, chopped

1 teaspoon vanilla
⅛ teaspoon salt
2 cups sifted flour

Mix all ingredients well. Use long pan and spread mixture as thin as possible. Cook at 325° for 28 minutes. (This should be lightly brown — your oven may vary — be sure the bread is just *tan* — do not brown too much.) Delicious.

Marie Baddour Albertson

LEAH'S COOKIES

¼ pound butter
1 cup flour
2 tablespoons sugar
2 eggs
1½ cups brown sugar, lightly packed
2 heaping tablespoons flour

1 level teaspoon baking powder
1 cup nuts, chopped
3 tablespoons butter, melted
1 cup confectioners sugar
1 teaspoon vanilla
Cold water

Cream butter. Sift flour and sugar together. Add to butter to make soft dough. Spread in greased 9″ pan. Bake in oven at 350° 10 minutes or till set. Beat 2 eggs. Add brown sugar, flour, baking powder, and nuts. Pour this mixture over first layer and cook 25 minutes at 350°. Cool. Combine butter, confectioners sugar, vanilla, and enough cold water to thin to cream. Spread over top.

Billy and Barbara Mills

OZARK DESSERT BARS

1   box yellow cake mix
1   cup light brown sugar
½   cup butter
2   eggs

2   teaspoons vanilla
1   6-ounce package semi-sweet
    chocolate or butterscotch pieces
¾   cup chopped dates

Mix all ingredients. Beat well. Pour into greased 9x13x2" pan. Bake at 350° for 25 minutes. These are chewy and may not look done but are. Cool and cut into bars. *Yields – 24 bars.*

Charles Baddour

MYSTERY BARS

1   cup white sugar
1¼ cups brown sugar
2   eggs
2   sticks oleo
1   teaspoon vanilla

3   cups flour
1   teaspoon baking powder
1   teaspoon soda
1   cup chocolate chips, and/or
    coconut, chopped dates

Mix well: sugar, eggs, oleo, and vanilla. Add dry ingredients and chips. Spread thin on baking sheets. Bake 350° about 15-20 minutes. Cut while warm.

CHEESECAKE COOKIES

⅓   cup brown sugar, packed
1   cup flour
½   cup walnuts, chopped
⅓   cup butter, melted
1   8-ounce package cream cheese

¼   cup granulated sugar
1   egg
1   tablespoon lemon juice
2   tablespoons milk or cream
1   tablespoon vanilla extract

Mix brown sugar, flour and chopped nuts together in a large bowl. Stir in the melted butter, and mix with your hands until crumbly. Remove 1 cup of the mixture to be used later as a topping. Place remainder in an 8-inch square pan and press firmly. Bake at 350° for about 12 to 15 minutes. Beat cream cheese with the granulated sugar until smooth. Beat in the egg, lemon juice, milk and vanilla. Pour into the baked crust. Top with the reserved crumbs. Return to a 350° oven, and bake for about 25 minutes. Cool thoroughly; then cut into 2-inch squares. These can be baked the day before. Cover with plastic wrap and keep refrigerated. *Makes about 16 cookies.*

Marie Baddour Albertson

This recipe is great.

TOFFEE PISTACHIO DELIGHT

1 3¾-ounce package instant
   pistachio pudding
6 ounces vanilla wafers, crushed
1 7-ounce carton frozen whipped
   topping

7 ounces Heath candy bars, finely
   chopped

Mix pudding according to package directions. In 9x9" pan, layer half of crushed wafers, half of pudding, half of whipped topping and half of chopped Heath bars. Repeat layers, topping off with Heath bars for garnish. Refrigerate overnight.

Fran Hilliard

CHOCOLATE PECAN SQUARES

½ cup butter
¼ cup white sugar
¼ cup brown sugar, firmly packed
½ teaspoon vanilla
1 egg yolk

½ cup sifted all-purpose flour
½ cup quick oats
6 small Hershey bars
1 teaspoon butter
½ cup pecans or walnuts, chopped

Work butter until creamy then gradually work in both kinds of sugar. Add vanilla and egg yolk. Beat until light. Next, stir in the flour and oats thoroughly. Spread mixture in a greased 8-inch square pan and bake 20 minutes in 350° oven. Remove from oven and let stand 10 minutes. Meanwhile, melt chocolate bars and butter over hot water. When smooth, spread over cookies and sprinkle with nuts. Cut into squares while still warm. *Makes about 18.*

Mary Lane Price

BLUEBERRY CRUNCH

2 cups flour
2 sticks oleo
1 cup pecans
1 box confectioners sugar

8 ounces cream cheese
1 large carton Cool Whip
1 can blueberry pie filling

Mix flour, oleo and pecans together. Spread in 13x9x2" pan and bake at 350° until brown. Mix sugar, cream cheese and Cool Whip and spread on crust. Top with pie filling. You may use strawberry or cherry pie filling instead of the blueberry.

Donna Poteet,
Grace Knolton

Or use as a salad.

NUT COOKIES

2 sticks oleo
1 cup sugar
1 egg, separated
2 cups flour

2 teaspoons cinnamon
½ teaspoon ground cloves
1 cup nuts, chopped

Cream softened oleo and sugar. Add egg yolk. Put spices in flour and add to oleo and sugar mixture. Pour into cookie pan, brush the top with egg white and sprinkle with nuts. Bake for 30 minutes at 300°-325°.

Mrs. Nick Nail

CHOCOLATE SURPRISE

1 cup flour
1 stick oleo, melted
½ cup nuts, chopped
8 ounces cream cheese, softened
1 cup powdered sugar

1 cup Cool Whip
2 4-ounce packages instant fudge
   pudding
3 cups milk

Combine flour, oleo, and nuts, and press into a 9x13" greased pyrex dish. Bake at 350° for 20 minutes. Cool. Mix cream cheese, powdered sugar, and Cool Whip. Spread over first layer. Chill. Mix pudding and milk. Beat with wire whisk until thick, spread on top and chill. When ready to serve, cut into squares, top with whipped cream and cherry.

Homazelle Ashford,
Mrs. Joe Bass, Jane Kinney

Even non-dessert eaters like this.

DATE DELIGHT CHOC-O-DATE DESSERT

1 package cream-filled chocolate
   cookies, crushed
1 8-ounce package pitted dates,
   chopped
¾ cup water
¼ teaspoon salt

2 cups tiny marshmallows or 16
   large marshmallows
1 cup Cool Whip
½ teaspoon vanilla
Walnut halves
½ cup walnuts, chopped

Reserve ¼ cup cookie crumbs. Spread remainder in 10x6x1½-inch baking dish. In saucepan, combine dates, water and salt. Bring to a boil. Reduce heat; simmer 3 minutes. Remove from heat. Add marshmallows. Stir in chopped nuts. Spread date mixture over crumbs in dish. Combine Cool Whip and vanilla; whip. Swirl over dates. Sprinkle with reserved crumbs. Top with walnuts. Chill overnight. Cut in squares. *Makes 8 servings.*

Helen Robinson

LEMON SOURS

¾ cup flour
⅓ cup oleo
2 eggs
1 cup brown sugar
¾ cup coconut
1 cup nuts, chopped

⅛ teaspoon baking powder
½ teaspoon vanilla
1 teaspoon lemon rind, grated
1½ tablespoons lemon juice
⅔ cup powdered sugar

Mix flour and oleo together to a fine crumb. Sprinkle in 11x7" pan. Pat firmly. Bake at 350° for 10 minutes. Beat eggs, brown sugar, coconut, nuts, baking powder and vanilla. Spread over first mixture. Bake 20 minutes more. Mix lemon rind, juice and sugar and spread over top as soon as you remove from oven. Cool. Cut in squares.

Lilly Baddour Icenhour

LEMON TORTE

1 package lemon Jello
1 cup hot water
1 can Pet milk, refrigerated
   overnight

½ cup sugar
½ cup lemon juice
24 graham crackers
¼ cup butter, melted

Dissolve Jello in water; let thicken. Beat canned milk to peaks. Add sugar, lemon juice, then Jello. Beat until thick and well mixed. Crush crackers and mix with butter. Line a 9x13" pan with cracker-butter mixture. Add Jello mixture. Sprinkle crumbs over top. Refrigerate. *Serves 8 or more light, high, fluffy, low-calorie desserts.*

Beatrice Rosenblum

CHOCOLATE OR LEMON SQUARES

1 package Pillsbury chocolate or
   lemon cake mix
3 eggs
1 stick butter, melted

8 ounces cream cheese
1 teaspoon vanilla
1 box powdered sugar

Combine cake mix, 1 egg and butter and mix well. Press into 9x13 pyrex pan. With mixer, mix remaining eggs, cream cheese, vanilla and powdered sugar until smooth and creamy. Spread on top of cake mix. Bake at 350° for 25-35 minutes. Cool and cut into squares.

Martha Whitington

LEMON BARS

2¼ cups flour	2 cups sugar
2 sticks butter	1 teaspoon baking powder
½ cup powdered sugar	2½ lemons
4 eggs	Powdered sugar

Mix 2 cups of flour with butter and powdered sugar. Spread in pan. Bake at 325° for 15 minutes. Beat eggs with sugar. Add remaining flour, baking powder, juice and rind of lemons. Spoon over batter. Return to oven and bake 20 minutes. Cool. Cut in bars, sprinkle lightly with powdered sugar.

Marilyn Baddour Aaron

PEANUT BUTTER DESSERT BARS

1 box yellow cake mix	2 teaspoons vanilla
1 cup brown sugar	6 ounces Reese's peanut butter
½ cup butter	chips
2 eggs	¾ cup pecans, chopped

Mix cake mix, brown sugar, butter, eggs and vanilla. Beat well. Add chips and pecans. Pour into greased 9x13x2″ pan. Bake for 25 minutes at 350°. These are chewy and may not look done but are. Cool and cut into bars. *Yields about 24 bars.*

Marie Baddour Albertson

MOCHA SOUFFLÉ

2 ounces unsweetened chocolate squares	1 cup milk, heated
¼ cup butter or margarine	1 teaspoon vanilla extract
3 tablespoons flour	3 egg yolks, well beaten
⅔ cup sugar	4 egg whites
1 teaspoon instant coffee	¼ teaspoon salt
	½ teaspoon cream of tartar

Prepare 1½ quart soufflé dish — ungreased. Set in shallow pan containing 1 inch hot water heated in 350° oven. Melt chocolate in top of double boiler (or use a pyrex cup in hot water). Melt butter or margarine in saucepan over low heat. Blend in flour and cook for 2-3 minutes. Remove from heat. Add ⅓ cup sugar and instant coffee, mixing well. Then slowly add hot milk and stir to a smooth mixture. Cook and stir over medium heat until sauce thickens and comes to a boil. Remove from heat. Blend in melted chocolate and vanilla extract. Cool 10 minutes. Gradually add beaten egg yolks, stirring briskly and thoroughly. Combine egg whites and salt and cream of tartar and beat to soft peaks. Gradually add remaining ⅓ cup sugar until stiff glossy peaks form and egg whites will not slip out of bowl. Gently, but thoroughly, fold chocolate mixture into egg whites. Pour into prepared soufflé dish while hot. Bake at 350° for 60-70 minutes.

BERNICE'S BANANA PUDDING

1 quart milk	1 tablespoon vanilla
4 eggs	1 small can Pet milk
½ cup yellow cake mix	⅛ teaspoon salt
½ cup flour	1 11-ounce box vanilla wafers
1 cup sugar	4 medium ripe bananas
½ stick oleo, melted	

Heat milk in double boiler until just before boiling. In mixing bowl, combine eggs, cake mix, flour, and sugar until smooth. Gradually add to milk, stirring constantly, and heat until it bubbles. Remove from heat and add oleo, vanilla, milk, and salt. Line bottom of 9x13″ pan with broken (not crushed) vanilla wafers. Slice bananas over wafers. Pour pudding over bananas. With your spoon, gently move some of the bananas slightly to be sure the pudding seeps through. Top with finely crushed vanilla wafer crumbs or whole vanilla wafers.

Bernice Alexander

FRUIT PUDDING

1	10-ounce package frozen strawberries, thawed
1	small can pineapple chunks
1	11-ounce can mandarin orange sections, drained
¼	cup coconut, shredded

1 ½	tablespoons cornstarch
½	cup brown sugar
2	tablespoons margarine or butter
2	tablespoons flour
¼	cup quick cooking oats

In a 1½-quart baking dish, mix strawberries, pineapple, oranges and coconut. Combine cornstarch with brown sugar and add. Heat in microwave until bubbly 3-4 minutes. Mix margarine, flour and oats together until crumbly. Sprinkle over fruit mixture and cook uncovered 3 minutes, turning dish once.

June Spotts

Taste of summer in the middle of winter.

ERNESTINE'S BREAD PUDDING

1	stick butter or oleo
4	eggs, beaten
1 ¾	cups sugar and cinnamon

2	cups milk
4 or 5	slices of bread, torn up
1 ½	teaspoons vanilla

Melt butter in pyrex bowl. Add eggs, sugar and cinnamon, milk, bread and vanilla. Sprinkle top with more sugar and cinnamon. Have oven preheated to 400°. Put the pudding in the oven and immediately reduce heat to 350°. Cook about 45 minutes.

Danette Watkins

Delicious.

LEMON CHIFFON PUDDING

5	tablespoons flour
1	cup sugar
3	tablespoons butter
3	eggs, separated

1	cup milk
¼	teaspoon lemon juice
¼	teaspoon lemon rind

Mix flour and sugar. Cream together butter and flour mixture. Beat egg yolks until thick. Add yolks and milk to mixture gradually. Add lemon juice and rind. Beat egg whites til stiff; fold in carefully. Pour into greased baking dish; place in pan with 1 inch hot water. Bake at 350° for 35 minutes.

Pam Baddour

RAW SWEET POTATO PUDDING

3 eggs	½ teaspoon salt
1½ cups milk	½ cup sorghum molasses
4 cups sweet potatoes, grated	1 teaspoon nutmeg
⅓ cup butter	1 teaspoon cinnamon
½ cup sugar	

Beat eggs and milk together. To the grated sweet potatoes, add melted butter, sugar, salt, molasses and spices. Pour into buttered pan and bake in moderate 350° oven. When crusted on top and side, turn under with spatula and let crust again. Do this twice and allow to crust again. Remove from oven and serve either hot or cold with whipped cream. Total cooking time 30-45 minutes.

Evelyn Spear

An old, old recipe.

NOODLE PUDDING

1 package egg noodles	¼ cup almonds, chopped
3 eggs	½ teaspoon salt
½ cup sugar	¼ teaspoon cinnamon
2 large apples	3 tablespoons butter
½ cup seedless raisins	

Boil noodles in salted boiling water 20 minutes. Drain in a colander and put aside. Beat eggs with sugar (if apples are sweet, omit sugar). Add cooked noodles, apples and raisins, nuts and seasonings. Heat butter in a heavy baking dish, add mixture to hot pan, drop bits of butter on top and bake at 375° for 1 hour or until well browned.

Ruby Alperin

If sugar is omitted, goes well with a meat or chicken entree.

SUNDAY EGG CUSTARD

5 eggs	2¼ cups milk
1½ cups sugar	Butter
2 tablespoons flour	

Preheat oven to 425°. Mix eggs, sugar, flour and milk together and pour in a shallow pyrex bowl. Then dot with butter. Cook for 25 minutes or until it will still shake a little in the middle. Can be served hot or cold.

Nell Boyd

PROFITEROLES WITH CHOCOLATE FILLING

1 cup water
½ cup butter or oleo

1 cup all purpose flour, sifted
4 eggs

Heat water and butter until butter melts and water comes to boiling. Add flour all at once; continue cooking and stirring until dough forms a ball and cleans sides of pan. Remove from heat; cool 5 minutes. Beat eggs in one at a time, beating well after each addition. Drop batter by teaspoonful, 2 inches apart onto greased cookie sheet. Bake at 350° for 30 minutes or until puffed and browned; cool thoroughly. *Makes 2½ dozen.*

Filling:

6 egg yolks
2 cups milk
1 cup sugar
4 tablespoons cocoa

2 heaping tablespoons cornstarch
2 tablespoons butter
2 teaspoons vanilla

Beat egg yolks; add milk and sugar. Add cocoa and cornstarch and cook until thick. Remove from heat; add butter, vanilla and beat well. Let cool thoroughly before putting in crust. This can be used as a pie filling also. To fill profiteroles, slice top, fill with filling and place top back on, or pierce each puff near the top with tip of paring knife. Fill pastry bag which has been fitted with a large round tube with chocolate filling. Press filling into puffs. Sprinkle with 10x sugar.

Marilyn Baddour Aaron

Absolutely fantastic for any entertaining!

HEAVENLY HASH DESSERT

½ envelope Knox gelatin
2 tablespoons cold water
16 ounces semi-sweet chocolate
   chips
4 eggs
¼ cup sugar

1 teaspoon vanilla
⅛ teaspoon salt
1½ pints whipped cream
1 large angel food cake, broken into
   2-inch pieces
1 cup pecans, chopped coarsely

Dissolve gelatin in water. Melt chocolate chips in top of double boiler, cool slightly and add dissolved gelatin. In separate bowl beat eggs with sugar until light and frothy. Mix eggs and chocolate mixture together thoroughly. Add vanilla and salt. Fold in ½ pint whipped cream. Place layer of angel cake pieces on bottom of a buttered 9x12" glass baking dish. Pour ½ of chocolate mixture over cake. Put remaining pieces of cake on top and pour rest of chocolate over all. Top with 1 pint whipped cream and chopped nuts. Put candied cherry on each piece when served, if desired. Very fancy, very tasty, very rich. *Serves 12.*

VIENNESE TORTE

1 6-ounce package semi-sweet
   chocolate pieces
½ cup butter
1 cup boiling water

4 egg yolks, slightly beaten
2 tablespoons confectioners sugar
1 teaspoon vanilla or 1 jigger brandy
1 12-ounce store bought pound cake

In a heavy saucepan, heat chocolate, butter and water over medium heat, stirring until blended. Cool slightly. Add egg yolks, sugar and flavoring. Stir until smooth. Chill until mixture is of spreading consistency; about 45 minutes. Slice cake horizontally in 6 layers. Cake will slice easily if frozen first. Spread chocolate filling between layers, then frost top and sides. Chill at least 45 minutes before serving. Cut in ¼-inch slices.

Freezes beautifully.

FROZEN RAINBOW DELIGHT

1 pint whipping cream
3 tablespoons sugar
1 teaspoon vanilla
18 to 20 coconut macaroons,
   crushed

1 cup nuts, chopped
1 pint raspberry sherbet
1 pint lime sherbet
1 pint orange sherbet

Whip cream. Add sugar and vanilla. Combine crushed macaroons and nuts. Fold into whipped cream. Line a 13x9x2-inch pan with half of whipped cream mixture. Chill. Spread a layer of each sherbet over whipped cream mixture, allowing each layer to freeze before spreading next layer. Top with remaining whipped cream mixture. Cover and freeze. Cut into squares to serve. *Yields 10-12 servings.*

Beth Vail

PINEAPPLE ICEBOX DESSERT

1½ cups confectioners sugar, sifted
1 cup oleo
1 #2 can crushed pineapple, well
   drained

2 egg whites, beaten stiff
1 cup pecans
Vanilla wafers

Mix sugar and oleo and cream until fluffy. Add pineapple and mix well. Fold in egg whites and add pecans. Line bottom of 9x9 pyrex pan with vanilla wafers, add a layer of pineapple mixture, then another layer of wafers, another layer of pineapple mixture and top with vanilla wafers. Chill at least 6 hours or overnight. Cut in squares and serve with whipped cream.

Sarah Smith

FROZEN CUP CAKES

1 pint sour cream
¾ cup sugar
⅛ teaspoon salt
2 bananas
2 tablespoons lemon juice

1 small can crushed pineapple,
   drained
¼ cup nuts
¼ cup cherries

Blend sour cream, sugar and salt. Mash bananas and sprinkle with lemon juice. Stir fruit and nuts into sour cream mixture, just until coated. Spoon into muffin tins lined with cupcake paper. Freeze.

Evelyn Smith

LOTUS DESSERT

2 cups milk
2 cups cream

2 cups sugar
4 lemons

Stir milk, cream, sugar to dissolve sugar. Pour in pan and freeze until mushy (about 1½ to 2 hours). Put in bowl, add juice from lemons and grated rind of lemons and beat; freeze again about 2 hours. Beat again. Freeze until ready to serve. Put Cool Whip on top. Add crème de menthe to Cool Whip.

Mrs. Billy Barrett

FROZEN FRUIT CUPS

1 pint sour cream
2 tablespoons lemon juice
¾ cup sugar
⅛ teaspoon salt
1 8¼-ounce can crushed
   pineapple, undrained

¼ cup maraschino cherries, chopped
3 bananas, peeled and cubed
¼ cup chopped pecans

Combine all ingredients, and pour into muffin tins lined with paper muffin cups. Freeze until firm; store in plastic bags. *Yield about 1½ dozen.*

Nancy Webb,
Mrs. Ray Sturrup

May also be used as a salad.

HOMEMADE VANILLA ICE CREAM

1 tablespoon flour	2 teaspoons vanilla
2 cups sugar	1 can Eagle Brand milk
3 eggs	½ pint heavy cream
Dash salt	½ gallon milk

Mix flour in sugar; stir in eggs. Blend in salt, vanilla, and Eagle Brand milk. Whip cream until barely firm. Fold cream into first mixture. Add half of milk. Pour into freezer and add the remainder of milk.

Mrs. Nick Nail

FREEZER PEACH ICE CREAM – UNCOOKED

4 eggs	3 or 4 cups milk – to fill line in freezer
2½ cups sugar	1 quart fresh peaches, mashed and
4 cups Half and Half cream	sweetened
2 tablespoons vanilla	6-8 drops red food coloring
½ teaspoon salt	

Beat eggs until light. Add sugar gradually and continue beating until mixture thickens. Add remaining ingredients and mix thoroughly. Chill in refrigerator 2-3 hours in freezer container before freezing in ice cream freezer. Makes 4-5 quarts. Substitute 2 pre-sweetened packages of frozen strawberries, thawed, or 1 quart fresh strawberries, sweetened, or 5 ripe bananas mashed. Omit fruit and add more milk to make plain vanilla.

Jane Baddour

HOMEMADE LEMON ICE CREAM

12 lemons	2 quarts single X cream
4 cups sugar	Homogenized milk

Slice 4 lemons into thin slices. Cut into quarters and remove seeds. Prepare juice from 6 to 8 lemons. Mix lemon pieces and juice with sugar. Cover and refrigerate overnight. Stir occasionally. Next day, add cream. Pour into freezer, churn and add homogenized milk to the one gallon mark. Freeze and eat.

Eulalee B. Dacus

NELLIE GEORGE'S ORIGINAL RECIPE FOR HOMEMADE VANILLA ICE CREAM

10 extra large eggs	½ gallon + 2 cups warm milk
2¾ cups sugar	5 teaspoons pure vanilla
½ teaspoon salt	1 large can Pet milk
1 cup cold milk	

Beat the eggs. Gradually add the sugar and salt. Stir in 1 cup cold milk. Add the warm milk gradually. Cook over medium heat, stirring constantly, until mixture coats the spoon. Pour *immediately* into a large pyrex bowl. (If left in hot pan it continues to cook and mixture will curdle.) Cool to room temperature, stirring occasionally, before refrigerating. (If refrigerated before it cools to room temperature it will separate). Refrigerate overnight or at least until mixture is very cold. At freezing time add vanilla and Pet milk. *Makes one gallon.*

Nellie George Baddour

GERMAN CHOCOLATE SAUCE

1 bar German chocolate	1 cup powdered sugar
1 tablespoon butter	Dash of salt
¼ cup strong coffee	½ teaspoon vanilla

Over low heat melt chocolate, butter in the coffee. When melted, add sugar, salt and vanilla. Beat with mixer.

Doris Lanford

CHOCOLATE SAUCE

1 6-ounce package semi-sweet chocolate	2 tablespoons sugar
¾ cup whipping cream	1 teaspoon vanilla

In saucepan over low heat, melt chocolate in cream, stirring until blended and smooth. Stir in sugar until dissolved. Remove from heat. Add vanilla. Serve warm over ice cream.

Louise Pearson

Excellent!

COFFEE ANGEL ICE CREAM PIE

2	egg whites	1	pint vanilla ice cream
1½	teaspoons vanilla	3	tablespoons butter or oleo
¼	teaspoon salt	1	cup brown sugar
¼	teaspoon cream of tartar	6-ounce can evaporated milk	
½	cup granulated sugar	Dash of salt	
½	cup pecans, finely chopped	½	cup white raisins
1	pint coffee ice cream	½	cup pecans, toasted (optional)

Beat together egg whites, ½ teaspoon vanilla, salt and cream of tartar until soft peaks form. Gradually beat in granulated sugar until very stiff peaks form. Fold in the nuts. Spread in well-buttered 9-inch pie plate, building up sides to form a shell. Bake at 275° for 1 hour. Turn off heat — let dry in oven with door closed for 1 hour. Let crust completely cool. Pile scoops of vanilla and coffee ice cream into cooled shell. Freeze. Let stand at room temperature for 20 minutes before serving. In small saucepan melt butter or oleo. Stir in the brown sugar, evaporated milk and salt. Cook and stir over medium low heat just until mixture boils. Remove from heat — add raisins, remaining 1 teaspoon vanilla and pecans and cool slightly. *Makes 1½ cups sauce.* Serve sauce over pie.

Marguerite Baddour

An elegant dessert!

Time clocks are punched and paychecks are earned in the Vocational Division of Baddour Center. Two workshops make up The People Factory, which employs most of the residents. The invaluable process of contributing to one's own welfare is denied no one at Baddour Center. As the name of The People Factory implies, the Vocational Division puts emphasis on developing people, as well as producing quality products.

"Thank God every morning when you get up
that you have something to do that day which
must be done..."
–Letters of James Russell Lowell

PICKLES & PRESERVES

THE
PEOPLE
FACTORY

Vocational Workshop

CRISP PICKLE SLICES or BREAD & BUTTER TYPE

4 quarts medium cucumbers,
  sliced
6 medium white onions, sliced
2 green peppers, chopped
3 cloves garlic
⅓ cup coarse-medium salt

5 cups sugar
1½ teaspoons turmeric
1½ teaspoons celery seed
2 tablespoons mustard seed
3 cups cider vinegar

Do not pare cucumbers; slice thin. Add onions, peppers, and whole garlic cloves. Add salt, cover with cracked ice; mix thoroughly. Let stand 3 hours; drain thoroughly. Combine remaining ingredients; pour over cucumber mixture. Heat just to a boil. Seal in hot, sterilized jars. *Makes 8 pints.*

Jeanette McCollum

CUCUMBER AND ONION PICKLES

3 pounds cucumbers, sliced
⅓ cup salt
5 cups water
3 medium onions, sliced
2 cups vinegar
1⅔ cups sugar

1 teaspoon celery seed
2 teaspoons prepared mustard
1 teaspoon ginger
¼ teaspoon turmeric
⅛ teaspoon mace
⅛ teaspoon red pepper

Combine cucumbers, salt and water. Let stand 24 hours. Drain well. Pour into a large pan and add onions, vinegar, sugar, celery seed, mustard, ginger, turmeric, mace, and pepper. Heat to boiling point and simmer for 3-4 minutes. Pack in sterile jars and seal. *Makes 4 pints.*

Marie Hartfield

DILL PICKLES

2 teaspoons dill seed or bunch
  of dill
2 pods garlic, chopped, or ¼
  teaspoon minced garlic
2-3 hot peppers or ½ teaspoon
  crushed red pepper

3-4 peppercorns
⅓ teaspoon cooking alum
1 quart cucumbers
1 quart cider vinegar
2 quarts water
¾ cup canning salt

In bottom of quart jar, place dill, garlic, pepper, peppercorns, and alum. Wash cucumbers and fill jar. In a saucepan, boil vinegar, water and salt. Pour boiling liquid over cucumbers and seal. Do not open for 5-6 weeks.

Jeanette McCollum

BREAD AND BUTTER PICKLES

25 to 30 cucumbers
8 large onions
2 large bell peppers
3 or 4 cups of cauliflower
  (optional)
½ cup pickling salt

5 cups cider vinegar
5 cups sugar
2 tablespoons whole mustard seed
½ teaspoon cloves
1 teaspoon turmeric

Wash and slice cucumbers thin. Chop onions and peppers and pull cauliflower into small pieces. Combine salt with above and let stand 3 hours. Drain. Combine vinegar, sugar and spices in large kettle, bringing to a boil. Add drained vegetables, heat thoroughly. Do not boil. Pack hot in sterilized jars ½ inch to top. Seal with hot sterilized lids and rings. *Makes 14 to 16 pints.*

Myrtle Burks

ICICLE PICKLES

7 pounds cucumbers or tomatoes,
  sliced
2 gallons water
3 cups lime

5 pounds sugar
4 pints vinegar
5 tablespoons pickling spice, in bag

Put cucumbers in water mixed with lime. Soak 24 hours. Drain and add ice water. Soak for 4 hours, changing water every hour. Boil sugar, vinegar, and spices together for 5 minutes. Pour over cucumbers and let stand overnight. Cook slowly for 1 hour — do not boil. Seal. *Makes 8 pints.*

Marie Hartfield

SWEET 14 DAY PICKLES

2 gallons cucumbers
3 gallons water
2 cups pickling salt
2 tablespoons powdered alum
2 quarts white or cider vinegar

3 quarts sugar
5-6 cinnamon sticks
3 teaspoons turmeric
4 teaspoons whole mustard seed

Slice cucumbers approximately 1 inch or cut in chunks. Boil 1 gallon of water with pickling salt and pour over cucumbers. Let stand 1 week. Pour this mixture off and WASH WELL IN CLEAR WATER. Boil 1 gallon of water, pour over pickles and let stand 24 hours. Pour off. Boil 1 gallon of water and alum, pour over and let stand 24 hours. Each day for three days pour this mixture into pan and heat, pour back over pickles. On third day, mix vinegar, sugar, cinnamon sticks, turmeric, mustard seed and bring to a boil, and pour over pickles. Heat this mixture each day for 4 days and pour back over pickles. On 4th day heat mixture, add pickles and heat until pickles are hot through and through. Pack in hot sterilized jars and seal. Remove cinnamon sticks from mixture and do not pack these. When pouring hot mixture over pickles in gallon jars pour very slowly so as not to break jars.

Myrtle Burks

SWEET CUCUMBER PICKLES

1 gallon cold water
1 pint lime
7 pounds cucumbers

4 pounds sugar
3 quarts vinegar
½ box mixed pickling spices

Combine lime and water. Slice cucumbers, put in lime water and let stand for 24 hours. Drain and put in ice water; let stand 2 hours. Make syrup of sugar, vinegar, pickling spices. Add cucumbers, bring to boil and boil 2 hours. Seal. *Makes 9 pints.*

Marie Hartfield

PICKLED GREEN BEANS

1 ½ gallons green beans
1 cup sugar

½ cup vinegar
Salt

Cover washed snapped beans with water. Add sugar and vinegar and boil 40 minutes in large pan. Pack beans in hot sterilized jars, adding 1 teaspoon salt to each quart. Seal, and do not pressure. When ready to serve, drain liquid off and add water, season and cook as usual green beans.

Myrtle Burks

PICKLED OKRA

6   quarts whole okra, medium to
    small size
6   teaspoons boxed dill seeds
6   cloves of garlic
6   small red peppers, fresh or dried

Powdered alum
2   quarts water
1   quart white vinegar
1   cup pickling salt

Wash okra and drain until dry. Pack whole okra in sterilized jars. Add to each jar 1 teaspoon of dill seed, 1 garlic clove, 1 pepper (or piece of one if very large). Make a brine of salt, water and vinegar; bring to boiling point, pour hot brine over okra, adding about ⅛ teaspoon powdered alum to each pint for crispness. Seal jars. Store 4 to 6 weeks before eating. Jars can be turned upside down in hot water and boiled several minutes to be sure of a very good seal, and avoid spoiling. *Makes 12 pints.*

Myrtle Burks

PICKLED OKRA

1   quart okra
2   cloves garlic or ¼ teaspoon
    minced garlic
2   teaspoons dill seed
½   teaspoon crushed red pepper

⅛   teaspoon alum
1   quart cider vinegar
1   cup coarse-medium salt
3   quarts water

Wash the okra and cut off top part of the stems. Put in crushed ice and water. Let stand until very cold. Pack in hot sterilized jars. Drain excess water out of jars. Add garlic, dill seed, pepper and alum to jars. In a saucepan, bring vinegar, salt and water to a rolling boil. Pour into jars. Seal. (Don't worry if it becomes cloudy; it will still be good.)

Jeanette McCollum

PICKLED TURNIPS

6   cups water, boiled
Turnips
3   cups white vinegar

6   tablespoons salt
1   hot pepper (optional)
2   beets, halved

Use enough water to measure 6 cups after it boils. After it boils, allow to cool. Wash and quarter turnips. Place in gallon jar. Add cooled water and other ingredients. Let sit for at least 10 days.

RELISH

1 gallon green tomatoes	4 cups sugar
3-4 ripe tomatoes	½ cup salt
5 bell peppers	2 teaspoons turmeric
6 (or more) hot peppers	1 teaspoon allspice
12 medium white onions	1 teaspoon cinnamon
1 stalk celery	2 teaspoons white mustard seed
1 medium head of cabbage	2 teaspoons cayenne pepper
3 pints white distilled vinegar	Juice of 4 lemons

Put tomatoes, peppers, onions, celery and cabbage through a food chopper. Pour into colander and allow to drip for about 15 minutes. In large container, combine vinegar, sugar and spices. Mix well. Add lemon juice and stir again. Add the drained vegetables, mix thoroughly, and let set for several hours. Place in sterile jars and seal. Keep refrigerated after opening. *Makes 16-18 pints.*

Jeanette McCollum

QUICK RELISH

1 onion	¼ teaspoon celery seed
½ cup vinegar	¼ teaspoon dry mustard
3 tablespoons sugar	1 12-ounce can Mexican style whole
1 tablespoon mustard seed	kernel corn
¼ teaspoon salt	

Slice onion paper thin. Place in small saucepan and add vinegar, sugar, mustard and seasoning. Cook 5 minutes and remove from heat. Stir in corn. Cool. *Makes 1¾ cups.*

Irma Jo Williams

APPLE RELISH

12 tart apples	3 large onions
6 red bell peppers	1 tablespoon salt
6 green bell peppers	1½ pounds brown sugar
2 hot peppers	1 pint vinegar

Put apples, peppers and onions through food chopper and then put in saucepan. Add other ingredients and let come to boil. Boil 15 to 20 minutes, stirring occasionally. Put mixture into hot sterilized jars and seal.

Elizabeth and Catherine Baddour

Real good and simple.

CORN ON COB FOR FREEZER

Pick good filled ears but not hard. Shuck, silk and wash corn. Have water in pan boiling, drop corn in and leave for 2 minutes only. DO NOT WAIT FOR IT TO BOIL. LEAVE IT ONLY 2 MINUTES. Quickly remove and drop into water with ice in it. Leave only long enough to chill. Lay on dry towels, dry and bag for freezer. When ready to cook do not thaw. Drop in boiling water to which has been added a little milk and half stick oleo, and boil about 7 minutes.

Myrtle Burks

PEACH PRESERVES

7 cups sugar
½ cup water

8 quarts fresh peaches

Put sugar, water and thinly sliced peaches in a saucepan over low heat. Simmer, stirring often, until tender and the juice is thick and waxey. Pack in hot sterilized jars, seal. Can be turned upside down to be sure of a proper seal.

As peaches are peeled drop into cold salted water to avoid fruit turning dark. Does not affect taste.

PEACH PRESERVES

2 quarts peaches
½ cup water

6 cups sugar
1 tablespoon vanilla

Cook peaches and water 10 minutes. Add sugar and cook 45 minutes. About 20 minutes before they are done, add vanilla. Pour in jars and seal with paraffin.

Jeanette McCollum

361

CANNED PEACHES

Select fully ripe fruit. Peel and slice or quarter peaches and drop into cold salted water. (Use about 7 teaspoons salt per gallon water). This solution keeps peaches from turning dark. Make syrup of 2 cups water to 1 cup sugar and heat until sugar is dissolved. Add drained peaches and heat until peaches are hot all way through. Pack in sterilized jars, filling with syrup to ½ inch of top of jar. Run knife down side of jar to remove any air bubbles. Seal. Process in cooker 8 minutes at 5 pounds pressure.

Myrtle Burks

If have much juice left after several cookings of fruit, make peach jelly.

PEACH JELLY MADE FROM LEFT OVER SYRUP

4 cups juice
½ lemon

1 box Sure-Jell
4½ or 5 cups sugar

Bring juice, lemon slices with seeds removed, and Sure-Jell to rolling boil. Have measured sugar set aside and quickly add all at one time. Bring to a fast rolling boil that cannot be stirred down and boil for 1 minute, stirring constantly. Remove from heat and let set a minute. With large spoon skim off foam, and pour into sterilized jars and seal with hot sterilized lids. I sometimes cook some of the peaches until tender and use in this. Use the small thin pieces of peaches.

Michelle Burks

PEACH POT

2 gallons chopped peaches and
    peach peeling

4 cups sugar
½ cup vinegar

Combine in a saucepan and cook down low. Put in container (I put mine in pints). Put in the freezer. They are good for fried pies or to eat on biscuits. They taste a lot like dried peaches.

Jeanette McCollum

SPICED PEACHES

2   29-ounce cans cling peach   1   cup cider vinegar
    halves   4   cinnamon sticks
1 ⅓ cups sugar   2   teaspoons whole cloves

Drain peaches, reserving syrup. Combine peach syrup, sugar, vinegar, cinnamon sticks and cloves in a saucepan. Bring mixture to a boil, then lower heat and simmer 10 minutes. Pour hot syrup over peach halves and let cool. Chill thoroughly before serving. Store in refrigerator. *Yield: About 4 pints.*

Mrs. Nick Nail

FIG-STRAWBERRY PRESERVES

3   cups figs, mashed   2   3-ounce packages strawberry
3   cups sugar   Jello

Thoroughly mix figs, Jello and sugar in a large saucepan. Bring to a boil over medium heat and continue boiling for 3 minutes, stirring occasionally. Pour quickly into glasses and seal or cover with ⅛ inch paraffin.

Sarah Smith

FIG JAM

6½ pounds ripe figs (weigh after   4½ pounds sugar
    peeling, removing only the   ¼   cup lemon juice
    peeling that easily pulls off   1   tablespoon cinnamon
    with the stem)   1   tablespoon cloves
1   #2½ can crushed pineapple   1   tablespoon allspice

Mash peeled figs to fine pulp, add other ingredients. Mix thoroughly and cook until thick, stirring constantly. Pour into hot sterile jars and seal.

Opal Deneke

STRAWBERRY PRESERVES

1 quart strawberries   3 cups sugar

Cover strawberries with boiling water. Let stand 5 minutes. Drain well. Add 1 cup sugar. Boil 5 minutes. Add remaining sugar and boil 15 minutes. Pour in shallow pan and let set overnight. In the morning pack in sterile jars and seal.

Mrs. John Mac Smith

PICKLED YELLOW SQUASH

6 cups yellow squash   3 cups water
2 large green bell peppers   3 cups sugar
2 large red bell peppers   2 cups white vinegar
2 cups white onions   3-4 dashes turmeric
¾ cup pickling salt   1 teaspoon mustard seed

Slice squash, peppers, and onions thin. Mix pickling salt with water and pour over vegetables. Let set 1 hour. Drain. Mix sugar, vinegar, turmeric and mustard seed and boil until syrupy. Add vegetables and bring to a boil. Remove from heat, put in sterilized jars and seal.

Myrtle Burks

The Pre-Vocational Program provides an important service to the residents of BMC, as well as many mentally retarded students from surrounding area schools. For those unprepared to enter a work setting and earn wages, this program analyzes their abilities and structures learning and practice activities which will enable them to assume an entry-level position at Baddour Center or another similar work place. Teachers stand ready to give assistance and a kind word. Praise and motivation play a big part in promoting good work ethics along with developing essential skills.

"We must open doors of opportunity.
But we must also equip our people
to walk through these doors...."
–Lyndon B. Johnson

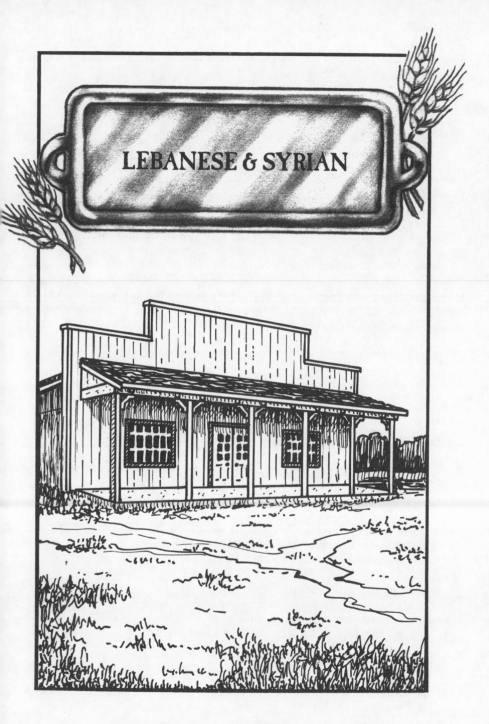

LEBANESE & SYRIAN

Pre-Vocational Center

Thanks to the ladies of St. Nicholas Orthodox Church in Bridgeport, Conn. for their help with this section.

CAULIFLOWER APPETIZER
(Kurnabeet)

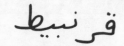

10 ounces frozen cauliflower,
   cooked and mashed
2 tablespoons tahini
2 cloves garlic, crushed

1 teaspoon salt
2 tablespoons lemon juice
3 tablespoons water

Combine the tahini, garlic, salt and lemon juice. Add the water and blend until smooth. Add mashed cauliflower and mix very well. This is excellent as an appetizer on bread or crackers, or a dip.

EGGPLANT WITH TAHINI

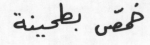

3 medium eggplants
3 tablespoons tahini
½ cup lemon juice

3 small pods garlic, minced
1½ teaspoons salt
1 tablespoon olive oil

Poke holes in eggplant and broil until skin is burnt. Peel and mash. Mix other ingredients together and add eggplant. Mix very well. Serve as dip. (Ingredients can be mixed in blender.)

Variation: Beans with Tahini

Cook beans till done, drain. Then do same as for eggplant, but decrease tahini to 1 tablespoon for 1 can of beans and use 1 lemon.

Variation: Cauliflower and Tahini

Boil cauliflower till tender, brown in olive oil, then do same as for beans.

Variation: Mashed Humus with Tahini

Use 2 cans humus. Make as eggplant.

Mrs. M. D. Baddour

MEAT PIES
(Lahem-be-Ojeen)

Dough:

2 pounds flour
½ teaspoon salt
1 yeast cake

½ cup warm water
⅛ cup oil

Filling:

1 pound meat (beef or lamb),
   chopped
3 onions, chopped
2 tablespoons butter

1 teaspoon black pepper
1 teaspoon tomato paste
1 teaspoon salt
1 tablespoon lemon juice

Add salt to flour. Dissolve yeast in ½ cup warm water. Add to flour, keep adding rest of water as dough is kneaded. Knead until the dough no longer sticks to hands, about 15 minutes. Cover and let rise in warm place until double in bulk. Punch dough. Dip fingers in ½ cup of oil and cut dough into pieces the size of a lemon. Let rest 20 minutes, spread each piece of dough to about a 6-inch circle — (using fingers dipped in oil). Spread ¼ cup of filling on each circle. Fold the edges over ¼ inch and flute, making an open faced pie. Bake in a greased pan 400° oven for about 25 minutes.

Filling: Mix all ingredients together. Sauté before putting on dough.

RICE WITH MEAT
(Riz Tajin)

1½ pounds beef, diced
1   large onion, coarsely chopped
¼   teaspoon cinnamon
Salt and pepper to taste

½ cup margarine or butter
½ cup pine nuts
2 cups uncooked rice
Grated cheese

Sauté meat, onions, and seasonings in margarine or butter until almost done. Add pine nuts and continue sautéeing for 5 minutes more. Place in an even layer in a casserole. Add rice and cover with 4 cups boiling water. Top with grated cheese. Cover and bake at 325° for one hour or until rice is tender. Remove and run knife around edge of pan. Turn upside down onto serving dish. Let stand for few minutes before removing casserole. *Serves 6-8.*

STUFFED CHICKEN
(Dgeej Muhshe)

دجاج محشي

5-6 pounds fowl for cooking	1 ½ tablespoons salt
2 cups beef, chopped	¼ teaspoon black pepper
1 cup uncooked rice	½ cup pine nuts

Prepare fowl for cooking. Combine the rest of the ingredients in the order given and stuff the stomach cavity, neck and between the skin. Sew. In a large kettle with boiling water and a teaspoon salt, add chicken and cook gently for about 2 hours. Take out of water and place in a roasting pan and brown in a 400° oven. The water from the chicken makes excellent stock for soup.

BAKED CHICKEN
(Djaj Mhammar)

دجاج محمر

¼ cup olive oil, or vegetable oil	½ teaspoon pepper
¼ cup lemon juice	¼ teaspoon cinnamon
1 teaspoon salt	1 chicken, fryer, cut into
1 teaspoon oregano	serving-sized pieces

Combine olive oil, lemon juice and spices in shallow baking pan. Roll cut up chicken in marinade. Bake in hot oven at 425°, basting occasionally. Bake until tender when pierced with a fork (approximately 30 minutes). Remove from oven and baste again. Serve around a bed of plain rice. Sprinkle rice with cinnamon or pine nuts sautéed to a golden brown. Chicken juices may be served in separate bowl to pour over rice. *Serves 4.*

CAULIFLOWER WITH RICE
(Yakhnit Al-Quarnabit)

يخنيت القرنبيط

1 pound beef shoulder, chopped or ground	2 ½ to 3 cups water
	1 cup uncooked rice
1 small onion, chopped	⅛ teaspoon cinnamon
1 medium head of cauliflower, cut into florets	Salt and pepper to taste

Sauté meat in a small amount of margarine. Add onions and continue sautéing until onions are limp. Add cauliflower and water (water has to barely cover the cauliflower). Bring to a boil, add rice and seasonings, and lower to medium heat. Cover. Cook until rice is tender, about 20 minutes. Let stand a few minutes before unmolding. Turn upside down onto platter. *Serves 4-6.*

CIGARETTE CABBAGE *(Stuffed Cabbage)*

4 quarts water	1 ½ teaspoons salt
2 ½ pounds cabbage (1-2 loose heads)	1 teaspoon cinnamon
1 cup long grain rice, uncooked	1-pound can tomatoes, drained (optional)
1 ½ pounds round steak, finely cubed	½ stick oleo
	1 teaspoon salt

Core cabbage and parboil in water until limp and easy to roll. Place in a colander and separate leaves. Slice each leaf in half on the rib. Slice rib off. Leaves should be roughly 4″ long and 6″ wide. (They can be other sizes as long as they are uniform.) Mix rice, steak, 1½ teaspoons salt, cinnamon, tomatoes, and oleo. Place a tablespoonful on each leaf. Spread lengthwise and roll as for jellyroll. Gently squeeze each roll when placing in pan. Arrange in compact rows over a layer of cabbage ribs. Cover rolls with water ½″ higher than the top. Sprinkle with 1 teaspoon of salt over top. Place a pottery plate over cabbage so the rolls will remain firm and intact. Cover pan and cook on medium fire for 30 minutes or until rice is done. *Serves 4 to 6.*

Oneida Baddour

STUFFED GRAPE LEAVES *(Muhshe Urreesh)*   محشي عريش

7 dozen grape leaves, fresh or pickled	1 small clove garlic, chopped fine
2 whole chicken legs and thighs	Salt to taste
1 tablespoon crushed dried mint	3 cups water
	Juice of 1 lemon

Filling:

1 ½ pounds coarsely ground beef	1 small clove garlic, chopped fine
¾ cup uncooked long grain rice	3 teaspoons tomato paste (optional)
1 ½ teaspoons salt	⅓ cup tomato sauce (optional)
½ teaspoon ground pepper	

Combine filling ingredients and mix well. Lay leaves right side down. Add 1½ teaspoons filling to each leaf. Roll with sides tucked in until approximately 3″ long and the width of a small cigar. Place chicken leg in pot to be used, plus a few leaves on top of chicken; this is to prevent sticking. Arrange rolled leaves on top of chicken. Sprinkle mint, garlic and salt over top. Add water. Place an inverted dish on leaves to keep them firm while cooking. Cover, cook 30 minutes. Add lemon juice and cook 45 minutes more or until leaves are tender. *Serves 4 to 5.*

STUFFED SQUASH
(Muhshe Koosa)

محشي كوسا

1 dozen medium size squash	1 teaspoon salt
1 ½ teaspoons salt	1 ½ pounds coarsely ground beef
1 small clove garlic, finely ground	¾ cup rice
	½ teaspoon ground pepper
3 teaspoons tomato paste	⅓ cup tomato sauce

Wash the squash and cut off stems. Scoop out insides of squash, being careful not to tear the outside skin. Wash inside of squash thoroughly. Make the filling by combining the beef, rice, salt, pepper, garlic, tomato paste and tomato sauce, mixing well. Stuff each squash to about ½ inch from the top. Arrange in pan, open side up. Add enough water to cover the squash. Add 1 teaspoon salt to water. Cover and boil on slow fire for 35 minutes or until tender.

EGGS FRIED WITH CHICKEN GIBLETS
(Bayd Ma Hwahis Ad-Djaj)

بيض مع حواصيص الدجاج

¼ pound gizzards and heart	3 eggs
Oil or margarine	Salt and pepper to taste

Cut gizzards and heart into small chunks. Sauté in oil or margarine, until tender. Add eggs and seasonings to giblets and cook like an omelet; or the eggs may be left whole on top of the giblets. In the Middle East, this is usually served for breakfast, but is excellent for lunch or any other time.

LEBANESE POTATO SALAD

1 button garlic
6 medium potatoes, boiled,
    peeled, and diced
Juice of 2 lemons
3 dill pickles, chopped

½ cup stuffed olives, chopped
1 onion, chopped
6 parsley sprigs, chopped
Salt and pepper
3 tablespoons olive oil or salad oil

Mash garlic button in a large bowl. Add potatoes, lemon juice, pickles, olives, onion and parsley and season to taste. Add the oil and toss carefully.

Elizabeth and Catherine Baddour

HOT POTATO SALAD
(Patata Imshehe)

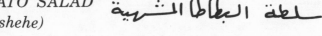

3 pounds potatoes
½ cup olive oil
3 large onions, sliced
1 green pepper, chopped
3 tomatoes, chopped
1 tablespoon finely chopped
    parsley

1 6-ounce can tomato paste
1 tablespoon salt
⅛ teaspoon black pepper
⅛ teaspoom cumin seed (optional)

Boil potatoes, cube, and set aside. In a large fry pan, cook the onions and green peppers in the oil until soft but not brown. Add the chopped tomatoes, tomato paste and spices. Cook gently for 30 minutes. Remove from fire, add the cubed potatoes and toss. Sprinkle with parsley. Serve hot or cold. *Serves 6 to 8.*

STRING BEANS WITH TOMATOES
(Loobee-be-Demma)

لوبيا بدّما

1 onion
½ cup oil
1½ pounds string beans or
    2 16-ounce cans green beans

1 teaspoon salt
3 fresh tomatoes or
    1 16-ounce can tomatoes

Brown onion in oil. Add washed and cut string beans (if fresh), salt, and toss lightly. Cover and cook about 10 minutes. Add tomatoes. Simmer until beans are cooked (about ½ hour). *Serves 4.*

MAJADRA مجدرة

1 cup dry brown lentils	3 tablespoons olive oil
4 cups water	¼ cup uncooked rice
1 large onion, chopped	Salt and pepper to taste

Wash lentils, and in a covered pot, boil lentils and water for 1 hour. Fry onion in olive oil until done, but not dark. Add to the lentil mixture, then add rice and salt and pepper. Cover and cook on low heat for 30 minutes. *Yields 1 quart.*

Oneida Baddour

LENTILS
(Adees Imkulla) عدس

2 cups lentils	1 onion
4 cups water	½ cup oil

Boil lentils in water until cooked thoroughly. Stir. Cook about 30 minutes. Brown onion in oil. Add to lentils mixture and stir very well.

BLACK-EYED PEAS لوبيا
(Yahnit Loobe)

1 cup black-eyed peas	1 tablespoon salt
1 quart water	½ lemon
1 cup onion, sliced	¼ teaspoon mint or sweet basil
¼ cup olive oil	

Cook washed peas in salted water for 20 minutes. Cook onions in oil until soft, and add to black-eyed peas. Add lemon juice and mint or sweet basil and cook 20 minutes longer. *Serves 4.*

SYRIAN TOMATO SALAD سلطة البندورة
(Salata Ahrabee)

4 large tomatoes, cut in small pieces	1 cucumber (optional)
1 large onion, sliced thin	½ teaspoon dried mint or 1 tablespoon fresh mint, chopped
¼ cup olive oil	1 teaspoon salt
Juice of 1 lemon	½ teaspoon oregano (optional)

Place onions and tomatoes in salad bowl. Add rest of ingredients and mix well. *Serves 4.*

THIN SYRIAN BREAD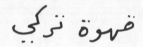
(Khubz)

5 pounds flour
1 yeast cake
½ cup warm water

1 tablespoon salt
6 cups warm water

Dissolve yeast cake in ½ cup warm water. Mix flour and salt in a large pan, add the yeast mix. Knead the dough, adding water as needed, turning often until dough is smooth and silky about 20 min. Cover and let rise until double in bulk. Divide dough into pieces about the size of a grapefruit. Let rest for 5 minutes. Roll each piece with rolling pin to a 12-inch circle. Let rise for 1 hour in warm place. Bake in 500° oven 8 to 10 minutes. *Yield: approximately 10 loaves.*

TURKISH COFFEE
(Kuhwee Turkee)

5 teaspoons Turkish coffee
2 teaspoons sugar

1 ½ cups water

Turkish coffee is made in a small, narrow, long handled pot called a JEYVE. To serve 4 in demitasse cups, measure 5 teaspoons of Turkish coffee and 2 teaspoons of sugar. Add cold water. Stir well and bring to a boil over medium heat. Pour into demitasse cups and serve piping hot.

FRUIT BREW
(Sharaab)

2 cups sugar
2 ½ cups water
Generous bunch mint

2 cups orange juice and rind
6 lemons
Ginger ale

Boil the sugar and water to make the syrup. Pour this syrup over crushed mint. Add the orange juice and rind and juice of 6 lemons. Let it stand covered for one hour or more. Strain. To make a drink, add ginger ale to ⅓ cup of this brew. This concentrated brew keeps for weeks.

DRIED PEPPERMINT LEAVES

Pick peppermint leaves off stems. Wash thoroughly and place in an open pan to dry. When thoroughly dry, place in jar. This is good for a stimulating drink or a seasoning for salads. As a drink, boil in boiling water like tea.

AUNT EMILY'S BAKLAWA بقلاوة

2 cups sugar	1 cup sugar
2 cups water	2 tablespoons orange blossom
Juice of one lemon	water
1 tablespoon orange blossom	1½ pounds prepared filo or
water	strudel-pastry leaves
4-5 cups finely chopped walnuts	1 pound butter, melted

Combine 2 cups sugar and water in saucepan, bring to boil. Cook at low temperature for 45 minutes. Add lemon juice and cook another 15 minutes, or until amber color and slightly thickened. Remove from heat, and stir in 1 tablespoon orange blossom water. While sauce is cooking, combine walnuts, 1 cup sugar and remaining orange blossom water in bowl. Set aside. In 11½x16½ jellyroll pan, begin layering the filo leaves, brushing each leaf with melted butter. Continue layering until 14 layers of pastry are used. Spread the walnut mixture on top, and begin the layers of dough again, with 13 more layers of pastry (each buttered). Butter top pastry leaf and trim edges if necessary. With sharp knife, make 8 diagonal cuts on long side at 1½-inch intervals. Then, starting at one corner, make 9 cuts on diagonal at 1½-inch intervals to form diamonds. Bake at 325° for 60 minutes, or until golden brown and puffy. Remove from oven and pour warm syrup on top. Cool in pan on wire rack. *Makes 35 pieces.*

Mrs. H. N. Haddad

BAKLAVA

1 ½ boxes filo dough
1   pound walnuts, chopped
½   cup sugar
⅔   cup confectioners sugar

¾   teaspoon cinnamon
2   tablespoons rose water
1   pound unsalted butter, melted

Syrup:

3   cups sugar
1 ½   cups water
Dash of cinnamon

3   tablespoons lemon juice
3   tablespoons rose water
1   cup honey

Thaw the filo dough 2 hours before using. Mix the chopped walnuts with both sugars, cinnamon and rose water. When working with the filo dough, be very careful, as the dough is thin. Lay 20 layers of dough in a deep cookie sheet, spreading each layer with melted butter. Work quickly so it doesn't dry out. Spread the nut mixture over the last layer. Then continue the layers of dough and butter until all layers have been used. Cut into diamond-shaped pieces. Brush top with butter. Bake at 300° for 1 hour. Pastry will be a light golden brown. While pastry is baking, mix syrup ingredients in a saucepan and bring to a slow boil. Cook until just before the soft ball stage. This will take about 45 minutes. When pastry is done, immediately spoon the syrup over the top. Serve cool.

Ann Al-Chokhachi

LEBANESE BAKLAWA POUND CAKE

3   sticks oleo, softened
3   cups sugar
5   eggs
3   cups flour
⅛   teaspoon salt
7   ounces orange juice

2 ½   cups walnuts, finely chopped
3   tablespoons orange blossom
      water
1 ½   cups sugar
1   cup water
Juice of half a lemon

Cream oleo and sugar. Add eggs, one at a time, beating well after each. Combine the flour and salt, and add alternately with the orange juice. Mix well. Combine the walnuts, 2 tablespoons orange blossom water, and ½ cup sugar in a separate bowl. Stir into cake batter. Pour into a well-greased and floured bundt pan, and bake 1 hour and 15 minutes at 350°. While cake is baking, combine water and remaining 1 cup sugar in saucepan. Stir until sugar is dissolved and cook 1 hour on low temperature. Add lemon juice and cook 10 more minutes. Remove from heat and stir in orange blossom water. Cool cake in pan 10 to 15 minutes. Remove from pan and spoon warm sauce over cake. Cover with cake-saver or other cover, and allow to "sweat" 1 hour.

Charles Baddour

BAKED KIBBY

4 cups fine berigal	2 teaspoons cinnamon
4 pounds round steak, ground fine	3 large onions, grated
¾ teaspoon pepper	¾ cup olive oil
3 tablespoons salt	

Soak berigal 20 minutes in cold water. Wash well to get the starch out. Drain all water off. Mix meat with pepper, salt and cinnamon. Add to berigal and mix well. Use a little ice water occasionally to keep meat from being sticky. Add onion and mix well. Grease 9x13 pan with oil. Put a layer of kibby about 1 inch thick in bottom of pan, then a layer of filling. Then add 1-inch thick layer of kibby on top of filling. Dipping knife in cool water from time to time, cut in diamond shapes. Pour remaining oil on top. Bake in oven at 450° 30 to 35 minutes.

Filling For Kibby:

1 ½ pounds round steak, chopped fine	Salt and pepper to taste
1 ½ pounds round steak, ground	1 teaspoon cinnamon
1 large onion, chopped	3 tablespoons olive oil
	¾ cup pine nuts

Fry meat, onion, seasonings in oil. When just done, add pine nuts. Let cool.

Mrs. M. D. Baddour

A popular program at Baddour Center is administered by the Performing Arts Department. Residents join the community choir, the handbell choir; they play in the orchestra, perform with the drama team in productions staged on campus and in Senatobia, and take individual lessons in piano, guitar, violin, etc. The joy of performing and receiving accolades is positive reinforcement for the self-worth, which Baddour Center seeks to evoke within each resident. The Miracles, a group of 20 BMC singers and instrumentalists, tour extensively and receive tributes and honors. They have recorded three albums.

"Music is the greatest good that mortals know,
And all of heaven we have below."
"Song for St. Cecilia's Day"
—Joseph Addison

HOLIDAY FOODS

Performing Arts Center

HOT CHRISTMAS CIDER

1 gallon sweet apple cider
Juice of 4 large oranges
Juice of 2 lemons
2 cups of sugar

½ teaspoon ground nutmeg
1 teaspoon ground cinnamon
3 teaspoons ground allspice
4 sticks of cinnamon

Mix the cider, orange and lemon juice. Add sugar and liquid to saucepan. Put spices in cheese cloth bag and add to liquid and let boil for about 5 minutes. Remove spice bag and float cinnamon sticks on top. Serve hot.

Mrs. Charles Carr

SPICED TEA

2 7-ounce jars of Tang instant
  orange juice
¾ cup Lipton unsweetened instant
  tea with lemon

1 teaspoon ground cloves
1 teaspoon cinnamon
1 cup sugar

Mix together and store in airtight container. Put 3 teaspoons tea mixture to every cup hot water.

Mrs. George Moore, Jr.

HOT SPICED PERCOLATOR PUNCH

3 cups pineapple juice
3 cups water
1 tablespoon cloves
½ tablespoon whole allspice

3 sticks cinnamon, broken
¼ teaspoon salt
½ cup brown sugar, lightly packed

Put pineapple juice and water in bottom of 8 cup percolator. Put spices, salt and sugar in basket for coffee. Perk 10 minutes.

Variation: Reduce water to 1½ cups and add 3 cups cranberry cocktail sauce and a few drops of red food coloring.

Beth Vail,
Grace Wesson

HOT DRINK

1 small jar cranberry juice	3 cinnamon sticks
2 quarts apple cider	1 ½ teaspoons whole cloves
¼ cup brown sugar	1 lemon, sliced

Bring to a boil and simmer for 15 minutes.

Nellie Baddour Pike

Good served before a meal or with dessert.

SALTED NUTS

1 cup nuts (meat halves look nicer)	1 teaspoon salad oil
	½ teaspoon salt

Put nuts in a pint jar. Add oil and shake to coat thoroughly. Pour nuts onto shallow baking pan and bake at 250° for 45 minutes to 1 hour, stirring occasionally. When done, sprinkle with salt. Store in refrigerator and reheat for serving.

Berenice Clemmer

TOASTED PECANS

2 pounds pecans	Salt
1 stick butter (or oleo) cut in 4 or 5 pieces	

Put pecans in large iron skillet and top with pieces of butter. Place iron skillet in 300° oven (do not pre-heat). As butter melts, stir pecans to coat. Stir every 10 to 15 minutes. Watch carefully as they will burn easily. Spread newspaper on counter top or table. Cover newspaper with paper towels. When pecans become medium brown, pour onto paper towels. Immediately sprinkle generously with salt. Stir and mix well so salt will stick to all of the pecans. Let cool completely. Store in air-tight container.

Eulalee B. Dacus

CHRISTMAS PECANS

1 egg white	1 teaspoon vanilla
¾ cup brown sugar	2 cups pecans

Beat egg white until stiff. Stir in brown sugar and vanilla. Add pecans, coating well, and place on cookie sheet, making sure they do not touch. Bake at 250° for 30 minutes.

Pam Baddour

ORANGE PECANS

1 cup sugar	1 orange rind, grated
½ cup hot water	Pinch of salt
2 tablespoons orange juice	3 cups pecans

Cook sugar and hot water until it spins a thread. Add orange juice, rind, and salt. Cook for 1 minute. Beat and add pecans. Pour on oil paper and break into pieces when cool.

Grace Knolton

THANKSGIVING CRANBERRY RELISH

1 package lemon Jello	2 cups whole cranberries
1 cup sugar	1 cup pecans
1 cup boiling water	½ cup cold water
1 Delicious apple, cored	1 small can crushed pineapple
1 orange	

Dissolve Jello and sugar in boiling water. Chop unpeeled apple, whole orange, and cranberries in blender. Chop pecans by hand. Add chopped fruit, pecans, water and pineapple to Jello. Refrigerate.

Billy and Barbara Mills

CRANBERRY SALAD

2   packages cherry Jello
2   cups boiling water
1   large can cranberry sauce
2   tablespoons sugar (optional)

1 ½ unpeeled red Delicious apples,
     chopped
¾   cup celery, chopped
¾   cup pecans, chopped

Dissolve Jello in boiling water. Add cranberry sauce and sugar and mash. Refrigerate until jelled. Add other ingredients. Let congeal in a flat pan overnight.

Mrs. Nick Nail

CRANBERRY SALAD

2   cups whole cranberry sauce
2   cups apples, chopped
1   cup sugar

1   pound marshmallows, quartered
2   cups whipping cream
½-1 cup pecans, chopped

Mix cranberry sauce and apples. Add sugar and marshmallows. Let stand 30 minutes or longer. Add whipped cream and nuts. Freeze.

Mrs. Billy Barrett

RAW CRANBERRY SALAD

4   cups cranberries
2   oranges
1   cup apple (unpeeled)

2   cups sugar
1   cup pecans (optional)
1   cup pineapple (optional)

Grind cranberries, one whole orange with rind and one orange pulp only, and apples. Add sugar. Let stand in refrigerator for at least two hours. This is great and pretty for Thanksgiving and Christmas. Keeps well. I add both optionals but good either way.

Evelyn Spear

AMBROSIA

12 medium size naval oranges
1   cup grated coconut

1   #2 can of crushed pineapple

Mix together. Cover tightly and chill.

Pat Baddour

CRANBERRY-PINEAPPLE SALAD

1 large package raspberry Jello
   (or lemon)
2 cups boiling water
1 cup cold water

2 cans whole cranberry sauce
1 #2 can crushed pineapple
1 can angel flake coconut (optional)
1 cup nuts, chopped

Dissolve Jello in boiling water. Stir in cold water. Chill until syrupy. Mix cranberries until soft and add to Jello. Add pineapple, coconut and nuts. Refrigerate until firm. Serve on bed of lettuce.

Mrs. Robert Homra
Beverly Reeves

A different cranberry salad, and very good.

APPLE AND CRANBERRY CASSEROLE

3 cups unpeeled apples, sliced
2 cups raw cranberries
¾ cup sugar
1 stick oleo

1 cup flour
½ cup brown sugar
½ cup nuts, broken

Combine apples and cranberries in baking dish. Sprinkle with sugar. Melt oleo and add flour, brown sugar and nuts. Spread over fruit. Bake at 350° for 45-60 minutes.

Variation: Eliminate the cranberries and use 5 cups of apples. Add ¼ teaspoon cinnamon and a dash of nutmeg in topping.

Mrs. Ervin Manning

BLUEBERRY MOLD

2 packages black raspberry Jello
2 cups boiling water

1 pint sour cream
1 can blueberries

Dissolve Jello in boiling water. Let cool until it begins to thicken. Add sour cream and mix well. Add blueberries; mix well. Pour into a Jello mold that has been rubbed lightly with oil to prevent sticking. Let this congeal.

Florence Belton

HOLIDAY SALAD

1 package lime Jello
1 cup hot water
1 8-ounce package miniature
  marshmallows
1 tall can crushed pineapple

2 teaspoons lemon juice
1 cup salad dressing
2 3-ounce packages cream cheese
½ pint whipping cream
1 package cherry Jello

Dissolve lime Jello in hot water. Add miniature marshmallows. Stir until almost melted. Add crushed pineapple and lemon juice. Cool. Cream salad dressing with cream cheese and fold with first mixture. Whip cream and fold into mixture. Congeal hard. Dissolve cherry Jello as directed on package. Cool. Just before congealing, pour onto other Jello mixture. Pour into slanted spoon so it won't make holes in Jello. Refrigerate.

Mrs. Harold Redfearn

Colorful at holiday season, as well as good.

CHRISTMAS SALAD

1 package cherry Jello
1 package lime Jello
2 packages cream cheese

1 can crushed pineapple
1 cup whipped cream

Make cherry Jello according to package directions. When partially set, make lime Jello in separate bowl, so when cherry Jello is firm, lime will be partially set. Combine cream cheese, pineapple and whipped cream. Spread over the firm cherry Jello. Carefully spoon the partially set lime Jello on top. Let set overnight.

Mrs. J. C. McCaa

CHRISTMAS SALAD

⅔ cup sugar
2 cups water
2 packages strawberry Jello
1 large can crushed pineapple

1 large box Dream Whip
1 8-ounce package cream cheese
1 cup pecans

Boil sugar and water, add Jello and undrained pineapple. Set in refrigerator until just beginning to gel. Prepare Dream Whip according to package instructions. Fold Dream Whip, cream cheese and pecans into Jello.

Mrs. Henry Harmon

EASTER NEST COFFEE CAKE

1 package yeast
¼ cup warm water
½ cup milk
¼ cup sugar
¼ cup shortening
1 teaspoon salt

3 cups flour
1 slightly beaten egg
Shredded coconut
Green food coloring
Confectioners icing
Candy decorations

Soften yeast in ¼ cup warm water. Heat milk, sugar, shortening and salt until sugar dissolves. Cool to lukewarm. Stir in 1 cup flour, beat until smooth. Add softened yeast and egg and beat well. Stir in enough of remaining flour to make a soft dough. Knead until smooth and elastic (8-10 minutes). Place in greased bowl, turn and let rise about 1 hour. Punch down and divide into thirds. Let rest 10 minutes covered. Shape ⅓ of dough into 6 "eggs," place close together in center of greased baking sheet. Shape remaining dough into two 26" "ropes" twisted together. Coil around "eggs" to form nest. Seal ends. Cover and let rise about 1 hour. Bake at 375° for 15-20 minutes. Remove from baking sheet, and cool. Tint coconut green. Frost with icing. Sprinkle "eggs" with candy decorations and "nest" with coconut. Serve.

Helen Younes

SUGAR PLUM PUDDING CAKE

2 cups flour
1½ cups sugar
2 teaspoons cinnamon
1 cup mashed up prunes (baby food)
½ teaspoon salt

1 cup sugar
1¼ teaspoons soda
1 teaspoon nutmeg
1 cup buttermilk
2 eggs

Mix and pour into bundt pan. Cook at 325° for 30 minutes or until firm. While cake is cooking mix glaze.

Glaze:

1 stick butter or oleo
½ cup buttermilk

1 cup sugar
1 teaspoon vanilla

Bring glaze to boil and pour over cake while hot.

Grace Knolton

CRANBERRY BREAD

2 cups sifted flour	2 tablespoons butter, melted
½ teaspoon salt	½ cup orange juice
1 ½ teaspoons baking powder	2 tablespoons hot water
½ teaspoon soda	½ cup pecans
1 cup sugar	1 cup whole cranberries
1 beaten egg	1 tablespoon orange rind, grated

Pierce each cranberry, so they won't burst. Combine flour, salt, baking powder, soda, and sugar. Add egg, butter, orange juice and water, and mix well. Stir in pecans, cranberries, and orange rind. Bake in greased loaf pan for 1 hour and 10 minutes at 350°.

Anita M. Slaughter

WASHINGTON CHERRY TREE LOAF

2 cups sugar	1 small pinch salt
2 ½ cups milk	1 cup walnuts, finely chopped
2 ½ ounces maraschino cherries	

Cook sugar and milk to soft ball, stirring almost constantly. Take from fire, add juice from cherries and cook again to soft ball. Take from fire, add salt, nuts and chopped cherries. Beat hard and quickly until mixture begins to cream. Then turn out on cup towel wrung out in cold water. Form in a roll and keep in refrigerator overnight. Slice with sharp knife for serving.

BISHOP'S BREAD

1 ½ cups sifted flour	2 cups nuts, coarsely chopped
1 ½ teaspoons baking powder	1 cup dates, snipped
¼ teaspoon salt	1 cup Glacéed cherries
1 cup semi-sweet chocolate	3 eggs
pieces	1 cup granulated sugar

Preheat oven to 325°. Grease a 10x15x3″ loaf pan well; line bottom with waxed paper. Into a medium bowl sift flour with baking powder and salt. Stir in chocolate pieces, nuts, dates and cherries until all are well coated with flour. In large bowl, with mixer at medium speed, beat eggs well; then gradually beat in sugar. Fold in flour mixture; turn into loaf pan. Bake 1 to 1½ hours or until done. Cool in pan on wire rack. When cool, remove from pan, wrap in foil and store. Serve in slices. *Makes one loaf.*

Linda Stubbs

UNCOOKED FRUIT CAKE

2 pounds graham crackers,
   crushed
1 pound candied cherries
1 pound candied pineapple
1 pound candied figs
1 pound candied citron
1 pound raisins
1 pound dates
1 pound pecans

1 pound English walnuts, broken
4 15-ounce cans sweetened
   condensed milk
1 cup dark brown sugar
4 tablespoons cocoa
1 teaspoon salt
1 teaspoon ground cloves
1 teaspoon allspice
1 teaspoon cinnamon

Mix graham crackers with fruit and chopped nuts in large bowl. Mix milk
thoroughly with sugar, cocoa, salt and spices. Pour over first mixture. Blend
well, pack firmly in a large fruit cake pan that has been lined with waxed
paper. It must set four days in refrigerator and it is better after 30 days.

Glenda Baddour Tribble

DARK FRUIT CAKE

½ pound butter or oleo
2 cups sugar
8 eggs
4 cups flour, sifted
1 teaspoon salt
1 teaspoon cinnamon
1 teaspoon nutmeg
1 cup wine or orange juice

½ pound raisins
½ pound currants
½ pound cherries
½ pound almonds
½ pound dates
½ pound pecans
½ pound pineapple
½ pound citron

Cream butter and sugar. Add eggs and beat well. Sift 3 cups flour, salt, cinnamon and nutmeg together. Add alternately with wine or orange juice. Mix
the fruits and nuts with remaining cup of flour. Add batter and mix well.
Bake in metal pans lined with brown paper, greased and floured. Bake at
250° for first hour, then reduce to 200° for 2½ hours or until done.

Mrs. Woods C. Eastland

FRUIT CAKE

½ cup buttermilk
1 teaspoon soda
1½ cups sugar
3 eggs
4 cups flour
1 teaspoon cinnamon
1 teaspoon allspice
1½ teaspoons nutmeg

1 pinch salt
1 cup whiskey
1 box raisins
1 pound crystalized pineapple
1 pound cherries
1 cup cherry preserves
1 cup nuts

Dissolve soda in buttermilk. Add sugar and eggs and mix well. Sift flour, cinnamon, allspice, nutmeg and salt together and add alternately with whiskey. Stir in fruit, preserves and nuts. Bake in tube pan at 325° for 3½ hours.

Mrs. Gerald Gibson

FRUIT CAKE COOKIES

8 ounces raisins
½ pound cherries
½ pound orange peel
1 pound pineapple (½ pound
   red, ½ pound green)
1½ pounds nuts (6¼ cups)
3 cups all-purpose flour
1 stick butter or oleo

1 cup brown sugar, packed
4 eggs, well beaten
3 teaspoons soda
1 teaspoon cinnamon
1 teaspoon allspice
1 teaspoon nutmeg
3 tablespoons sweet milk
½ cup whiskey

Cut fruit and nuts and mix with one half flour. Cream butter and sugar, add eggs. Sift remaining flour with soda and spices and add milk and whiskey. Add to fruit. Mix thoroughly. Drop onto greased cookie sheet and bake at 350° for 15 to 20 minutes. *Makes 10 to 12 dozen.*

Lynda Akil

"TIPSIES"

1 package chocolate chips
2½ cups vanilla wafers, crushed
1 cup nuts, chopped

½ cup powdered sugar
3 tablespoons white Karo
½ cup whiskey

Melt chocolate chips over hot water; then add vanilla wafers, nuts and powdered sugar. Mix Karo with whiskey and pour over wafer mixture. Mix well. Let stand for 30 minutes. Roll in balls about the size of a walnut or smaller.

Mrs. Albert Thomas

CHOCOLATE COVERED STRAWBERRIES

1   quart large firm strawberries   1   8-ounce package semi-sweet
¼ cup vegetable shortening   chocolate (not chocolate chips)

Wash strawberries (leave hulls on). Dry completely on paper towel. Place shortening and chocolate in top of double boiler. Place over hot, not boiling, water and stir until chocolate is melted and smooth. (Do not allow water in the chocolate). Holding the strawberries by the hull, dip them into melted chocolate until they are ¾ covered. Hold over double boiler until excess chocolate has dripped off. Place dipped strawberries on a cookie sheet covered with waxed paper. Chill until chocolate hardens. This can be done the morning of the party. *Makes 48.*

Marilyn Baddour Aaron

ROSALYNN CARTER'S FRUIT CANDY

½ pound dates   1   pound dried apricots
1   pound dried figs   1   teaspoon orange zest, grated, or
2   cups walnuts or pecans,   sesame seeds or unsweetened
    chopped   shredded coconut
½ cup seedless raisins

Grind together dates, figs, nuts, raisins and apricots. Press into a buttered pan; cut into squares, and sprinkle with orange zest or sesame seeds, or coconut.

Rosalynn Carter

DIVINITY CANDY

4   cups sugar   4   egg whites
1½ cups water   1   teaspoon vanilla
1   pinch salt   2   cups pecans, broken
1   cup white Karo syrup 1 jar cherries

Boil sugar, water, salt and Karo syrup until it forms a soft ball in cold water. Beat egg whites until they form stiff peaks. Pour small amount of boiling syrup slowly over the beaten egg whites. Beat constantly. Cook the remaining syrup until it forms a hard ball in cold water. Pour slowly over the egg whites. Beat constantly until it begins to thicken. Add vanilla and nuts. Keep beating until it becomes creamy. Drop on wax paper. Top with cherry halves.

Mary Moore

Beautiful and delicious.

388

MOLASSES POPCORN BALLS

1 cup molasses
1 tablespoon butter or margarine

1 cup sugar
4 quarts unsalted popcorn

Combine molasses, butter and sugar in a 2-quart saucepan. Place over low heat and stir until sugar is dissolved. Cook over medium heat until syrup, when dropped in very cold water, separates into threads which are hard but not brittle; or until candy thermometer reaches 270°. Pour syrup over popped corn, stirring to coat each kernel. When cool enough to handle, shape into balls with lightly buttered hands.

Mrs. Frank Baddour

I made these when I was a child.

POPPY COCK

1 ½ cups sugar
⅓   cup white Karo
1   cup margarine

1 cup raw peanuts
2 quarts of popped corn

Bring sugar, Karo and margarine to boil. Add peanuts. Cook 15 minutes. Then add the popped corn. Mix, then pour out on waxed paper. When cool, break up and put in plastic container.

Mrs. Hershel Christian

Makes an excellent snack treat.

FUDGE BALLS

2 12-ounce packages chocolate
   chips
1 can Eagle Brand milk
1 cup flour

1 cup nuts, chopped
2 tablespoons butter
2 tablespoons vanilla

Melt chocolate chips with milk over hot water. Remove from heat and add flour, chopped nuts, butter and vanilla. Let set 10 minutes and drop by table-spoon on greased cookie sheet. Bake at 300° for 5 minutes.

Helen Baddour Deneka

389

ROCKY ROAD HALLOWEEN SQUARES

1 12-ounce package semi-sweet
   chocolate chips
1 14-ounce can sweetened
   condensed milk

2 tablespoons butter
2 cups dry roasted peanuts
1 16-ounce package miniature white
   marshmallows

In top of a double boiler, over boiling water, melt chocolate chips with milk and butter. Remove from heat. In a large bowl, combine nuts and marshmallows. Fold in chocolate mixture. Spread in a waxed paper lined 13x9-inch pan. Chill 2 hours or until firm. Remove from pan, peel off waxed paper, cut into squares. Cover and store at room temperature.

Mrs. John Sanders

NUTTY NOODLY CLUSTERS

2 6-ounce packages semi-sweet
   chocolate chips
2 6-ounce packages butterscotch
   chips

2 3-ounce cans La-Choy Chow Mein
   Noodles
½ cup peanuts or cashews

Melt chocolate and butterscotch chips in a heavy saucepan over low heat, stirring constantly. Remove from heat and quickly stir in noodles and nuts so they are covered. Drop by teaspoon onto waxed paper. Chill and refrigerate. *Yield 24 clusters*.

Variation: Eliminate chocolate chips and use 4 packages butterscotch chips.

Mrs. John Sanders, Joy Melton
Mrs. Wayne Bridwell

HOLLY WREATHS

½   cup butter or oleo
30 large marshmallows
1 ½ teaspoons green food coloring

3 cups corn flakes
Red hots

Melt oleo over low heat; add marshmallows. Stir until melted. Remove from heat and stir in green food coloring. Add corn flakes and stir gently until completely coated. Spray your hands and waxed paper with Pam then shape wreaths. Dot with red hots. *Makes 12 or more.* Let wreaths sit for about 3 hours before wrapping with Glad Wrap. Sometimes I have to let the wreaths sit overnight.

Marilyn Baddour Aaron

390

WHISKEY PUDDING

9 ounces vanilla wafers
1 stick butter
1 cup sugar

4 eggs
1 cup pecans, chopped
½ cup bourbon whiskey

Crush vanilla wafers fine. Cream butter and sugar together; add eggs one at a time and beat well after each one. Add pecans and bourbon. Place in greased pyrex dish, 8x10", in layers, ending with layer of crumbs on top. Refrigerate for 48 hours. Serve topped with whipped cream. *Serves 10.*

Homazelle Ashford

VELVET BOILED CUSTARD

5 or 6 eggs, separated
½ gallon milk
4 heaping tablespoons cornstarch

1 cup sugar
Nutmeg
1 teaspoon vanilla

Beat yellow of eggs in saucepan. Add ½ cup of milk and stir. Add cornstarch and sugar. Mix well and add remainder of milk. Let come to a boil. Remove from heat. Beat egg whites stiff and gradually add to the custard. Let cool, add sprinkle of nutmeg and vanilla when ready to serve.

Mrs. C. S. Sanders, Sr.
Mrs. M. D. Baddour

BOILED CUSTARD

4 eggs
8 tablespoons sugar
1 quart sweet milk

1 teaspoon vanilla
½ pint whipped cream

Beat eggs and sugar, adding sugar gradually. Add milk. Cook in double boiler until it coats spoon. Keep in refrigerator until cold. Add vanilla flavoring and whipped cream.

Mrs. Fort Daniel

WALTER'S EGGNOG

1½ pints whipping cream   1 pint straight bourbon whiskey
2   dozen eggs, room temperature   Nutmeg
1½ cups sugar

Whip the cream stiff. Beat egg whites until stiff, but not dry. Gradually add sugar to whites and beat until they hold a point. Beat yolks until light colored, then add bourbon very slowly. This cooks the eggs. Stir constantly to prevent curdling. *Fold* yolk mixture into whites. Do not beat. Fold cream into the mixture, being careful not to beat. For the extra touch, sprinkle with fresh grated nutmeg.

Walter Scott
Here's fifty years of holiday tradition at the home of Walter Scott in Duck Hill, Miss.

The beauty of Nature calls forth an instinctive closeness to God. All who observe the fields and trees, the lakes and winding roads of the Baddour Center grounds sense that quality. The beauty of the mentally retarded adults who live there is observable also: It is found in their courage to face a world which does not always understand, in their sensitivity to others' feelings, and in their dependence on the Holy Spirit for strength and guidance.

"Afoot and light-hearted I take to the open road
Healthy, free, the world before me..."
–"Song of the Open Road"
Walt Whitman

INDEX

God's Beauty in Nature